If You Don't Pay
You Don't Play

JAMES R HOGGETT

IF YOU DON'T PAY, YOU DON'T PLAY
Copyright © James R Hoggett 2006

All rights reserved.

ISBN 978-XXXXXXXXX

Published 2007 by
BUSTER PUBLICATIONS
Whittlesey, England.

First published by Authorhouse 2006

Printed by Print-on-Demand Worldwide Ltd.

Chapter One
Weekend

John leant against the doorway of the building site cabin surveying the site. He tutted and shook his head ponderously. Why hadn't he trained to be a brain surgeon, lawyer, or maybe a MP? In retrospect he knew now that all those years back he should have listened to his mother and father, and honed his failing educational skills. When he was a lad education at that time didn't have the allure for him that the girls round the back of bike sheds had, or smoking, but if he had attained the higher levels as a brain surgeon, lawyer or MP, unquestionably the work would certainly have been a lot easier than being a poxy plumber. It was hard to believe that he'd been in the plumbing game for twenty-eight years, man and boy.

The week had been the normal yardstick for English weather, rain, rain and more rain. Scanning the sky, John mulled over the week's mayhem as he looked forward to his weekend at home. The dark clouds that had darkened the site all week had at last parted and it was looking much more promising for an excellent weekend at home. He'd seen so many changes since he'd started his working life in the plumbing game, some good and some bad. But now his hair was greying, receding, he was in his forties and sorted. As he'd grown older he found life more difficult to adhere to, particularly in today's society of the Americanised system of quick change as he embraced change like a Rottweiler embraces a postman's neck. 'Why on earth do we need all these changes?' he muttered, shaking his head at the thought. 'Like Plasma Screen TVs, face lifts, Botox, boob jobs, the word COOL, and who's got the bloody smallest mobile phone.' He looked at his hands wondering how he'd ever got his pigs' tits that double as fingers to press those pinhead buttons on his daughter's minuscule mobile phone. Apparently, so Kaylie, his daughter, informed him last weekend, mobile phones now took bloody photographs, and showed films. John put his finger to his lips. *In fact she's right,* he thought, Rod's got pornographic films on his mobile. Maybe that's so that when he's not actually participating in the sexual act, he can sit and watch it. 'Sick bastard,' he mumbled to himself again. *Big Mac's,* he thought, they seemed to have taken the place of wholesome cooked Sunday roasts, like roast beef, with horseradish sauce, Yorkshire pudding and roast potatoes; he licked his lips at the thought of the weekend's ritual roast. He shook his head again. 'Big Mac's,' he mumbled again. No wonder there is so many 4x4s on the road, transporting this generation of overweight children and mothers around. Well done Gordon Brown, One Hundred and Ninety pounds road tax, at least he's making them pay for the bloody privilege. 'Whatever,' he muttered. *They can throw all the changes they liked at me,* he thought, *it wouldn't make any difference.* He wasn't having any of it at all, Hoggett's don't do change.

Plumbing had always been his life and he never really wanted to do anything else after his failed education. He loved plumbing; at least the money was better now than it was in the past. *But some things will never bloody change though,* he thought, scanning the site again; the site was in its normal state of disarray. Pallet loads of bricks had been dropped where they wanted the sand, and two fifty-five-ton piles of sand reached up into the sky like the humps of a Mongolian Bactrian camel. The sand had been dropped where the bricklayers had wanted the bricks. There was at least one saving grace though. *Thank God I'm a plumber, and not a bloody bricklayer,* he thought. Still, thank Christ it was the end of another week. *This week had been a particularly long haul,* he thought, rubbing the crotch of his trousers, repositioning his sore testicles. Thank God they'd all gone; now he could get on, then pub, beer and home. 'Thank, f… f… f… fuck, it's f… f… f… Friday,' he mumbled to himself as he turned and walked into the cabin to shut up shop for the weekend. Mick, the site foreman, had already checked the site and left for the pub with the rest of the lads for their end of the week pint: Mick's way of saying thanks to them for their hard work. Everyone had been accounted for. He eyed the cabin with distaste. Switching on the toilet light he flushed the chemical loo and rolled the trailing toilet paper back onto its roll. 'The dirty bastards,' he mumbled, picking up the soap off the floor and placing it back into the chrome-wire soap rack. Washing out the sink he noticed the remnants of five scum marks at different levels. Was that one line for five days of the week or just five dirty lines that the lazy dirty bastards hadn't bothered to wipe a cloth around? *Am I becoming the paranoid plumber/cleaner,* he thought. *No, it just pisses me off cleaning up after five grown bloody men.* He shook his head trying to eradicate his anger. *F...f.... f... for...f...f...fucks sake John get a grip of yourself mate, why should I give a shit, I'll be out of here soon and home for the weekend.* He stood up, straightening up the towels. In fact, he'd take the towels home, get Linda to wash them and bring a couple of clean ones back on Monday. 'If it wasn't f... f...f...for me they would never have got the site bloody cabin in the f...f...f...first place,' he mumbled, looking around, nodding his head. 'It's a shit hole.' He wondered what the other lads' homes must look like as he gathered the scattered newspapers into a pile, placing them in a neat pile on the end of the bench. Snatching up the JCB digger's ignition key from the table, he placed the key in the key safe and shut it. He ran his hands along the top of the safe looking for the key. 'Shit.' The key was missing. Mick must have it in his trousers' bloody pocket again,' he mumbled. 'What's the point of having a bloody key safe if Mick's always got the bloody master key in his pocket.' He shook his head and bent down, unplugging the wall heater and the coffee machine and dropping the plugs onto the floor. He threw the used coffee cups into the bin, looking round the cabin at his efforts. *Now why didn't the lazy bastards do that before they left? It would only have taken them a second and it would have made his life a lot easier.* He clapped his hands together. *Right, now he could have a drink in peace without worrying about the mess.* He switched the lights out, picked up the dirty towels, locked up and made his way to his car.

⋆ ★ ⋆

Mick and the lads bowled through the pub doors making a beeline for the bar, their customary end of the week drink. Drinking away all their frustrations of the week's work before they went their separate ways. The pub seemed to be full of like-minded people. Mick smiled at the lads. 'Well done,' he shouted over the noise. 'Another excellent week's work lads. I've checked our progress sheets for this week and we are well on our way to keeping our target on track. Right, who's getting the drinks in then?'

They all looked at each other.

'You are, you f...f...f...fucking tight f... f... f... fisted bastard,' shouted John from the back of the pub as he walked towards the bar, the state of the site cabin still in the back of his mind. 'You can take the drinks out of the f...f... f... fucking f... f... f...fat bonus you're going to get, f... f... f... from all our bloody hard work.' John was the master at straight talking.

'That's right, you tell him John,' the lads shouted in unison.

Mick held up his hands in defence, knowing that there's one thing you didn't do, and that was cross John. 'Ok...ok...' he said, embarrassed at John's outburst, trying to ignore the people in the crowded pub who were now looking towards him. Producing his wallet from his back pocket, he shook the wallet at them.

'All cleared up Mrs Mop?' shouted Rod.

'Bollocks,' shouted John.

'Hope you didn't forget the towels?'

John stuck his finger in the air.

'Well, what's it going to be then, lads?'

'Don't give a shit,' shouted John, 'as long as it's wet, but not f… f… f… fucking warm, like the one I had last F… F… F… Friday.' John pointed his finger at the bar lady. 'And Betty, I wish you'd clean out your bloody pipes. I'm sure I saw rat shit f… f… f… floating in my beer last week,' he said, pulling out a chair and sat down. You could have heard a pin drop as the other customers turned their heads, looking towards Mick again. Mick smiled sheepishly and looked away from their stares, lowering his head. 'Glass of orange, and five pints of your best, please Betty.'

Betty leant across the bar, and whispered. 'Joe's going to bar him one of these days.'

Mick smiled at Betty, and held up a hand in John's defence. 'Take no notice, that's just John, Betty.'

They all sat in the corner as Mick passed round the beers and sat down. 'Betty said that Joe's going to bar you one of these days, John.'

'I've been barred f… f… f… from f… f…f…fucking better pubs than this one Mick.'

'Well, what are doing this weekend, Sean?' Mick asked, ignoring John's reply.

Sean smiled. 'Well, it happens to be my birthday on Saturday, and Cathleen's buying me a new set of golf clubs.'

'Cheers, happy birthday for Saturday, Sean.' Rod said, raising his glass.

Sean raised his glass in appreciation. 'Thanks Rod, I think a few holes on Saturday afternoon with my new clubs will be the order of the day, and then a few pints down the local in the evening. I think the girls and Cathleen have arranged a surprise party for me, but I'm not supposed to know. You're all welcome to come down lads, and have a few beers, of course, that's if you've got nothing else on,' replied Sean.

'Cheers, we'll be there,' Paul and John said in unison, raising their glasses.

'I'll be there, might be a bit late though, got something on,' Rod winked, 'but I will definitely be there, Sean.'

'I'd love to Sean, but I'm sorry, I can't, not this Saturday,' said Mick.

'Come on Mick,' said Rod, 'it'll do you good to get out more, and meet some nice totty.'

'I said NO, Rod,' snapped Mick looking sternly at him.

John glanced at Mick's harsh face, and then at Rod. John shook his head at Rod, warning him not to pursue his invite.

'I'm sorry Sean,' said Craig, 'maybe some other time, we've got to go round to Marie's mum and dad's on Saturday night.'

Sean held up a hand. 'No problem, Craig,' he said.

'So you're a golfer then?' asked Craig.

John yawned.

Sean nodded his head. 'One of the best games in the world.'

'He's right,' agreed Paul.

'Golf is a waste of a bloody good walk, if you ask me,' mumbled John.

'We wasn't asking you,' Rod snapped, looking back at Sean. 'What's your handicap then Sean?'

'I've just got into single figures.'

'Wow, no shit, you must be good then.'

Sean shrugged his shoulders. 'Let's say, Rod, that when I play I don't rent a cart. I don't need one. When I hit the ball I need a taxi.'

Rod smiled. 'I've swung a few irons myself in the past.'

John smiled. 'How far did you hit your balls then Rod?' he asked.

'I can hit my balls further than you go on bloody holiday John, that's for sure,' Rod replied. 'Anyway,' he said, turning back to Sean, 'I'm afraid I don't seem to get that much time to play now.'

'There's a surprise,' mumbled John, 'too busy looking in the mirror.'

'Right,' said Sean, ignoring John's remark. 'Oh well, that's too bad,' he continued, 'but we should definitely play a round sometime. What's your handicap then Rod…?' 'His knob,' interrupted Craig.

'Nice one, Craig,' laughed John.

Rod sneered at Craig choosing to ignore his remark. 'It's not all about handicaps, it's how you play the game, *mate*.' He said the last word as if it was a synonym for *twat*.

Sean nodded his head in agreement. 'Your absolutely right, Rod,' he agreed.

'What's this now a bloody gentleman's club…?' 'He's right though, John,' interrupted Sean, 'it's all about how you play the game.'

'It's a serious game, John!'

'Ok…let's put your little game to test then, how serious Rod?' asked John.

Rod gripped his hair with both hands and tutted, pushing back his hair. Looking around he looked back at Sean. 'Right ok, Sean, what if you had to choose between Cathleen and your favourite putter, what would you do…?'

'I'd miss her,' replied Sean.

'There you are,' laughed Rod, 'proves my point.'

'Doesn't prove a thing,' disagreed Craig looking at Sean, 'in fact Sean, that's quite sad…' 'Just a joke,' interrupted Rod giving Craig a resigned smile. 'I expect you've played a lot of golf in your time then, Monkey man, you look like somebody who'd look good with a bloody club in his hand.'

'Afraid not,' replied Craig nodding his head. 'Would like to though,' he said, not taking in the significant innuendo that Rod suggested about the club. 'It looks an interesting game, but unfortunately I've never had time to pursue outside sports, what with a very demanding wife to support at the moment.'

'Rod's right,' interjected Paul. 'I play golf,' he said, 'builds character you know, you can forget all about football.'

'Thank God f… f… f… for that,' mumbled John.

'Golf is the beautiful game,' continued Paul. 'In fact, I became a full-fledged member of the B.M.G.A. just last week.' Paul stood and did a run through putting shot. 'Practising at the moment for the Danish open, the first Saturday in September.'

'Absolutely, golf is a beautiful game,' agreed Sean again, looking impressed at Paul's putting stroke, although he was confused by the B.M.G.A. 'Surely you mean the P.G.A. Paul?' he asked.

John looked up from the magazine he'd picked up on the way in. 'P.G.A., B.M.G.A., what the f...f...f...fuck are you two going on about?'

Sean gave John a surprised look, as if everybody knew what the P.G.A. meant. 'They are golf membership clubs' overseers,' he replied. 'P.G.A. is the Professional Golfers' Association,' he shook his head, looking back at Paul. 'But the B.M.G.A. well, that seems to elude me Paul.'

'British Minigolf Association,' replied Paul.

Rod laughed. 'That's bloody crazy golf, windmills, castles and novelty bloody obstacles and all that,' he said, looking at Sean, 'that's a bloody kids' game. I've seen them playing it at the seaside. Believe me Minigolf is a load of bollocks, kids stuff.'

'Laugh all you like mate,' replied Paul. 'It's water off a duck's back. Anyway, how can it be bollocks, just because I prefer Minigolf to golf?'

'Because it's the wrong preference my son, believe me. If I say it's bollock's, it's bollocks.'

John shrugged and smiled.

Rod looked at John. 'What? What? What's that bloody smug smile for?'

'Nothing, but Paul does seem to have got under your skin Rod. Anyway, just leave him alone, it doesn't matter, golf or Minigolf, who gives a bloody shit, we're not listening to you, so give it a bloody rest.'

'Since when did you become a leader of this Non-Golf fascist regime John?'

'Since you started talking a load of f...f...f... fucking bollocks.'

Paul wasn't about to give up with Rod, shaking his head in disbelief. 'Well that's where you're wrong Rod, it's not a bloody kids' game,' he snapped, defending his sport. *I must admit when I was a child and dad took us on holidays mostly to the seaside dad and I spent hours on the Minigolf links in Cromer.* Paul smiled at the thought... Rod looked at Sean. 'Shit, Sean, I do think he's bloody serious,' he said, looking back at Paul. 'So, Peter Pan of the Minigolf course, you never grew up then?'

'As I've said, there's nothing wrong with crazy golf,' interjected Paul, 'Minigolf is now a world-wide acknowledged sport, and attracts competitors from all around Europe, Germany, Denmark, Austria, Holland, even America and Japan....' 'Does it really,' interrupted Rod, yawning and looking decidedly bored now.

'There's even a World Minigolf Sport Federation.'

'Nice, sure you don't mean W.F.F.W.?' said Rod sarcastically.

'What's W.F.F.W.?' asked Paul, looking puzzled.

'Worldwide Federation of Fucking Weirdo's, I think. 'Don't knock it, Rod,' interrupted Craig. 'But do you really consider Minigolf as a sport then?' Craig asked, turning towards Paul.

Paul didn't pause. 'Yes, it is,' he said, without a hint of doubt.

'But don't take this the wrong way, but don't you feel just a little bit…silly though?' asked Craig.

'Certainly not,' replied Paul. 'Never, no, it's all a test of skill. It may not conform to Rod's idea of a sport, but we all know the sort of sport he's into. But I can't see where you are coming from Craig, that maybe fundamentally Minigolf is very different from other sports that people might take part in. But I'm telling you, it requires co-ordination and decision-making.'

'Why don't you take it up then Rod, that's two of the many things you haven't got,' said John sarcastically.

'No chance, shooting bloody balls at windmills, wouldn't want to lose my street credibility,' replied Rod.

'Anyway, whatever,' continued Paul. 'It's very competitive, we take Minigolf very seriously, mate.'

Rod rolled his eyes. 'I bet you do,' he replied, shaking his head, 'do you all wear anoraks, when you play?' he laughed.

Without a trace of a smile Paul replied. 'Hooded cagoules actually, designed to European Minigolf specifications… 'You don't see many of them around… I bet,' interrupted Rod. 'You'll have to wear it to work one day and give us all a laugh. And,' he added, 'I couldn't think of a sadder sight in the world than a grown man in an anorak.'

'Cagoule.'

'Whatever,' said Rod, he continued, waving an unconcerned hand. 'Playing on a crazy-golf course. God,' he said, rolling his eyes again. 'You can't possible call crazy golf a real sport now, can you Sean?'

'Every man to his own, Rod,' replied Sean.

Rod looked at John and Mick. 'Apart from Paul and Monkey man, that leave's you two.'

Mick shrugged his shoulders. 'No, I've never played golf myself,' he held up his hand. 'Hang on though, come to think of it though, my dad played a little golf in my younger days, he took me to the em…emm…a golf…' He shook his hand…. 'Course,' interrupted. Sean.' That's it Sean, the golf course. I can remember one day after a game Dad and I were walking back to the… emm…' he waved his hand again…. 'Club-house' suggested Sean… 'That's it, top man Sean, back to the clubhouse. Well, as I said, on our way back to the clubhouse my dad held up this golf ball, and said to me that he'd had this extraordinary golf ball for some time. He said, if it goes in the rough, it sends out a high-pitched bleeping noise.'

'Fascinating,' yawned John.

'That's not all;' continued Mick, 'apparently if the ball falls into the water it rises to the surface…. 'No,' interrupted Craig. Mick waved a hand, 'And believe it or not, that's not all and when you play at night, the ball glows in the dark.'

'Amazing, I could do with a few of them myself,' said Rod. 'Where did he get it from?'

'He found it.'

Craig, Paul and Sean roared with laughter.

'Twat,' mumbled Rod, red-faced. 'John, what about you?' he said, ignoring their taunting laughter.

John looked up from his magazine. 'As I've said, a waste of a bloody good walk, but I can understand why Rod has taken up golf as his particular sport.'

Sean smiled. 'Why?'

'He likes tucking his balls into tight little holes.'

'John, please,' replied Mick, 'do you have to be so crude.'

'Well it's bloody true Mick,' snapped John, shaking his magazine.

On that note Rod leant back in his chair, scanning the pub for some local talent. He sported handsome features, his longish jet-black hair tied back into a long ponytail, piercing dark but small eyes, chiselled face well proportioned, and small nose and ears tightly tacked back. His cosmopolitan complexion came from *Easy Tan* in the high street and was topped up every Saturday morning. His Saturday preparations were like that of a well-trained Olympic athlete; the preparation was for his one endeavour, his Saturday night pull. His aim in life was to shag as many women as he could in the world, from consensual age to when he believed they weren't worth a second glance. Rod looked back at Mick, John and Sean. Or at least until he'd reached their age, in fact he'd consider giving up sex forever at their age. Almost certainly they had. Especially John, that's why he was such a bloody grumpy twat. But until that time shagging was Rod's buzzword.

Craig nudged Paul. 'Shit, look at them two birds at the bar.'

Rod had already clocked them. Looking back at the bar, 'Christmas crackers,' he said.

Craig raised his eyes. 'What do you mean Christmas crackers Rod?' he asked, looking puzzled.

'Yer,' replied Rod, 'ready to pull, my son, ready to pull. Jesus Christ,' he continued. 'I've got bigger handkerchiefs than those skirts they're wearing and look at those bloody legs, they go right up to their arses. I hope one of them crosses their legs, we might get a glimpse of the old beaver.'

'You dirty bastard,' mumbled John.

Craig fleetingly looked at the girls again; his personality was completely different from that of Rod's, his attitude to his looks was like that of a young girl with anorexia. When she looked into the mirror she believed she was fat, instead of being painfully thin. When he looked in the mirror he believed he was ugly, and that his ginger hair and his long arms made him akin to an orang-utan, the nickname Rod had given him, Monkey man, at times sapped at his already diminishing confidence. But what did he care, orang-utan or not, he had a beautiful-looking wife, Maria. He turned back to Rod. 'What are you going to be doing tonight then Rod?' he asked.

'Them,' Rod replied, holding his glass out towards the two young girls sitting at the bar, envisaging that he had an automatic right to a girl's compliance, just because they had breasts.

John nodded his head and tutted loudly from behind his magazine.

Rod scraped back his chair. 'What,' he paused. 'So you don't think I can pick them up John?' he asked. He stood. 'Right, we'll see,' he said, picking up his beer.

'Do you think you can?' asked Sean.

John looked up from his magazine, and looked at Craig.

Craig shrugged, nodding towards Sean. 'It's a rhetorical question Sean, it doesn't really require an answer.'

'Certainly,' continued Rod. 'No problem,' he looked round at the girls and winked.

They both smiled.

'What makes you so attractive towards women then, Rod,' asked Mick. 'What's your secret?'

Rod had never been asked that before. He paused, scratching his head, 'Good question Mick.'

'He hasn't a clue, but I'll tell you this Mick, they are impressionable young, not ladies but girls, Mick, young girls,' John muttered from behind his magazine, 'not like mature women.'

'Well if you asked me,' interjected Sean.

'We didn't,' mumbled John.

'I would say it's Rod's sense of humour,' Sean said, ignoring John's remark.

Rod held up his thumb towards Sean and smiled at Sean's compliment. 'You've hit the nail right on the head their Sean my son,' he rubbed his chin thoughtfully. 'Yeah, you're right Sean, I never really thought of it that way,' he said. 'That's what women like about me, it's my sense of humour, as opposed to some of us,' he said, looking straight at John. 'Make em laugh John, and they drop into bed, like confetti at a wedding. When was the last time you made your Linda laugh John' he paused.

John looked sternly over his glasses at Rod without saying a word.

Rod moved on quickly holding his hand out towards Craig. 'You stay here Monkey man, we don't want to frighten them off now do we.'

'Bollocks, very funny,' replied Craig.

'Why does everybody get the arse with me when I tell the bloody truth,' said Rod, smiling as he turned towards the bar.

'Because you're a twat,' said Craig to his disappearing back.

'Shit, he's only going to talk to them,' said Paul as Rod moved towards the girls.

'Oh Rod,' shouted Sean as an afterthought. 'Hang on a minute.' He pulled out his black book from inside his overalls pocket. 'Before you go off on your quest to find your perfect soul mate. Come on, don't forget Saturday's lottery draw.' He tapped his black book. 'I need a pound from you, now. You know the score, if you don't pay, you don't play' winked Sean.

'Shit,' said Rod, making his way back to the table. 'I know, if I'm not in it, I can't win it.' He turned towards Sean, rummaging in his back pocket. 'Right there you are,' he said, sliding the pound coin across the table. 'I'm telling you, it's a waste of bloody time, how long have we been doing this bloody lottery?'

'Four years,' replied Sean, flipping back the pages of his black book.

'Four bloody years,' said Rod, thinking back. ' And we haven't won a bloody thing. Not even a tenner. Are you sure you're putting the bloody money on, Sean, and not in your back pocket?'

'G.G.R.,' said Sean.

John's brow furrowed suddenly. 'What the f... f... f... fuck's G.G.R.?' he asked, looking up from the magazine.

Sean looked at John. 'Good God Rod,' translated Sean, looking back at Rod, as John shook his head, lifting up the magazine.

Sean shook his head in disbelief at what Rod had suggested. 'Your accusations Rod, they are like an arrow to my heart, you hurt me Rod,' continued Sean holding his hand to his heart. 'To think, that's what you were thinking. I put the lottery on religiously, ever weekend mate. Same shop, check if you like *Costcutters* in the high street. Every Saturday Seven pm, in fact, it's the same young girl called Amanda who takes our money every week, and a P.Y.T. she is as well.'

John looked up from his magazine again. 'Sean, I wish you wouldn't bloody do that.'

'What?' asked Sean shrugging his shoulders not conscious of what he'd said.

'Jesus Christ, here we go again,' grunted John. 'Ok...ok...I'll play your game again Sean. What the f...f...f... fuck's, P.Y.T.?'

'Pretty young thing,' replied Sean.

John grunted and hoisted up his eyebrows. 'Of course it is,' he said, nodding his head, pulling up the magazine again.

Rod was deep in thought, biting his lower lip. ' How old would you say she is Sean?' he asked with interest.

'Who?'

'This girl in the shop, Amanda?'

Sean shrugged. 'I really didn't take that much notice Rod.'

Rod waved a hand at him. 'Think.'

'Oh…I don't know Rod, maybe 21, 22.'

Rod was in deep thought again; giving what Sean had said some serious thought. 'Hum…. 21, 22 you say.' Biting the corner of his mouth, he looked towards Sean again. 'Is this P.Y.T. married?' he asked.

'I don't know,' replied Sean, 'didn't see any rings on her fingers when she passed over the lottery ticket, and I can't say I really took any notice Rod.'

Rod's face dropped again, 'Kids?'

'For God's sake Rod, enough of the inquisition, I only go in there to put on the bloody lottery, not to learn all the girls' life histories that work on the tills.'

Rod bit his bottom lip again; he wasn't moving off the subject. 'Interesting though,' he said, *'Costcutters* you say? Might pop in there, and have a gander for myself.'

Sean ignored his answer, looking over at the two girls at the bar thinking that he already had enough on his plate, what with the two young girls already eyeing him up from the bar. 'Anyway,' continued Sean. 'I'm in the same boat as you lot, you know, if you don't win, then I don't win, do I… And might I add,' he said, as an afterthought, 'I put in all this work,' tapping his book, 'collecting your lottery money every week, and putting it on, and what the hell do I get for all my efforts.'

'Jack shit Sean,' they all shouted in unison. 'Just mark us down,' said the others, all throwing their pound coins across the table.

'Come on Sean,' said Rod looking at his watch, 'I'm losing precious chat up time here. Can we get a move on Sean, and don't forget to mark me off.'

John looked up from his magazine. 'Is that all you think about. How can a young girl with any sense ever think of giving themselves emotionally or sexually to you, you're an animal,' he said.

'Grrrrrr,' Rod winked. 'I know, thanks for your support John.'

'I don't know John,' said Sean, 'I think if I was a woman I wouldn't mind going out with him.'

Rod smiled at Sean's appreciation of his sexual prowess, even if it was coming from a man. 'Thanks Sean,' said Rod.

'That wasn't a bloody offer, Rod,' Sean said, pointing his finger at him.

'Sean for Christ sake don't bloody encourage him, that's all he thinks about, is bloody sex. There's more to life than sex.'

Rod shrugged his shoulders. 'And of course you'd know, John, seeing as you have plenty of time to spare.'

John held up his hand to ward off an answer.

'Is there anything else to think about than sex, John?'

John looked up. 'As I said, there's more to life than sex, Rod.'

'Is there?' said Rod sarcastically. 'What d'you mean like plumbing?'

'There's nothing wrong with plumbing mate, plumbing has f... f... f... facilitated a lot of your sexual grati... f... f... f... fications, so I've heard.'

Mick looked at John. 'What… what… have you heard John?' he asked.

John shook his magazine at Rod, 'Go on Rod, tell the lads about your private jobs then, the cat's out of the bag mate,' he said with a smile.

The lads' ears pricked up. 'Well?' asked Mick.

'Come on Rod, what happened?' asked Craig. John was glad the others were joining in.

Rod looked round at them all. 'It was nothing, just the overflow in Mrs Denton's loft, that's all, I was repairing the tank, the tank had sprang a leak in her house.'

'Go on,' smiled John.

'Come on, so what happened?' asked Mick, encouraging him to continue.

'As I pulled out the tank, the tank had some residue of slimy water left in the bottom and as I was getting the tank down the ladder from the loft the slimy water went down the front of my trousers.'

'It's all bollocks, if you ask me,' said Craig.

'Well I know what happened,' said John, 'anyway how can you say what he's saying is bollocks Craig?'

'Easily, because he talks bollocks.'

'Whatever, anyway Craig, bollocks does come into it, go on,' John said, waving his hand at Craig. 'Tell them what else happened Rod.'

Rod turned red. 'I went into the bathroom to change my trousers, and Mrs Denton had taken my trousers and was washing the slimy residue off my trousers in the bath…' 'Dressed in what, Rod?' interrupted John.

'Well it was early in the morning John…' 'What was she dressed in then?' interrupted Mick. 'Ok… Ok,' replied Rod, 'she was in her dressing gown; I'm telling you she was only washing my trousers.'

'Yer, right,' said Paul and Craig in unison. 'Come on, Rod tell them the rest,' interrupted John. 'Wait lads, it gets better. That's not the best bit, carry on Rod.'

'You managed to keep that quiet, Rod,' said Mick, watching Rod closely. He didn't know why, but he needed to know what had happened next. 'Well come on then Rod, tell us what happened,' urged Mick.

'Did you score?' asked Craig.

'No,' Rod said determinedly. Which caused John to burst out laughing. 'Are you going to share with us what happened next, Rod?' Mick asked, wondering if John had laughed precisely because Rod had scored.

'Well I never heard the car stop, outside the house,' continued Rod.

'Probably because of all that running water,' said Paul smiling.

'Yer,' agreed Craig, nudging Paul. 'And all that scrubbing to get the slimy gunge off his trousers,' they both laughed sarcastically.

Mick held up his hand to shut up Craig and Paul. 'What car Rod?' he asked.

John held up his hand. 'Wait Mick,' he said, 'the best bit's coming.'

'The next thing I saw,' continued Rod, 'was her husband standing in the doorway, believe me, you wouldn't have got a fag paper between him and the door frame.'

Craig's mouth gaped. 'Shit, so what did you do?'

'Well obviously Monkey man I never charged them for the job, did I.' Rod laughed and shrugged his shoulders. 'Apparently they were going through a divorce anyway.'

'Did her old man hit you?' asked Craig, hoping that he had. 'I would have, if I found you in my bathroom with my wife holding your trousers in her hands.'

Rod smiled. 'I'm amazed you haven't already Monkey man, and no he didn't hit me, I know that must be a disappointment to you,' he said.

'Bollocks,' replied Craig.

'You sure that wasn't what Mrs Denton had in her hands Rod?' asked John.

'What!'

'Your bollocks.'

'Piss off.'

'Hang on Rod,' Mick looked puzzled. 'As you said, you hadn't done anything wrong,' he paused, 'what I don't understand is… why didn't you just explain to her husband what had happened.'

'Good God Mick, you didn't see his face; round, red and blowing. I'm telling you he was like a volcano ready to erupt.'

'Jesus,' gasped Mick. 'So how the hell did you get out of the bathroom then, if her husband was standing in the doorway?' he asked.

Rod tapped his head. 'In those situations Mick, there's only one thing you can do. Think fast, think on your feet…' 'Pity, if he came in a bit later, maybe you wouldn't have been on your feet?' interrupted Craig.

'Well he didn't, and I was on my feet,' Rod said. 'What I did was I used this,' he said, tapping his head again, 'used this, and got out. Thank God there was two doors to the bathroom mate, I just did a runner.'

'Bollocks,' Craig mumbled under his breath.

Mick shook his head. 'You're one hell of a lucky bloke Rod.' 'Lucky,' interrupted Rod sharply, a little puzzled at what Mick had said. He looked sternly at Mick and snapped. 'Why?'

Craig looked up at the pub ceiling. *'Please God,'* he said under his breath, and looked at Rod. He hesitated and then suddenly grinned. 'What! Don't say her old man caught you?'

'Sorry Monkey man, but no, he didn't, maybe in your dreams you would have liked him to, tough luck no he didn't, unlike you mate, I'm fitter than a butcher's dog, he didn't stand a chance. Sebastian Coe wouldn't have beat me out of that house.'

'Pity,' whispered Craig.

'I'm telling you Rod, you were bloody lucky there,' said John.

'How's that,' asked Rod. 'Why the hell does everybody keep saying I'm lucky, nothing went on?'

'Right,' said John, 'I'm only saying that because I know David Denton you didn't need to be doing anything with his wife, it was enough for you just to be in his bathroom.'

'Why is that so unusual John, I am a plumber and I might add we've all been in peoples bathrooms.'

'A plumber with no trousers on though,' Craig held out his hands I think we keep out trousers on Rod,' he reminded him.

'Right,' agreed John, 'not a good start to a lasting friendship,' John said. 'Ex A.B.A. boxing champion, as I recall winner in1996, 97 and 98,' he continued holding up his fists. 'Went under the name of the D.D.T.D.D. when he was in the ring.'

Mick sighed heavily 'Here we go again,' now John's bloody doing it.'

John held out his hands. 'What?'

'D.D.T.D.D. What's it stand for then John?' asked Mick.

'Yer right, sorry Mick, D.D.T.D.D. stands for Dynamite Dave The Dark Destroyer. I'm telling you Rod, if he had caught you, you wouldn't be standing here telling us all about it, he'd have caved your head in f… f… f… for sure, divorce or not. I'm telling you he's one hell of a jealous man. I saw him f… f… f… floor eight blokes in a pub one night, with no help all on his own.'

Mick tilted his head to one side, not understanding the concept as to why somebody would floor eight blokes. *Eight blokes, Christ, that in itself would have been suicide*, he thought. 'Why?' he asked.

'Apparently,' continued John, 'Mrs Denton's one hell of a nice-looking woman,' he nodded his head. 'What the hell she sees in him I haven't got a bloody clue, God he's so ugly, mind you I wouldn't say it to his f…f… f… face though. He'd make the Hunchback of Notre Dame good looking.

Craig looked at John, puzzled. 'Who's he?' he asked.

'Who?'

'The Hunchback of Notre Dame.'

'Over to you Mick,' said John. 'Tell him.'

'Quasimodo *was* one of the ugliest persons that ever lived.'

Rod smiled. 'What you mean uglier than Monkey man?'

'Bollocks, Rod.' Craig looked back at Mick. 'Take no notice of the twat, Mick, go on.'

'Well, Quasimodo lived in Notre Dame...' Craig went to speak. Mick held up a hand, 'And before you ask me, Notre Dame is a church in the centre of Paris, France.'

'I known that Mick.'

Rod smiled. 'Must be one of your descendents Monkey man.'

'Why did you say *was?*' asked Craig.

'Past tense Craig,' explained Rod. 'Because he's dead you twat, shame though, Craig, you could have gone to his funeral if you'd known.'

Craig ignored Rod's remarks. 'How did he die then, Mick?' he continued.

Mick shrugged.

'Who gives a shit,' replied John.

Rod held up a hand. 'No.... no...John,' he said, 'I'm glad that Monkey man is taking such an interest in his ancestors....' 'Bollocks,' interrupted Craig. 'Go on,' interrupted John, wanting to hear the story. 'Well,' continued Rod, 'I know how Quasimodo died, apparently it's said he died a horrific death.' He looked round at them all, he was holding their interest.

'Apparently,' he continued, 'so it was said, a Parisian was walking past the Notre Dame. That's a Frenchman to you Monkey man.'

'I know what a bloody Parisian is,' snapped Craig.

John held a finger to his lips. 'Schuss,' he said, 'let him finish the story.'

'Anyway,' continued Rod, 'the Frenchman noticed a crowd had gathered around this man laying on the cobbled street in front of the Notre Dame, blood trickling from his ears, his face distorted. As the Frenchman pushed his way through the crowd, the man on the floor looked up at him. The Frenchman looked down at him and said, 'I think I know you, your face rings a bell.' Rod paused thinking he might have got a laugh. Nothing dead silence. He continued. 'Yes said the man on the floor, 'I'm Quasimodo the father of Monkey man.'

'Bollocks.'

'Sssh,' they all said in unison. Rod continued, 'and he said, 'I live in the church,' half-heartedly Quasimodo tried pointing towards the church. 'My God what happened to you?' asked the Frenchman. "Well I was up there, in the belfry, he pointed towards the belfry, 'and I was about to strike the bell for the hour, when... Esmerelda... came... into the belfry.' Sucking in air, he panted, finding it difficult to get out the words.

'What happened, asks the Frenchman, "what put you in such a grave position?

"It was something I said to Esmerelda," replied Quasimodo, "as you said, that put me... in... this... grave... position."

"My God, what did you say to her?" asked the Frenchman looking puzzled.

"I... said...I... said... toss me off Esmerelda, and she did," and he died.'

They all roared with laughter, except for Mick who found the story inappropriate. 'When you have finished lads,' said Mick, 'let John finish what he was saying... 'Where was I,' prompted John still laughing... 'Mr Denton and how ugly he is,' answered Mick. 'Yes right, thanks Mick,' he said, pointing at him. 'Yes boxing that's what it was, it must have been all them years of boxing, his f... f... f... face had paid the price, he has a f... f...f... face that looks like he'd f... f... f... fallen out of the ugly tree, and hit every branch on the way down. Anyway, his wife Mrs Denton was coming back f... f... f... from the toilets,' he held up a finger, 'one of the eight blokes whistled at her. And at that precise moment the landlord rung the bell f... f... f... for last orders,' he shook his head slowly. 'Bad move, on the landlord's part, he should never have rung that bell.'

Paul looked at the others and then back at John, he had to ask the question, he knew they all wanted to ask. 'Ok John, why shouldn't the landlord have rung the bell?' he asked, holding out his hands.

'Well, it was the combination of the two things, coming together at the same time that sent him into a f... f... f...frenzy, tables and chairs f... f... f...flew across the bar, women screamed, blood everywhere, anyway he f... f... f... floored the lot of them.'

'No...you're... joking,' said Craig. *I wish he had bloody caught Rod now,* he thought. Craig turned to Rod.

'Imagine what he'd done to you if he'd caught you Rod, I mean there's a big difference between whistling at her, and her having your bollocks in her hands. You're one hell of a lucky bastard.'

'Up yours Monkey man, anyway I've told you she never had my bollocks in her hands at any time,' replied Rod looking round at them all. 'Anyway, why the hell do you all keep saying that I was lucky, I wasn't bloody lucky at all; it was all a bloody big disaster...' 'Why?' interrupted Mick. 'Apparently it seems you got away with your life, according to what John says...' 'Because, think Mick,' interrupted Rod. 'I had to buy a new pair of trousers and a whole set of bloody tools.'

Craig smiled. 'Why didn't you go back and get them?' he asked, 'then Mr Denton could have had a real pop at you.'

John heaved a sigh. 'I'm not so sure that it was as innocent as Rod says.' He shook his head. 'I think Rod got exactly what he went there f... f... f... for.'

Rod held up an unrepentant hand. 'Whatever John, whatever you want to believe. Anyway, I suppose to you John, sex is quite a strange phenomenon. I expect you must have given up sex a long time ago.'

'No I haven't.'

'Have you checked the expiry date on your Durex packet?'

'For your information Rod, me and Mrs H don't use them,' John replied.

'There you are,' laughed Rod. 'That proves my point.'

'That proves f...f...f...fuck all,' snapped John. 'Mrs H and me don't shag around like you do mate, especially with girls like that,' he said, laughing as he looked towards the girls at the bar.

Mick held up a hand at John. 'John don't encourage him.'

John could barely restrain his temper. 'Piss off Mick, I'm going to have my say,' he snapped. 'Believe me Rod I've had my moments.'

Rod laughed at John's belligerence.

'Oh yes, go on Rod, you can laugh, but you should have seen me in my heyday, a real lady's man. With me around you wouldn't have stood a bloody chance,' John said pushing back his thinning hair.

'I'm amazed you can remember that far back John,' replied Rod. 'Have you looked at Mrs H's beaver lately, you sure it hasn't healed up, like the hole in my ear did when I had my stud removed?' he said, touching his ear.

John lifted a fist in mock warning. 'I'm warning you mate, you're standing on thin ice,' he snarled.

'Hit a raw nerve there then, have I John?'

'John's right Rod,' warned Mick. 'You're going to push him too far one of these days.'

John looked at Rod, gritting his teeth. 'It's about time you grew up Rod.'

Craig laughed. 'You'd have more chance, John, of stopping my dog licking his bollocks, than Rod acting like a grown-up,' he replied shaking his head. 'I'm afraid that's never going to happen mate.'

Rod looked sharply at Craig. 'Bollocks.'

'See what I mean,' said Craig holding out his hands.

Rod wasn't going to let John get the last word. 'Tantric Sex John, that's what you and Mrs H want. Sting does it you know?'

'What the f...f...f...f... fuck's Tantric Sex and Sting?' asked John.

Sting was the lead singer of the pop group Police, and as I've said he practices Tantric sex.

'You don't say,' said John without looking over the top of his magazine.

'I've tried it myself, the only trouble is it gets in the way of drinking time, but it's ideal for older people like yourself and Mrs H. It's very, very slow sex, and has a lot of different positions.'

'A bit like Yoga with sex,' said Paul

'Right, I'm really not interested,' said John pulling up his magazine.

'Did you have a favourite position?' asked Paul.

'Mmm...' Rod thought, 'now you've asked, yes in fact I did have a favourite position, it was called the plumber.' Rod pointed at John. 'You should try it some day John.'

John nodded his head uncommitted.

Paul looked puzzled. 'Why the plumber?'

'Because you stay in all day and nobody comes'.

Sean laughed, pulling a pencil from behind his ear waving it in the air, hoping to get things back on track. 'Right, so you're all paid up, except for John,' he said, tapping John's name with his pencil. 'Let's hope we win.'

'Ok,' Rod turned towards the two girls. 'Here we go, here we go,' he sang, clapping his hands together and picking up his pint. 'Oh by the way, Sean,' he said over his shoulder as he walked towards the girls. 'About soul mate you said earlier Sean, believe me mate, its just shag.'

Paul looked at Rod's disappearing back and then at the girls. 'He will you know, he will,' he said, turning back towards the lads.

'Will what,' said John, looking up from his magazine and squinting at Rod as he made his way to the bar.

'Shag them,' replied Paul. 'He's scored with more women than David Beckham scores penalties. It's even said that in his local pub he's got a waiting list of women waiting to go out with him.'

'Sad bastard,' said John.

'Lucky bastard,' said Paul and Craig simultaneously.

Everyone nodded slowly, and rolled their eyes at Rod.

'That's all he bloody thinks about,' tutted John. 'Pity he never puts that much bloody effort into his work,' he grunted, looking over the rim of his glasses towards the girls at the bar. 'Dirty little bastard.'

'Don't you mean lucky little bugger John?' said Mike as he looked round at the girls. 'Maybe that's why he got a job as a plumber.'

'Why?' asked Sean not able to see the connection.

'Because he likes tapping up young girls,' replied Mick.

'Right…right,' said Sean pointing his pencil at Mick. 'I never thought of it that way.'

Paul and Craig laughed at them both.

John shook his head in exasperation and laid down his magazine on the table, running his hand along the back of his neck. 'Don't you bloody encourage them Paul…f… f… f… for Christ sake,' he continued, 'although it pains me to say this lads,' he paused, 'there is one thing that Rod has got right.'

'What's that?' asked Sean.

'It's this bloody lottery thing,' John paused gathering his thoughts 'Let me try to explain, Sean. Apparently I'd have more chance of f... f... f... finding f... f... f...fucking Jordan naked, draped up my stairs at home, pleading f...f...f... for me to make mad passionate love to her as I walked through the f...f... f...front door, than winning this bloody lottery,' he said, throwing his pound across the table at Sean.

'You never know John,' said Sean making a mark against his name.

John looked over the rim of his glasses at Sean. 'Sean, I'm telling you now,' he said, shaking his head. 'It's never going to bloody happen.'

'How do you know?' asked Sean.

'Because his wife wouldn't let him,' laughed Mick.

Paul laughed.

Sean never got the joke.

John scowled at Paul and returned to his magazine.

Paul ignored John's intent look. 'But they're fake,' he continued. 'She told everybody on the television,' he said quickly.

Confusion tightened Sean's eyes. 'Who? What's fake?' he asked, looking puzzled, not following Paul's train of thought.

Paul replied with an exaggerated eye roll. 'You know Sean, Jordan's things. Them!' said Paul pointing at his chest.

Mike's eyes widened. 'What, you don't mean her breasts?'

John blew out his breath and shook his head, throwing down his magazine. 'For Christ sake, will you all get a bloody life,' he said, gulping down the last of his beer. 'Jordan's tits he tutted, as much as I would like to stay here f... f...f... for the whole weekend and listen to your useless, pathetic, meaningless babble, I'm afraid,' he stood up banging his glass down on the table, 'I must go home to my f... f... f... family and some sane f... f... f... friends,' he said, looking at Paul. 'Paul, have you ever heard the song *Eve of Destruction?*' he asked.

'No, why?

'*Even the Jordan river had bodies floating,*' does that sound f... f... f... familiar?' John laughed, 'just remember that Paul,' he continued. 'Paul, you're in,' said John, looking towards Rod and the girls at the bar.

'I've already got them in,' said Paul.

'Not the beers, you twat, the bloody girls,' John said. 'You're in there mate.' He nodded towards the bar.

The girls were looking back at their table, as one of the girls winked at Paul.

Paul was tall, six foot, good-looking, short well-groomed blond hair, round face, and large saucer blue eyes, but his height made him painfully shy, in fact he walked with a stoop to make himself look smaller.

Paul blushed. 'Shit, I think John's right Mick,' he said. Leaning across the table towards Mick he whispered. 'One of the girls fancies me.'

'No!' gasped John, 'you're quick.' Looking back at the girls, 'I'm sure I didn't see a blind dog lying down next to them when I came in, did you Mick?' he asked.

Rod waved Paul over.

'Piss off John, talk about boosting a bloke's confidence.' said Paul.

'I don't think it's your confidence that they are after Paul, go on lad fill your boots,' said John as Paul stood up.

'Oh, Paul,' shouted Mick as he shyly stooped off towards the girls.

'What?'

'While you're up there, it's your round,' shouted Mick, holding up his glass.

Paul held up a finger.

'I'll take that as a no then,' shouted Mick. He breathed deeply. 'John, stay and have a swift half,' he pleaded. 'I'll get them in.' He was never keen to break up these Friday get together. He hated weekends; as for him it was the start of his lonely weekend waiting for Monday to return. His work was his solace, and he loved the banter with the lads. He dreaded going back to that house, after losing Kathleen and Elizabeth some three years ago in a fatal car accident, the outcome of one of their weekend shopping trips. Their house that was once so full of energy and love now it was empty, like his heart. The house had become his prison, and he descended into sadness and shyness that was forced upon him. He'd become so lonely he'd become introspective.

John waved a hand. 'Sorry Mick, but no, I've really got to get going,' he said, looking at Sean. 'Look, he's already dropping off to sleep,' he looked at his watch. 'Anyway, must go,' he said, tapping his watch, 'got Jordan waiting for me at home, mustn't keep the young lady waiting, must I?'

'You wish,' said Sean, through one half opened eye.

'Go back to sleep Sean,' said John placing his glass on the table. 'I'll see you all again on Monday. Oh and by the way,' he said as an afterthought, 'the key, Mick, to the wall safe...' 'Sorry John,' interrupted Mick, tapping his jacket pocket, 'right, busy day, forgot to put it back in the lock.'

'Well as long as you know we have all the spare keys to the houses, the spares for the porter cabin, and the machinery...' 'Don't worry John,' interrupted Mick. ' The crime rate is very low in that area.'

'Well as long as you don't f... f....f...forget to bring it back on Monday.' John looked at his watch. 'Must f... f... f... fly Mick. I hope and pray Rod doesn't get a shag this weekend, and you lot have a poxy weekend.' On his way out John slapped Rod and Paul on the shoulders. 'Take a word of advice f... f... f... from a wise old man lads,' he paused. Wagging a finger at Paul and Rod. 'Wear a Durex, you never know these days, better to be safe than dead.'

'Of course!' was the positive reply from Rod as if no such recommendation was necessary. John smiled sarcastically at the girls, as if it was them that had started the whole AIDS epidemic single-handed. 'What do you suggest John, teasers, ribbed or ticklers?'

John never supported what they'd asked with a reply, as he turned on his heels to leave the pub.

'Cheers John, thanks for your advice,' shouted Rod, 'we'll buy those edible ones, strawberry flavour,' he said, licking his lips.

'Give our love to Jordan,' shouted Paul.

John looked over his shoulder at the girls as they both pointed to their breasts, giggling.

'They're real,' shouted the lads in unison, pointing at their breasts.

John glanced back, 'Bollocks,' he shouted back. 'You dirty little bastards, *you just can't help some f... f... f... fucking people, the bloody arrogance of youth,'* he mumbled, sticking up two fingers, and was gone. He pulled out of the pub car park in his BMW, and sped towards Peterborough thinking not of sex, fake breasts, or flavoured Durex, but of Sundays, roast beef and Yorkshire pudding.

Chapter Two
Monday : The Start Of
Another Week

Monday 7:00 am John unlocked the cabin and flicked on the light's, the fluorescent light flickered into life and lit up the site cabin. *That's strange* he thought as he entered the cabin, it was unusually warm for a cold Monday morning. Throwing his lunch bag on to the table, he bent down to plug in the heater and the coffee machine; he padded the floor with his hand, looking for the plugs. 'That's strange,' he mumbled to himself, checking the plug sockets in the wall, both plugs were already plugged in. Lines appeared in his forehead, *I'm sure I unplugged the heater, and the coffee machine on Friday when I left,* he thought. *Maybe I didn't,* he dismissed the thought and drew himself a cup of coffee from the machine. He sat, shook out his newspaper, his eyes roving over *The Sun*'s page 3 naked beauties. He was into his second Styrofoam cup of coffee as the rest of the lads started to drift in.

'Morning John good weekend?' asked Paul.

John groaned a reply, and shook his newspaper at him.

Paul slipped onto the bench beside him, glancing at page 3. 'I'd bet you'd like to get your hands on them,' he said, 'instead of fitting in that bloody boiler today.'

John shrugged, turning the page of his newspaper, looking around the cabin. Most of the lads were sitting quietly, bleary-eyed; none of them looked fit enough to do a day's work, let alone a week's work. 'You all look like you're glad to be back.'

'I've got some good news,' said Craig softly as he entered the cabin, hiding his embarrassed face as he drew a coffee from the machine.

'What's the good news then Monkey man?' asked Rod, yawning. 'You haven't found another job.'

'Bollocks,' replied Craig. 'All I'm trying to do is cheer us all up on this wet bloody Monday morning. That's all. Very sorry.'

John grunted into his newspaper. 'Ignore him Craig.' He looked up at him. 'What's the good news, you have f... f... found another job, one down f... f... four to bloody go.' He smiled in anticipation.

'John don't stoop to Rod's level. It wasn't funny the first time'.

'I'm not being funny, I'm serious Craig.'

'No ...no... don't worry, I'm here for life mate, no it's not another job,' Craig replied, waving a placatory hand.

'Well?' asked Paul.

'Maria's expecting.'

Intrigued, Rod angled his head. 'Expecting...expecting what Monkey man, a letter?' he asked.

Paul rolled his eyes at John. 'John, remember it is early in the morning,' he said, turning towards Rod. 'Maria's with child, Rod,' he explained, 'something I thought you might have known about, what with all the women you've had sex with, I bet you've had a few near-misses.'

John smiled, nodding his head in agreement.

'Nobody's come knocking on my door yet, mate,' Rod replied. 'I'm too bloody careful.'

'Yer, he moves house a lot as well,' Craig informed them all.

'No, I don't Monkey man,' Rod answered with feeling. 'I haven't moved for ages. Anyway,' he continued, 'shit, a baby you say Craig, didn't I tell you to wear a Durex?'

Craig shook his head in marked bewilderment, looking at Rod. 'What the hell are you going on about Rod, Maria and I planned this baby.'

'Yer…yer … right, that's what they all say mate, that's their last line of defence. That's how they trap you into marriage. I know you lot won't believe it, but I have a really healthy attitude towards permanent relationships.'

'And what's that then?' asked Paul.

'Avoid them like the plague.'

Craig look puzzled. 'Getting back to what you said earlier Rod, before all the relationship bollock's. I am married, and have been married for the past five years,' he said.

Rod waved a hand at Craig. 'Whatever, I'm telling you now that hell would freeze over before a woman trapped me and tied me down. They wouldn't bloody catch me out like that, making out that we'd planned a bloody sprog,' pointing a finger at Craig, 'Planned, be bollocks,' he smiled shaking his head, 'planned you said,' he repeated.

'Maybe it happens in your world, Rod. Probably that's the case,' replied Craig, 'but not in ours.'

'It will happen to you one day, believe me.'

'I'm telling you it will NEVER... NEVER happen to me mate.'

'We'll see,' replied Craig. Shaking his head at John and Paul, he held out his hands and nodded towards Rod. 'Where the hell's he coming from, he hasn't got a bloody clue, has he?'

'That's right,' said John agreeing with Craig, 'he obviously knows f...f...f...fuck all about marriage.'

They both nodded their heads in agreement.

'In fact,' continued Craig, 'Maria's six-and-a-half,' he paused, scratching his head, 'or...maybe, seven months pregnant.'

'Christ Craig, seven months pregnant you said,' answered John, 'and you've only just told us.'

'Well Maria's had a lot of trouble in the past,' whispered Craig, see-sawing his hand, 'so we didn't want to get our hopes up, you know.'

Rod slapped his hand on the table. 'There, I rest my case,' he said looking at Craig. 'Why's that then Monkey man, you weren't firing blanks,' he asked. 'Were you?'

'Bollocks Rod, anyway,' Craig turned back to the others and continued, 'so Maria's having a baby; I thought that might brighten up your Monday lads. That's good news for the start of the week, isn't it?' he asked, looking at them one at a time, smiling at the thought of being a dad.

Paul smiled, 'Well done Craig.'

'Doesn't do jack-shit f… f… f… for me,' replied John. 'Babies are babies and, Mondays are bloody Mondays,' he said, watching the disappointed expression on Craig's face. 'No… no… Joke. I'm joking. Take no notice of me Craig, that's really good news, well done my son.'

Craig's smile appeared back on his face, at John's approval.

'Who's the daddy then?' asked Rod smiling.

'Thanks,' said Craig smiling half-heartedly.

'That wasn't a compliment Craig,' smiled Rod, 'I meant, who's the daddy!'

Paul smiled and looked at Craig. 'You sure Rod hasn't been round your house, has he?' he asked.

Rod laughed, 'If I had, I'd guarantee that the baby would be good-looking, and that's a fact, anyway, people always say that ugly people shouldn't have children.'

'Bollocks,' replied Craig.

'See lads, he's lost his sense of humour, look at him he's a fucking wreck.'

'What do you expect? We're having a baby!'

'Anyway, enough about babies, how was your weekend Rod?' asked John, quickly turning their attention off the subject of babies.

'Bloody champion,' smiled Rod. 'Remember those two birds in the pub on Friday?'

John nodded his head.

'Only thing was, that he bloody let me down,' said Rod, pointing a finger at Paul.

'Why?' asked John, looking at Paul.

'Because I'm married John, that's why,' Paul shrugged his shoulders. 'I wasn't about to jeopardise my marriage for a bloody quick roll in the hay.'

John tapped Paul on the shoulder. 'Good lad, that's what I like to hear, a man with principles.'

'Principles, be bollocks, he had pangs of bloody guilt,' said Rod. 'See, once again, if that's what bloody marriage does to you, as I said before, you can stick it. Treat women like cars, that's what I say.'

'Why?' asked John, trying not to show too much interest.

'Because they all need a good servicing now and again, and I'm just the mechanic to do it.'

'Rod the great philosopher of women I don't think so Rod,' said Paul.

'Look at my face Paul does it say I give a shit what you think.

'Paul's right Rod. Anyway, what did happen to the two young girls in the pub on Friday?' inquired John.

'I don't think we need to be privy to Rod's sexual experiences, do we lads? Asked Craig.

'I'm intrigued,' said John.

They waited for him to elucidate, so he did. 'Right, so if you'll all let me finish,' replied Rod. 'Anyway, it didn't make any difference to me whether Paul stayed or not. I took them both out to dinner that evening, and back to my place for a coffee, and you'll never guess what happened.'

John definitely didn't want to ask, but had to admit he was inquisitive.

'What?' Rod asked reluctantly, as if he needed any prompting.

'The weekend.'

'Right the young ladies, well, when we all got back to my house, I found out that they were twin sisters; would you believe it, bloody twins. Mind you, not identical twins though you wouldn't have known. One of them had long dark hair and the other one had short blonde hair, and the one with blonde hair,' Rod raised his eyebrows, 'her hair was dyed you know!'

'How did you know the blonde one was dyed?' asked Craig, 'the blonde could have been natural, and the dark-haired one could have had her hair dyed.'

Rod nodded his head. 'No chance,' he replied.

'And how the hell did you know that then,' asked Paul.

'You don't get out much, do you Paul, think,' said Rod. 'That's a good sign,' he said, pointing at his private parts.

John looked back at his newspaper and mumbled. 'You dirty little bastard.'

Paul's mouth gaped open. 'You mean you took the blonde one to bed,' he said, 'what about the other sister?'

'Couldn't leave her standing out in the cold, wouldn't have been gentlemanly thing to do now, would it? So I took them both to bed with me,' Rod said smiling at the thought of the previous night. 'They were both gagging for sex.'

Paul looked swiftly at John, and Craig, then back at Rod. 'Both, you said. You mean… both… both of them together, at the same time, in the same bed!'

John's mouthed gaped open, endeavouring to get his mind around the concept of getting two women into the same bed, at the same time, the very idea struck him as impossible. 'You're winding us up, you dirty little bastard,' he said finally, from behind his newspaper.

'No…. no…. I'm not winding you up at all John, why would I do that?' replied Rod.

'I think he's telling the truth John,' agreed Paul.

'Well,' inquired Rod, holding out his hands. 'Do you want to hear what happened to me, or not?'

Paul shook his head enthusiastically.

Craig shrugged his shoulders, not happy at the thought of Rod getting lucky with anything at all, let alone the two girls.

'Well, as I said, they were twins,' continued Rod, 'and Sam told me that whatever her sister George felt, she felt it too.'

John looked up from his paper. 'George,' he said. Rod held up his hand. 'Before you come to any conclusions which are unfounded John, George is short for Georgina.'

John smiled. 'So George is short for Georgina. Good, we're glad you cleared that one up Rod.'

'Anyway,' said Rod, 'I thought I might as well make the most of them both.' Rod gyrated his hips. 'So I shagged the both of them, and bloody good they both were too.' He stopped gyrating his hips and looked at John, seeing the look of revulsion on his face. 'Don't tell me John you never had sex with more than one woman,' inquired Rod.

'In the past John's had more sex than a policeman's torch has seen,' replied Paul in John's defence.

John nodded towards Paul and smiled, and nodded looking back at Rod. 'What the hell is that suppose to mean Rod?'

'More than one woman John,' Rod repeated.

'Well, once again you're wrong Rod,' answered John, pausing for a moment in mock contemplation. 'Bollocks, in f... f... f... fact, I have made love to two women,' he replied, 'but they weren't sisters, and not both at the same bloody time, and certainly not in the same bloody town. In f... f... f... fact Rod, a word of advice here, you should never shit on your own doorstep mate.' Furrows appeared in his forehead. 'Anyway what intrigues me is,' he paused and shook his head contemplating the answer, 'what was George doing while you were making love to her sister?'

'Well while I was making love to Sam, George was tickling my balls John,' replied Rod.

Craig half-heartedly laughed, trying not to give Rod the idea that he approved. 'Thanks for helping us get our heads round that one Rod.'

'They certainly did,' replied Rod.

'Certainly did what? Asked Paul.

'Got their heads round this,' Rod said, rubbing his groin.

'Ok, ok Rod,' said Craig quickly. 'Thanks for sharing that with us.'

'Yes, we're all really glad you shared that with us Rod,' agreed John turning up his nose at the thought of the girls tickling and getting their heads round Rod's balls.

Rod grinned. 'No problem John glad to be of service.'

'Shit, where's Sean?' John asked, turning towards Craig and Paul, swiftly moving away from Rod's sexual activities and shoving Rod's licking and balls tickling escapades to the back of his consciousness without the slightest anticipation of it conceivably resurfacing ever again.

'Holiday I think,' replied Craig.

'No Craig, Sean's not on holiday until the end of next month,' said Paul, 'I'm sure he said he was going to Disney World.'

John looked up from his newspaper. Page 3. 'Disney World Paris?' he inquired.

'No, Disney World Florida, I think,' replied Paul.

John threw his newspaper on the table. 'Did you say, F… F… F…Florida, f… f… f…fuck me, F… F… F… Florida the lucky bastard.'

'Anyway, whatever,' answered Paul. 'Sean's not turned up for work.'

'Well, get Mick to phone him,' said John, ' you know Sean hates Mondays, he's always late…'

'It's done,' interrupted Paul. 'I've already seen Mick on the way in, apparently he's already rung Sean's mobile,' he said, 'there was no answer.'

Mick walked in, 'Morning lads, good weekend?' smiling at the thought that he was back in the place that he enjoyed so much.

'Apparently Craig's wife's having a baby,' said Rod.

Mick smiled at Craig. 'Well done lad.'

Craig smiled back, blushing. 'Thanks Mick.'

John looked over the top of his paper. 'Silly question Mick, but did you came back to the site over the weekend?'

'No,' replied Mick.

John looked puzzled.

'Why?' asked Mick.

'No reason,' John said waving a hand, 'f... f... f... forget it, it's not important.'

'Ok lads, right the itinerary for today,' said Mick, holding up his itinerary board. 'John you're in number 55, first fix.'

'Mick, you gave me f... f... f...fifty f... f... f... five's f...f... f...first f... f...f...fix because of my...'

'Yer Mick,' interrupted Rod, 'That's not fair you know John's going to have trouble with that all day. Give the first fix to Craig. He can swing around the joists all day and he needs the bloody experience.'

'Bollocks Rod.'

'Just trying to help John out, Craig,' smiled Rod.

'Cheers Rod f... f... f... for your support,' said John. 'Anyway, you know I bloody hate f... f...f...first f...f...f...fixes no money in them, and I still haven't recovered from the bloody accident.' He tilted his body to one side squeezing out a fart.

'Jesus Christ John, was that you?' said Mick, standing by the coffee machine waving the air in front of his face with the itinerary board.

'That's what the bloody accident left me with, bad guts,' replied John. 'Anyway, better out than in.'

'Jesus Christ, d'you think so,' said Rod, turning towards John waving his hand in front of his face. 'We ought to stick a pipe up your arse, and provide the whole bloody estate with free gas. Jesus, open the door Paul for Christ sake. Anyway, what bloody accident are you talking about?' he asked, looking round at the lads puzzled.

'Apparently John said it was my fault,' answered Paul, opening and closing the door and looking sheepishly at John.

'It was your bloody f…f…f…fault you numpty,' said John, shifting his arse on the bench.

'I know John, and I felt terribly about what I did, but I didn't know,' Paul said in his own defence hold up his hands.

'Well what happened?' asked Rod

'Well, John was doing a first fix in number 42: he'd laid his boards out across the joist to get to the airing cupboard on the other side of the room. While he was downstairs getting the boiler out the van,' Paul raised his hands again, 'I didn't know he'd gone to the van… Anyway, I took the first board away from the doorway to work on a water tank in the loft. John came back up the stairs, with the boiler in his hands, and bang, boiler and bollocks, fell through the floor.'

'No shit,' winced Rod from the other end of the cabin…. That's not the worst of it,' interrupted John. 'In retrospect, I'd wished I had f… f… f… fallen straight through the bloody f… f… f… floor joists.'

'Why's that?' asked Rod puzzled, *thinking that falling through the joist would have been bad enough.*

'Because my legs went either side of the f.... f.... f....
fucking f... f... f... floor joist.'

'Jesus,' they all said in unison, wincing, holding their
testicles in front of their trousers.

'Mind you, John,' said Rod, 'I did notice that you
were walking a bit funny lately, but I just put that down
to your old age.'

'Bollocks Rod, it wasn't my bloody age, just
incompetent bloody plumbers that don't give a shit about
anybody else,' replied John.

Paul held out his hands. 'John, I've said I'm sorry,
what else can I do,' he replied.'

'You could massage his bollock's for him.'

John ignored Rods remark and nodded his head at
Mick. 'He's bloody sorry,' he said, looking at Paul,
raising his hands. 'Because of your stupidity I was in pain
f... f...f... for bloody weeks, and still am, in
f...f...f...fact,' he said, shifting his position again on the
bench.

'That would never have happen to Monkey man,'
Rod informed Craig.

'Why not?' asked John.

'Not with those bloody arms, look at the length of
them,' said Rod, grunting and striding round the cabin
giving his impression of a strutting ape.

Craig stood up making his way to the cabin door.
'Fuck off Rod, you're a simpleton. D'you know what I
like about you?'

'What?' asked Rod smiling.

'Fuck all,' replied Craig. 'Mick, I'm off outside for a
smoke before I bloody chin the bastard,' he said.

'He doesn't mean it, Craig,' said Mick as Craig slammed the cabin door, nearly taking the door off its hinges as he left the cabin.

'Feeling's mutual,' shouted Rod.

'I don't think Craig likes you Rod!'

'That's not a problem, anyone who doesn't like me is obviously too uptight.'

'Lots of people don't like you!'

'That's because lots of people are too uptight.'

John threw down his newspaper. 'Hey Rod, you toss pot; you haven't got a clue have you? Don't beat around the bush, why don't you, just say what you mean.'

Rod smiled. 'I did, didn't I. Anyway as you said that's where Monkey man should be.'

Paul looked at Rod puzzled. 'Where?'

'Beating around the bush deep in the Amazon jungle.'

Mick frowned at Rod. 'That's enough Rod, zip it.'

'Rod you're a real twat sometimes, d'you know that?' John said.

'Funny, that's what Mick said about you John.'

John looked sternly at Mick.

'Don't bring me into this squabble, Rod,' Mick said, looking at John. 'I've said nothing of the sort John.'

'I know Mick,' said John, looking back at Rod. 'You're an insensitive bastard,' he said, 'you certainly know how to make f...f...f...friends and influence people. Diplomacy has never been one of your strongest points, has it? You'll get your comeuppance one of these days my f...f... f... friend.'

Rod shrugged his shoulders. 'Well he's a twat. Anyway, hark at you John,' replied Rod. 'Mr bloody sensitive, talk about the kettle calling the pot black.'

John looked at Mick. 'What the f... f... f... fuck's he talking about, Mick?'

Mick raised his eyebrows, and rolled his shoulders. 'I haven't a clue John.'

'Have you ever thought of working in social care Rod?' asked John.

'I do, you're all social retards, especially Monkey man.'

Craig poked his head around the site door. 'I know what he's talking about John, bollocks as usual,' he said.

'You're right Craig,' John shouted back at Craig as the cabin door slammed shut again. 'Anyway,' said John, turning back to Rod, 'you shouldn't take the piss out of Craig. He can't help having long arms,' he whispered. 'You've bloody upset him now,' he said.

Rod shrugged. 'Well, I'm fed up with looking at his long bloody face, and arms.'

'Maybe it's the new baby,' said Mick, 'he could be worried about the birth.'

Rod held both his palms up in mock-surrender. 'Ok,' he continued, looking round at them all, seeing that he hadn't gained their approval with his remarks. 'Right then,' he held out his hands, 'how do you suggest I put a smile back on his face?'

The cabin door opened. 'Go and play on the M25 Rod,' said Craig, pulling the door shut again.

Rod held out his hand towards the door. 'See what I mean?' He looked back at John. 'Talking about chivvying people up, how's your balls John?' he asked, knowing that they were John's two sore points.

John shifted uncomfortably on the bench. 'Black as bloody Newgate's knocker, in f… f… f… fact they were throbbing like hell on Saturday night,' he said, 'I had to get Mrs H out of bed to check them for me. I had to bend over, with one f…f…f…foot on the bidet, while Linda inspected them f… f… f… from behind, with a torch.'

Mick and the lads gave an involuntary shiver as the image filled their consciousness.

'Jesus,' said Rod screwing up his nose. 'By the way John, she didn't find your wallet up there, while she was looking up your arse, did she?'

'Bollocks, I'm warning you Rod,' spat John pointing a finger at him, making a move to get up…. 'Oooh. I'm so scared,' said Rod as John made his move. 'Ok… ok…' said Mick, holding up a hand trying to defuse the situation. 'For God's sake the pair of you, will you cool it, and sit down. Mind you,' he continued, looking back at John, 'that was definitely too much information John.'

Craig put his head round the door. 'Mick, it's here.'
'What?'
'Sand, Mick?'

'Shit,' muttered Mick, 'its bloody bricks we want not more bloody sand. Right, cheers Craig,' he said, raising a hand. 'Anyway, I've got a first fix at number 55, is that all right with you Craig?'

Craig shrugged his shoulders. 'Whatever, Mick,' he replied.

'F... f... f...for f...f... f... fuck sake Mick, who's the bloody f... f... f...foreman here, don't f...f...f...fucking ask him, you've got to show some sort of authority around here you know, or they'll wrap you round their little f... f... f... finger. Bloody tell him.'

Mick raised an authoritative hand and raised his voice an octave. 'Ok John,' he said, turning towards Craig. 'Craig, first fix in number 55.'

Craig slammed the cabin door shut.

'Not Monkey man's day, is it?' said Rod laughing.

'John, 69 second fix.'

John held up his thumb. 'Consider the job done Mick.'

Paul stood at the mirror combing back his hair.

'Paul, we need the lead-work finishing on number 75's roof.'

'Shit,' said Paul. 'Mick have you seen the bloody weather out there?' He pushed the comb into his back pocket.

'Force 8,' said Rod laughing.

John laughed and looked up from his newspaper. 'That'll f... f... f... f... fuck your hair up Paul.'

He who laughs last, laugh longest thought Mick. 'I'm afraid Rod you're going to have to double up on your work load today, we've got to finish number 84 before dinner. We've got clientele moving in this afternoon.'

'Why do I have to double my work load?' asked Rod, pulling his shoulder-length hair into a ponytail and securing it with an elastic band.

'Because Sean was supposed to be working with you today and as you can see he hasn't turned up.'

'Mick, I'm knackered, I had a bloody busy weekend you know.'

'He should have kept your old man in your trousers then,' said John, looking at Mick. 'Don't you go bloody soft on him Mike, it's bloody self-inflicted you know, serves him bloody right.'

Mick rubbed his chin, and held out a hand towards Rod. 'I'm afraid John's right Rod, that's your problem, but I will give you a hand later.'

'What!' said John, 'you, bloody plumbing, Mick?'

'You know I used to be a plumber once John, and a damn good plumber at that.'

'You're a bloody F…. F…. F….C.P.,' said John.

Paul looked puzzled. 'What the hell's a F.C.P. then?' He asked.

'Mick's a bloody f… f… f…Father Christmas plumber Paul,' John said. 'Only does it once a bloody year.'

They roared with laughter.

Mick's face stayed unresponsive. 'John, what did you just say about authority? That's it, take the piss, they aren't going to take too much notice of me if you come out with remarks like that, now, are they?'

John waved a contrite hand. 'You're right, sorry Mick,' he said, smiling. 'Anyway Mick, when you phoned Sean what was the outcome?' Paul asked.

'Yer, strange,' replied Mick, rubbing his chin. 'It's very strange, I did ring him on his mobile earlier this morning,' he said, rubbing the back of his neck. 'But I got no reply, it was switched off, anyway,' he waved his itinerary board. 'I'll ring him back later. Right lads, when you're ready can we make a start, preferably today if that's all right with you lot,' inquired Mike.

John eased out another silent fart.

Paul wrinkled his face. 'Whew,' he said. 'God was that you again John?'

John smiled. 'It must be all that sitting around at the weekend, gas build up I think.'

'Oh…oh…Jesus Christ John have some mercy here,' cried Mick, waving his itinerary board again. 'Jesus, I'm out of here, I'll see you all back here at 12:30 for dinner.'

John folded his newspaper and clapped his hands together making Rod, who had fallen asleep in the corner of the canteen, jump. 'Ok lads, you heard what Mick said, let's make a move,' he said, 'sitting here isn't going to put food on the table, and keep the kids off the streets, is it? Anyway, sitting here is giving my bollocks some gip,' he said, squirming in his seat. He stood rearranging his lower regions. 'Oh, lads, do me a favour before you go, just have a quick gander at the old tackle.' He turned his back to them and smiled.

The site cabin was empty by the time John had dropped his tracksuit bottoms and his boxers.

12:30 dinnertime. Paul shook his head. 'Everybody for coffee?' They all raised a hand. He passed the coffees round and sat next to John.

'How's the balls John? asked Rod sipping his coffee.

'Bloody sore,' replied John, pulling a sandwich from his lunch box and pulling the two slices of bread apart.

'F… f… f…for f…f… f…fuck's sake cheese again,' he went on, 'I hate f…f…f…fucking cheese,' his eyes darting to Mick and Paul for support.

Paul fell into line. 'You had cheese all last week didn't you John?' he asked.

'I did.'

Rod looked at John with a puzzled look on his face. 'Why don't you make your own sandwiches then John?' he asked.

'I do,' said John, as John and Paul roared with laughter, pointing at Rod.

'Bastards,' Rod said, pulling up his 4 X 4 magazine to hide his embarrassment of being sucked in by them both.

'You were very quiet this morning John. Apart from the testes, is there something else worrying you?' inquired Paul.

'Sometimes, I bloody despair Paul,' John paused, throwing his crusts back into the sandwich box. 'She's bloody been caught smoking again,' he said, pulling his tub of fruit from his bag.

Paul raised his eyebrows. 'Who, the wife? I didn't know Linda had given up smoking,' he replied.

'No she hasn't, and it's not the bloody wife,' replied John, 'it's Kaylie.'

'Jesus, what, not your daughter, she's smoking!'

'The very one,' replied John.

'How did you find out?'

'Bloody school teacher caught her smoking outside the school gates.'

'What did she say when you found out.'

'Who the teacher?'

'No Kaylie.'

'She says she smokes because she wants to be a supermodel when she leaves school. She thinks that smoking will keep her thin f...f... f... for Christ sake. She's always been thin. What do you think Paul?'

'Well, I must say I've seen more meat on a butcher's apron, but as you say a supermodel, I must admit for a sixteen-year-old she's a bit of a stunner.'

Rod's ears picked up at the word stunner.

John pointed a finger at Rod. 'Don't you even think about it, mate. I blame it on the television,' John continued. 'Disgusting f...f...f...fucking habit.'

'What's disgusting?' asked Rod, 'the television or smoking?'

John looked sternly at Rod. 'F...f...f...fucking smoking of course,' he replied.... Ok...ok...John, keep your hair on.' interrupted Rod... 'Has he got enough?' interrupted Craig.

Paul and John ignored their remarks. 'Well, what did you do then John?' Paul inquired.

John shrugged. 'What could I do?' he asked, pausing for thought. 'Mind you, I did bloody ground her f...f...f...for a week. Anyway Paul, what the bloody hell do I know about teenagers? Apparently Linda and Kaylie said that I know Jack shit, about teenagers.' What John did know was that he'd brought into the world the equivalent of Harry Enfield's portrait of Kevin the teenager, the female variety. He shrugged his shoulders again. 'So there you are, two against bloody one as usual, I can't win,' he said.

'Don't worry it's no big deal John; smoking in your teenage years is just a minor setback. We've all done it haven't we?'

'You're right,' said John, nodding an agreement 'She'll probably grow out of it.'

'I'll tell you what though,' said Paul. 'Tell her it will ruin her nice new pink lungs, age her skin, and she'll die young of lung cancer. But, for God's sake, don't tell her it will make her look older or she'll be on sixty cigarettes a bloody day.'

'Good point,' said John, pointing at Paul.

'Anyway,' Paul continued, 'think yourself lucky it wasn't none of the other stuff, Jesus,' he said, shaking his head.

John stared at him loosely. 'Come again…. What other stuff?'

'I mean,' Paul paused to allow John to prepare for his next revelation. 'Well, it could have been something much more dangerous than cigarettes.'

'What's more dangerous than cigarettes? They will kill you, it says so on the packet for Christ sake.'

'You're right,' Paul nodded his agreement, 'but cigarettes will only kill you slowly, but the other stuff, instantaneously.'

'What?'

'You know, drugs, smack…'smack interrupted John.

'Heroin John, and there's crack cocaine,' Paul shook his head, 'or even heroin, look what drugs did to, Naomi Campbell and Westwood, Kate Moss and her twaty boyfriend.

'Fucked old Westwood's snout up,' said Rod….

'Right Rod,' continued Paul, and it sent all of them to rehab, and as Rod said Westwood nearly lost her nose.'

'I know what drugs are, and what they bloody do Paul,' said John, nodding in agreement. 'You're right though.'

'You sure Paul don't mean Snap Crackle and Pop?' said Rod.

'Bollocks Rod, this is serious stuff we're talking about here,' said John, turning back to Paul.

'Well,' Paul continued, 'drugs have a triple addiction.'

John silently counted on his fingers. 'I can only think of two, your health, and money.'

'One,' Paul tapped his finger. 'There's, as you say, your health. And Two,' he continued, pulling at his second finger. 'As you said again money. Three, and this is the bloody worst one of them all,' he paused, tapping his third finger, 'the most dangerous, that's because of the long-term affects…. 'What long term effects?' interrupted John impatiently.

'On the brain John, the brain, believe me, I know… I'm telling you, I know,' Paul said, shaking his head.

'Don't tell me Rod's taking drugs,' said John looking across at Rod.

Paul waved a hand in the air. 'No…no…' he smiled. 'Rod's really quite fortunate.'

John pulled another cheese sandwich for his box. 'Why?'

'Firstly, said Paul, 'you need to have a brain, and Rod's pea-sized brain is only his second main organ.'

Mick lowered his newspaper. 'What's his first main organ then,' he inquired, coming into the conversation looking puzzled.

'In his trousers Mick,' laughed Paul.

'You're right,' agreed John smiling.

Paul's face and voice took a more serious tone. 'I'm afraid drugs are much closer to home for me.'

John frowned. 'Why's that then Paul?'

Mick spoke. 'I'm sorry to hear that Paul. Do you want to... have a chat about it, kind of thing?' he asked compassionately.

Paul lifted his head and frowned. 'Piss off Mick, you're joking of course,' he answered. 'Believe me Mick, you lot would be the last individuals I'd tell anything to.'

John dropped his newspaper and held up his hands. 'Thanks Paul, for your vote of confidence,' he replied. 'Mick was only trying to help.'

'Right,' Mick continued, 'then let's get back to the issue in hand then. Is she sexually active?'

John looked down at the page 3 model again, puzzled at Mick's question. He looked up at Mick. 'Who?'

'Your daughter Kaylie of course,' answered Mick.

'How the f...f... f... fuck did we get f... f... f...from smoking cigarettes and taking drugs to the sexual activities of my daughter? Anyway what the f... f... f... fuck's it got to do with you Mick?'

Mike flinched at John's outburst; he could see he'd irritated John. He continued. 'You never know,' he said, 'if she was, and I'm certainly only suggesting,' he held up a hand, 'not that she is, as I said, maybe if she is sexually active, you could have Rod banging on your front door.'

Craig nodded in agreement. 'Even worse she could bring home Rod's baby,' he suggested.

'Bollocks, I'm telling you that's never going to happen Craig.'

'God forbid, let's hope that all the banging he'd be doing would be on your front door,' said Mick, pointing at Rod.

Rod threw his hands up. 'That's life, it happens all the time, lads!'

John's eyebrows shot up. 'You're treading on thin ice here my son, not with my daughter you f… f… f… fat f… f… f… fuck,' he shouted. Rod wasn't fat, but John thought that remark would wind him up.

Rod completely ignored John's remark, but looked down at his stomach anyway. 'Anyway,' said Rod looking at Mick, 'let's get back to Sean, why isn't he at work?'

'Oh, right…right,' said Mick, banging his forehead with his hand. 'Oh, I nearly forgot to tell you. I rang Sean's house, and apparently his wife said that he'd come home Friday night, but on Saturday evening late about 10:00 pm he got a phone call from *me* saying he had to get back to work a day earlier. He told her it was something to do with work deadlines.'

Paul's jaw dropped.

Craig dropped his coffee.

Rod would have dropped his trousers if there had been a girl in the site hut, but there wasn't so he didn't.

John lowered his newspaper. 'You sure Sean never came back here on Saturday?' he asked.

'Yes I'm sure.'

'How do you know he didn't come here,' inquired John.

Mick frowned. 'Because why would Sean come back to work early, I never rang him at all,' replied Mick. 'Why did you ask me that John, whether Sean came back to work on Saturday?'

John waved a hand. 'No reason, it was just a thought,' he said. 'Why would Sean tell his wife he was coming back to work early, and who rang him then if you didn't?'

'How do we know whether somebody rang him or not?'

'Anyway, shit, Mick, what did you say to Sean's wife?'

'I told her that I must have missed him this morning. I told her I'd have another look round the site, and get back to her later. You're right though John, it's bloody strange. As you said why would Sean say that to his wife, if he wasn't here on Saturday?' Mick spread his arms. 'It's a complete mystery.'

'Maybe he's sick,' said Paul.

'Right,' said John, tapping his head. 'Think Paul, if he'd been sick, then he would have been at home with his wife, and he would have spoken to Mick, am I right?'

'Of course, you're right John,' Paul agreed, nodding his head.

'Maybe he's on holiday,' said Rod…. 'That's the trouble with you Rod, you don't listen,' interrupted Paul. 'I told you this morning that he's not on holiday until next month.'

'Right sorry,' replied Rod, 'only trying to help.'

'Don't bother Rod, get me another coffee,' said John, sliding his cup across the table.

Rod snatched up John's cup and shrugged his shoulders. 'Well, I'm only saying there's got to be a good reason why he's disappeared.'

'Maybe he's found another job,' said Craig.

'There, are you listening Rod?' said John, 'now those are the sort of suggestions you should be coming up with,' he said, pointing back to Craig. 'Now, that is a possibility.'

'I think he would have told us though, don't you?' said Paul, looking around at them all. They all shrugged their shoulders.

'There's another possibility,' said Craig.

'You listening, Rod?' said John, 'you might learn something,' waiting with interest for Craig's suggestion.

Craig scratched his head. 'It's just a thought... but it's possible that,' he blew out his cheeks. 'What's the betting Sean's playing away from home and found another woman, and he's run off with her, and that's why he isn't at work, and maybe that's why his wife doesn't know where he is.'

John pointed from Paul to Rod. 'See Rod he's bloody good,' he said, turning his attention back to Craig. 'You're in the wrong job Craig, you should have been a copper,' he looked back at Rod. 'You want to take a leaf out of Craig's book Rod, that's what happens when you use your brain.'

'Bollocks John,' replied Rod, looking sternly at Craig for coming up with such good suggestions.

'Well, it's only an opinion but I think you're on the wrong path there,' said Mick, giving what Craig had suggested some serious thought. He shook his head. 'No... no... that's not possible, disappearing without a simple explanation is definitely out of character for Sean.'

Paul nodded his head. 'Yer Mick, you're right,' he agreed. 'There's got to be some simple reason for Sean's disappearance.'

Mick shook his head to clear any doubts. 'I don't know.' He paused. 'You all saw him on Friday in the pub, there was no indication he was going anywhere, he even talked about his birthday,' he said, nodding his head again. 'Any thoughts?' he asked, lifting his brow in invitation to each of them in turn.... 'Hang on, Rod,' Mick continued, turning back towards him. 'Don't you live close to Sean? You know his wife I believe.'

'I do,' Rod replied, 'what's your point Mick?'

'Were they getting on alright?'

Rod paused at the question. 'Hum...' He smiled. 'You're right Mick, Monkey man's bloody suggestions are ridiculous. I certainly haven't heard any rumours about Sean and any other woman; no it's not possible that Sean would have had another woman,' he said, looking round at them all. 'Have any of you heard anything about Sean and another woman then?'

Silence.

Rod went on, taking everyone's silence as a no, 'I couldn't imagine Sean going off with another woman or leaving Cathleen. No matter what the enticement. He would never allow anything to come between Cathleen and his marriage, especially with another woman. I'm telling you all now, you couldn't get a more loving couple than Sean and his wife, and in genetic terms they're as close as any two people could ever be, like two peas in a pod. Plus, she's one hell of a beautiful-looking woman, I'm telling you.'

Paul shook his head and rolled his eyes. 'Here we go John,' he said.

'What!' asked Rod, scanning Paul's face, as if for any clues.

Paul held out his hands. 'Go on Rod, don't disappoint us all.'

'What!' said Rod again, looking around at them all. They all knew what was coming. Rod raised a hand and continued. 'Anyway, as I was saying, Cathleen is a very beautiful-looking woman for her age, and if she wasn't married to Sean and just a little bit younger...' Rod never finished what he was going to say as they all shouted in unison, 'I'd give her one.'

'You was right Paul,' John said, looking at Paul and Craig, 'he didn't disappoint us.'

'You're so predictable Rod,' said Paul.

Rod shrugged his shoulders, trying to ignore their interruption. 'Whatever,' he said, waving an unashamed hand. 'Anyway Sean and Cathleen both drink down my local boozer, you know. On Saturday nights they sing karaoke together, karaoke King and Queen they are, they both do a good version of *Fairytale of New York*; you know the one by the Pogues and Kirsty MacColl...' I know... I know it,' said John. 'Sung it many times myself.'

'Is that right, John,' inquired Rod. 'Which one were you then Kirsty MacColl?' he smiled. 'Anyway, did you know this then John?' pointing a finger at him. 'That before the Pogues became famous they used to be called Poge Me Hone.'

' Is that right, Rod,' said John, knowing exactly what it meant, but not wanting to be drawn in by him.

Rod waited for a reaction.

Paul raised his eyebrows, looking puzzled at Rod.

John smiled to himself, *go on, go ahead Paul, ask him.*

'Ok... ok... Rod,' said Paul, looking at him. 'So what's Poge Me Hone?'

'It's Irish Gaelic,' Rod informed Paul, glad that somebody had asked.

'Well, what does it mean then?'

'Quite appropriate for you Paul,' said Rod, 'Kiss my arse, that's what it means,' he said, pointing at his arse. 'No, in fact,' he said, pointing at John, 'kiss John's arse.'

John went to pull down his tracksuit bottoms.

'For God's sake John, no,' shouted Paul, waving a hand vigorously in John's direction.

All the lads looked away.

Paul turned up his nose at the thought of John's hairy arse stuck in the air. 'No, thanks for the offer but I think I'll give that a miss,' he said... 'Can we get back to the point,' interrupted Mick.

'You're right Mick,' agreed Rod so childish, 'we seem to be going off the track a little bit here. Cathleen and Sean, no... no... certainly no problems in that quarter Mick.'

'I'll tell you what is strange though,' said John, 'I've never know Sean to have a day off work since I've worked here.'

Mick agreed with John. 'Nor since I've been here.' Rubbing his chin, he shook his head. 'I must admit it's a bit of a puzzle.'

Paul stood and paced the cabin. Thinking. 'God, no,' he gasped and stopped as if he'd walked into a brick wall. 'No, it's not possible,' he said, shaking his head. 'Shit, no… no… not Sean, it's not possible,' he repeated. *He could be wrong, he kept telling himself. It's probably nothing to do with Sean, but where was he? A simple answer would help but it wasn't coming from anyone.* He turned and walked back towards them. *He could be, and hoped he was, completely wrong about the whole idea. Maybe it was Sean; it must be Sean, he's not here is he?*

Mick held out his hands and hunched his shoulders, looking round at the lads. 'What the hell's he going on about?' he asked.

'What,' blurted Rod.

'Paul for fuck's sake spit it out. What's not fucking possible?' asked Craig.

He turned and faced them. 'Hang on a sec,' he pleaded, and started pacing the cabin again. He turned back towards them all again. 'Don't take this the wrong way it's only a thought,' he said. 'Maybe something, but probably nothing,' he said, pulling the back of his head with his hands. 'But… Jesus no…' he said, scratching the back of his head.

They all sat, waiting in anticipation, hanging on his every word.

John's face turned red, eyes blazing. 'Paul f… f… f…for f… f… f… fuck's sake, what!' he roared, throwing down his newspaper.

'It's just a thought...' Paul said again, his hands pulling at the back of his neck, as he started pacing the cabin again.... 'I think I'm experiencing a bit of déjà vu here,' interrupted Rod.

'F... f... f... for f... f... f... fuck's sake shut up Rod, Paul what is it?' John shouted again.

Paul held up a hand and shook it at John. 'Hang on don't rush me... I think it's Sean.'

'I think it's Sean, what's your point? Craig asked with a bored tone in his voice.

'Paul, what do you want: 50/50, ask the audience, or phone a friend,' said Rod, holding out his mobile phone.

Mick frowned at Rod sternly, and then looked back at Paul. 'We've guessed that much, that it's bloody Sean you're talking about, but what about, you think its Sean,' he asked. 'Come on...come on Paul. We're all losing the will to live here, for Christ sake spit it out,' he continued in a get on with it tone of voice.

'I think its Sean and the lottery,' Paul stated, slipping his hands into his pockets.

John's jaw dropped, pre-empting his next answer. 'Shit, you're not suggesting that we've won the lottery, and Sean's disappearance has something to do with the lottery?' He looked at Mick. 'And that's why he's not at work. What do you think Mick?'

Mick shrugged his shoulders at John. 'Might be coincidence, but all the same I suppose it's possible,' he replied.

John scratched his head. 'So you're suggesting Paul that... that's why Sean's not at work,' he said again.

Paul shook his head, and shrugged his shoulders. 'I don't know, it's all just guesswork,' he admitted lamely, holding out his hands in a vague gesture. 'I said it's just a thought,' he repeated.

'That's a new experience for you Paul,' mocked Rod.

Paul looked at Rod sternly. 'Ha... ha... bollocks,' he said sarcastically, turning back to the others. 'I hate saying it, or even thinking of it, but it...is... possible, what do you all think?' raising his hands and shoulders again... 'No...no... not Sean,' interrupted Craig, shaking his head, 'I'm telling you Sean wouldn't bloody do that to us...' 'I don't know, but it does seem sensible to me, what he's saying,' interrupted Rod. 'What Paul's suggesting is possible. I've had lots of people rip me off loads of times,' he said. 'And they were supposed to be my so called friends.'

'Why are we not surprised at that statement Rod,' replied John.

'Anyway,' said Craig, giving Paul's suggestion some thought. 'Paul may well be right, and what he suggests does seem to make some sense, I suppose, but I'm still not convinced that Sean would do as he suggests.' He paused. 'Anyway, if, and... I... don't say this lightly,' finding it difficult to say. 'If... Sean did... take the money, then you've got more of a chance of seeing a formation of pigs flying over the building site, than seeing Sean or our money ever again.'

John could see the value in Paul's suggestion. 'Paul's right,' he said. 'Let me elaborate on what's the bleeding obvious is here lads. Sean's done a runner with our money.'

Mick lifted his shoulders in a slight shrug. 'John whatever you might want to believe, we still don't know if it was Sean. Hang on a minute,' he said, holding up a hand. 'We... could... check Saturday's draw numbers.' He looked around at them all. 'Does anybody know the numbers?'

Paul had already read Mick's thoughts, pulling a pad from the inside pocket of his overalls, and flipping the front cover open. Flipping over the pages, one after the other. He paused. 'Yes, here they are,' he said, '2. 16. 19. 21. 36. 48. That's the six numbers.'

'How the hell are we going to know if those numbers were Saturday's winning numbers?' asked John, scratching his head.

'I know,' said Rod. 'A thought just crossed my mind.'

'Short journey then Rod?' smiled Craig.

'Bollocks,' replied Rod. 'Do you want to hear what I've got to say or not?'

John waved a hand at Craig. 'Go on Rod, what?'

'Ok, well aren't the winning numbers in Sunday's newspaper?'

John clapped his hands. 'Well done, you're right Rod, Sunday's newspaper,' he said, pointing at him, ' and what's to-day Rod.'

'Monday,' replied Rod, looking at John puzzled.

'Right Monday,' repeated John.

Rod waved a hand and smiled. 'That's not a problem John,' he said, 'I brought Sunday's newspaper with me from home.' He rummaged in his rucksack. 'I never had time to read it, because of the busy weekend, you know,' he winked, 'if you know what I mean.'

'We know what you bloody mean,' spat John, 'you dirty little bastard. Just get on with it.'

'Here we are,' he said, pulling the newspaper from his bag, waving it at John.

John looked at Rod sternly. 'You're a smart twat.'

'Thanks, I know,' teased Rod, 'well, do you want to know if we've won the lottery, or not,' he said, spreading the newspaper out on the table, as they all gathered round.

'Page 53,' said Paul, as Rod turned the pages.

'There you are,' said John, placing his finger on the numbers.

Paul laid his pad on the newspaper, as they checked the numbers. You could hear a pin drop as they all stood frozen to the spot. John broke the silence. 'F... f... f... for f... f... f... fuck sake,' he said, 'we've got all six bloody winning numbers.' he ran his finger along the numbers again, just to make sure. 'That f... f... f... fucking bastard Sean's done a f... f... f... fucking runner, with our f... f... f... fucking winnings.'

Rod nodded his head in disbelief. 'I don't believe it,' he said, 'he's so quiet, a shy retiring type, always been as straight as an arrow, not Sean.'

'Believe it,' John said. After seeing the numbers, he was now completely convinced that Sean had done a runner with the winnings. 'We're going round and round in circles here. Why can't you all just accept the f... f... f... fact that Sean's done a f...f...f...fucking runner with our money, the bastard has taken early retirement with our money.'

Mick smiled. 'How much money didn't we win then?' he asked.

John looked across the table at Mick's face. 'It's not bloody f... f... f... funny Mick,' he said, looking back down at the newspaper again. 'It doesn't bloody say, I haven't a f... f... f... fucking clue. I know what we can do though,' he added. 'Mick you ring Camelot and f... f...f... find out how many winners they had Saturday, and how much they paid out.'

'Will Camelot give us that information?' queried Mick, pulling out his mobile phone.

'Of course they will,' blurted Rod.

'Ok...ok...give me the number then?' asked Mick.

Paul read the telephone number from the newspaper, as Mick punched Camelot's hotline digits into his mobile. The phone rung three times, as a disembodied voice spoke, 'Camelot hotline, how can I help you.' Mick gave them the thumbs up sign; they all stood in stock silence as he spoke. After a few seconds Mick dropped his itinerary board on the table; they saw the colour draining from Mick's face as he was receiving the information.

'Thanks very much,' said Mick, slowly pressing a button on his mobile to disconnect the call. He dropped his arm and sat down on the bench, his legs had given in. His blood turned to ice.

'The... bastard...' said Mike slowly shaking his head. John peered across at Mick, noticing his brow furrowing and beads of sweat standing out on his brow. 'What Mick? He shouted.

Mick rubbed desperately at his forehead. 'Apparently, there was only one winner,' he answered.

The lads looked anxiously from one to the other. 'Well, Mick how much?' they all shouted in unison.

Mick cleared his throat and gave a non-committal answer. 'Apparently it was a rollover from Wednesday night's draw.'

'Mick for fuck's sake, how much,' they all shouted again.

Mick stood up, dumbfounded, breathing heavily. 'Eight.... t...e...e... n million fucking pounds.'

Everyone looked flabbergasted at what Mick had said.

'That's...' John did a quick summary in his head. 'That's three million pounds each.'

The figure seemed to hang in the air for a moment as they collected their thoughts; they all shook their heads as if to clear their thoughts. Spontaneously three raucous fucks hit the ceiling in unison, John's finished two seconds later.

'What are we going to do?' asked Mick.

'The pub,' said John.

Chapter Three
Three Million Pounds

Paul placed the tray of drinks on the table and sat down.

Mick took his orange drink from the tray. 'Right, this is the way I see it,' he said, taking a sip from his drink. 'We've three courses of action here. One,' he tapped his index finger, 'if Sean did do a runner with the winnings, we could let him keep the money.'

'F... f... f... fuck off,' said John 'if you think I'm going to kiss my share of eighteen million pounds good-bye, you better think again Mick. But, yer,' he looked around at the lads, 'but, if you lads think that's a good idea, then go ahead, give the bastard your money, but not mine.'

'As you said Mick, if Sean has taken our money, or if he hasn't, whatever the case is, then I must admit that I'm intrigued as to what might have happened to the money,' said Paul.

John shook his head at Paul, 'Paul's got a point,' he said, turning his head to face Mick. 'I haven't got a clue either what's happened to the money, but I'll be interested in finding out.'

'I'm going to have to go along with what John said,' Paul interjected.

Rod gave a low grunt, not wishing to side with them both. 'John and Paul are right Mick, eighteen million pounds is big money,' he agreed, 'I've got to go with Paul and John.'

Craig half-heartedly nodded his approval.

'I'll take that as a no then lads, letting Sean keep the money, that's if he has done a runner with it,' asked Mick.

They all nodded in unison.

' Ok… here's option two then, we can go back to work and forget all about the money.'

John went pale with the thought of going back to work.

'Fuck off,' they all said in unison; John finished his fuck off a few seconds behind them.

'Right, then I'll take option two as a no go also. And, option three… we can go and find where our money went.'

'What would Jordan…I mean your wife, think about that then John?' whispered Paul.

'Very f… f… f… funny,' said John smiling sarcastically. 'I haven't a clue; I'll ask her when I see her next,' he said.

'So you all think Sean really has done a runner with the money?' asked Paul, looking around at all the lads.

'That's the eighteen million pound question Paul,' said John, looking around the pub. 'But I can't see Sean in here can you? You're not exactly brain of Britain Paul,' John inferred.

'Well John,' said Paul defending his question. 'We still don't seem to have the proof that it was Sean who took our money.'

Mick interjected. 'Paul's right John, we haven't anything concrete,' he said, 'Camelot didn't give me a name, they just said only one winner,' he paused. 'Let's say, that if Sean didn't put the lottery money on that Saturday night, then the winner isn't Sean.' Mick raised his eyebrows. 'You never know, it could be somebody else.'

John shrugged. 'It's possible I suppose.'

'See, Mick's right, that's what I was trying to say John, we don't know if it was Sean that took the money,' said Paul, smiling at John. 'But if, and that is only if, Sean did take the money, and at the moment I say that very loosely, then the money will be well gone, and as Mick said we're just going to have to let the money go.'

John stuck his finger in Paul's chest. 'I've told you, there's no f... f...f...fucking way I'm going to let the bastard get away with it, if he has done a runner with our money!'

Paul sat back in his seat. 'John c'mon. Calm down.'

'What's wrong John? Is it your time of the month or something?' said Rod. 'Things aren't that bad.'

John looked around the table at the lads. 'Things aren't that bad,' he snarled. 'I've got a bloody teenager that smokes, and I haven't got a pot to piss in, and' he continued, waving his hand at them, 'and the chance of me not ever looking at all your ugly f... f... f... faces ever again. Bullshit! Bullshit! Bullshit!'

'Cheers for that John,' said Paul as he stood and paced the bar. 'Firstly, we need to find out if it was Sean that did a runner with our money.'

'Yes,' agreed Mick.

'You've got more chance of finding a virgin in Leeds than finding Sean,' Craig informed them.

'Certainly not if Rod's been there f... f... f... for the f... f... f...fucking weekend,' smiled John. The smile left his face as quickly as it came. 'So we've hit a bloody brick wall then?'

Mick folded his arms and smiled without humour. 'Stop taking the piss out of each other for two seconds and give this predicament some thought.'

'You're right Mick, well said,' Rod agreed, slapping the tabletop and standing up. 'No we haven't hit a brick wall, not yet John, hold on, wait here,' he said as he made his way to the bar, and spoke with Joe the barman.

John looked at them all. 'Where the f... f... f... fuck does he think we're going.'

They all shrugged their shoulders.

Rod made his way back to the table 'That's it,' he said, throwing a phonebook onto the table.

'Good one,' said Paul, 'Right, the Yellow Pages phonebook, so how the hell will that find Sean and our money?' he asked.

Rod sat down. 'It may not find our money or Sean, but it will find out if Sean brought a ticket on Saturday, and this,' he said, tapping the book, looking round at them all, 'I'm telling you, it will definitely tell us if Sean put the lottery money on.'

John looked at Rod, puzzled. 'As Paul said, how the hell is that going to tell us if Sean put the lottery money on, Sherlock bloody Holmes?'

'Easy,' replied Rod. 'Just use your head. Didn't Sean say Friday afternoon that he put the lottery on at *Costcutters,* let me see,' he said, flicking through the telephone book.

'I haven't a f…f…f…fucking clue,' said John, 'I never listen to you and Sean's bloody ramblings.'

'Costcutters,' Rod mumbled, running his finger down the list of names. 'Here it is *Costcutters,* Right, here we are,' he said, punching the number with his finger. 'Mick, phone, might as well use your mobile, eh?' he demanded, shaking his hand at Mick. Mick handed over his phone. Rod punched in the numbers. Tapping his fingers on the table. 'Hello, right,' he sat up straight, 'Is that *Costcutters,'* he nodded his head… 'Can I speak with Amanda please; she works on one of your tills…' Rod nodded his head again. 'I'm sorry, but I do need to speak with Amanda it is very important; I'm Doctor Holmes from Peterborough District Hospital… Yes, I'm afraid it's about her brother, I need to speak to his next-of-kin,' he said, tapping his fingers on the table again. Holding the phone away from his ear he whispered, 'they've gone to get her now; he placed the phone back to his ear. 'Oh, hello Amanda, I'm Rod, sorry to bother you, you don't know me, but I needed to speak to you… Oh, so you do have a brother then? No….no…. ' Said Rod, shaking his head…. 'No… no… your brother's fine, I needed to say that just to get you to the phone, sorry if I panicked

you…I'm not really a doctor, in fact I'm not anything at the moment.'

'F… f…f… for f…f…f…fuck sake Rod get on with it,' John whispered, waving a hand to get Rod to move on.

Rod held up an outstretched hand towards John. 'I'm just ringing to find out if you processed a lottery ticket on Saturday evening at 7:00… I'm sure you did… Yes it was a man, his name is Sean…. yes…yes…' he said, nodding his head in response to whatever was being said. He looked at the lads and held the phone away from his mouth. 'Bastard,' he mouthed silently at the lads, replacing the phone to his ear. 'Oh, by the way Amanda,' he said, as if it was an afterthought. 'What are you doing on Saturday night?' he said, not missing the chance of shag. He smiled… 'Champion, we'll go for a drink… Right, a black Porsche 911.'

John looked at Mick, Mick looked at Paul, as Paul looked Craig and Craig looked at Rod.

'I don't believe it, he's going for a shag,' whispered Paul

John nodded his head towards Rod. 'You lying little bastard, a 911 Porsche,' he looked at the others, 'he drives a f… f… f…fucking rusty old F… F… F… Ford bloody, F… f… f… Fiesta.'

He's a cunning, sneaky little bastard when there's a shag in the offing,' said Paul.

'Shush,' Rod said, holding his hand over the mouthpiece. He shrugged and smiled to himself, *he's not bloody wrong,* replacing the mobile to his ear. 'Right, sorry, Amanda I'll pick you up after work on Saturday evening

8:00 pm if that's ok,' he nodded, 'Ok, bye, see you Saturday,' he said, pressing the off-key with his thumb disconnecting the call and passing the phone back to Mick. 'Shit, it was definitely Sean who bought the ticket.'

'The bastard,' the other four said in unison.

'Well, so, what have we got so far?' said Mick. concentrating. He raised his hands and started to tick points off on his fingers with exaggerated gestures. 'One, Sean didn't turn up for work. Two, he bought a lottery ticket on Saturday. Three, he left the pub that night after the lottery draw. Four, his wife hasn't seen him since…'

'F… F… F… Five,' added John, tapping Mick's fifth finger. 'Each of us is now three million pounds f… f… f… fucking worse off.' He always felt he was under constant pressure money-wise, nothing had come to him easily, now it had and he had the chance of an easier life, it had all gone. He let his mind wonder a little on the prospect of recovering the money that had been stolen.

Craig looked down into his glass. 'Well,' he said, looking up at them all. 'What are we going to do about it?'

'*Ubi juis, ibi remedium,*' said Rod.

'What the f…f…f…fuck's he talking about?' asked John, looking at Mick.

Mick shrugged his shoulders.

'Latin,' replied Rod.

'Well what the f…f… f… fuck does it mean?'

'Hang on,' said Paul, holding out a hand towards John. 'Can you speak Latin, Rod?'

'Doesn't everybody speak Latin?' replied Rod sarcastically.

'Not the bloody school I went to,' said John, 'half of my class couldn't speak bloody English, in fact, the school's bloody goldfish and hamster got a better education than me.'

'Why doesn't that surprise me,' replied Rod.

Paul laughed. 'Where did you learn Latin then Rod?' he asked.

'School of course.'

'What bloody school?' asked Craig, 'we never did Latin at our school, did you Mick?

Mick nodded no.

'What about you Paul?' asked Craig.

Paul nodded no.

'How about you John?' asked Craig.

'I bloody just told you; we had trouble getting through English, come on Rod f...f...f...for f... f... f... fuck sake put us out of our bloody misery, where the f...f...f...fuck did you go to school then.'

'Eton.'

Paul took a sharp intake of breath. 'What!' He said. 'Not Eton, the public school?'

'The very one,' replied Rod.

'Not so public,' said John, 'that must have cost a bloody f... f... f... fortune, what a waste of money, look at you, a bloody plumber.'

'Goes to show you John, that not all plumbers are stupid,' replied Rod mockingly, 'in fact,' he said as an afterthought, avoiding John's glare, 'I was in the same class as Prince William.'

'What! Prince you're joking William you say,' said Mick, 'Prince Charles's son.'

Paul looked puzzled at Mick. 'Everybody knows that Prince William is Prince Charles's son, Mick.'

John laughed to himself.

'What you laughing at John?' asked Mick.

'Wish we could say the same about Harry,' replied John.

Mick looked at John sternly. 'You can't say that,' he said, finding what John had said offensive, as he had been a royalist all his life; he'd never missed the Queen's speech on Christmas Day.

'Why! I'm not saying anything that 39 million other people hadn't already thought about Harry.'

'Whatever,' said Mick, 'let's get back to the point, what this...*Ubi... Ubi...*' '*Ubi juis, ibi remedium,*' interrupted Rod, 'where there is a wrong, there is a remedy.'

Craig frowned. 'Like what?'

Rod rolled his eyes at the lads. 'Why don't we just all sit right here Monkey man and wait for Sean to bring back our money? It's never going to happen.'

'Working with a know-it-all is never dull, is it?' said Craig, looking around at the others for their approval.

'It's not a joke,' snapped John.

Rod smiled at John's displeasure. 'You're right John, we're going to have to find Sean. We can't sit here wondering whether Sean took the money or not, we need to find him, it's not like we have a lot to lose at this point,' he replied.

John was becoming thoroughly exasperated at the thought of the money and Sean. He turned to him. 'Look Rod's right f... f... f... for once in his bloody life,' he said, 'wondering will get us nowhere; we've got to do something, *got to!*' He repeated. 'Not knowing would drive me out of my mind. As Rod said we need to f... f... f... find him f... f... f... for our own sake's.'

Mick snapped his fingers, knowing where the conversation was taking them. 'Whoa, Whoa, hold your horses lads,' he suddenly called out, unfolding his arms and raising them. 'Let's all slow down here,' he said. 'Don't be too hasty, what about the site, we've got contracts you know, clientele, and you've got jobs that need finishing,' he explained.

They all looked round at Mick. 'Are you going to tell him John, or shall I?' asked Paul. 'No, in fact,' Paul continued, 'you tell him John, and use your favourite word.'

'F... f... f...fuck off Mick,' said John, 'if I could put three million in my back skyrocket, and get me out of that shit hole of a cabin, then I'm afraid, Mick, your jobs haven't got a f... f... f... fucking cat in hell's chance of getting done, think about that one Mick.'

Mick scratched his head, and raised his eyebrows. 'Well if that's how you see it, what are we going to do then?' he asked.

John's face was turning redder by the minute. Breathing in deeply and puffing out his cheeks, he exhaled slowly. 'I'll tell you what I'm going to bloody do, F... f... f... first I'm going to f...f...f...find the thieving little bastard and get my three million pounds back. That's what I'm going to do,' he said.

'That's not going to be easy, finding him, and getting the money back is it? Easier said than done,' said Paul.

'Hang on, when you find him John, why don't you kill him, and we could claim his life insurance,' said Rod.

'Rod why don't you give up your childish sense of humour....' 'Oh,' interrupted Rod, 'and you'd know all about childish humour then, John. I thought it was rather funny.'

Rod's remarks went straight over John's head. 'This is three million pounds each we are missing out on and that's not funny.'

They all nodded in agreement.

The thought of the three million pounds made Rod do something that he thought would never happen. 'Ok, then I'll go along with what John said,' he informed them.

John looked quickly towards Rod, his voice taking a note of interest. 'Well I'm shocked, that's a bloody f… f… f…first,' he jibed, 'your agreeing with me Rod.'

Rod, ignoring John's jibing turned towards Mick. 'Shit, Mick, think what you could do with three million pounds, you could splash out, and buy your own bloody building site.'

Craig buried his head in his hands; he knew the direction John and Rod were going in. *It's all right for John, his house was paid for, his wife worked, and one teenage daughter, he was sorted. Whereas I have a mortgage, a secure job, a wife, and now a new baby on the way.* He shook his head, looking around the table at them all with a doubtful expression on his face.

They all looked at Craig.

'What, Craig?' they said in unison.

Craig shook his head. 'I don't know,' he answered. 'I have responsibilities you know. John, you're all right, money-wise. Mick's got no dependents only himself. Paul's wife's father loaded, and well,' he shook his head again. 'Look at Rod, he don't give a shit about anything, or anybody, only himself. Lads,' he held up his hands in placatory gesture. 'As you know, I have a baby on the way to think about.'

'We know,' replied John. 'F... F... F... For Christ sake Craig it's not bloody born yet. Just think Craig what you could buy with three million pounds for your new baby when it's born. Just think, baby would start life with his or her daddy being a millionaire. I wish when I was born that my f...f...f...father was a bloody millionaire, maybe I wouldn't be a f...f...f...fucking plumber now.'

'You're not a plumber,' Rod reminded him.

'Too true John,' Paul agreed with him holding up a thumb. 'He's not wrong Craig, just think three million pounds, it's got to be worth a go, after all, we've all got nothing to lose.'

Craig couldn't argue. *They were right,* he smiled relishing the thought of being a millionaire, 'Ok, shit or bust,' he said, relenting. ' I suppose I can always go back to plumbing if it doesn't work out. Ok, count me in,' he agreed, raising his shoulders. 'As Paul says, what have we got to lose?'

'Only three million pounds down the drain,' replied Paul, 'if we don't do what John says. Anyway, I'm certainly in. We all know that finding a decent plumber is as elusive as rocking horse shit. As you said, Craig, we can always get another bloody plumbing job if finding Sean goes bloody pear-shaped.'

'It won't go bloody pear-shaped,' replied John, looking at them all. 'I'm telling you. Well Mick,' he asked. 'What's it going to be, the ball's in your court?'

Mick sat silent, pulling his mobile from his jacket pocket, punching in a number and nervously tapping his fingers on the table. 'Hello, Ken it's Mick, I've got the lads here, I'm going to hand them over to you one at a time... I think they have got something to tell you.' He handed the phone to John.

John mouthed silently at Mick. 'Who is it?'

'The boss, Ken Grey,' mouthed Mick.

John sniggered as he put the phone to his ear. 'Hello Mr Grey it's John Hoggett your senior plumber... Not too bad, thanks,' he said, 'but getting better by the minute...because you can stick your f...f... f...fucking job up your arse.' He punched the air as he handed the phone to Craig.

'Hello... Mr... Mr Grey, it's Craig,' he spluttered, 'I'll go along with what John said,' he said, quickly passing the phone over to Rod as if it was an unexploded bomb.

Rod put the phone to his ear. 'I'll be back,' he said, putting on his best Arnold Schwarzenegger voice... All the others heard the bellowing voice coming from the phone.... 'Ok,' replied Rod when the bellowing stopped... 'Maybe I won't then,' he said, sticking up a V sign at the phone and handing the phone to Paul.

Paul put the red-hot earpiece to his ear. 'Hello, it's Paul, I think the others have said it all, bye,' he said, passing the phone back to Mick.

'Hello,' said Mick tentatively, holding the phone away from his ear. The lads leant forward and Mick held out the phone as they heard, 'Where the fuck is Sean?' Mick put the phone back to his ear. 'That's our problem Ken, Sean seems to have done a runner with our lottery winnings.'

'Bit over the fucking top for a fucking tenner isn't it?' spat Ken.

'More like eighteen million pounds,' replied Mick. The line went dead. Mick pressed the disconnect button and scratched his head. 'Consider yourselves out of the plumbing game lads, I think we've all just been fired,' he said, replacing his mobile in his jacket pocket.

Rod gulped down his beer. 'Well, what are we going to do now we're free spirits?' he asked.

They all sat silent, giving it some thought. John broke the silence. 'F… f… f… firstly we've got to tell our wives we've lost our jobs.'

'I'm not, I'm a free spirit,' said Rod.

'Shut up Rod,' said Paul and Craig. 'Then what, John?' Paul asked.

John ran his hands through his thinning hair and held out a hand. 'Over to you Mick,' he said.

'Why me,' said Mick sipping his orange.

'Because you're the f… f….f… foreman.'

'Right…right…ok, firstly, we need to get a seven-seater van.'

Rod looked puzzled. 'Why?'

'We can't run around in five cars, now can we Rod?'

'He's right,' interjected Paul.

Rod bit his bottom lip looking even more puzzled. 'Why?'

'For f... f...f...fuck's sake Rod you sound like my daughter,' snapped John. 'Why... why... why,' he mocked. 'Use this,' he continued, pointing to his head.

Rod shook his head. 'I'm an ex-plumber, not a bloody fortune-teller. 'What!' he asked.

'We're really making progress now,' said Craig, 'he's gone from whys to bloody what.'

'Your brain,' they all shouted in unison.

'In f... f...f...fact, make yourself useful,' said John, 'and get the beers in.'

'I wish you'd be more specific,' mumbled Rod, as he picked up the glasses and made his way to the bar.

Mick looked over his shoulder. 'Public school would you credit it, what a waste of money. You're right when you said that Rod's brain was his second organ,' he said, 'now I believe you. Right,' he said, turning back to them. 'So we all agree that we buy a seven-seater van.'

'Why?' said John now that Rod had gone.

'We won't have to run five cars then,' Mick informed him. 'And now that we're out of a job, it will save on petrol.

John pointed his finger at Mick. 'Good thinking Mick,' he said as they all nodded in agreement.

'Look,' said John. 'There's got to be a way to get to the bottom of all this, this is what we need to do,' he paused.

They all looked puzzled.

John continued, 'We need to find Sean, someone has to know where he's gone.'

'How the hell are we going to do that,' said Paul, 'and where do we start, it's going to be like looking for a bloody needle in a haystack... 'Good God,' interrupted John. 'If you don't believe Paul, that we can find Sean, then we're not going to find him, are we? 'He snapped.

Paul held out his hands. 'I'm only saying John, where do we start?'

'I know,' Mick continued. 'We've got to call on Sean's wife and find out as much information as to his whereabouts.' They all nodded in agreement again as Rod placed the beers on the table.

'Right,' said John. 'Ok Mick, it's agreed then that you'll get the van, and we'll all meet round mine.' He paused. 'No, hang on, we'll meet round Rod's at 9:00 am, I don't want him anywhere near my daughter.'

'Right, whatever,' said Rod as he returned, putting down the tray of drinks carefully on the table. 'Well, what's happening then?' he asked.

'You don't need to know at the moment Rod,' said Mick, 'you just be ready at 9:00 am tomorrow morning.'

'I know what am means Mick.'

John laughed. 'Good, then you'll be in then. Cheers,' holding out his glass. 'Ok lads, may the f... f... f... force be with us,' he said as all their glasses chinked together.

Chapter Four
Visiting Sean's Wife

John stood outside Rod's house glancing around the small tree-lined Mews, deciding whether he should knock or wait for the lads. He shook himself to keep warm, hopping from foot to foot to keep warm. It was freezing. Properly, unbelievably freezing, *He wasn't sure which was Rod's house. No he'd wait for he others,* he thought, stamping his feet impatiently waiting for them to arrive. He pulled up the collar of his coat against the bitter wind and blew into his hands, *a bloody thermal vest wouldn't have gone amiss,* he thought. He looked at his watch. 'Well, at last,' he mumbled to himself as Paul pulled into the Mews. He dug his hands into his coat pocket, playing with the packet of cigarettes he had found in Kaylie's school bag.

Paul got out of the car, and clicked the remote, as the orange light flickered. 'What up?' he asked.

'For a start it's f... f... f... fucking f...f...f... freezing, and I've been hanging around for Rod to show for the last f...f...f...fifteen f... f... f... fucking minutes.' He took his hands out of his pockets and blew into his cupped hands.

'Did you knock?' inquired Paul, looking down the path at the house.

'No, I thought I'd wait for you lot to turn up,' replied John, looking back at the house. 'The curtains are drawn, and there doesn't seem to be any movement inside.'

Craig pulled up behind Paul. 'What's up,' he shouted, jumping out of his car.

Apparently it's Rod,' said Paul, 'John says he's not in.'

'He's got to be in,' replied Craig.

'Is this actually Rod's house?' asked John.

Paul and Craig shrugged their shoulders. The blazing horn got their attention, as Mick turned into Baxter Mews in a white seven-seater van, beeping his horn enthusiastically.

'Here's mad Mick, the white van man,' said John, as he pulled up behind Craig's car.

'Not bad is it?' shouted Mick, as he jumped out, slapping the bonnet with his hand. 'Got this beauty off my brother-in-law, he's in the motor trade, a snip,' he said, looking over his shoulder at the van as he walked towards them. Mick's eyebrows lifted. 'Why are you all standing out here, it's bloody freezing,' he said, pulling up the collar of his coat and rubbing his hands. 'Didn't you tell him 9:00 am?' Mick looked at his watch. 'It's nine bloody fifteen. Where the hell is he?'

'Haven't a clue,' said John shrugging his shoulders. 'I did tell him nine o'clock sharp, the same as I told you lot. I'm telling you half the time he doesn't pay attention.'

'Is this his house Mick?' asked John.

Mick shrugged his shoulders.

'Mick, have you got Rob's telephone number on your mobile?' inquired Craig.

Mick pulled out his mobile. 'Yes, it's here somewhere. He pressed phone book and scrolled through to Rob's number.

'Hang on,' said John, looking puzzled. 'Doesn't anybody know where he lives?'

'We thought you'd know his house number John.'

'No!' said John quickly. 'Why the hell should I, and I don't bloody want to know. Don't any of you know it?'

They all looked at each other, and shrugged their shoulders again.

'I'm sure it's this one,' said Craig. 'Mick, mobile,' he coaxed Mick with his hand to give him his mobile phone. Mick handed the phone to Craig. 'Right,' said Craig. 'This is our plan of action. Paul, you bang on the front window. Mick, you hang on the doorbell, and John, you shout through the letterbox, and I'll ring his mobile. That'll get the bastard up.' They nodded in agreement. 'Ok,' continued Craig, smiling. 'Don't do anything until I say go, right.' They all nodded in agreement again, as they walked up to Rod's front door. Craig looked round as they all stood in position. 'Right go,' he said, pressing call on the mobile phone. Paul rapped on the front window. Mick hung on the doorbell. John pushed the letterbox flap open, holding back the firm stiff springs and shouted through the door, 'Rod we know you're in there you lazy little bastard, get your arse out of your pit and open this bloody door it's f...f...f...fucking f... f....f... freezing out here.'' For added effect he rapped the door knocker.

A Rottweiler emerged from the back of the house growling and showing its teeth, racing towards the front door scratching and barking through the frosted glass. 'F... f... for f...f...f...fuck sake, that f... f... f...fucking dog nearly f...f...f...fucking bit my f...f...f...fucking f...f... f... fingers off,' John shouted, jumping back.

The window of the house next door opened.

'I didn't know Rod had a f...f... f...fucking dog,' shouted John, shacking his hand, and checking his fingers.

'I haven't, are you looking for me?' Rod shouted out of the upstairs window of the house next-door, holding his ringing mobile out of the window.

They all looked up in surprise at the next-door window, and then at each other. Mick's hand fell off the bell. Craig's fingers pressed disconnect call as Rod's mobile stopped ringing. Paul stopped banging on the window and they all pulled away from the front door. 'Shit,' they all said in unison as they all turned and ran down the path and into Rod's front garden, huddling themselves inside the cover of his front porch. The top window of the house they had just evacuated flew open. 'What the fuck's going on, down there,' somebody roared, leaning out of the window looking down at the front door. A bloke with a Grant Mitchell haircut, 21 stone in weight, maybe more, with a face full of piercing, ears, nose, eyebrow, lips and nipples, with enough tattoos on his torso to have spent half his life in a tattoo parlour. Half dressed he leaned out of the window; he could have been naked owing to the fact that you couldn't see below the windowsill.

Rod held up his hand. 'I'm sorry, mate,' he shouted, in defence of the noise they'd been making.

'So… so… am I,' whispered Craig huddled in the porch.

The window shut with a bang.

John felt it was safe as he stepped back out of the porch, and pointed at his watch and mouthed, 'Get the f…f…f…fuck down here now.'

Rod opened the front door in his Hawaiian sarong as they all bundled in; nobody spoke until he'd shut the front door.

'We told you f…f…f… fucking nine o'clock am sharp Rod,' spat John, looking at his watch. 'It's now nine bloody twenty.'

'Sorry,' replied Rod.'I must have overslept,' he said, wiping his eyes in a futile gesture. 'I've had a very busy night.'

'Rod who was it?' shouted the naked girl at the top of the stairs, shaking the long ruffled blonde hair from her face. 'God,' she screamed, trying to cover herself with her hands. Too late: John, Mick, Paul, and Craig had looked in the direction of the scream and their eyes opened as wide as possible as their four mouths gaped open.

John tilted his head to one side and stood in rapt contemplation for a moment. 'Shit, that's… that's… bloody amazing,' he said, almost unable to get his words out. 'Now I can bloody see you've had a busy night,' he concluded. 'What do you think Mick?' asked John, not looking away, not wanting to miss any of the opportunity of looking at a naked young lady as the naked figure jumped out of sight.

John sighed. 'Shit, what the hell can I say; I'm lost for bloody words,' he said.

Rod felt himself swell with pride. 'That's not like you John.'

'It's not every bloody day you see that,' John replied, pointing up the stairs.

'It's a dirty job, John, but somebody's got to do it. So you like it?'

'Bloody right I liked it, who wouldn't f...f... f...fucking f...f... f.... fancy looking at that,' replied John.

'Tristram wouldn't.'

'Who the hell's Tristram?' asked John.

'Doesn't matter,' answered Rod. 'Any chance she'll give us a repeat performance?' interrupted John. 'I haven't seen such a large pair of pert tits and a nice tight arse like that f... f... f... for years.'

'No bloody chance,' came a voice from up the stairs.

Mick shook his head and pointed up the stairs. 'Who the hell was that?' he asked.

'Not that it's any of your business Mick,' replied Rod, shrugging his shoulders. 'But her name is Michelle Fuller.'

'Certainly got the right surname,' said Paul holding his hands up to his chest. 'Fuller by name Fuller by nature, I bet you don't get many of those to a pound.'

'Piss off Paul and make yourself useful, do the coffee, and take bloody Monkey man with you.'

'Wahoo,' said Craig, rolling his eyes, and smiling at Paul. 'I think you've upset him,' Craig said. 'Let's get some coffee, while the big girl's blouse gets out of that skirt. Nice tits though, Rod,' they said in unison as they made their way to the kitchen.

'Nice, full tits, that's what I like,' said Paul as he followed Craig to the kitchen.

John smiled. 'Very nice to see you Michelle, hope to see more of you,' he shouted up the stairs. 'I'm telling you Rod she'd be an ideal candidate f... f... f...for a f... f... f... fancy dress party. That's if you ever get invited to one.'

'In fact we have,' Rod sneered. 'We are invited to one next weekend.'

'Good,' said John rubbing his hands together. 'Then both go naked.'

Rod raised an eyebrow. 'Why?'

'Why! What, with a name like Michelle, you're made mate.'

'I don't get the connection,' said Rod shaking his head.

'Right,' continued John. 'It will be the best f... f... f... fancy dress costume ever if you both go naked.'

Mick nudged John.

'What!'

Mick looked puzzled. 'How can it be a costume if they're both naked?'

'Good point Mick,' said Rod, pointing a finger at him.

'Bear with me for just a minute Mick,' smiled John. 'Anyway Rod,' he continued, looking back up the stairs, hoping he'd get another glimpse of Michelle although she didn't look like she was going to make another appearance. He looked back at Rod. 'As I said, both go naked.'

'Why?'

John pointed at his head. 'Use this Rod. Because then you can both go as a tortoise.'

'How's that!'

'Well, when you get to the front door naked, get her to jump up on your back,' John said, pointing up the stairs.

'Why's that?'

'Because when your hosts answer the door, which they will, they're bound to ask you what you've come as. Believe me, they always do Rod. And then when they do, you can say we've come as a tortoise.'

'They won't ask, they'll probably slam the door in our faces and ring for the bloody police.'

John waved a finger from side to side. 'No they won't Rod, I'm telling you they won't ring the police, I promise you they will ask what you've come as.'

'You think so.'

'I know so Rod, Ok, have you got the picture,' continued John. 'You naked with her upstairs on your back.'

'No,' replied Rod, shaking his head in bewilderment, wondering where this conversation was going.

Mick was already sniggering.

'Shit, you are bloody slow Rod. Anyway, when they ask you what she is doing on you back, you can say that you have come as a tortoise and that's Michelle,' he said, pointing at his back. Mick and John roared with laughter.

Rod shook his head, his face never altered.

John shook his head at Mick. 'Lost Mick, bloody lost,' he said, pointing at his watch again, as Rod made his way back upstairs, dumbfounded. 'Just get dressed, Rod, and you haven't got time for a shag.'

'He'd probably be quicker at the latter,' said Mick. 'No you go ahead have a shag Rod,' he shouted up the stairs, still laughing at John's previous joke.

'Right, quick coffee then Mick. Did you see her beaver's pocket Mick?' asked John as they both made their way to the kitchen.

'What the hell's a beaver's pocket?' asked Mick, looking puzzled.

John rolled his eyes and raised his eyebrows. 'You know Mick, the thing that women have.'

'What thing that women have?' replied Mick, looking even more confused.

'You know, that, Mick, that,' said John, pointing at his groin.

'John, please, I am too much of a gentleman to even so much as look at her.'

'Right,' replied John. 'That's why you miss out half the time. 'Well Mick I wasn't, and I'm telling you I will take that vision of her beaver and tits to my grave.'

They all stood at the bottom of the stairs: they had given Rod enough time to get ready. John shouted up the stairs. 'For Christ sake Rod, come on we haven't got all day.' He looked at his watch. 'We need to be at Sean's house, I told Sean's wife ten o'clock.'

'Ok...ok...' shouted Rod. "It's not that far from here,' he said, bounding down the stairs. 'Have I got time for a coffee?'

'No,' they all shouted in unison halfway out of the front door.

'Michelle, don't forget to do the washing up, and put the key on the hall stand when you leave,' Rod shouted up the stairs.

'Always the gentlemen,' said John as Rod shut the front door.

'Well you don't want them getting too comfortable do you,' replied Rod, waving up at Grant Mitchell next door. Grant looked down at them surlily as they made their way towards the van.

'I bet you didn't say that last night Rod, when you were coaxing her through the front door and into your bed. You're a sexual vampire, that's what you are.'

Rod smiled. 'Needs must Mick, needs must mate.' He was one of those men who always managed to wriggle away from responsibilities with women, and Michelle was no exception.

'Who's the gorilla next door?' whispered John as he slid in the front passenger seat next to Mick.

'Nice van Mick,' Rod said as he looked back at Tristram's house. 'Oh, that's Tristram.'

'Thanks,' said Mick, rubbing his hands on the steering wheel. 'What sort of name is Tristram?' Mick asked, laughing.

'It's short for turmoil,' replied Rod, jumping in the back of the van.

'What the f…f…f…fuck's turmoil when it's at home,' asked John.

'Turmoil means uproar, riot, agitation, violent emotions, to name a few.'

'Well he's certainly got the right name the ugly bastard,' whispered John, half looking up at the bedroom window.

'You're quite lucky actually,' said Rod. 'If you were a woman, he'd have kicked your tits in.'

John turned in his seat and looked at Rod in surprise. 'Why?'

'Because he's gay.'

'No,' John protested. 'F… f… f…For f…f…f…fuck's sake, a f… f… f…faggot, no shit, you're saying he's gay and you're living next door to a gay-lord.'

'Yes gay, John,' repeated Rod, 'that means he likes men.'

'I know what bloody gay means Rod,' snapped John. 'What man in their right mind would go out with an ugly bastard like that, it would be like going out with a walking art gallery?'

'Hang on a minute John. You've got tattoos John,' said Paul.

John pulled up his sleeve and swung round towards them. 'Yer, I have, look,' he said, throwing his arm over the seat. 'But not all over my f…f…f…fucking f… f… f… face.'

Rod nudged Paul. 'Maybe not John but he does like men with tattoos.'

John pulled down his sleeve sharply.

'And he likes men that swear a lot, and it seems to me like you fit the bill nicely, John.'

'Bollocks,' replied John, holding his hand up to his mouth, hoping Tristram couldn't lip-read. Not realising that his swearing might be a sexually attractive to other men. 'He just doesn't look the type to be gay, Rod,' he said, looking round at Mick. He winked, 'That's probably why he's got a dog, Mick.'

Mick turned up his nose and gnawed the inside of his cheek. 'Probably that's all he can get, the dirty fat hideous looking bastard,' said Mick.

'It takes all sorts,' said Craig.

'Shit,' laughed Paul. 'Well, I wouldn't like to meet him up my back passage on a dark night, not if, as Rod says, he has violent emotions, no way Hosé, no entry, back passage closed I'm afraid,' he said, clenching his rectum muscles and looking out of the passenger window at him.

'Don't knock it lads, if you've never tried it,' said Rod.

They all looked quickly towards Rod in silence. It was John who broke the silence. 'Have you then Rod?'

Rod looked at the lads, rotating his head quickly. 'NO, I bloody haven't,' he snapped. 'Shit, I was just saying don't knock it, that's all.'

They all smiled in unison.

'Actually,' Rod continued. 'He's a very nice guy; appearances can be very deceiving.'

'Gay,' said Craig.

'Hang on Rod, you mean like Howard Jones' lyrics in his song *I'd like to get to know him well*, sang John. 'You sure you haven't, have you, got to know him well, I mean?' inquired John.

'No, I've told you, certainly not, he's just a good friend, and believe me, you don't ever want him as an enemy.'

'I said the back passage was closed,' said Paul only half listening. 'No enema for me.'

'Not enema, I said enemy Paul. An enema is cleaning out your arse with fluid.'

Paul shrugged. 'Same thing,' he replied.

Rod looked puzzled. 'Tell me Paul how do you get to enema and enemy to being the same thing.'

'Didn't you say that Tristram is gay?'

'Right,' said Rod.

Paul pointed a finger at Rod. 'And you said that you didn't want Tristram as an enemy, right.'

'Correct,' said Rod, still not following his direction.

'Well what if he was your enemy then,' asked Paul.

Rod shrugged. 'So what, what's your point?'

'Well if he caught you up a back passage on a dark night and he was your enemy, the sheer size of him would overpower you, right.'

John nodded. 'He's right there you know, he bloody would.'

'I still don't see his point,' said Rod.

'Nor do I Rod,' replied John. 'But, he is right.'

'Go on Paul,' said Mick who was now intrigued.

'Well, Mick think, him being gay and all that, probability is that he'd take you from behind. So that's where the similarities are between enema and enemy.'

John looked at Mick and shrugged his shoulders. 'Where?' he asked, looking back at Paul.

'You get a long thing shoved up your arse and you're squirted with warm fluid.'

John roared out laughing.

Mick turned up his nose. 'Paul please,' said Mick. 'Don't drop down to John's level.'

'What do you mean Mick?' said John. 'You must admit that it was bloody f... f... f... funny.'

'Jesus Christ, I don't believe what I'm hearing; I'm in a van full of retards. Anyway,' continued Rod, steering the conversation away from warm fluids up the back passage, 'I like women too much for that sort of thing. Why the hell do you all keep going on about me being gay?' he inquired, looking confused.

'That skirt you were wearing this morning,' answered John.

'That wasn't a bloody skirt at all, that only goes to show how ignorant you are,' snapped Rod. 'You've never travelled much, have you John?' he asked.

'Yes I have,' smiled John.

'Where?' asked Rod.

'We go on holiday every year to Scarborough.'

'Right, Scarborough you say?' sighed Rod, looking at Paul and Craig. 'See what I mean,' he looked back at John. 'I mean abroad.'

'No way, why should I go abroad... anyway everywhere abroad is f... f... f... full of bloody f... f... f... foreigners.'

'That's the point of going abroad John, seeing different cultures, foods, life styles, people. Anyway you should try it some time, it might widen your small bloody horizons.'

'If I want to see other cultures,' replied John, 'I'll go to Camden Town, Nottingham, or bloody Birmingham, I don't need to go abroad.'

'Change of surroundings John, Camden Town, Nottingham or Birmingham, that's not like seeing people in their own countries,' Rod said, shaking his head. A thought had just struck him, *no not John. It could be though, it happens to a lot of people, in fact his mum, dad, and uncle Joe are just the same as John, they won't go abroad.* 'John are you scared of flying, is that it?' he smiled as he saw the blood drain from the back of John's neck. *Yes,* he thought, he'd found John's Achilles heel.

John felt his heart race; his legs trembled at the word flying. Rod had hit the nail on the head.

'You don't suffer from aerophobia John, do you?' inquired Paul.

John partly ignored Paul's question. 'What the f...f...f... fuck's aerophobia,''Fear of flying,' interrupted Rod. 'Paul's right,' continued Rod, 'Steve Wright said that 25% of airline crews and would you believe it, that some pilots have a fear of flying.' 'No shit,' interrupted Craig. 'Jesus, you say pilots have a fear of flying ...who the f...f...f...fuck's Steve Wright?' asked John.

'Steve Wright in the afternoon, the DJ on Radio Two, it was on the other day, it's factoids.' 'What the f...f...f...fuck's f...f...f...factoids,' interrupted John.

'Factoids are just facts John,' answered Mick, waving a hand at him. 'Right, f... f...f... facts you say,' said John, nodding his agreement but not letting them know that he didn't have a bloody clue what they were going on about.'Also,' continued Rod, 'Steve said that one out of six adults have a fear of flying.' 'That counts you out then Rod,' interrupted Craig.

Rod looked at Craig, puzzled. 'Why,' he asked.

'Adult was the word Rod,' replied Craig.

'Bollocks,' replied Rod. 'Anyway air travel is the second safest mode of mass transportation in the world.' 'Ok, smart arse,' interrupted Craig, making a yawning motion. 'So, if flying's the second safest mode of transport, then what's the first,' he asked, trying to catch him out.

'Escalators and lifts.'

'Escalators and lifts, that's bollocks,' said Paul, 'you're pulling our pissers, I'm always travelling in lifts and up and down escalators, when I'm shopping with Gale in Westgate House.'

Thank fuck Hoggetts never did the shopping, John thought. 'You'd just have to watch yourself in the f...f...f...future Paul,' he said.

'Thanks for your concern John,' replied Paul. 'I will, I'll use the stairs in future.'

'Do you know the chances of you being in a plane crash?' continued Rod.

'Who cares,' replied John, as he was never going to be in a plane and he was getting bored with the whole subject.

'I care,' said Mick, 'I fly quite a lot, I'd like to know my chances, go on Rod.'

Rod smiled. 'Cheers Mick, I'm glad somebody takes an interest in life.'

'Ok, go on then Rod, bore us,' said John, trying to speed up the whole conversation. 'What are your chances then?'

'One in eleven million.'

That still didn't make John feel any better about flying. 'One in eleven million, as opposed to what then?' he asked.

Rod rubbed his chin...hum...I know, as opposed to one in five hundred thousand chances of getting killed in a car accident, in fact you'd have more chance of dying on your drive to the airport, than in a plane crash.'

John tapped Mick's arm. 'Slow down Mick and keep your eyes on the road.' He still wasn't impressed by Rod or Steve Wright's factoids, but he wasn't about to let them all know about his fear of flying. Not even the car drive to the airport, because it was never going to happen. He wrapped his arms very tightly across his chest, taking a defensive position. 'What you said earlier about me flying,' he shouted, affirming his position. 'John Hoggett frightened of flying, never.'

'Have you ever been on a aeroplane then?' asked Rod.

'Have I ever been on a plane,' replied John, staring out of the front windscreen.

'Have you?' asked Paul.

John laughed. 'Have I ever been on a plane,' he repeated.

'Jesus Christ John,' said Mick. 'Well have you, or haven't you?' he asked.

'What?'

'Been on a fucking aeroplane John,' snapped Craig.

'No,' John replied, looking at his watch. 'Come on Mick or are we going to sit here all day chatting about my f... f... f... flying habit.'

'Or not, as the case may be,' replied Paul.

He pulled down on his seat-belt, making some slack so he could turn to face them. 'Anyway,' John said, moving on quickly, 'what's all this got to do with Rod wearing a bloody skirt?'

'Sarong.'

'Whatever Rod,' replied John.

'Well,' continued Rod, 'because, if you did travel John then you would know that that skirt as you call it, is a Hawaiian sarong, the Hawaiian's national dress.'

'What did you say Rod?' asked Mick, only half listening, 'did you say national skirt or national dress?'

'Dress, I said, cloth ears.'

'National dress you say Rod. Well I never John,' replied Mick. 'You learn something every day,' he smiled at John and half turned in his seat towards Rod. 'Rod did you get a matching handbag and Alice band to go with the dress?'

They all roared with laughter at Mick's remark.

Rod snarled, giving Mick the full force of his scowl. 'Ha...ha... very funny Mick,' he said, 'I don't know why I bother sometimes.' He turned to peer out of the window, looking back up at Tristram's window. 'Anyway,' continued Rod, 'you really should all get to know Tristram, you know.' He paused in deep thought and finally he said, 'I'll tell you what. I'll invite you all round mine one evening; maybe we could all have a game of cards. Tristram loves a game of cards.'

'They all shouted, 'NO,' in unison, shaking their heads.

'I bet he does,' jibed John. 'What card game does he play then, crabs?'

'That's crib, John,' said Rod looking back up at Tristram's window again, deciding to get his own back on John. 'Tristram's pointing at you John,' he said, 'I think he fancies you.'

'F... f...f...for heaven's sake Mick pull away.' John wound down the window and waved, and mouthed silently, 'You're not having my back passage, you dirty fat bastard.'

Tristram moved away from the window.

Rod slouched back in his seat and smiled to himself. 'John,' he said, 'I think Tristram's coming to get your telephone number.' He continued to taunt John. 'I saw him picking up a pad and pencil from his windowsill.'

John's face went pale. 'Go Mick, f...f... for Christ sake go,' he bellowed, as he watched the front door open.

Mick smiled round at the lads, and gunned the accelerator.

Chapter Five
No, Definitely Not The Girls

'Mick for Christ sake remember the factoids, slow down for Christ sake.'

Mick half turned in his seat. 'I hope you know the way to Sean's house, Rod,' he asked.

'Of course I do,' replied Rod, looking back at Tristram standing in the middle of the road.

'Right Rod,' Mick said as he pulled out of Baxter Mews.

'Does the bloody heater work Mick?'

'Yeh, why?'

'Well switch the bloody thing on then, it's bloody f... f... f... freezing in here, it's like sitting in a f... f... f...fridge.'

'I don't know where you switch it on,' replied Mick, fiddling with the dashboard switches. 'I haven't had the van long you know.' John slapped his hand. 'For God's sake watch the road, I want heat not bloody death. Shit, there it is Mick,' interrupted John, turning it all the way up. 'There you are, that's better,' he said, holding his hands against the blower and rubbing them together.

Mick looked into the rear-view mirror where he could connect with Rod's eyes, and sighed. 'Well Rod, are you going to tell me, or not?'

'Ok sorry, right Mick, left,' said Rod.

The van swerved from the right to the left side of the road as John grabbed the dashboard.

'For Christ sake Rod was that a right or a left?' asked Mick. 'Just say bloody right or left, not the bloody two together, or you're going to get us all bloody killed.'

'Ok…ok, sorry Mick, next left,' answered Rod.

Mick turned left.

'Ok Mick, stop at the lights.'

'I know I'm going to stop at the lights, Rod, they're red.' Mick rolled his eyes at John as he pulled up at the lights.

Rod peered out of his side of the van. 'Shit,' he roared, 'I'm certainly going to get me one of these vans, Mick,' he said.

'Why?' asked John.

'Well look at that Mini next to us, you can see right inside the car, and look at the babe that's driving it.'

'So,' said John, craning his neck across Mick to look into the car.

'She's a beauty,' said Rod. 'Mini car, mini skirt, I've got hankies bigger than that skirt. Look at those bloody beautiful legs, they are like a giraffe's neck; they go right up to her arse.'

'That's a wonderful analogy of a pair of legs Rod.'

'You've got to admit it though John, that was a pretty good analogy. Christ Rod's right, look at them,' Paul said, looking into the interior of the Mini.

John craned his neck. 'So what, they're only a pair of legs f… f… f…for Christ sake. Is that all that runs through that pea-sized brain of yours Rod, bloody sex?'

'Well, now that I'm out of a job, what else have I got to think about John?' replied Rod.

'He's right though,' Mick remarked, looking down into the car. 'She has got a lovely pair of legs John.'

'Don't side with him,' whispered John, 'you'll make him worse than he is.'

'Is that possible,' mumbled Mick.

'I heard that Mick,' said Rod, smiling at the girl in the car. He waved at her as the lights changed to green. She winked at him, and roared off.

'Shit, I'm bloody in there Mick,' said Rod grabbing the back of his seat. 'Follow that Mini,' he shouted, pointing at the disappearing Mini.

'Piss off Rod,' replied Mick.

'Ok, I'll take that as a no then, shall I?' said Rod, sinking back into his seat. 'Right, take the next left, and you'll pass two sets of traffic lights, and when you hit the roundabout take the second exit, on the left you'll see Toys R Us...' 'Don't tell us you want to go in there Rod,' interrupted Paul.

'Ha...ha...very droll Paul,' replied Rod sarcastically.

'Good one Paul,' said Mick laughing.

'What's the plan of action, when we get to Sean's then John?' asked Craig.

John shrugged his shoulders. 'Over to you Mick, you're the diplomat.'

'Why me?'

'Because Mick you're the foreman!'

'Was, not any more John, have you forgotten we're out of a job?' replied Mick.

'I know, but Mick you know what to say, we can't leave it to these three in the back now, can we?'

Mick glanced round quickly at their faces. 'I suppose you're right John. Ok, I'll do the talking. But let's get one thing clear.'

'What's that,' replied the lads in unison.

'Firstly, Rod you keep your gob shut, we don't want you putting your foot in it now, do we,' said Mick.

Rod heaved a sigh and shook his head. 'Ok if that's what you want, I won't say a bloody word,' replied Rod. He watched the approaching left turn. 'Hang on though, before I go into a complete silence mode. Is that only when we get there?' he asked.

'Of course,' replied Mick.

'Ok left, NOW,' roared Rod.

The tyres screeched as Mick took the corner on two wheels swerving the van right, just missing an oncoming lorry. Brakes hissed, the driver hung on his horn as he yelled a barrage of abuse from the lorry window and Mick pulled the van to the left. They all piled to the right side of the van. 'For Christ sake Rod,' shouted Mick. 'I'm sure you're trying to get us all killed, so you can keep the bloody eighteen million for yourself.'

'I'm going to throttle the bastard when we f...f...f... fucking get there,' screamed John tearing his white knuckles from the dashboard. He touched Mick's. 'F... f... f...factoids Mick, remember the f...f...f...factoids, one in f.... f.... f... five hundred thousand,' he said.

Mick eased his foot off the accelerator.

'Don't blame me,' shouted Rod, 'it was Mick's bloody fault, he told me to keep my gob shut for Christ sake,' he mumbled as he felt a warm trickle of blood running down his cheek. 'Jesus Mick, thanks to you, I've bloody split my head open here,' he shouted, looking at his bloodstained fingers where he'd hit his head on the window catch. 'Look,' he shouted, holding out his hand to show Craig.

Craig took a sharp intake of breath. 'Jesus Christ Mick he has, he's gashed his head open,' he said. 'Put your head down Rod, and let's have a look.'

'Don't touch his blood Craig,' shouted John. 'You might f... f...f...fucking catch something.'

'Oh my God,' Craig said. 'Jesus Christ Rod,' he said again for effect, smiling at Paul.

'What...what...' bellowed Rod looking at Craig's face. 'Does it need stitches?'

' Maybe,' said Craig. 'It looks like you're going to be scarred for life, just keep some pressure on it, you'll need the bleeding to stop.'

Mick half looked over his shoulder at Rod. 'Shit Rod, don't you go bleeding all over the bloody cloth seats, for God's sake, use these,' he shouted, throwing over a box of tissues.

'I've always said he was a bleeder,' said John.

Rod ignored John's remark and looked out of the window shaking his head. *Were those two cars in front of the van the same or was he,* he looked at the number plates, they were the same numbers, 'shit, I'm getting bloody double vision here, I think I'm going blind,' he shouted.

'Rod, we don't give a f... f... f... flying f...f... f...fuck, as long as you don't go f...f...f... fucking blind before we get to Sean's,' shouted John.

Mick pulled back on the accelerator as the van slowed down. 'Come on Rod, where the bloody hell are we going then?' shouted Mick.

'Shit Mick, I can hardly bloody see here,' said Rod, squinting through the front windscreen, holding the wad of tissues tightly to his head. 'Next right, if I'm right you should be in Goodfellows Road, number fifty-five.'

Mick flicked the indicator pulling into Goodfellows Road. 'Fifty-five you said.'

'Fifty-five,' repeated Rod.

Mick pulled up outside number 55. The driveway of 55 was empty, except for two Persian blue cats lying huddled together on the driveway. They all got out and walked up the drive.

Rod tripped over the cats and they hissed at him. He bent down but as his free hand went to stroke the cats, they both lashed out at his hand scratching him simultaneously. 'Shit,' he gave a muffled shout, pulling back his hand and licking the wounds on the back of his hand as the cats made a beeline to the front door.

'Remember Rod,' said Mick, 'not a bloody word.'

'Not a bloody word Mick,' snapped Rod. 'Shit, thanks to your driving, and the bloody cats,' he showed Mick the bloodstained wad of tissues and the back of his hand. 'I've got enough to worry about,' he said, placing the wad of tissues back on his head.

Mick turned towards Craig and Paul. 'You two, remember not a word from you either, let me do the talking.'

'Right,' said Paul and Craig in perfect unison, nodding to each other and tapping their noses with their index fingers. 'Mum's the word, our lips are sealed.'

'Sealed lips, that reminds me John,' Mick said, pointing at him, 'you can talk, but watch your language.'

'That's fine by me,' replied John, raising his eyebrows and a hand. 'Never again, I'm a new man,' he replied in his deepest voice. 'Especially after Rod's revelations about gay men and swearing, I don't think I'll ever swear again.'

'Yer, right,' said Paul, cupping his hands and peering through the garage window as the others made their way to the front door. 'There's a car in here,' said Paul, squinting his eyes against the frosted pane of glass. 'I think it's a VW.'

'That's not Sean's car,' Rod informed them, 'he's got an old white Vauxhall Astra van.'

'No bloody Sean,' Paul mumbled to himself as he made his way to the others, 'and now no bloody car.'

'You didn't expect to see Sean sitting in the front seat of his car, with our eighteen million on the front seat did you?'

'Good one Mick,' said John, laughing.

'Right, then,' said Mick, 'we've all agreed that I'll do the talking.'

They all nodded their agreement as Mick rang the front doorbell.

They all waited, pulling up the collars of their coats against the cold wind as a frosted figure appeared through the glass window. The door opened.

Mick's jaw dropped. 'Hello,' he smiled. *If this was Mrs Walsh* Mick thought *she was certainly everything that Rod had said about her, and more, in the flesh. He was definitely right what he'd said earlier about Cathleen, the age thing never even came into question with Mick, she was certainly one hell of a beautiful woman, her eyes sparkling with shyness, high cheekbones, a full wide mouth, skin comparable to an alabaster doll. Three words span around in his brain, he shook his head trying to rid himself of the thought, but it was very inappropriate that he had even thought of it. But, she was definitely shagable...*John interrupted his thoughts as he nudged him in the ribs. 'Sorry,' said Mick. 'Are... are... you Mrs Walsh?

'Of course she is, you silly twat,' whispered Rod.

'She heard that,' whispered Craig to Paul, who had to stifle a snort of laughter.

'Sorry,' said Mrs Walsh as she looked over the heads of the others, recognising Rod's voice.

'I'm sorry Cathleen... I...I... said are these your cats?'

Cathleen gave a slight shake of her head. 'Yes,' she said in her soft Irish accent, as the cats made their way through the front door. 'That's the King and I,' she said, 'Sean named them after the film. Well Rod, to what do I owe this pleasure? *She'd always had a soft spot for Rod, in a motherly sort of way, but of course she would never have let it be known.*

'Cathleen we're sorry to trouble you,' said Rod. They all turned and looked sternly at Rod. 'But we're looking for Sean....' Mike interrupted. 'As Rod was saying, Mrs

Walsh, we are looking for Sean, I spoke to you on the phone yesterday.'

'Ok, right, you must be Mick then, the foreman from Sean's work.'

'Pleased to meet you,' said Mick, holding out his hand.

Her soft hand touched his; he withdrew his hand quickly embarrassed by the roughness of his skin.

'I can only tell you what I told you on the phone; Sean's supposed to be at work, he went back to work late Saturday night. He was quite annoyed that he'd missed out on his church day on Sunday; you see he never misses church. He told me it was something to do with a deadline...'

Who would of thought it, Sean a bible puncher, going to church; he never said thought John...Paul nudged John, interrupting his thoughts. 'What was Sean's favourite saying,' he whispered, 'if you don't pay, you don't play.'

'Pardon,' asked Cathleen looking at Paul.

'Sorry,' said Paul, looking over Mick's shoulder. 'I said, it's not a very nice day, cold,' he said, sinking further in to his jacket.... Mick interrupted Paul and spoke softly. 'Would it be ok Mrs Walsh if we come in and talk?' he said, looking left and right at the other houses to see if the neighbours' net curtains were moving, and then back at Cathleen. He rubbed his hands together against the cold.

'Yes, of course, sorry, come in,' Cathleen said. She smiled and held the door open, standing away from the door allowing them to enter. 'Just go straight ahead, the sitting room is facing you,' she said. 'We have a fire already made up in there. Can I take your coats?' she said, shutting the front door.

They all removed their coats and handed them to her. 'Go through,' she said, holding out her hand towards the sitting room, and hung their coats in the hall cupboard.

Paul nudged Craig. 'Sean would never have left for another woman,' he whispered.

Craig raised his eyebrows and whispered. 'Why!'

Paul nodded towards the hall cupboard. 'There's his new set of golf clubs.'

They all sat holding out their hands towards the roaring fire, feeling their cheeks turn red in the heat from the fire, except for Rod who only held out one hand as the other was still applying pressure to his laceration. Quickly the warmth of the blazing fire engulfed the whole of their bodies.

'Right,' said Cathleen, sitting down holding her hands demurely in her lap, as if in prayer. 'Well, you know who I am, so please, introduce yourselves.'

'Ok,' said Mick, leaning forward. 'Apparently you already know Rod.'

Cathleen nodded.

'And as you know I'm Mick Elliott, and this is John Hoggett, Paul Lane and Craig Hill.'

They all simultaneously made a gesture of *hi* with their hands. Cathleen waved a petite hand in return.

'Well, we all work on the building site with Sean, we are all plumbers...' 'I must say you don't look like plumbers,' Cathleen interrupted softly, looking them over.

John had never really heard that before, *what did she mean, don't look like plumbers, what do plumbers look like* he thought looking at Mick, *anyway we aren't plumbers anymore, for God's sake Mick get to the bloody point or else we're going to be here all day...*Cathleen interrupted John's thoughts. 'So gentlemen how can I help you. Where's Sean?'

'I don't really know how to put this Cathleen. You don't mind if I call you Cathleen, do you?' asked Mick.

'Of course not,' replied Cathleen nodding her approval.

For f...f...f...fuck's sake John mumbled under his breath.

Mick looked sternly at John and continued. 'I'm afraid to say as far as we know Sean never returned to work on Saturday night.'

Cathleen looked puzzled. 'He must have,' she said, 'Sean said he had a call from you late Saturday night.'

'I'm afraid if he did get a call on Saturday night to come in to work, then it wasn't from me... was you with him when he received the call?'

'No, I wasn't with Sean when he got the call,' replied Cathleen. 'All I know is that I packed him some lunch, and he left late Saturday night.' She was beginning to panic now. 'Is... is... Sean all right?'

'I'm sorry Cathleen, but we don't know,' replied Mick softly. Cathleen crossed him. 'Where is he then?'

'We don't know,' answered Mick, 'we haven't seen him since last Friday, at the pub, we'd hoped you might have had some idea about where Sean might have gone to?'

Cathleen shook her head, placing her head in her hands. Obviously by Cathleen's reaction she also had no clue of Sean's whereabouts. 'Where is he then?' she pleaded. 'I haven't heard from him since Saturday, no phone call, nothing.'

'We're all as stumped as you are,' said Mick looking at the lads, as they all held out their hands. Mick continued, 'Well, as you know, Sean runs the work's lottery syndicate and all of us are members of that syndicate.'

Rod shuffled in his seat trying to get attention. Nobody seemed to be worried about the gaping wound in his head.

Cathleen raised her head from her hands, tears in the corner of her eyes; she listened intently as Mick explained the position. She found it difficult to get her words out. 'Jeez...surely... You're... not suggesting... that... my Sean would run off with your lottery winnings.' She nodded her head. 'My Sean would never ever do that, he's as honest as the day is long,' she said.

'Mind you, I did say that too, Cathleen,' said Craig, confirming what she had just said. 'Not Sean.'

The others held out their hands again, except for Rod whose head had dropped as he dabbed the top of his head with the tissue, which was fast becoming redundant, soaked in blood. In the anticipation of getting to the house nobody had remembered to bring the tissues with them.

Cathleen looked at Rod, puzzled. 'Oh, my God,' she said. Standing up, she walking towards him and removing the tissues she parted the hair on his head to look at the injury. 'What's happened to your head Rod?' she asked.

'When Mick swerved in the van, I banged it on...' 'Oh it's only a little scratch, Cathleen, it will stop bleeding soon,' interrupted Mick. 'You said it would stop in the van, and it hasn't, it's getting worse,' interrupted Rod.

'Wait,' said Cathleen. 'I'll get one of the girls,' she said as she walked towards the door.

Rod's ears picked up on the word girls.

Cathleen stopped at the door and turned. 'Sinead is a practising doctor, I'll get her to look at it for you Rod.'

Even better, thought Rod, *at last I'm going to see a practising doctor.*

With that Cathleen called up the stairs. 'Sinead, can you come down for a moment, somebody needs your professional help here. In fact Kerrie, Caitlin and Una, you come down as well, there's something you need to hear.'

Four girls thought Rod *even better.*

The girls had already heard most of what was being said, albeit muffled. They came down the stairs, and entered the lounge. 'Ha, right girls,' Cathleen said, half sitting as the girls entered. Now this is our eldest, Sinead is the doctor.'

'Not yet Ma,' said Sinead.

'Sinead can you have a look at Rod's head, he seems to have had a nasty bump.'

Rod lifted his head slowly and looked round at the four girls.

'Jesus, I've died and gone to heaven,' Rod mumbled.

'Here we go Mick, isn't there any time when his brain doesn't rise above his waist?' John whispered.

'Shush,' whispered Mick, putting his hand over his mouth and coughing.

Rod looked up at Sinead. *Jesus,* he thought, *Sean never said a word about these four beauties, especially this one, five-feet-nine of sheer beauty. Those deep green eyes seemed to lock onto his with an unsympathetic look, and that auburn hair tied back into a bun he couldn't see how thick it was, but he could imagine it spilling down around her face, encircling her faultless skin, so perfect, not a blemish, and all without the aid of make-up. He couldn't see much of her figure owing to the white coat she wore loosely wrapped around her body, but he imagined the contents of the package to be as perfect as her exterior. Her overall look gave her a gentle look that he found irresistible.*

Sinead held out her hand towards the kitchen. 'Will you come to the kitchen and I'll take a look.'

Her voice was gentle, and the faint soft Irish accent appealed to Rod. Without any resistance he stood as Sinead showed him the way to the kitchen.

Paul rolled his eyes at John *My God, it's like a kid in a sweet shop, trouble with Rod though he's never got any money* thought Paul, *lamb to the slaughter. He wanted to shout out to Cathleen not to leave Rod out there alone with her...*Cathleen interrupted Paul's thoughts. 'And this is our second oldest, Kerrie, she's a freelance computer analyst, works for banks all over the world sorting out all their computer problems. She's a clever young lady, and a wizard on a keyboard, used to spend all her time in her room. Sean and I used to worry about her, and hope she would do something else, at least unrelated to Bits and

Bytes, fax-modems, Rams and Roms, and of course the World.Wide.Wed, but then at last she found herself a boyfriend, nice lad…' Kerrie crossed her. 'Ma, please,' she said. 'I'm sure they never came here to hear about our life histories.' She smiled shyly at them all.

Good for her thought Paul *that will take Kerrie out of Rod's clutches seeing as she has a boyfriend. One young lady out of Rod's equation, one down Rod, three to go.*

Cathleen touched her daughter's hand gently. 'Kerrie, darling would you be an absolute love, and make these young men a cup of coffee, use the tray. Oh, and bring in some of that soda bread I baked this morning.'

Kerrie counted them, smiled and made her way to the kitchen.

Good, thought Paul smiling *that will piss Rod off, not getting Sinead on her own.*

'And these are our youngest, twins Caitlin and Una.' They both sat on the arms of the small sofa. 'Una is studying marine biology at university.'

'Isn't that a posh fisherman?' asked John.

Una ignored John's remark, and just shrugged and grinned at them all.

'And Caitlin, she's studying law at Cambridge.'

Shit thought John *I better not tell her that all I've got is a teenager who smokes.*

'Sean never told us that you had four such beautiful young ladies,' said Mick. 'They certainly don't get their good looks from him, their beauty definitely comes from their mother.'

'Thank you,' Cathleen smiled, and blushed.

'Interesting names,' said Mick.

'Do you think so?' replied Cathleen.

'Irish names aren't they?' asked Paul.

John and Mick didn't say a word, but just looked at Paul and nodded their heads in unison.

'Yes,' answered Cathleen, nodding her head, 'Sinead's name is the female version of Sean. And Kerrie came from County Kerry in Ireland, that's where Sean and I were born and married. And Caitlin comes from Kathleen, but the Irish version of Kathleen is the way I spell my name Cathleen with a C, not a K, and last is Una that's a very old Irish name for *lamb*. Cathleen touched Una's arm, 'because she's the baby of the flock.'

'Ma, please,' hissed Una, blushing.

Cathleen looked back at the lads. 'Have you any children Mick?' she asked.

The question hit Mick like a time bomb. For some years he had tried not to forget, but put the accident in the back of his mind. He spoke softly. 'Sadly not any more. That's a strange thought though about your name,' he continued. 'My late wife was called Kathleen also, but with a K, the English version I suppose,' he shrugged, 'although I'd never really thought of her name in that way.' Mick dropped his head; the memories hit him harder than he'd expected as a tear appeared in the corner of his eye. 'Anyway,' his voice shook as he tried to finish what he had started. 'Sadly… my… wife… was killed some time ago.' He dropped his head further, rubbing his eyes with the back of his hand. 'With… our… only child Elizabeth, she was only nineteen-years-old, so vibrant and a very happy young lady In fact on the day it happened, they were shopping for Elizabeth, she had just been accepted into Cambridge University.'

'What happened, if you don't mind me asking,' asked Cathleen softly.

'No,' said Mick half-heartedly smiling. 'A car accident, some drunk driver veered over their side of the road, head-on collision, they never knew what happened, apparently. The police said they must have both died instantly. Within a fraction of a second my whole life was swept away.' *Time had passed since his wife and daughter had died, but the wounds still dug deep. They say time is a healer, but for Mick it wasn't, it still hurt as much now as it did at the time of fatal accident.*

Cathleen tilted her head to one side, trying to get a better look at Mick's dropped face. 'That is so sad, I'm… so… very… very… sorry, Mick,' she said slowly, and she meant it, as the tears showed in the corner of her eyes. 'It must have been so very painful for you,' she continued, dabbing the corner of her eyes with her crisp white handkerchief. Mick half-heartedly smiled again at Cathleen, seeing the pain in her face. 'Thank you, it was and is still very painful,' he replied. *Never in his life had he felt so alone since the days after the accident.* 'I have my good days and bad days.'

John's mouth gaped open as he was galvanized by Mick's unexpected revelations. 'My God, poor sod I didn't know that' He patted Mick gently on the shoulder, trying in vain to imagine what he had gone through. John's interior dialogue with himself resumed. *You just can't tell about people. It's amazing how well you think you know somebody. Even the ones you think you know inside out.*

Then Mick comes out with that. He shook his head vigorously; it was amazing how unimportant Kaylie's smoking habit had become. *But you can have my smoking teenager if you like Mick...* 'And... you.... John,' asked Cathleen, interrupting his thoughts. He was still in shock at Mick's revelation. 'Just... the same as Mick said John. 'I'm sorry, what your wife died as well?' *He would normally have said no such luck, but didn't feel it was appropriate.* 'No...no ... just a...' He paused, *not wishing to go into the smoking teenager syndrome, not after the explanation of Cathleen's daughters' academic abilities.* 'No...no... no children.'

Paul looked at John gobsmacked, *what about the smoking teenager...* Cathleen interrupted his thoughts. 'Paul, and you?'

Paul shook his head. 'What... yes... sorry Mrs Walsh?'

'Such a polite young man,' said Cathleen, looking at John. 'Paul, please, Cathleen is fine. Any children!'

Paul smiled at John and turned to Cathleen. 'Thank you, yes Cathleen, we have two little girls, Melissa and Ally, but of course the girls' names aren't as profound as your girls' names. Melissa our oldest was named after her grandmother, and our youngest is called Ally.'

'Ally...Uhmm... how sweet...' said Cathleen, 'now that's a strange name, Ally, where did that come from?'

Paul opened his mouth to explain. John blurted out before Paul could reply, 'She was conceived up a back ally, Cathleen.'

'Cathleen laughed– a gentle warm laugh; it was the first time they had heard her laugh.

As if it was possible Cathleen was even more beautiful when she laughed, Mick thought.

Cathleen looked at Craig. 'Sorry, Craig was it?'

Craig nodded and went to speak. John spoke as Craig's mouth opened. 'Yes his wife is expecting a baby.'

'First one?' asked Cathleen.

Craig opened his mouth and went to speak again as John said, 'Yes.'

Sinead shook the bottle. 'This might sting a bit,' she said, tipping up the contents of the bottle of TCP onto a swab to allow it to soak in. She had small hands, he noticed, as he watched her emptying the contents of the bottle onto the swab, quick, clever fingers. She averted her eyes, *shyness,* he thought, *but he decided a doctor can't have a rusty sense of socialising skills, all the nurses that he knew, same profession, and all the nurses' house parties he had been invited to, the one thing he'd learnt was that they were very sociable creatures.*

'Right here we go,' said Sinead, interrupting his thoughts. Grinning, she dabbed the wound.

Rod grabbed the worktop. 'Jesus Christ, what's that?' he shrieked, ducking his head trying to get away from whatever she was dabbing onto the wound. 'That stings like buggery.' His whole head stung like a thousand bee stings.

Kerrie turned and looked, giggling as she laid the tray.

'Sorry, it's just TCP,' said Sinead, showing him the bottle and smiling. 'I know it stings, but it will clean the wound, that's it, all over,' she spoke like she was reassuring a hurt child, pulling his head towards her, drying off the wound. 'The bleeding has almost stopped, you'll live.'

Rod smelt the soft scent of her body; he would have liked to stay in this position forever, he'd never smelt anything like it before, he breathed in deeply.

'There you are,' she said, abruptly pushing his head away. 'Take this pad, just keep the pressure on; we can't put on a plaster, unless we shave the affected area. She pulled a razor from a jar on the windowsill.

'No...no...' said Rod quickly, holding up a hand in defence of the razor, not wishing to walk around looking like bloody Friar Tuck. That wouldn't give his street credibility a boost.

'Ok,' said Sinead, replacing the razor in the jar. 'Use this pad then,' she said as she moved to the sink and washed her hands.

Kerrie was looking timidly at Rod as she cut the soda bread. 'Are you married?' she asked.

Rod laughed, 'God no.'

'Partner,' said Kerrie, placing the cut slices of soda bread on a plate.

'Nope.'

'Kerrie, don't be so nosy,' snapped Sinead.

'That's ok,' said Rod, waving his free hand.

'Girlfriend,' Kerrie said as she had been given the invitation to continue the questioning.

'No...no girlfriend,' *technically no, he thought, hoping that Michelle would be gone by the time he'd got back home. So that wasn't a lie.*

'Have you any brothers?' Kerrie asked, pulling a packet of sugar from the cupboard, filling the bowl, and taking the milk from the fridge.

'One brother, Chris, in fact he's about your age.'

'Kerrie for God's sake,' Sinead snapped again, 'what did I say?'

'Ok...ok...that's it, that's all I need to know,' Kerrie said, pulling the cups from the cupboard.

'It's ok,' Rod said, smiling at Sinead. 'What about you?'

'What?' asked Sinead.

'Married?'

'God no, much too busy with my career, anyway it wouldn't be fair.'

'Anybody waiting in the wings?' *God please make her say no.*

She bit her lower lip, nodding her head from side to side, wanting to get away from the question, and checking the wound on Rod's head. 'That looks fine, the bleeding has stopped.'

Shit thought Rod *that's not what he wants to hear, sod the wound.*

'Any admirers?'

'Nope, the only man in my life is my da.'

'And a very lucky man Sean is too.' *Thank you Sean, and of course, thank you God.*

Kerrie giggled.

Rod smiled. 'Whoa, so you're a doctor Sinead?' he asked; he looked fascinated and impressed. 'I am impressed,' he said. *Come to think of it he'd never been out with a doctor. In fact the girls he'd been shagging didn't need to be above the IQ of a Tesco's shelf-filler. That was ok, they didn't need a high IQ for what he was looking for, there wasn't a lot of talking to be done, sex, that's all he wanted. After all, sex was just animal instincts; you didn't need to be an intellectual. Sinead was different though, she was something else, this wasn't going to be a walk in the park he* thought. Rod continued before Sinead could answer. 'It must be one hell of a job, being a doctor.' *What a twat of a line he* thought *why couldn't he'd just say what he wanted to say, that I think you're bloody fantastic, what about a shag. It normally worked that way for him.* He silently nodded his head up and down, *but somehow he knew she wouldn't go for that.*

Sinead frowned. 'No, it's not hell, to be a doctor would be fantastic, but I'm not a doctor yet. I've got my finals next week, then, if I pass, as you say, then I will be a doctor. But today has been particularly tiring.'

'Amazing, will you let me know if you pass?' asked Rod.

Sinead shrugged her shoulders. 'Why?' she asked.

Kerrie poured the hot water into the coffee pot, looked at Sinead and giggled *because he fancies you, you doughnut.*

Rod held up his hands. 'Because I'd just like to know, that's all, I've never met a doctor before.'

'Ok.'

'Cool,' said Rod, pulling a book from his back pocket and pulling a card from the back of his book. 'That one's my home phone, and that one's my mobile,' he said, pointing at the card. He hit his head, 'Ouch,' he said as he handed her the card. 'My God, why am I telling you that, you're nearly a doctor.' They both laughed.

Kerrie pulled the tray from the worktop.

'Let me take that for you,' asked Rod. 'It's heavy.'

'Thanks,' said Kerrie smiling shyly, passing over the tray.

'Ok, lead on McDuff,' said Rod, pushing the tray towards the door as they all made their way back into the lounge.

'Have you got any children Rod?' asked Cathleen as they entered the lounge.

The cups, saucers and plates rattled as Rod nearly dropped the tray. *Where the hell did that come from, shit, I've only been in there with Sinead for five minutes.* 'I'm afraid Cathleen,' John said, looking at Rod, 'he's just about getting out of adolescence himself.'

Rod looked at John sternly.

Cathleen smiled at Rod. 'I can't believe that,' she said. 'I'm sure that he would make a wonderful father, don't you think?'

They all nodded, NO.

Rod looked at Cathleen. 'Thanks for your vote of confidence Cathleen,' he said. 'Where shall I put the tray?' he asked.

'Over here,' said Sinead, clearing the large table by the front window.

'Kerrie dear, would you pour, please,' asked Cathleen.

Kerrie poured, handing them a coffee each.

'Please help yourselves to sugar and milk and of course try the soda bread, it was freshly baked this morning.'

'This bread smells wonderful,' said Mick, taking a slice of soda bread and a plate.

John nudged Rod, and whispered. 'It's got bloody currants in it; bread with currants in it, that's not bread, that's cake isn't it?'

Rod looked up with a grin. 'Travel John, that what I said to you in the van, travel, that's what you lack my son, travel and culture.'

'What's that got to do with bloody bread that looks like cake?' John whispered.

Rod leant into John. 'John you're irritating me now,' he whispered. 'It's not bloody cake, take my word for it, it's bloody bread, baked in the traditional Irish way.' Rod turned towards Cathleen. 'Cathleen, this bread is absolutely delicious,' he said, holding up the soda bread.

'Thank you Rod.'

John wasn't going to let it go, he nudged Rod. 'I'm telling you Rod this is cake,' mumbled John, 'look at it; it crumbles in your hand as soon as you touch it.'

'You're really annoying me now,' said Rod through gritted teeth, turning towards John. 'I'll give you bloody cake,' he whispered, tapping the underneath of John's plate, as his cake/bread flew up into the air. Rod smiled and walked off towards Cathleen, as John scrambled on the floor picking up the exploding cake/bread as it hit the floor.

Cathleen waved a hand at John. 'Don't worry about that John,' she said. 'The girls will sweep that up later, help yourself to some more.'

'Right,' said Mick softly, 'let's get down to business, after all, that's what we came here for.' They all sat down. The girls sat next to Cathleen.

Mick placed his plate on the coffee table. 'Mmm… Cathleen that was absolutely delicious,' he said, licking his fingers and nodding his head from side to side.

Cathleen approved of Mick's approving smile. 'You're welcome,' she nodded back.

'Ok to business,' said Mick, turning towards the lads. 'But bear with me lads, I'm going to have to go through this again for the girls' sake.'

The four girls nodded their agreement.

'Right,' continued Mick. 'This is what we've got at the moment. One; Sean, your dad, collected the lottery money from us last Friday before we left work for the weekend.' The girls listened intently as Mick spoke. 'Two; as your mum said, Sean was telephoned by me late Saturday night, but she wasn't with him when he supposedly took my call…' 'What,' interrupted Caitlin the legal student. 'Are you suggesting that my da never got your call?'

John nudged Mick. 'You've got your work cut out here Mick,' he whispered, 'she's a legal beagle, you know.'

'I know John… I know,' whispered Mick, turning back to Caitlin. 'Well, Caitlin firstly I'm not suggesting anything about your dad; I'm just relaying the facts that I have to you. I know that I didn't phone your dad. I can show my phone bill if you don't believe me. Anyway if I did call your dad on Saturday to start work on Sunday and he'd started work, then we wouldn't be here having this conversation now, would we?'

Caitlin was pursing her lips, giving Mick's answer serious thought 'I suppose so,' she said finally, raising her eyebrows.

'Good one Mick,' whispered John.

Mick continued. 'Three; your dad never turned up for work on Monday morning, that was when I rang your mum and asked her where he was, and your mum said that she hadn't seen him since that Saturday night. Four; well lucky or not our lottery syndicate's numbers came up, all six of them...' 'How did you know your numbers came up if Da had the ticket,' asked Caitlin.

'She's bloody good Mick,' whispered John. 'I keep the set of numbers in my book,' said Paul, pulling the book from his jacket pocket, flipping it open to the lottery numbers and holding the book towards Caitlin. 'See for yourself.' 'And we checked those numbers in Sunday's paper,' interrupted Mick.

'Well, I don't do the lottery myself,' said Caitlin, looking at them all one at a time, 'mugs' game...correct me if I'm wrong, but doesn't the one who holds the ticket win the money?' 'That's my point,' said Mick, crossing her. 'What you've said is right, so if your dad held the ticket, then he had to be the one who collected the money.'

Caitlin held up a hand. 'Hang on a minute though,' she said, furrows appearing on her forehead, in deep thought. 'Right, so what you're saying is you've got the six numbers, because you checked them in the newspaper, but that doesn't tell you that it was Da who picked up your so-called winning money. There may have been more than one winner.'

John pointed at her. 'She's good,' he whispered, nudging Mick again.

Mick ignored John's comment and continued. 'Yes, you're right Caitlin, good point,' he said, 'but we've covered that avenue as well, we rang Camelot's hotline on Monday, and guess what?'

Sinead looked at them firmly. 'What?' she asked.

Rod smiled at Sinead; she didn't return his smile but looked at Cathleen.

'Camelot told us there was only one winner,' said Mick.

'Did they give you the winner's name?' asked Una.

'I'm afraid not Una, Camelot are not allowed to give that sort of information out.'

Kerrie looked puzzled. 'Well that winner could have been anybody; my da might not have put the syndicate's money on,' she said.

'So what you're saying is that your dad has disappeared because he didn't put the syndicate's money on,' asked Paul.

'It's possible,' said Kerrie.

'Don't think so,' replied Craig.

'He may….' Rod went to speak. Paul nudged him, as Mick continued. 'We have that covered as well, because your dad told us all in the pub that he always bought the ticket at *Costcutters* here.' 'That's right,' answered Cathleen. '7:00 on the dot, every Saturday without fail, then we'd go for a good old sing-song down the pub, karaoke, Sean loved a bit of karaoke...' 'Sorry to interrupt you Cathleen, but she's right,' said Rod, 'I remember now, Sean did get a call on Saturday night, he was on his mobile, while you were in the ladies'.'

Mick angled his head. 'But that could have been a call from anybody Rod,' he said, playing the detective.

'It's possible, I suppose,' replied Rod, shrugging his shoulders, 'but all I'm saying is that Sean did get a call on Saturday evening.'

'Hang on,' said John, holding up his hand as if he was back at school and about to ask a question. 'Cathleen, is Sean's mobile still here, we could check the numbers.'

'No,' replied Cathleen, 'I'm afraid Sean took it with him on Saturday night.'

'Damn it,' said John. 'Sorry ladies,' he said, putting his hand to his mouth.'

Craig gave John a quick stare, *God he's not apologising for damn it, only 10 minutes ago and he would have said f... f... f...fuck it. Now you'd apologise for that.*

'Anyway let's try not to get side-tracked,' said Mick. 'As I said earlier, we, I mean Rod, rang *Costcutters*, and the girl on the till said that she had definitely served Sean on Saturday evening around 7.00pm, so he definitely bought the ticket there, and this is the crunch. When we rang Camelot, as I said before, Camelot said there was only one winner, but this is the interesting bit, apparently it was a roll-over from Wednesday's draw, and the jack-pot for that Saturday's draw stood at eighteen million pounds.'

Cathleen gasped, as her hands went to her mouth, and there were four sharp intakes of breathe, as the four girls' jaws dropped.

Mick waited for a reply, but none came so he continued. 'So now you see our predicament,' he said. 'We have no Sean, no ticket…' 'And worst of all,' John interrupted, 'no money, and that's a share of three million pounds each.'

'Mary, mother of Jesus,' gasped Cathleen. 'This is just a thought but you've had winnings before, have you not?'

'Yes, tenner here, and a tenner there,' answered Mick, nodding, 'nothing really big.'

Lines appeared in Cathleen's forehead, as she spoke to Mick. 'And when Sean collects the winnings he has to give in the ticket, right.'

'I suppose so,' agreed Mick, not following Cathleen's thinking.

'Right, wait here,' said Cathleen, holding out a hand as she got up and left the room.

'What's up?' Rod mouthed silently to Mick.

Mick shrugged his shoulders.

Cathleen returned with a black folder and an envelope. She placed them on the coffee table and flicked through the folder. 'Sean always took a copy of the ticket because he knew that if he'd won he'd have to give the ticket up. As you can see, there's no ticket for Saturday nights draw you're talking about.' She twisted the folder towards them.

Mick flicked through them. 'As you said, there's not one for Saturday night's draw.'

Cathleen tipped out the contents of an envelope onto the coffee table, passports, medical insurance etc. She picked up the passports one by one; her fingers trembled as she flicked through them. 'There's only five passports here, the four girls' and mine. Sean's has gone.' Tears appeared in the corner of her eyes, as she dropped the passports on the table and sat down heavily on the sofa, trying not to believe what she was thinking. Caitlin and Kerrie put their arms around Cathleen to comfort her.

'Sorry Ma,' said Sinead.

Sinead looked at them firmly. 'Shite,' she screamed, looking around at the lads. 'I still don't believe that our Da would never have stolen your money.'

'I know how you feel, and I'm really sorry,' said Mick, 'but, with all the evidence we have, it's very difficult to believe that he didn't.' All the lads nodded in agreement. Even Caitlin had stopped asking questions.

Kerrie intervened. 'Well, maybe we should wait until we know for sure. That it was our da, who you believe took your money.'

John held out his hands. 'And how do you propose we do that then Kerrie?' he asked, 'because as sure as eggs is eggs, sitting here isn't going to tell us anything.' He put the question in for general debate.

Una took a deep breath. 'Maybe we could call the police,' she said, 'let them deal with it.'

'Shit,' said John. 'Sorry,' he said, putting his hand up to his mouth again, 'No good, it's only that the police took two weeks to get round my house when it was burgled. Something like this, it would take them months, and all we have at the moment is a missing person.'

'Maybe years,' agreed Paul, nodding.

Mick nodded his agreement. 'The lads are right I'm afraid,' he said, 'I don't think the police are an option.'

'Oh my God, sorry Ma,' said Sinead as she stood up suddenly in exasperation and snapped her fingers to bring their attention to her. 'This is so stupid. I can't believe I'm hearing this.' She paused. 'I know what we're going to do,' she informed them.

'What!' asked Mick.

Sinead rattled her well-manicured fingers in everyone's direction, but mostly at Mick. 'We're going to find my da, and I'll prove to you all that my da never stole your money. Da would rather give you money than steal it from you,' she snapped.

Rod smiled at Sinead, *that's my girl, you tell them* he thought. 'Sinead's right, let's all keep an open mind,' he said, looking at Sinead.

They all rolled their eyes at Rod.

Craig nudged Paul. 'He wants to shag her,' Craig whispered in Paul's ear.

Paul nodded. 'No chance,' he whispered back.

Mick flapped his hands tentatively, looking back seriously at Sinead. 'Oh, we didn't want to suggest that Sean took the money, and we hope you're right Sinead, but things are not looking too good for him… so what do you suggest we do then?' he asked, confused at her outburst.

'Well Da's passport is missing so we must assume that Da may well have gone abroad.'

John's face went pale as Sinead mentioned abroad, *shit that probably means a bloody aeroplane,* he thought.

'Ma,' Sinead said, turning towards Cathleen. 'You've got hundreds of photographs of Da.'

Cathleen nodded.

'A photograph would be helpful,' agreed Mick, nodding at the rest of the lads.

'Why Mick?' asked John, lifting his shoulders.

Mick rolled his eyes. 'You'll see,' he replied.

'He doesn't know,' Paul whispered to Craig.

Sinead flapped her hand towards the ornate cabinet against the wall. 'In there Ma, sort us out six recent photographs of Da.'

Cathleen knelt down at the cabinet, pulling out an overweight photograph album and laying it on the coffee table; she flicked through the pages pulling out six photographs and handed them to Sinead. Sinead flicked through them, one by one. 'Jesus, not that one Ma,' she said, handing it back.

'Why?' asked Kerrie, snatching the photograph from Ma.

'Because it shows me in a bikini,' Sinead said, thumbing over her shoulder at the lads, 'and I'm not having that lot gorping at me in a bikini.'

'You're right,' said Kerrie, looking at the photograph. 'It is a little bit revealing.'

Shit, thought Rod *I almost got to see what was under that white coat.*

'Sensible move Sinead,' smiled John, looking at Rod's crestfallen face.

'There you are dear,' said Cathleen, passing Sinead another photograph, 'that's a better photograph, it's of you and Da, taken last Christmas, you're well wrapped up.'

'Bugger,' murmured Rod.

Sinead turned and handed each one of them a photograph.

Rod snatched the photo that Paul had of Sinead in his hand and gave him his one of Sean and Sinead; he certainly didn't want to look at Sean's bloody face all day, especially after he had nicked all their money.

'Right,' Sinead explained, giving them her I'm in control look. 'Now, what we are going to do is, we are going to go down to the town centre and ask in every travel agency if they have seen my da, ok.'

Without any word in response, they all just nodded.

Sinead made her way to the living room door, and turned. 'Right let me just change my coat, and we'll be off.'

As she rushed through the door Mick looked at Cathleen. 'Is she always like this?' Mick whispered, hoping she was out of earshot. 'Not that I'm moaning, in fact I find it extremely appealing.'

'She's almost a doctor,' was all Cathleen said.

'Right, come on, are you all ready, or not?' Sinead shouted from the hallway.

Rod shot to his feet, as if he had been sitting in an electric chair and somebody had just thrown the handle and shot 50.000 volts through him. 'Come on lads,' he said, 'she who speaks, must be obeyed.'

'You've got no chance their Rod,' whispered Paul as they left the room.

Rod whispered, 'He who dares wins mate.'

Craig watched Sinead disappear through the front door. 'Only in your dreams mate,' he whispered.

Rod looked around for Cathleen and the girls. They hadn't followed them to the front door. 'Bollocks Monkey man,' he whispered, taking his coat from the hall cupboard, and making his way to the front door.

Chapter Six
Travel Agents

Mick pulled the van into the town centre's long-stay car park. Rod hadn't taken his eyes off Sinead since they had left the house. Sinead jumped out. 'Right, we'll go in pairs. Mick you go with Craig, and John you go with Rod.'

'Fuck,' mumbled Rod under his breath. John was thinking exactly the same thing.

'And I'll go with Paul.'

'You might have got her photograph, but you'll never get the girl,' whispered Paul, smiling.

'Poge ma hone,' said Rod.

'Right,' said Sinead, 'we'll go to the four corners of town, start from there and work our way back to the middle of town, and we'll all meet at Costa's coffee shop in the town centre.'

They all nodded in agreement.

Sinead smiled. 'Ok, and remember no pubs, travel agents. Right let's go Paul,' she said, as she strode off to their designated area.

Rod tried to catch Sinead's eye, but she was having none of it. Instead he stuck his fingers up at Paul as Paul followed her obediently. Paul pointed to his arse and mouthed. 'Kiss My Arse Loser.'

★ ★ ★

'Right we'll start from here then,' said John as they walked slowly through the shopping concourse scanning the shop fronts for potential travel agents. 'Just as a matter of interest Rod, what would you do with your 3 million pounds? That's if we ever do get to f… f… f… find it,' he asked.

'Hmmm… good question John,' replied Rod. 'If you'd asked me that yesterday, I would probably have said I'd buy a black 911 Porsche and take up shagging as a profession,' he shook his head, 'but now I don't know. I've changed my mind.'

'When you say you've changed your mind. What about the Porsche or being a professional shagger, which d'you mean?'

'No, it's not the Porsche 911, that's still in the bag, No… no… It's more the profession, if we ever get the three million pounds, it's the shagging that I've had enough of.'

John rolled his eyes. 'I'm sure you have,' he smiled, thinking of Michelle's naked body at the top of the stairs. 'Rod don't f… f… f… forget I've seen the evidence of what you're proposing to give up, and very nice it was too. Good God don't tell me that's what you've changed your mind about. I'd give my bloody right arm to sleep with a girl like that.'

'It's not sleep John, its just sex.'

John frowned. 'I know it's sex,' he replied, 'but I just didn't like putting it that way. Anyway, is that what you intend giving up?'

'Sort of, but I wouldn't say it was me that has changed my mind, more like my mind has been changed for me.'

John took a sharp intake of breath, as he looked at the expression on Rod's face. 'Good God Rod, you are, you're serious about giving up shagging. I'm telling you Rod there'll be wailing in the streets, you mark my words,' he smiled, shaking his head. 'And tell me this then Rod. What's going to happen if the great Valentino gives up shagging, then tell me, who the hell's going to service the whole world's f… f… f… female population?'

Rod looked up. 'You're trying to make me sound as if I'm a sex maniac or something. I can control my sexual emotions, and you know that John.'

'Do I,' said John, rolling his eyes, 'I'm telling you this Rod, there must a good reason f… f… f… for your denial of sex.'

John shook his head, ' Hang on,' he pointed a finger at Rod, 'you're not…. you're not sweet on Sean's girl, that Sinead?' he said.

Rod never answered. The answer showed in his face.

John looked at Rod full in the face; he'd never seen that expression before. 'Come on Rod, I've known you f… f… f… for some time, I've watched the way you look at Sinead, there's something there, am I right?' 'I don't know, maybe,' said Rod, shrugging his shoulders, 'early days yet.'

'My God Rod, you are, aren't you,' he said, 'I'm telling you now you're wasting your time there mate, I've seen it in Sinead's eyes.'

'When?'

'Not now, later Rod, we've got more important things to do at the moment, like looking for Sean, your love life can wait.

Look over there,' shouted John, pulling out the photograph from his inside pocket. '*Going Places Travel Agents*, lets go.'

★ ★ ★

Mick and Craig pulled up the collars of their coats, sinking their hands deep into the pockets of their coats as they walked down Market Street.

'I'm sorry to hear what you said back there Mick, at Sean's house, I didn't know you lost your wife and a daughter,' said Craig.

'Thanks,' said Mick. 'It's not something,' he paused for a moment then added, 'that I find easy to talk about, Craig.'

'I bet… do you mind talking about it now?' Craig asked. 'Tell me to shut up if you think I'm prying Mick.'

Mick tapped his shoulder. 'No lad… it's not so bad now, it doesn't hurt so much.'

'How long ago did it happen?' inquired Craig.

'5 years, 4 months,' he looked at his watch, '7 hours, 30 minutes and 25 seconds,' replied Mick.

'Christ Mick, you've got it down to the last second.'

'That's how it gets you Craig, when you love people as much as I did, my Kathleen and Elizabeth were two wonderful people, they meant everything to me,' said Mick.

'I bet… you've never found somebody else.'

'No,' replied Mick. He would only see that as a betrayal to Kathleen's memory.

'Why don't you find somebody else?'

'No…no…' replied Mick, 'I just couldn't, nobody would ever be good enough, I couldn't anyway, I wouldn't know how to look for anybody else, look at me, I'm too old in the tooth for all that… anyway I've forgotten how to do that since Elizabeth and Kathleen.'

Craig flicked back his forelocks of ginger hair and shrugged to say, 'Do what?'

'How to chat up women, of course, and if I did where do I take them?' Mick paused, thinking he was being a bit too open, but out of all the lads he knew he could trust Craig. 'Don't tell the lads.'

Craig made a gesture of zipping his lips.

Mick looked around, and lowered his voice. 'I've virtually forgotten how to make love to a woman since Kathleen.'

'God, is that a fact,' said Craig. 'Anyway, Mick I'm sure there is somebody out there for you, you're a good person, I'm telling you there is somebody out there for you. You deserve somebody.'

'Thanks Craig you're a good lad. Maybe, over there,' shouted Mick.

Bloody hell that was quick. 'Who!' asked Craig.

'Lunn Poly.'

'Who the hell's Lunn Poly?'

'The Flight Shop,' smiled Mick. 'Come on Craig,' he shouted, pulling the photograph from his inside pocket.

★ ★ ★

Paul stopped again and waited as Sinead looked into another shop window. He stood patiently aiming a desultory kick at an imaginary stone.

'What do you think of that,' Sinead asked him, 'smart or tarty, what do you think?'

'Christ Sinead,' Paul held out his hands in a gesture of non-committal. 'I'm a man for God's sake, what do I know about woman's clothes, shall we move on?'

'Don't put yourself down,' replied Sinead. 'You're married aren't you Paul?'

Paul looked puzzled at her question. 'Yes I'm married, so what's that got to do with it?'

Sinead raised and eyebrow, and tutted. 'Well you do go shopping with your wife then, don't you?'

Paul hated going shopping with Gale – women shopped differently to men. 'So what's your point?' he asked, raising his shoulders.

'Well, my point is that you're smartly dressed for a man, good dress sense, so who chooses your clothes?'

'I do, why!'

'That's my point, Paul, if you can choose your own clothes then you have got good dress sense.' Sinead stopped abruptly in front of a large shop window. 'Just look at yourself in this window Paul, smart or what?'

Paul stood looking at his reflection in the window; he shrugged his shoulders, not really knowing what he was looking for.

'See, smart,' said Sinead again.

'If you say so,' said Paul, moving off.

'Here... here...' said Sinead, pulling at his arm to stop him.

'What! Good God, not another shop,' Paul tutted, 'I thought we were supposed to be looking for travel agents, remember.'

Sinead never let go of his arm, just in case he got away. 'I know...I know... but I've got my doctorate exams next week, and if I pass, they throw a party after, and I have to buy a dress for the party, so just look at that, isn't it beautiful?'

Paul held both hands up to the window. 'It looks a bit clingy,' he said. 'Nice but it's got a slit right up the side. Do you think you could carry a dress like that off?'

Sinead elbowed him in the ribs. 'Cheeky sod,' she said, tossing back her hair. She took his elbow in a firm grip, much like a mother with a stubborn child and pulled him into the shop. As she strong-armed him into the shop, she walked him to a row of seats in front of some cubicles. 'Right, now you sit down there,' she said, pointing to a seat. ' I'll go and look for an assistant, isn't this wonderful?' she said as she wandered off looking for some assistance.

Paul sat down rubbing his ribs, looking around the shop. Half a dozen fawn-curtained changing-rooms faced him, some open, some closed; he picked up a magazine from the side table, *Jesus Christ* he thought as he flicked through the magazine. *Why do woman pay so much money for clothes, and put so little on, he couldn't understand their logic. Men, now they have a very different attitude when they go shopping for clothes, they want to get as much material as they can for the smallest amount of money.*

'Here we are,' said Sinead, followed by an assistant with arms full of dresses who disappeared into one of the cubicles.

Christ, thought Paul, *I'm sure I only looked at one dress through the shop window; she seems to have cleared the whole bloody window display.*

'Right, Paul now I want your honest opinion, please,' she said, diving into the cubicle, pulling the curtain across. He looked back at the magazine and waited.

Sinead made her entrance from the cubicle. 'Well, what do you think, don't forget, your honest opinion,' she asked, feeling the contours of the dress against her breasts.

Paul looked up from the magazine. 'My God,' he said, throwing the magazine on the table, his mouth gaped, gob-smacked, silent for a few minutes looking from her feet to her head, trying to take it all in. And this had nothing to do with the dress it was her. *She would look good in a black plastic bin liner* he thought.

Sinead spread her hands. 'Well, what do you think,' she said again, getting impatient.

'My God you are something else, did you put on a dress or just spray the colour on, you should be in this magazine,' he said, picking up the magazine from the table, and waving it at her.

'You like it then.'

'What?'

Sinead stamped her foot. 'The dress… the dress.'

'Oh right, the dress, yes, I hadn't noticed it.'

'Do you like the slit,' she said, pushing out her leg.

A man whistled at her, behind him. Paul spun round in the seat and stared at him, as the whistler quickly walked off. He watched him until he was out of sight, and turned back to Sinead. 'You... look... absolutely stunning.' He couldn't open his eyes wide enough.

'Well, thank you Paul, that is very sweet of you.'

She gave him a twirl. 'No panty lines,' she said, 'well what do you think?'

Paul looked closer, *my god she's only naked under that dress*. 'Right,' he said, blushing at the thought that she knew he was looking at her. 'What can I say; I take back what I said outside the shop. You are that dress, very... very... elegant,' he said. 'Neckline a touch Victorian, but beautifully finished.'

'Let me try on another,' she said, disappearing back into the cubicle and drawing the curtain across.

Paul looked at the magazine. He sound of a dropped hanger inside the cubicle made him look towards the curtain; he noticed a slight slit in the curtain and saw the reflection of Sinead's naked body in the mirror. He stared; his eyes were like magnets to iron filings, not able to take his eyes off the view in the mirror. Now that is a figure of perfect proportions. He'd never ever seen anything like it. He smiled thinking of John and Rod walking around the town, they would have given their right arms to be in the position he was in. Although he was married, he was feeling a bit of jealousy that Rod might at sometime get a chunk of this beautiful woman, and he certainly didn't deserve her. He was fixed, unable to take his eyes away from the slit in the curtain. *My God, here she comes again* as he saw her hand fold around the curtain. He dived his face behind the magazine as the curtain was pulled sharply back. He could sit there all day, just looking at this *Venus de Milo*. There she was again, this red apparition stood in front of him. Chris De Burgh's record swam into his head, *The Lady in Red*.

'Well?'

'Wow… that dress…. looks amazing on you,' he said, putting his fingers to his lips and pushing out a kiss. 'Now that's one hell of a dress, it's just perfect, love the colour,' he said, crossing his legs and laying the magazine over the stirring in his trousers, hoping and praying she wouldn't notice. 'It was made for you; it fits you like a glove, highlights your hair and brings out the best in your eyes. I'm telling you, that dress is perfection. You must get it,' he added.

'I'll take this one then,' she said, making her way to the cubicle; she turned and faced Paul before she disappeared. 'I'm sure you're right, this is the right dress, but,' she paused, 'I've never seen that before when I've put a dress on.'

'What?' Paul looked over his shoulder to see if the man had reappeared. He looked back at her. 'What do you mean, when that man whistled at you?' he asked.

'No, the car keys in your trouser pocket,' she smiled, as she disappeared behind the curtain.

Shit, she did notice Paul mumbled to himself, trying to rearrange the offending article.

'I'm sorry about what happened back there,' Paul said, thumbing over his shoulder like a hitchhiker as they exited the shop. His face was almost as red as the dress she'd tried on. 'I'm not a pervert you know; I'm a married man. God I don't know what came over me.'

'Me,' Sinead replied. 'Still, no problem Paul,' she said, smiling as she slipped her arm through his. 'In fact, I'm very flattered, if that's the reaction I'm going to get every time I put this dress on, then I'll be one very, very happy lady. Anyway, think of it this way.'

'What?' said Paul, quickly looking at her.

'You're certainly alive, your two main organs are working in perfect unison, trust me, I'm going to be a doctor.'

They both laughed.

'Here we go,' said Paul, pointing across the concourse, pulling the photograph from his inside pocket. He felt a lot more comfortable now that the thing in the shop had been brought up, so to speak.

The bell rang as they both walked into the travel agents.

Costa's 12:30. The place was packed with lunchtime diners. 'We've picked the right bloody time,' said John, looking at his watch and looking around the café over the heads of the other customers. 'We seem to be the first to have arrived.'

'Quick then,' said Rod, 'get the drinks in before the others arrive.'

'Good thinking Rod,' said John pointing at him, 'what you having,' he asked.

'Seeing as it's a coffee shop, I'll have a beer.'

'Wicked, do they do beers then?' enquired John, smiling.

'No,' Rod smiled. 'But a coffee will do though.'

'Piss off, you smart twat,' said John waving a hand. 'You go

and f…f… f…find some seats, while I get the coffees,' he said, as he pushed his way to the counter. Tapping his fingers impatiently on the counter, he raised his hand when he thought he'd caught the eye of a server on the off chance that he might get served today. He had lost interest in being served today as he rested both elbows on the counter; mesmerised by the disorder of people clambering to get served, his thoughts went back to the travel agents'. *It was the fist time he'd been in a travel agents', not the sort of place you'd go to book a week's holiday in Scarborough, wondering if the other had been more successful than they had…*'May I help you sir,' said the server, dressed like an inboard flight attendant. Leaning across the counter she touched John's arm, interrupting his thoughts… 'Right… yes… sorry, I was miles away, so to speak,' he said. 'Right, two coffees please.'

The flight attendant took a deep breath. 'Will that be two Cappuccinos, Café Lattés, Carmel Macchiato, Café Americino, Espresso, Café Misto, Café Mocha or Decaffeinated?'

John looked at her mesmerised as she reeled out the list. He'd now learnt that coffee wasn't just a case of opening a jar of Nescafe, dumping a spoonful of coffee into a mug, pouring on boiling water and Bob's your uncle, a cup of coffee. No, apparently not, you had to go through this ritual of decaffeinated etc…etc…etc… he shook his head, clearing the extensive list of different coffees. 'Just two normal coffees will do, if that's possible.'

The young flight attendant tilted her head to one side and looked at him strangely as if he'd just landed from another planet. She smiled, 'Of course sir, two normal coffees coming up.' He'd thrown her. 'Oh, and would that be large or small?'

'Large,' answered John.

'That's five pounds please sir,' she said, sliding the coffees across the counter.

'Pardon?' said John, straining to hear above the noise, pulling his wallet from his back pocket.

The flight attendant leaned across the counter. 'That's five pounds sir,' she repeated.

John shook his head in amazement. 'F… f… f… five pounds, for two cups of coffee, that's what I thought you said,' John grimaced, passing over a five-pound note. 'Keep the change,' he smiled, replacing his wallet in his back pocket and pulling the two coffees from the counter. He looked around for Rod. The waving arm indicated where he was. 'Shit,' he said, placing the coffees on the table. 'F… f… f… five bloody pounds, f… f…f…for two coffees.' He sat down with his back to the wall. 'Now I know why they call it bloody Costa's.

Rod pulled two sachets of sugar from the bowl in the centre of the table and tipped them in his coffee. Raising his eyebrows he stirred his coffee. 'Why?' he enquired.

'Because it cost us a bloody f…f…f…fortune.' There was a short silence. 'Right… got it,' said Rod smiling, holding up his spoon. 'Costa and cost us,' Rod laughed louder. 'Very good, John,' he said, stirring his coffee again. He sucked his spoon and pointed it at John. 'They're Italian you know?'

'Who?' asked John, looking round the café wondering who Rod was referring to.

'The Costa's.'

'Right.' John shrugged and nodded, trying to give the impression that he gave a toss, pulling two sugar sachets from the centre of the table and tipping the contents into his coffee.

'Two brothers you know,' continued Rod, 'Sergio and Bruno Costa.'

John stirred his coffee. 'Right, interesting, two brothers you say,' he said, tapping the spoon on the side of his cup.

'Anyway,' said Rod. 'Let's get back to what you were saying outside the travel agents.'

'Remind me,' said John, playing with the two empty sachets of sugar. 'That was bloody ten minutes ago, I've f…f…f…forgotten.'

'About the eyes, you were saying it was in the eyes. You see whatever you saw in Sinead's eyes, and I asked you when.'

Sitting back a little, John took a sip of his coffee thinking over what he had said earlier. 'Right, yes Sinead. It was back at her house, when she took you to the kitchen.'

Rod shuddered at the thought of the TCP. 'So what was in her eyes… what…' he asked, rippling his forehead in puzzlement.

'Haven't you heard the song?' John said, placing his coffee cup back on the saucer.

Rod shrugged. 'What song?'

'I only have eyes f… f… f… for you' sang John.

Rod looked round the café. 'For God's sake, shut it, people are looking.'

'A bloody good song,' said John, 'very appropriate!'

Rod looked puzzled. 'A bit before my time I think, mate.'

'I'm telling you it's all in the eyes Rod, eyes are the windows to the soul you know,' said John, pointing at his own eyes.

Rod looked closely into John's eyes. 'I know what you're eyes are saying mate.'

'What's that then?'

'Bullshit.'

John hunched his shoulders with irritation, and went back to playing with the sugar. 'Ok,' he said. 'If you're not interested in what Sinead's eyes said,' he picked up his coffee, 'then enough said.'

'Ok… ok,' said Rod. 'Sorry, I'm intrigued.' He looked pleased at the possible outcome, and then gave him a raised eyebrow. 'So what did Sinead's eyes say for Christ sake?'

'Ok,' said John, putting his cup down again. 'I'm sorry to say this Rod, but you've got two hopes.'

'What…what… are they then?' demanded Rod in anticipation.

'Bob Hope and no bloody hope, I'm telling you she's not interested in you, or men in general. Anyway,' he continued, waving his coffee spoon at him, 'she's too bloody clever f... f... f...for you mate, she'd tie you up in intellectual knots.'

Rod agreed that John was probably right about Sinead's eyes. They were bright, but he did detect starkness in her eyes; he'd never had to contend with a refusal from the opposite sex before, and he was finding that a bit of a complex concept. Maybe he wouldn't be too hasty at giving up sex completely, but just review the situation at a later date. He nodded his head in agreement. 'I can't argue with that, you're bloody right there. She's got to be clever to be a doctor, I'll give you that.'

'Yes a doctor, and you are just a plumber, no chance my son.'

'Rephrase that John, a bloody unemployed plumber,' Rod said, tracing an imaginary line on the table with his spoon.

'Right,' said John, concentrating. 'But,' he paused, thought and continued, 'you have to look at it her way.'

'What way?'

'Well, she probably thinks that you look at her as good entertainment value, that's all, and of course another scalp for your sexual totem pole.'

'I wouldn't do that,' said Rod.

John shook his head. 'Rod, this is the f... f... f... first thing you have to do.'

'What's that?'

'Be truthful with yourself. Look at your past record Rod, enough said, anyway it would only be a matter of time after sex that you would move on to pastures greener. You must agree looking at it, at her point of view, that would hurt, and I'm right.'

Rod nodded in agreement.

'So Sinead has made a defensive move,' John paused and sipped his coffee.

'How's that, what do you mean by a defensive move?'

John tapped his finger. 'One, protect herself, and two,' he tapped the other finger, 'don't let him get close, arm's length mate.'

Rod nodded his head in agreement again. 'Jesus, and you can see all that in the eyes?'

'Eyes and experience Rod, that's all it is,' replied John. 'Anyway, if you did, and I say this loosely, work on winning Sinead's affections, what about Michelle?' he asked, 'now she's an uncomplicated cracker, why don't you stick with her?'

Rod shook his head. 'No, there's no comparison at all John,' he replied, 'Sinead and Michelle are poles apart.'

John smiled. 'You're right Rod, as you say, they are poles apart, you couldn't take Sinead to a f…f…f…fancy dress party as a tortoise, the name just wouldn't work,' he stammered, nodding his head. 'This coffee's not bad,' he said, taking a sip from the cup. 'Not worth two pound bloody f… f…f…fifty a cup though.'

'Over three hundred outlets, you know,' continued Rod.

'What?' asked John, still wondering where Rod was getting his information from; it certainly wasn't in his head.

Rod continued. 'Costa's sell approximately three point seven million cups of coffee a week.'

'Jesus,' said John, looking impressed. 'They must be worth a bloody f… f… f… fortune, at two pound bloody f… f… f… fifty a cup. Three hundred outlets you say, that's one hell of a lot of coffee. Two pounds f… f… f… fifty a cup.' He worked it out in his head *three point seven million times two pound fifty*. 'Jesus,' John whistled. 'That's bloody, nine point twenty-five million pounds a week.'

'Yer, that's some turnover,' agreed Rod, looking at the two young ladies in deep conversation on the table next to theirs.

'Italians, you know,' said Rod.

'I know, I was listening,' answered John, 'you said the two Costa's brothers…' 'No, not them,' interrupted Rod, 'them,' he kicked John's leg under the table and nodded his head towards the other table, 'the two women on the next table.'

John gave them a sideward glance; he had to admit they were startlingly beautiful women as one of them played delectably with a strand of her long black flowing hair. They were thin with dark complexions, as if they'd both spent their whole lives on sun beds.

John leant across the table and whispered. 'Now those two ladies' eyes on that table are definitely saying something.'

Rod looked puzzled. 'Oh yer, what are their eyes saying then John?'

John tutted, and waved his spoon. 'I'm not saying, I thought you'd given all that up,' he asked.

'I… I… I'm trying,' said Rod, looking back sharply towards John. 'Just looking at what I'm trying to give up, anyway, what, come on, give me your words of wisdom.'

'Ok… no… I really shouldn't say.'

'For Christ sake John you can't just leave that statement hanging in the air, come on.'

John leant closer to Rod and whispered, 'their eyes are saying take us to bed Rod.'

'Shit no,' replied Rod, looking back in their direction and smiling. He looked back at John. 'Really, so you can tell all that by their eyes,' he said.

'I swear by it.'

'You would!'

'I would.'

'So where did you get this priceless information from?'

'I wasn't f… f… f…fucking born in my f… f… f… forties, you know, and believe it or not Rod, I was young once.'

'Wasn't you John, I thought you were born old.'

'Whatever,' said John, waving a hand. 'I was a good-looking bloke when I was young, although I say so myself.'

'Hard to believe,' said Rod, holding John's gaze.

'Bollocks,' mouthed John, 'and might I add,' he said, 'I've been out with a few ladies in my time.'

'That's hard to believe as well,' laughed Rod.

John held up his spoon. 'Ok, if you're going to take the piss, then it's your loss Rod.'

'Ok sorry,' Rod said, waving his spoon. 'Carry on.'

'I gave up going out with other women when I met my Linda. I'm telling you now, it was in her eyes, she winked at me from the other side of the pub and kept winking at me until she got my attention.'

Rod laughed out loud. He really didn't want to make a remark, but he couldn't help himself. 'You sure she didn't have something in her eye?'

'No, she didn't have anything in her eye, you smart twat. Anyway, I've told you, do you want to hear me out, or just take the piss, I'm trying to help you out here, I don't want you wasting my time.'

Rod took on a more serious expression. 'Okay John, go on.'

'I'm telling you Rod, that when I walked over to her, she spoke with her eyes.'

'What did her eyes say then?' asked Rod.

'They said John take me to bed, and make mad passionate love to me.'

'Did you?'

John screwed up his face. 'That's none of your f…f…f… fucking business.'

Rod laughed. 'That means you didn't.'

John pointed his spoon at Rod, giving him a severe look.

'Anyway, whatever,' said Rod. 'My brother actually works for Costa's,' Rod said. 'That's where he works between terms at University.'

So that where he's got his information from, his brother thought John. 'He must like the job then,' he asked.

'Who?' asked Rod, looking back at the other table, not being able to get out of his head what John had told him. All he could think of was Sinead. But he smiled at the two young ladies again anyway.

'Keep up Rod, your brother I said. I suppose your brother told you all about Costa's then.'

'No,' replied Rod, trying desperately not to cast sideways glances at the women on the other table.

'I'm impressed,' said John. 'Well, how the hell do you know all this information about Costa's?'

'It's all in here,' he said, touching his head with his spoon.

'Well I'm impressed Rod.'

'Thank you,' said Rod, pointing his spoon at the wall. 'It also says it on the wall behind you.'

John turned round quickly, and sure enough there on the wall was the Costa's life history.

'Twat,' said John.

Rod laughed. 'Anyway John, what would you do with the money, that's if we ever get it,' he asked.

'That's an easy question for me to answer,' John said. 'I'd get rid of this f...f... f...fucking stammer, as you've probably noticed Rod that I have trouble with the letter f... f... f... f's.'

'You don't say, I must admit you do seem to swear a lot, and unfortunately you seem to use the only word that gives you so much trouble...' 'No I f... f... f...f...fucking don't,' interrupted John.

'You don't say,' smiled Rod. 'Anyway, you don't need to pay any money to get rid of that stutter at all,' he replied.

John's eyes lit up at the thought of getting rid of the F-word problem without paying a penny. He pushed his cup gently to one side and leant forward. 'You reckon, how?' he asked.

'How long have you had trouble with your f's?'

'Uhmm…that's an interesting question Rod, never really given it much thought, but all my life I think,' he said. 'As long as I can remember, in f… f…f…fact my f…f…f…father suffered with the same problem.'

'Right,' Rod tapped his fingers on the table. 'What I'm going to do is tell you how to get rid of your problem,' he explained. 'Ok, when you come to the letter F, what I want you do is, before you say the word, take a deep breath and count to ten, then say the word…' 'Really,' John interrupted, 'will it work?'

'No guarantees, but you can only try,' said Rod as Mick and Craig approached the table. The two ladies on the other table stood to leave. John kicked Rod under the table. 'They're on the move,' he whispered.

They both smiled at Rod and discreetly slipped him a piece of paper as they walked past him. He watched their backs as they departed and raised his eyebrows at John in approval.

Mick and Craig took their seats.

'What was that all about Rod?' asked Mick.

'What's this?' said Rod, holding up the folded piece of paper, unfolding the note and reading it.

'Well,' asked John, 'what is it?'

'It says, "Donna, give me a ring" and she's left me a phone number,' he said, playing with the piece of paper, in two minds whether to phone or…. he tore it into little shreds and dropped it in the ashtray.

Mick and Craig looked wide-eyed at Rod and rolled their eyes at John… 'Don't ask,' said John, holding up a hand. 'Apparently Rod has seen the errors of his ways and is changing his life; he's renounced sex and is going into a life of celibacy.'

'I'm not,' shouted Rod, as he leant forward and whispered 'bollocks,' to John. 'Is that what I get for helping you out mate, let me remind you, John, of your Fs.'

John felt guilty at what he had said and moved on quickly. 'Well how did you do at the travel agents' Mick?'

'Not a sniff, we went into six travel agents', we showed them all the photograph, and they all said they never recognised him, how about you?'

John raised his hands. 'The same,' he said, 'and if the other two don't come up with anything, we're...' he paused. Mick looked at Craig and waited as John counted to ten '...fucked.'

'Get yourselves a coffee while you're waiting, Mick,' said John, smiling at Rod.

'What about you?' said Mick, pointing to John and Rod's cups.

'Please,' John and Rod said in unison.

'Give us a hand Craig,' said Mick, making his way to the counter.

'He's not going to be a happy chappy,' said John as they both laughed.

The cups rattled in the saucers as Mick placed the coffees on the table. 'Jesus Christ,' he whispered, placing the cups on the table. 'Ten quid for four coffees, daylight robbery,' he said, looking back at the counter at the flight attendants, 'no wonder they can afford those posh bloody frocks.'

'Just sit down and drink Mick, before you have a bloody heart attack,' smiled John.

Paul and Sinead entered the café and Paul shouted over the heads of the diners, 'We've got him,' waving a piece of paper in the air. Sinead walked behind him: her expression and her pale face showed she didn't share Paul's excitement.

Paul pushed his way to their table through the crowd of waiting customers and slapped the piece of paper on the table. 'That's bloody it,' said Paul. 'Venezuela, Sean's gone to bloody Venezuela, and if he's still there, then we can probably find him.'

John went pale. 'Venezuela... is... that abroad?' he asked, hoping it was somewhere near Scarborough. If it was, he couldn't place the name on his holiday trip to Scarborough, and Venezuela didn't sound like a Northern town.

Paul looked puzzled at John. 'Of course it's abroad,' he answered.

'F... f... f... fuck,' John inaudibly muttered under his breath, *two weeks ago he would never have envisaged any alterations to his status quo, and now Paul was talking about going a...fucking...broad...flying...* Craig interrupted his thoughts. 'Have you ever been abroad John?' he asked.

John shook his head. 'Of course I've been abroad,' he replied belligerently. 'I always went on the school trips, you know.'

'Where?' asked Mick.

John searched his brain. 'We... we... had a week's holiday on the Isle of Wight, and a week on the Isle of Sheppy.'

'Did you have a passport?' asked Craig.

'No,' John replied.

'Then I'm sorry to inform you mate that that doesn't constitute going abroad John, you've been misled, no passport, no abroad,' said Rod.

'Well it seemed like abroad to me,' sneered John.

'Why?' asked Mick

'Because we went on a boat.'

'Well take my word for it,' said Rod, 'going on a boat, isn't going abroad.'

John shrugged his shoulders. 'Well it seemed like abroad to me,' he mumbled again, not letting Rod get the last word on the subject.

'Sorry,' said Mick as he stood and held out his hand, offering Sinead his seat, 'please take my seat.' He saw the disappointment on her face. She was obviously in deep shook at the realisation that her dad had run away with their money. He tapped the table. 'Lads show a bit of respect here, this is Sinead's father we're talking about.' Rod put out his hand to touch her, to reassure her if he could, but she refused to be comforted, brushing his hand away and shivering. Rod stared at her as if straining to read her face. Nothing.

Silence went around the table as they all took on a sombre tone. Mick broke the silence. 'Paul, would you get Sinead a coffee, please, it looks like she needs one.'

'Anybody else?' asked Paul, pointing at their empty cups.

They all raised their hands.

'That'll take the bloody smile off his...' John counted to ten, '... face,' he said, as Paul pushed his way through the crowd towards the counter.

'I'm sorry Sinead, as I'm sure we all are,' said Mick softly. 'It must have come as an awful shock to you.' He reached over the table, gently tapping her hand. Her eyes appeared to have tears in the corners. 'Here,' said Rod, giving her his handkerchief and gently rubbing her shoulders. Sinead turned to look at him, opened her mouth to speak, but changed her mind and ignored him completely, shrugging off his hands. 'I was so sure that Da would not have stolen your money,' she said, blowing her nose into the handkerchief.

'Don't you worry,' said Mick. 'I'm sure it will all work out fine, we'll get your dad back, and the money.' She reached up and placed her hand on Mick's and half-heartedly smiled.

'Jesus Christ,' said Paul, placing the tray of coffees on the table. 'I don't believe it...' 'Fifteen quid,' they all said in unison, except for John who was ten seconds behind.

Paul dragged a vacant seat and sat next to Sinead. Rod pulled a vacant seat from another table and sat down.

'Ok then,' said Paul, 'so we've established the fact that Sean's in Venezuela.'

Mick rapped the table with his knuckles looking sternly at Paul, putting his fingers to his lips. 'Shush.'

'No it's fine,' sobbed Sinead, taking Mick's finger away from his lips, 'we are going to have to talk about it sometime.'

'Are you sure?' said Mick softly.

'No...no... it's fine, you go ahead Paul.'

'Only if you're sure,' repeated Paul.

'I'm sure, you go ahead.'

'Thanks,' said Paul, 'and let me say I think you are a very brave lady,' he smiled at Sinead. 'Anyway, as I said, Sean's in Venezuela.'

'Where the hell is Venezuela?' asked John. 'Is that anywhere near Scarborough?'

'You mean Scarborough, Yorkshire?' asked Craig.

'Is there any other, then?' asked John.

'No, John,' said Paul, 'Venezuela is not in Scarborough, it's in South America.'

John gulped the air like a goldfish out of water and gripped the table at the very thought of South America and *flying*. 'That sounds like it's abroad to me,' said John.

A faint smile appeared on Sinead's face.

Rod watched John's face drain of blood. 'Very much so, just look at it this way John, as I've said, the travel will broaden your mind.'

John looked at Rod sternly.

'What! What did I say!' asked Rod, lifting his shoulders.

John held up a fist. 'I'll broaden your bloody face in minute, with a,' he paused, 'fat bloody lip, Rod.'

'Later John,' said Paul quickly smiling, 'and after you've fattened Rod's lip, then go and get yourself a passport and a visa.'

'So we're taking off then?' asked John.

'Well, as you said all along John, the bloody money's not going to come to us is it?'

John's face turned ashen. 'In a plane?' he asked.

Rod noticed the fear in John's face and seized the moment. 'John d'you know how many people actually survive in a plane crash?'

'How many?' asked John nervously.

Rod laughed. 'None.'

John looked at Rod sternly, and then at Sinead. 'Excuse me,' he said and looked back at Rod. 'Rod, bollocks.'

Paul ignored their comments, but smiled. 'Yes we are, that is the normal mode of transport when you fly John, yes a plane,' Paul said smiling.

'We don't all have to go do we?' asked John. 'I could stay here and look after the ladies.'

Paul looked at John in amazement. 'John you're bloody joking, it was your idea all along, that we went looking for Sean, and now we've got this far, you're saying you don't want to go. I'm telling you, you're going.'

The skin around John's eyes drew tight with embarrassment as he realised he was the author of his own destiny. 'When... when...?' he enquired.

'Ok,' said Paul. 'No time like the present, we've booked a flight; the earliest we could get was in two weeks' time, for seven, to Caracas. Anyway we could all use a little holiday,' he pointed a finger at John. 'So, you can get your arse in gear and get yourself a passport.'

'Hang on Paul, did you say seven?' asked John.

They all looked at each other.

'Yes,' answered Paul.

'Well,' said John pausing, 'forgive me,' he paused, 'for asking Paul, but who's the other two?' he inquired.

Paul went to speak as Sinead coughed to get their attention. She shook her head. 'As I've said all along Da never took your money, so I guess we'll just have to prove it to you all. Kerrie and me are going with you.'

John looked at Sinead amazed. 'What!' he groaned, 'two girls?' He sounded astonished by Sinead's revelation. 'I don't know about Caracas, more like bloody crackers. No offence Sinead,' he said, raising a hand, 'but Jesus, two girls.'

'No offence taken,' said Sinead, smiling at him.

'John's right though, why?' asked Craig.

Paul went to speak again as Sinead put a hand on his arm. 'Because,' she said, 'and my sisters and I have a vested interest in our Da's interests, and Kerrie's coming with me so that I'm not travelling alone.'

'Hang on Sinead, but you won't be alone,' said Rod, 'you'll be travelling with us lot.'

'That's what I mean, especially with you lot. Anyway, Ma wouldn't let me travel alone. She's Catholic you know, and very... very... Irish.'

'Ok that's a fair comment Sinead,' said Mick. 'Ok is that agreed then lads, that the girls come along?' he said, looking around the table.

They all looked at each other and murmured their agreement, and nodded yes, in unison.

'Right then, that settles it, the girls go,' said Mick. 'Now we'll take Sinead home and explain to Cathleen what's happening, or does anybody want another coffee I believe it's John's round.'

John held up his hand to speak, and paused. They all waited for an answer... 'Fuck off,' he said as he stood up, 'at those prices we're going.'

★ ★ ★

Rod waited for Sinead's call. Nothing. Rod would not have admitted it, not to anybody, not even to himself. He longed to call her and ask her how everything was going. He'd waited long enough, he'd ring her on the pretext that they had got the flight tickets, and would pick them up from their house. To have there passports and baggage ready. In fact he was taken aback by the fact that Sinead hadn't bothered to ring him. She should have, all-said-and-done he had given her his number. He'd never seemed to have trouble with women before.

He punched in her number. She answered after the third ring. 'Hi, it's Rod, you didn't ring me,' he said. He frowned. 'I don't think I should ask you now as you never bothered to get in touch, but I will anyway. How did you get on with your exams?'

Sinead tensed at the thought that she knew Rod's game plan. 'I sailed through my PhD oral, and my practical examinations. You are now speaking to Dr Sinead Walsh.'

'Well done, Doctor,' said Rod with true excitement. 'I bet your dad will be pleased, when we find him... sorry,' he apologised, putting his hands to his lips.

'That's ok, as you say when we find Da,' repeated Sinead.

'We'll pick you and Kerrie up on Monday, is everything in order your end?'

'Ok, everything's fine,' Sinead replied. The line went dead.

Rod flipped his mobile shut looking forward to seeing her again. In the short time since they had met, he had thought about her almost continuously. His attraction for her was more than just about sex. This phenomenon for him was a strange one. There was something else about her that fascinated him. He sat back on the sofa, and sipped his beer mulling over every word they had exchanged in her kitchen.

Chapter Seven
Venezuela

The snow-capped Andes glittered like teeth as their plane approached Caracas. Rod leant forward. 'Check them out John,' Rod said, looking out of the window down at the peaks 20,000 feet below the aeroplane.

Mick stretched his face and pulled at his nose. 'Whew,' he whispered. 'Smells like somebody's farted in here.'

John half-heartedly smiled. 'Nerves Mick, nerves.'

'Well for God's sake hold it in John,' said Mick, waving his in-flight info book in front of his face. 'We can't open the windows you know, and I don't want the stewardess thinking it's me.'

John had grown pale as soon as he'd stepped on the plane, as though haemorrhaging.

'How the hell are you going to educate yourself John, for Christ sake, if you don't look out of the window,' said Rod.

'I am…I am…' John snapped, looking quickly out of the window and then back at his hands. They were trembling, his stomach churned, he didn't know the cause of his irrational fear as he had never flown before. Now he was going to have to conquer it, whether he liked it or not. He told himself that it was silly and stupid to be afraid, that was until *Aeroplane II* was shown on the small cinema screen. His heart pounded as he clenched his jaw and rectum muscles, and he put his sweating forehead against the small porthole window, looked down and vomited into a paper bag which had been provided by a benevolent stewardess as he got on the plane. He tried regaining control of himself. Closing his eyes, he did some deep-breathing exercises to calm himself. *Be bold confront your enemy, engage in battle* he thought, as the drinks trolley passed him down the aisle. 'Double whiskey please,' he shouted at the stewardess. 'I'm telling you now Mick,' John whispered as the stewardess passed him his drink. 'And you sir?' said the stewardess. 'The same, please,' said Mick, holding up his hand. He was sure he saw the stewardess's nose twitch; he inhaled deeply, maybe he was just imagining it. 'Telling me what?' said Mick as the stewardess laid his drink down on his tray.

'I'm going to deck the bastard when we find him, making me go through all this,' John said, throwing the whiskey down in one gulp.

In a jubilant mood the lads retrieved their hand luggage from the overhead lockers. John didn't join in: his feet had swollen, his eyes had puffed up, and his body felt as if he was dehydrating by the minute, turning him into a prune. Rod, on the other hand, looked refreshed as he stepped into the blanket of heat at the top of the steps. John stepped into the plane doorway and broke out into a full scale, all-over body sweat, as he sniffed the hot air disapprovingly.

'Weather's ok,' said Rod as if the meteorological conditions were somehow his personal victory.

A bit of colour was creeping back into John's cheeks as they got into the air-conditioned airport, cleared customs, and made they way towards the taxi rank.

'*Lleveme no al Hilton Avenida Libertador, por favor,*' said Rod to the taxi driver, as they all jumped into the taxi.

'I didn't know you could speak Spanish Rod,' said Mick, looking at John.

Rod held out his hands.

'He's been abroad before,' said John, looking at Rod impressed.

'Well, John, I've been to France,' said Craig. 'But I can't speak bloody French.'

The taxi pulled up outside the hotel. Rod passed over the fare, and smiled, '*quedese con el cambio.*'

'Smart twat,' said Paul pulling his luggage from the trunk of the taxi.

They had all forgotten the simple pleasures of sunshine as they booked into the hotel. The cool dark aqua blue sea to cool off in, fine clear golden sand, and an unspoilt landscape.

Rod smiled round the table at the lads as he sat down for breakfast. 'Good night lads and ladies?'

They all nodded.

'What about you then, grumpy?'

John looked up. 'I think it would have been nice to have Mrs H to cuddle up to; I missed her, it's the first time I've ever slept without her. But I must admit I didn't miss her snoring.'

'Right,' Rod whispered. He looked at Mick who was looking at him. Then Rod moved his glance to Sinead who looked away. 'Apparently,' Rod continued, 'Sean stayed here some time ago.'

'And how did you find that out, Inspector bloody Colombo?' asked Craig.

Rod smiled. 'Easy Monkey man, I just used this,' he said, pointing to his head. 'You should try it sometimes. Anyway I showed Sean's photograph around, and apparently he stayed here for one night, and then moved on.'

John looked up from his bowl of fruit. 'I don't blame him,' he said.

Mick looked at John puzzled. 'Why's that?' he asked.

'The bloody price of the rooms here Mick, for Christ sake, I could have stayed two weeks in Scarborough with the whole bloody,' he paused, 'family,' he paused, 'for the price of one night here.'

Rod waved a hand. 'Whatever John,' he said. 'Anyway, apparently he's gone to Barcelona.'

'Where's he gone to in Barcelona,' asked Mick, munching his way through a mouthful of wholemeal toast.

Rod shrugged his shoulders. 'I don't know Mick, the clerk just said Sean booked a taxi for Barcelona, and apparently it's about a thirty-minute drive from here.'

'Where did the taxi taken him to then when he reached Barcelona?' asked Craig.

Rod shrugged his shoulders again. 'He said he didn't hear the destination, that's all he knew.'

'Bloody Inspector Colombo,' said Craig, 'is that all you found out, that he actually stayed here?'

'That's more information than you found out Monkey man.'

'Lads please,' said Mick looking at them both. 'Anyway well done Rod,' he said, waving his spoon at him. Silence went around the table. Paul broke the silence. 'Isn't Barcelona in Spain?' he said. 'I know, because I've been there.'

Rod frowned. 'So! There's also a Valencia in Spain,' he said.

'You're right,' said Paul, pointing his knife at him, 'been there too.'

'Is there anywhere you haven't been?' asked Mick.

'Yer,' replied Paul. 'I haven't been to Scarborough,' he laughed.

John frowned and concentrated on the bowl of fruit in front of him.

'Well, continued Rod. 'I'm talking about Barcelona and Valencia in Venezuela.'

'That's a strange coincidence having Valencia and Barcelona here in Venezuela, isn't it?' said Paul.

'No… not really,' Rod nodded his head. 'History Paul history, didn't you ever do history at school?'

'Yer, we did Henry the VIII,' replied Paul.

'What the fat ginger twat that cut off women's heads because they wouldn't divorce him, nice,' replied Rod.

'I bet there's a few women you wish you could have cut the heads off, Rod,' laughed Craig.

'Funny, Monkey man, very funny, I'll cut your bloody head off in a minute.'

'Whatever,' said Mick, defusing the looks between Rod and Craig He was intrigued by what Rod had said about the Spanish. 'Well, what have Barcelona, Valencia and Venezuela have in common with Spain?' asked Mick.

'Conquistadors,' answered Rod looking at the two girls. 'Conquistadors,' he said again, this was a chance for him to impress them both, especially Sinead. He continued. 'For years the Incas or American Indians had live peacefully in South America and spoke Quiches, not Spanish, and were ruled peacefully by their Emperor I'ncan.'

The girls looked at Rod wide-eyed.

'Smart twat,' whispered Craig to Paul.

Rod pushed out his chest and smiled at them both, and continued. 'That was until 1527 when Francisco Pizarro set off with a bounty from the King of Spain...'

'Was that a coconut bounty?' interrupted Paul... 'Excuse me ladies,' said Rod, looking at Paul. 'Bollocks, anyway let's carry on. The King of Spain at that time was Charles who ruled from 1516 to 1558 and he gave Francisco Pizarro a substantial bounty to find the New World...'

'You're right Rod,' interrupted Craig, not letting Rod get all the attention. 'Didn't we have a Charles around about that time?'

'Yes, you were almost right,' answered Rod. 'In fact it was Charles I.'

'Smart twat,' mumbled Craig under his breath.

'So now can you see the connection?'

Mick nodded, 'so what you're saying Rod, is the Spanish came here many, many years ago.'

'Got it in one Mick,' replied Rod. 'It's nice to converse with somebody on the same intellectual level.'

'We knew that, didn't we?' said Paul sarcastically looking at John.

John looked at Rod dumbstruck, and just nodded.

Rod waved a hand at them both, 'I don't know why I bother,' he said. 'Anyway,' he looked around the table at the others, 'I've booked a taxi for us all, tomorrow morning 6:30am, and I've booked us into a hotel in Barcelona.'

'Jesus, 6:30,' said John.

'It's best to get there before the sun gets up.'

'No sightseeing then, apparently they've got the Semana Santa carnival tomorrow, plenty of bare-breasted women,' said Craig.

'Sod the Semana Santa, and the bare-breasted women,' said John. 'When we've found Sean, and we've got our bloody money, then you can do all the sightseeing you feel like, Craig.'

Rod looked wide-eyed at John. 'I don't believe it you're bloody cured, I told you it would work,' he said.

They all looked at John.

'What!' said John, looking at them all, raising his eyebrows and placing his spoon in his fruit bowl. 'What did I say!' he said again, looking at Rod.

'It's what you didn't say,' said Rod. 'You said found and feel without pausing, or stuttering.'

'Did I?' said John, trying to recall what he had said.

'Try this one,' said Rod, tapping his knife on the table. 'Fresh fruit falls freely in the fallow fields, go on, go on, say it.'

John repeated what Rod had said, 'Fresh fruit falls freely in the fallow fields,' without a pause or a stammer. 'For fuck's sake you're right Rod, I'm fucking cured.'

They all laughed in unison.

Chapter Eight
Barcelona

The sapphire sea spread out beyond the veranda. Rod sat on the lounger staring out into the moonlit sky in disbelief that they were actually there, and listened in happy silence. The only sound to be heard was the rasp of the crickets. Below the veranda the moonlight shimmering in reflection was a perfect accompaniment to the timid lapping of the docile sea on the sandy beach, the moonlight catching the crest of the waves as they hissed and languished lazily back into their warm source. The evening was beautifully warm: the warm salty air could be smelt coming up from the sea, across the beach and up onto the veranda. Rod took a swig of Cuzco beer, its tart chill sinking deliciously into his hot chest, and felt a swell of happiness glow inside him. This was right for him. He was in the right place. Hypnotised by the lapping waves. His feet up on the wooden rails, he tilted his head further back as he looked up again into the clear dark starlit sky, thinking, while the ice in the makeshift cooler was turning slowly back into water. *This is what he needed, he never realised there was a place like this, it felt like being as close to heaven as anybody could ever be. Even if he didn't get the lottery winnings he could always sell his house back home and buy a beach bar in a place where he could find a bit of peace, and get away from it all, besides he had nothing to go back home for anyway.* He never heard John walk onto the veranda, flapping at the insects that swarmed around his head. He slapped the back of his neck. 'It's so quiet here,' his hands gripped the railings as he looked out to sea. 'I didn't expect it to be this quiet,' he said, pulling a beer from the bucket and slumping into the lounger next to Rod.

Rod sighed loudly, 'Quiet was the operative word John.'

John's eyes narrowed. 'I'll go, if you want to be alone,' he said. He stood up. 'I'll go.'

'No… John sit,' said Rod casually swigging his beer. 'Don't be so bloody sensitive, I didn't mean anything by it, I was just agreeing with you. You're right though, this is the life, and does it get any better than this, does it? He said, sipping his beer thoughtfully. 'I could definitely get used to it. I can't believe we're actually here.'

'It will when we get our money,' said John pushing his head back and looking up into the inky black sky. 'The stars are so bright here, I've never noticed how bright the stars were before.'

'No ambient lights mate, that's why,' replied Rod looking back up into the sky.

John looked puzzled. 'What are ambient lights?'

Rod looked at John. 'Street lights mate, that sort of thing.'

'Right, you mean that sort of artificial light.'

'Right.'

'Why didn't you say artificial light in the first place, I'm not thick you know.'

Rod rolled his eyes, and mumbled under his breath, *that's a matter of opinion.*

John looked back at Rod. 'What?'

'Nothing,' Rod smiled. 'John… you know…. when we were back home, looking for the travel agents'.'

'Yer.'

'You asked me what would I do with my share of the money,' Rod paused. 'That's if we ever find it.'

'Yer,' answered John, rolling the cold beer bottle across the back of his neck. 'A Porsche, and shagging comes to mind.'

Rod laughed. 'So juvenile,' he said. 'Freud said once that the only things you need to make you happy are work and love…' 'And a Porsche convertible maybe,' interrupted John.

Rod ignored John's remarks and continued. 'Well, work seems to be out of the equation, and as for love I don't think I'm ever going to find out about love, as Prince Charles so famously said once, 'whatever that is' 'Jesus,' interrupted John. 'How could a man not fall in love with a wonderful woman like Lady Diana, she was some beauty, he must have been mad. I fell in love with her straightaway, theoretically speaking of course. But as for you, this time I'm willing to agree with you Rod,' he replied.

'Cheers John,' said Rod, waving his bottle at him. 'Anyway, what I wanted before I came out here…' he paused. 'Well, that's all changed, well and truly in the past now.'

'So what's your point,' said John matter-of-factly, sucking the top of the bottle.

'What I'm going to do now... is,' Rod sipped his beer. 'That's if we ever do get the money, I'm going...' He sipped his beer again; sucking the neck of the bottle knowing that what he was about to say John would probably take the wrong way.

John eyes sparkled with interest as he took a long pull on his beer, and looked at Rod. 'Well get to the point?' he said, wiping the foam from his mouth with the back of his hand.

Rod sipped his beer reflectively. 'Well, I'm going to find a nice young woman, settle down, and plough my money into a bar out here, on the beach, and fuck the plumbing.'

'I know this is a silly question Rod, but do you... you know what?'

Rod looked at John, puzzled at his answer and frowned. 'I'm not with you. Do I what?'

John enjoyed the bemused expression on Rod's face. 'Fancy her!'

'Fancy who,' asked Rod pausing. 'Do you mean Sinead?'

'Of course I mean bloody Sinead, unless there is somebody else.'

'John, is snow white?'

'Not if you piss in it, it's not,' he laughed.

Rod smiled. 'Be serious, of course it's Sinead, I haven't been out with anybody since I clapped eyes on her, she's all I seem to be thinking about these days, But!'

*Even from Rod, John hated but*s, he thought. 'What?' he asked.

Rod pulled another beer from the bucket of melting ice, flipping off the top. 'I don't think the feelings are mutual though, you know, she doesn't seem to look at me like other women did.'

'What?' said John, as another mosquito decided to dine on his arm. 'Shit, what a bummer,' he said, slapping his arm. He smiled. *Good for her. So she hadn't let him yet, seeing as he was without a doubt and consistently trying to get into her knickers.* 'Mind you, I must say that she's got bloody good taste, then,' he laughed. He looked at Rod disapprovingly. 'What's the matter Rod?' he asked. 'Lost your sense of humour?'

'Ha, ha John,' Rod replied. 'It's not funny.'

John looked at Rod's crestfallen expression. *He really did fancy her.* He rolled his eyes. 'What d'you mean Rod, you're saying she hasn't fallen for the charms of the great Casanova.' He exhaled. 'I'm telling you Rod, there's not much that I don't know about women.'

'You reckon John?' Asked Rod. 'I'm curious... so where does all this knowledge about women come from then?'

John tapped the side of his head with his bottle. 'It's all in here mate. And I'm telling you, you don't get every girl that comes along to fall into your arms at the drop of a hat. Let me give you some good advice here. With some girls you have to work at it, and those are the ones that will fall in love with you forever, believe me I know.' He nodded his head, and shook his bottle at Rod. 'Take my Linda for instance, she wasn't easy,' he said nodding his head again, his thoughts going back to the first time he had meet his wife, Linda. 'Believe me, she wasn't easy.

Sinead will come around Rod, you'll see, but you're just going to have to work harder at it, if you have any chance of winning her over.'

Rod raised his eyebrows. 'And how the hell am I going to do that?'

John took a sip from his bottle and scratched his head. 'Well firstly you are going to have to discover and redefine exactly who you are mate.'

'With regards to what?' Rod asked looking puzzled 'I know exactly who I am.'

'Oh really? So do we Rod, we know exactly where you're coming from, and with regard to women, look at the way you chased women and fell in and out of love every two seconds, that isn't impressive...' 'I know,' interrupted Rod... 'Hang on, let me finish,' John said, holding up a hand. 'In fact it's immature and patently it shows you're scared of commitment.' 'I know...I know...' Rod interrupted again, he knew that John had hit the nail on the head. 'But I'm telling you John that's all changed. I've got away from all the vain, insincere, selfish crap.'

'Maybe... maybe... but that's not going to help you win Sinead's heart is it?'

Rod had never heard John speak with such intelligence. 'Ok Solomon, so how the hell am I going to win her over then?'

John scratched his head again. 'Firstly, you must,' he paused and waved his bottle at him again, 'I know you've got to start treating young ladies with more respect and, as you said, stop being such a selfish twat...' 'But,' interrupted Rod. That was all he could say because he knew John was right. 'What?' asked John.

Rod waved a hand without a word. 'Carry on,' said Rod.

Shit he's actually listening to me thought John. 'Right, once you have mastered the respect, then you must gain her confidence, and encourage her so that she can trust you completely. The important thing is simply to spend time with her, getting to know her and what really makes her tick, and what you say to one another at first is oddly secondary. Then if there is a relationship, it will only blossom if you base it on honesty and trust.'

'How?'

'I've always found a girl is more flattered if you pay her more attention, especially when she least expects it.'

'Like when?'

'First thing in the morning is a good time, when they think they are at their worst, and haven't put their make-up on. I'm telling you mate, girls like that kind of stuff.'

'Do they?' said Rod glumly.

John nodded his agreement.

'Sinead doesn't wear make-up.'

'Yer… Shit, you're right … she doesn't, does she…' replied John.

'Well, what's next then?' asked Rod, testing John's knowledge further on women.

'Right…what… what you've got to do is give her the impression that she has seen you for the last time.'

Rod held out his hands. 'And how the bloody hell am I going to do that, when we're all here together?' 'Difficult I know Rod,' interrupted John, scratching his head. 'Difficult, but, you're just going to have to stay away from her. You know the old saying, absence makes the heart grow fonder.'

'But you said that I need to get to know how she ticks.'

Shit he's sussed me. 'Get to know her from a distance, you can do that, can't you?'

Rod could see the logic in that. 'Ok...ok,' he agreed, 'and when we've got over that hurdle. Then what?'

'You're going to have to show her that you'll always be there for her,' John said, waving his bottle at Rod again. 'And her only,' waving the bottle from side to side. 'And definitely no other women, let's face it, as I've said before, you scarcely have a background where these things are very encouraging!'

Rod bit his lower lip. 'Right, I know... point taken earlier, I'll give what you say a go.'

'If you are going to give it a go, then you're going to have to start from square one, you've got nobody on the scene at the moment.' John looked at Rod and frowned.

'I haven't... I haven't... you know I haven't got anybody, we've all been together since we left the UK,' he said, nodding his head.

'Point taken, but it's early days yet mate. Anyway, you've got nothing to lose then, have you? You never know, miracles might happen. I mean,' John swept his beer bottle across the veranda. 'Just think, who'd imagined six weeks ago we'd have all been out here.'

Rod squinted at him. 'Maybe... maybe' he replied to that glimmer of hope from John. Rod smiled, rolling the cold beer between his hands. 'Anyway,' he said, looking at John. 'I thought you'd turned in for the night?'

'You're right I had,' answered John, 'but I couldn't bloody sleep. I've been bitten to fucking death ever since I got here, look,' he said, thrusting his arm in front of Rod. 'What the bloody hell is that?'

Rod looked at his arm, at the small red blistering bumps. 'Mosquitoes,' he said.

'Well how the fuck do you get rid of the little bastards?'

'Pull down your mosquito net.'

'I did, I pulled the net down, but the little bastards seem to get through it.'

'Ok, when you go back to bed, direct the air conditioning towards your bed; the mosquitoes are too light to fight against the strong current of air. That will do the trick.'

'Shit, I bloody hope so,' he said, slapping the back of his neck again. 'You don't get these little bastards in Scarborough you know.'

'You don't get any bloody sun in Scarborough that's why,' replied Rod.

'Yes, you do,' replied John defensively, looking out to sea, pulling another beer from the ice bucket and rattling the cubes. 'Sometimes you do.'

Paul sat down to breakfast. 'It's all set for today,' he said excitedly.

'What?' asked John, getting up for another bowl of fruit.

'Michelle's,' said Paul holding his breasts. 'That's what we're going to see today, Michelle's, and a bit of sightseeing. This is the city of the three S's sun, sea...' 'And Sean,' interrupted John. 'Bear in mind Paul, that's what we're here for. We haven't come for the scenery, we're here for money that our mate stole,' replied John, moving off to the breakfast counter to fill his bowl with a second helping of fruit.

Paul leant towards Mick. 'For God's sake Mick, tell him, will you,' he pleaded, pointing his spoon at John. 'I haven't come all this way to spend the whole time going from hotel to bloody hotel looking for Sean. My bloody feet are killing me. We've got to have a bit of fun you know!'

Craig sneaked a glance at Mick who was working away at a crust of toast. 'Paul's right Mick,' he agreed. 'I wouldn't mind another gander at a pair of Michelle's, all work and no play makes Jack a dull boy, you know.'

Mick stared back at them both. 'Ok...ok...' he said, waving his knife at them. 'I'll have a word with him when he comes back.'

Mick reached for his coffee, preparing to wash down the mouthful of toast. 'John,' he said as John sat down. 'It would be nice to get out and see a bit of Barcelona...' John interrupted Mick, looking sternly at him. 'Don't you go siding with them. Don't forget what we've come here for Mick, we need to find Sean.'

Mick tilted his head to one side. 'John, just one day,' he replied.

'Come on John, just one day that's all,' pleaded Paul, 'and I promise you that we'll get straight back on Sean's case tomorrow.'

'Go on,' said Rod, 'we've checked all the taxi drivers and all the hotels, bars, and the railway station, and we've had no joy yet, as they say, let's give it a rest, for just one day.'

John looked around the table and focused his eyes on the girls.

Both the girls smiled. Sinead said, 'Go on John, it won't do us any harm.'

John smiled and nodded at the girls, looking back at Paul. 'Ok, you've obviously got something in mind.'

Paul smiled. 'I have,' he said, looking excited and jigging about in his seat. 'It's carnival time, partying, four days of drinking.'

John waved his hand and held up a finger. 'You said one day, and that's all you're getting, just one day.'

Paul held up his hands in capitulation. 'Ok…ok…one day, I suppose it's better than none at all. Yes,' he whispered, scooping up a spoon full of cornflakes.

Paul was up front leading the way as if he'd lived in Barcelona all his life, trekking through the labyrinth of streets. The music started off as a whisper. As they moved through the streets, the music increased.

'Nearly there,' shouted Paul. They could smell the carnival and breathe it in the air. The music grew louder and louder, the sound of what seemed like thousands of whistles piercing the air.

'You sure it's not a bloody football match?' asked John. 'I hate bloody football.'

'It's definitely not a football match,' replied Paul

John checked his arms for mosquito bites as they walked through the streets. 'Oh by the way I did as you said and moved the air conditioning. That did the trick with the mosquitoes,' he said, showing him his arm. 'See not a bite, cheers for that Rod.'

'No problemo John,' replied Rod.

'What the bloody hell's that music?' John shouted.

'Samba,' Mick shouted, holding his arms out in a dancing mode and shuffling his feet to the beat of the music.

'I didn't know you could samba, Mick,' shouted Kerrie, jumping into his arms as they both danced down the street together.

'Go, Mick go,' shouted Craig.

'Reminds me of Gloria Estefan, shouted Paul. '*The rhythm is goner get yer*,' he sang.

The music began to swell to a crescendo, drowning out the noise of the city as they emerged into the main street. The air was hot and dusty although it was only eight o'clock in the morning, and it was hot. The roasting air was thick with competing smells of cooking. Falling into the mass of partying people felt like falling into a gushing river, and there was only one way to go: with the flow. There were wonderful sounds, smells, and most of all the colours.

'Now this is what I'd call bloody culture,' shouted Paul. 'Look at it.'

The perpetual chorus filled the air. 'Shit, there must be thousands of people here,' shouted John, looking over the celebrating masses of heads; there were people as far as the eye could see. Everywhere he looked all he could see was a sea of faces, and all sporting what one might call a carnival smile. The place had opened up into a vibrant display of colour, dance and music. 'Yeah, guys,' shouted John. 'I don't want to stick a spanner in the works.'

'And your point is?' shouted Paul.

'I don't know. Just you know. Maybe look out for Sean…' 'Day off, John,' shouted Paul. 'Come on lads,' he shouted, 'let's go. We're in heaven.'

'Look at that,' shouted John, pointing to a group of people.

'What?' shouted Paul, jumping up in the air to look over the heads of the crowds.

'I don't believe it,' shouted John, 'young and old people dancing together. If that was at home they'd be robbing the old people for drugs money,' he shook his head. 'And over here they dance together, I've seen it all now. You sure they aren't robbing them?' he shouted.

Paul laughed. 'Chill John, just chill and watch the carnival,' he shouted. The whole area was filled with rich colours, reds, blues, yellows and greens of the elaborate costumes flashing past, standing out against the crowd. Ladies in huge, lacy hoop dresses, people dressed in costumes looking like a large multicoloured butterfly with massive wings flapping, a physical presence to the music as they danced to the rhythm. Green costumes depicted the destruction of the rainforests, men following them with chainsaws. Girls danced on high platforms wearing very little but high headgear. 'There they are,' shouted Paul, jumping up and down like an excited schoolboy, pointing up at the platforms. 'I said we'd see them, didn't I.'

'What are we looking at?' shouted John.

'Michelle's,' shouted Paul, 'look, on the platforms.'

'Where?'

'There.' Pointing at the platforms he pointed straight up in the air towards the floats, and they followed his finger.

John looked up at the ladies dancing, and his eyes widened as their bodies gyrated to the music, *shit I've never see that in Scarborough,* he thought. 'Oh, oh my goodness,' said John. 'You dirty little sod Paul, don't look,' he shouted.

'Right. …. Right… John, sod off,' Paul shouted. 'They're great, aren't they, look at them move to the music,' he yelled, throwing his hands in the air, feeling the carnival spirit, and the rhythm of the music vibrating through his whole body. The rhythm never let up for a moment, it was mesmerising, oscillating between hysterical and hyperactive and back again, so full of energy it seemed as if it was going to explode at any moment.

John pulled them out of the flowing stream of people into a bar. 'Drinks,' he shouted, looking around. 'Where's Sinead and Rod?' They all looked round. 'Kerrie, do you know where they are?' John asked. Kerrie shrugged her shoulders, and held out her hands. 'I don't know, they were behind us a few minutes ago,' she said, looking around. 'We must have lost them back there in the crowd.'

'Crafty bugger,' shouted John.

'What?' asked Mick.

'Nothing, Mick, get the drinks in.' *Rod must have took on board what he had told him the other night,* John thought, *he's working on her.*

The carnival music seemed to follow them into the bar. The bar was thumping, and the glasses rattled on the counter. 'What you having to drink Kerrie?' Mick shouted.

'Whatever you're having Mick,' Kerrie shouted.

Mick smiled at Kerrie. 'That's my girl,' he shouted as he turned to the barman and held up five fingers. '*Quiero cinco cerveza por favor.*'

'Your Spanish is good Mick; in fact with your tan you actually look a little bit Spanish,' Kerrie said, rubbing his face.

Mick blushed. 'Not as good as your samba, though,' he replied.

'Yer, we'll have to start calling you Julio Iglesias,' shouted Paul.

'Bollocks,' whispered Mick, in perfect Spanish.

After John's fourth pint he was slowly being seduced by the rhythm of the music, at last his foot was tapping and he was ready to dance.

They were all well oiled and back into the street, raring to go. The dancing horde was hypnotic. 'Come on John,' shouted Paul and Craig as they danced to the music following a very, very pregnant young lady, trying to keep up with her. 'God she's fast,' Craig shouted.

'Not that fast Craig, look she's pregnant.' Being pregnant didn't seem to matter to her; she danced with as much grace as all the others. Although it looked like her baby was going to pop out at any moment, nothing seemed to stop the carnival. Paul's and Craig's arms, hips and legs were moving expertly with the music 'Come on John,' Paul shouted again as the others joined in.

Mick and Kerrie danced in perfect rhythm. 'It's only when you dance with such a beautiful young lady that you realise what a carnival really is like,' said Mick. Then Mick released what he'd said. He blushed, pushing her at arms' length. 'Jesus Christ, Kerrie please, I hope you didn't take what I said the wrong way, I only said that as a father/ daughter thing.'

'I know, don't be so silly Mick,' replied Kerrie. 'Come here,' she said, pulling him in closer.

'Does your mother dance?' asked Mick, moving on quickly *wishing it was Cathleen he was holding in his arms.*

'Yes Mick, Ma and Da are first-class samba dancers, that's who us girls learnt our dancing from.' She looked puzzled. 'Why did you ask me that?'

Mick shrugged his shoulders. 'No reason, I just wondered,' he replied.

John jumped in; dancing like a marionette, like somebody else was pulling his strings. 'How the hell do you dance like that Kerrie?' he shouted.

'Copy the person in front of you,' Kerrie shouted back.

John followed a man who he thought to have been at least 110 years old. Sporting a Clint Eastwood poncho and the largest sombrero he'd ever seen, his dark tanned wrinkled face appeared from under the sombrero. He smiled at John revealing a mouth full of missing teeth and the odd ones he had left were black. *Mind you, he was dancing a lot better than me* he thought. He smiled back.

'Get with the rhythm John, swing your arse about,' Mick shouted.

'Ok… ok… I'm swinging my arse, thank you, bloody Julio.'

Craig danced up to the side of John. 'Throw your arms around in the air John, and keep smiling, at least if your upper half looks good people won't notice your uncoordinated feet.'   'Right,' shouted John as Craig moved off, pairing with a young lady with large castanets.

John looked down at his feet and nearly fell over the 110-year-old man in front of him who had stopped to catch his breath.

Chapter Nine
Bloody Lost Him

Rod scrutinised Sinead's face; she didn't look as if she was enjoying the carnival as they followed the tidal wave of people. Sinead's main priority was finding her da. 'How the hell are we supposed to find Da in the middle of fifty thousand people?' she asked Rod.

'Good question,' said Rod, looking around. 'This is something else though,' he smiled, trying to lighten the moment. 'Would you like to dance Sinead?' he asked as he held out his hand.

She shivered as she held out a shaking hand towards him.

If anything she's bound to be seduced and liberated by the carnival, he thought hopefully. He felt her cold hands sweating against his. They rigidly followed the dancing crowd, her body unyielding to the rhythm of the music, her body rigid and taut, cold.

Rod stopped and looked into her eyes, *it was right what John had said, there was something in her eyes that showed fear.* 'You're not enjoying this one bit, are you?' he asked.

She shrugged, looking around as if looking for the comfort of the other lads.

Rod clapped his hands together. 'Ok, right, let's eat,' he said, looking around for a restaurant. 'Over there,' he said as they pushed their way through the crowd towards the restaurant. Rod held open the door as Sinead pushed her way through the crowded restaurant to the stairs leading to the upper level. The upstairs was as crowded as downstairs.

'*Hola,*' said a waiter.

'*Una mesa para dos, por favor,*' Rod asked.

'*Si senor,*' he held out a hand.

'*Nos gustara una mesa junto a la ventana,*' asked Rod.

'*Esta el camino,*' he said, his hand still outstretched. He moved them towards a table where two diners were vacating a table by the window. Sinead was already on the move pushing her way through the crowd. Sitting down, she glanced out of the window down into the street keeping her eyes on the moving crowd.

'*El menu, por favor,*' asked Rod.

' *Si senor,*' said the waiter as he pushed his way through the tables. The waiter handed Rod the menus, clicking his fingers at a waitress.

Rod passed Sinead a menu; he smiled as a waitress appeared pen and pad in hand. '*Que quieren beber?*'

'*Una botella de vino de la tirra,*' replied Rod, nodding his thanks at the waitress as she wrote down their order and took it to the bar.

Rod lifted his glass. '*Salad!*' Rod said as the waitress poured out Sinead's wine. Sinead half-heartedly lifted her glass in response to his gesture and took a sip, her eyes never straying from the street. He noticed Sinead facial expressions relaxing a little; *maybe it was the wine* he thought.

She looked out of the window again down into the mass of people in the street below. Sinead stood abruptly.

'Rod, there's Da,' she shouted with joy, pointing in the direction of the crowd outside.

Rod spun his head so fast; he'd swear his head had done a complete circle like Regan, the girl from the film *The Exorcist*. 'Where?'

'Outside,' shouted Sinead, pointing out of the window.

Rod scanned the crowd. 'Where?'

'There,' Sinead pointed again, 'across the road, Da's just going into that bar over there, *Les Mercedes*.'

'Jesus Christ yes, I see him, you sure it's Sean? I can only see his back.'

'It's Da, I'm telling you its Da.'

'Right,' Rod shouted, 'forget the order, let's go.' He waved wildly at the waitress, *'Lo siento mucho, deje el cambio,'* he said as the waitress came over to the table, pressing a wad of notes into her hand, hoping it would cover what they hadn't had. Snatching Sinead's arm they barged their way out of the restaurant, apologising as they barged into the other diners, falling down the stairs out into the street, hurrying, pushing through the crowds, breaking through the crowds; they ran into the road. Tyres squealed as a carnival float screamed to a halt nearly running them down. The driver hammered on the horn from the abyss of the float... beep... beep... beeeeep. 'Bollocks,' screamed Rod as he returned the confrontation with two fingers in the air, and continued pushing through the crowd on the other side of the street towards the bar. His heart was pumping in his chest as they slowed down and entered the crowded bar, both scanning over the heads of the customers looking for

Sean. They moved slowly forwards, their heads going from left to right. The bar was crammed from wall to wall with bodies.

'Damn! Damn! Damn!' shouted Rod. 'Where the hell has he gone?'

Standing on tiptoe Sinead scanned the bar. 'There...there...' she shouted. 'Upstairs,' pointing in the direction of the stairs. 'Look Rod, Da's going upstairs.' Sure enough it was Sean. Rod recognised him; he shouted out Sean's name. Sean continued up the stairs, not so much as a glance back as the noise in the bar swept Rod's voice away.

'Come on,' shouted Sinead, grabbing Rod's arm. As fast as she could she plunged through the ocean of bodies pulling him towards the stairs. She was eager to meet her da; there were so many questions she needed to ask him. They fought their way to the top of the stairs, looking frantically around the mezzanine floor as people crowded past them going up and down the stairs.

Rod held out his hands, and shouted, 'Where's the hell's he gone, now?'

Sinead jumped up and down looking over the heads of the customers.

'There,' shouted Rod. They hadn't noticed the other set of stairs in the corner of the mezzanine floor that went back down to the ground floor, into the bar. 'Sean must have gone down those steps, that's why we lost him,' he shouted as they pushed through the crowd towards the steps, and descended back into the bar and out into the crowded street. The music and throng of people hit them again. 'Shit... shit... shit,' shouted Rod, 'shit,' his head rotating left and right looking desperately around at the crowds of people, pulling back his hair with his hands. 'Shit, Sinead we've bloody lost him.'

The carnival was petering out, as the lads walked through the open-air bazaar. The crowds had thinned out slightly. 'What's that?' asked Paul, stopping at the cart, pointing at the array of displayed fruits.

Craig stopped next to him. 'Which one?' he asked.

'That one,' replied Paul, pointing at the odd-shaped fruits.

'This one,' said Craig, picking it off the cart and throwing it into the air. 'That's a mango papaya fruit, absolutely delicious they call it *iechosa*, and that's avocado, *aguacate*. He pointed at the oranges…. Paul interrupted him, 'Don't tell me, let me guess these are oranges.' 'Ok, what are they called in Spanish?' asked Craig…. John interrupted him. 'They're called *naranja*.'

Craig looked round in surprise at John. 'You're right,' he said. 'How the hell did you know that then?' he asked.

'Because I've seen them in Tesco's supermarket,' John replied. 'I don't know why, but they seem to put the Spanish name underneath the English, maybe it's because we're in Europe now.'

'I didn't think Hoggett's did shopping John,' asked Paul.

'We don't but I do, I like to do the fruit shopping. Let's buy some,' he continued. 'You can't beat fresh fruit. And those,' he continued, picking up a hand of bananas, 'these are called *cambur*.' He handed them over to the girl behind the cart. 'And that's *coco*, coconut,' he said, shaking the fruit next to his ear, putting it back on the cart, and picking up another to repeat the operation. 'This one has plenty of milk,' he said, passing the coconut over to the girl. He watched Paul as he moved along the cart. Picking up a handful of passion fruit he twisted them in his hands, and smelt them. 'Just right, and these are *parchita*. Wow,' said John, passing the passion fruits to the girl. 'Look at those melons,' he said, as Paul looked at the young Venezuelan girl behind the cart. 'Not her you fool,' he said, 'these,' he continued, picking up two melons one in each hand. 'Now that's what I call melons,' he said, holding them up in the air. 'Aren't they lovely,' he said, stroking their light-yellow skins, as if they were alive. 'Just look at the colour.' He pressed them to his nose, taking in deep breaths. 'You can tell how fresh they are, you know, just by pressing them lightly with your thumb, and the skin retracts back to its present form,' he said, pressing them with his thumbs. 'There you go,' he said, showing them. 'Perfecto.'

'We're impressed John,' said Mick, watching the skins retract.

'Have you ever seen such perfect melons,' John continued, showing them to the lads again.

Paul raised his eyebrows, and rolled his eyes at Mick, nudging him in the ribs. 'You mean recently John?,' he said, shrugging his shoulders.

'Yes, recently,' replied John.

'Only Michelle's melons,' laughed Mick.

John's face creased into a smile. 'Right,' he said. Blushing, he quickly passed one of the melons over to the girl and put the other melon back on the cart now that Mick had transformed the two perfectly formed melons into sexual objects.

'Anyway, why this obsession with fruit John?' asked Craig.

'It's not an obsession Craig,' replied John, 'I just love fruit.'

'We can see that but why?' asked Paul.

'Pay the girl Craig,' said John, taking the bag of fruit from her and walking them away from the cart. He looked sternly at Paul, and looked around, then back at Paul. 'If you must know,' he whispered, looking around again, 'it helps with my constipation, it makes... me... loose.'

'Loose,' sniggered Paul. 'When did this obsession start?' he asked... 'Paul, I'm telling you, I don't have an obsession with fruit, now can we drop this subject...'

'Hum... hang on though, John, this is interesting,' said Mick, 'when did you find out you had this liking for fruit?'

John looked puzzled at Mick's question, and wondered where his question was leading.

John held up his hands. 'Oh... I don't know, some time ago now. Ok, as I said, let's just drop it, end of subject.'

'I know John,' said Mick, holding up a hand. 'Do you remember when we got the company to supply us with a site cabin?'

'So?' replied John.

'It was when the cabin was brought on site, that's when it was.'

'Was what!' asked Craig, catching up with them and handing John the bags of fruit.

'When John started bringing in tubs of fresh fruit to work, sliced apples, grapes, melon slices, pineapple chunks and slices of banana. Do you remember John?'

'Yes…yes… I remember Mick. So?'

'Well, that's when your constipation went away,' said Mick.

'Shhhh…' John looked around. 'Kerrie's listening.' He waved a hand at Mick to quieten him down. 'Ok, all right everyone, what did I say, that's enough, end of discussion,' John whispered in an authoritative voice as he walked off.

Mick held up both hands as they all walked through the bazaar.

John stopped abruptly, turning towards Mick. 'Hang on Mick,' he said quietly, 'a,e you suggesting that it wasn't the fruit that cured my constipation?' He held up the bags of fruit.

Mick looked at the lads. 'You told us not to discuss it John.'

'I know…I know…' said John, waving the bag of fruit in the air, 'but it intrigues me, how the site cabin and these bags of fruit seem to you to have a connection.'

'Well, as I tried to say, it wasn't the fruit that cured your constipation.'

'Ok then Doctor Mick, the expert in constipation, what do you think it was that cured my constipation?'

'Well,' replied Mick, holding his hand to his mouth and sniggering, 'nothing concrete, but just a feeling I had, you know I said that it was when we got the site cabin.'

John nodded.

Mick looked at the lads. 'Well,' he continued, 'that's when John stopped using empty cement bags to wipe his arse.' Mick and the lads roared with laughter. They walked passed John, laughing. John dropped the bags to his side; turned and shouted at their backs, 'fuck off.'

'It's amazing what you find out when you scratch the surface of anything, if you know what I mean,' said Craig, 'and you'll find there's more to John than meets the eye...' 'You can't make omelette without cracking eggs,' interrupted Mick.

John overheard Mick. 'Very profound Mick,' he said as he caught them up. He looked at Paul, and lifted his eyebrows. 'What the fuck's he talking about Paul?' he whispered.

'You tell me John,' said Paul, shrugging his shoulders.

'Bollocks to it, it's bloody hot,' said John, wiping the sweat off his forehead with back of his hand. 'Let's go back to the hotel. Who's for a swim and a cold beer then?'

They all nodded in agreement as Mick hailed a taxi.

John wiped the sweat from his forehead with the back of his hand, squinting into the sun. 'Shit does it get any hotter?'

Mick looked at his watch. 'It's twelve o'clock. Mad dogs and Englishmen come to mind.'

'No Sinead and Rod then?' asked John, slipping off his shirt.

'No, she wasn't in her room when I left the hotel for the beach,' replied Kerrie. 'They're probably still at the carnival. I know Sinead said she was looking for a skirt.'

'Who would that be for, Sinead or Rod?' asked John.

They all roared with laughed, except for Kerrie who never got the joke. Kerrie frowned at their laughter, feeling slightly embarrassed. 'What did I say, that was so funny?' she said, holding out her hands.

'It's nothing you said Kerrie,' replied John, 'it's just a private joke. What are you having to drink?' he asked.

'Later,' Kerrie said, 'it's too hot at the moment.' She rubbed the sweat from her forehead. 'I thought we were all going for a swim, coming Mick?' She nodded her head towards the sea.

'No thanks Kerrie, I'm not a very good swimmer,' said Mick, trying to get out of it.

Paul winked at Mick. 'Go on Mick, when was the last time you had the offer to swim with such a beautiful young lady.'

'Well thank you Paul,' she said, holding out her hand-coaxing Mick. 'Come on Mick, I'll teach you.' Reluctantly Mick took off his shirt, and held out his hand, folding his hand into hers, wishing it were Cathleen's hand as she pulled him out of his chair.

Craig and Paul raised their sunglasses and looked wide-eyed at Mick as they both walked towards the sea.

'He's cracked it,' said Paul.

'Lucky bastard,' agreed Craig.

'Hark at you two,' remarked John, 'he's old enough to be her bloody father; it's nothing of the bloody sort. They only look to me like father and daughter.'

'Whatever,' said Paul. 'It's amazing you know, when people take off their clothes,' he said, smiling at the thought of Sinead's beautiful naked body in the cubicle back home.

John watched Paul's expression. 'What the hell are you smiling at Paul?' he asked. 'You look like the cat that got the cream.'

Paul pointed at John. 'That's for me to know, and for you to wonder John. There are some things that a gentleman just doesn't talk about.'

'Where's the gentleman then?' asked John looking around… 'Very funny John, but wouldn't you like to know,' he replied.

John looked puzzled by Paul's remark about people and clothes. Craning his neck upward, squinting into the sun, he watched Mick and Kerrie making their way down to the sea. 'Anyway, what's so amazing about people taking their clothes off?' he asked.

'Well,' said Paul, 'I didn't want to say anything while Mick was here. I might have embarrassed him.'

John rolled his eyes. 'There's a first,' he said, looking at Craig.

'Take Mick for instance,' Paul continued, holding his beer glass out towards Mick. 'We've never see him with his shirt off before have we? I've seen you lot,' he said, waving his hand at them, 'but never Mick.'

'So what!' said John.

'Did you see his six-pack?'

'He's got to have worked out,' said Craig.

Paul nodded his agreement, looking down at his stomach, flexing his stomach muscles.

John peeped at Mick again, his hand shielding his eyes from the sun, ignoring what Paul had said about Mick's six-pack, and his working out. 'That's because Mick's the bloody foreman, an office worker, he doesn't need to remove his shirt,' he said. 'Anyway Paul, what's your point?' he asked.

Paul pointed his glass at Mick again. 'You must admit, when you look at him from behind, he doesn't seem that old. For a bloke of his age, he hasn't got an ounce of fat on him, you know, he's what you'd call a lean machine, some blokes of his age and younger would give their right arm for a physique like that.'

John pulled in his stomach as he stood up to refresh their glasses. 'That's because Mick cooks for himself.'

'What!' said Craig, raising his sunglasses, looking up at John squinting away from the sun. 'What the hell's that got to do with the way he looks? Do I detect a little bit of jealousy here John?' he asked.

'Of course I'm not jealous,' replied John. 'You'll see, it's happening to you right now.'

Craig and Paul looked at their stomachs.

'You'll find out later,' continued John, 'it creeps up on you, as you get older. Women feed you up so you get out of shape so you are not attracted to the opposite sex, you know what I mean.'

'What! You mean like you John,' replied Paul.

'Bollocks Paul, I'm not out of shape,' John replied, running his hand over his pulled-in stomach.

'Right John,' said Paul laughing. 'Next time you're in the hotel, take a look in the mirror. I thought I noticed a little extra fat around your belly, plus you're going a bit grey at the edges.'

John raised his eyebrows. 'A little extra fat around the middle, you say, and going grey, anything else?'

'Maybe the beginning of a double chin,' said Paul smiling.

John stroked his neck deciding to ignore Paul's remark, but somehow he thought there was some element of truth in what he'd said. When he got home he'd book a session in the gym. 'What are you having to drink Paul?' He bent down and whispered in Craig's ear, 'remind me to piss in it, will you.'

Mick grabbed a towel from his chair and passed it to Kerrie, 'Thanks Kerrie,' he puffed, 'that was absolutely marvellous.' He turned to the lads. 'This young lady is one hell of a swimmer, and she swims like a dolphin.'

'And you swim like a whale Mike,' said John.

'No, I won't have that,' said Kerrie. 'In fact Mick's a good swimmer, he just needs a little confidence that's all.'

Kerrie looked up the beach. 'Good, here's Rod and Sinead,' she said.

Rod and Sinead ran down the beach towards them.

John laughed. 'Rod never bought a skirt then,' he said.

'How do you know that?' asked Kerrie.

'Because he's still got his shorts on,' John replied with a smile.

Rod and Sinead halted; Sinead was obviously fitter than Rod as he bent forward, hands on both his knees, gasping for breath.

'What… what's happened?' asked John.

'We've… we've seen… Sean,' gasped Rod. 'Your… dad… Kerrie.'

'I think Kerrie knows who her dad is Rod,' said Paul.

Kerrie face filled with excitement. 'Where?'

'You won't believe it, but he was at the carnival,' replied Sinead.

Mick looked puzzled. 'If you saw him, then why didn't you bring him back here?' he asked, looking around as if Sean might pop round the corner at any minute.

Rod dropped his head. 'Because… I'm… afraid we lost him.'

'Nice one Rod,' said Paul sarcastically. 'We can always rely on you to do sod all.'

Craig nodded his agreement. 'Too interested in trying to get his end away with…' Mick interrupted Craig quickly. 'Well there's one good thing that came out of it,' he said… 'What's that Mick?' interrupted John.

'At least we know Sean's in Barcelona.'

'We couldn't help losing him,' said Rod, 'you were all at the carnival, it was bloody crowded.'

Mick waved his towel at Rod and Sinead. 'Hang on Rod,' he said, 'Sean didn't see you, did he?'

'No,' answered Rod.

'Phew…thank God for that,' said Mick, looking round at the lads. 'Good, so he doesn't know we are here then.'

Rod looked puzzled. 'Why, I thought that's what we wanted?'

'Think Rod,' said John touching his head. 'Don't take this the wrong way girls, but if he did see you, and he did take the money, then he's bound to do a runner. Are you sure he never saw you?'

'I'm positive.'

'Good,' said Mick, putting him arm around Rod's shoulder. 'Right Rod, your punishment for losing Sean is beers all round, while Sinead explains to us all what happened. Off you go lad and get them in.'

★ ★ ★

'A beer's fine Mick,' said John, sliding onto the stool, 'it's bloody roasting out there.'

'That's why I'm in here,' replied Mick, holding his hand up to the barman. *'Dos grande cerveza por favor.'*

'Si senor dos cerveza.'

'Where is everybody?' asked John looking around the bar.

'After Rod and Sinead's surprise revelations yesterday they're all Sean hunting.'

'Right,' said John, sipping his cold beer. 'Let them carry on, young feet you know.'

'And don't I bloody know it,' replied Mick, rubbing his feet.

Chapter Ten
Shit, It's Him!

S inead and Kerrie walked in for breakfast.
'Were you girls out late last night?' asked Mick.

'It was just a girl thing Mick, we needed to look for Da...' 'Next time,' interrupted Mick, 'take one of the lads with you,' he said, waving his spoon at them. 'I don't trust these bloody foreigners.'

'He's right,' agreed John. 'Anyway, how did you get on?' he asked.

'Not a thing,' replied Sinead, pouring herself a glass of fresh orange juice.

'What happened to you and John then, Mick?' asked Kerrie. 'It was the heat,' Mick replied, 'too bloody hot for us, the heat got to us, so we had to come back.'

'Two guesses where you two ended up. The bar I bet,' said Rod as he came into the dining room from the foyer area.

'Looks like another bloody hot day,' said Craig as he sat down with a plate full of fry-up.

'How the bloody hell did you get that fry-up?' asked John.

Craig winked. 'It's not what you know John my son, it's who you know; Maria in the kitchens.'

'Got a bit of a thing for monkeys has she?' asked Rod.

Craig looked at Rod severely, and ignored his comment as he spoke to Mick, 'I swear, one of these days Mick, I'm going to chin him.'

'You'll have to get in the queue Craig,' said John.

John and Mick laughed.

Kerrie rolled her eyes at Sinead. 'Boys will be boys,' she said.

'Where's Paul?' asked John.

Everybody shrugged.

John made a gesture of too much to drink with his glass of orange.

'Well, what's on the itinerary for today?' asked Mick.

'Sinead and I are going to continue our search for Da,' said Kerrie.

Paul stood supporting himself against the dining room door, his face white as a sheet.

John nudged Mick and pointed his spoon at Paul. 'Look at the bloody state of that, I told you he'd too much to drink,' he said. Mick looked up. 'Shit, are you all right Paul too much to…' 'I… I…don't believe it,' interrupted Paul, finding it difficult to get his words out… 'What, Paul what?' snapped John, 'you look a little shaky my son; I've told you to control your drink intake…' 'Ha… ha…' interrupted Paul sarcastically and continued, 'he didn't bloody recognise me…' 'Who,' snapped Mick, 'Lord Lucan or bloody Shergar…' 'I'm telling you, you all better take me seriously,' interrupted Paul, looking round the table. 'I'm telling you he didn't recognise me. I walked straight past him,' he continued, holding his hands out towards the foyer. 'I even said good morning to him, he just returned it with a good morning, and that was that, I stood there gob-smacked, no reaction at all.'

'For Christ sake who?' snapped Rod.

'You won't believe me if I told you.'

John stood up. 'If he doesn't bloody tell us who it is, I'm going to bloody strangle him,' he said, pushing back his chair.

Paul held up his hands towards John. 'Ok…ok… all right, it was Sean,' Paul replied.

Craig's jaw dropped, revealing chewed up bacon and egg yoke. The sound of falling utensils filled the dining room as the rest of them stood up in unison.

'You didn't let him know who you were for Christ sake,' snapped Craig.

Paul rolled his eyebrows. 'Of course I didn't. Anyway, as I said, he didn't recognise me,' he repeated, 'that's why I came and told you lot.'

'Thank Christ for that,' said John, staring at him. 'You're sure it was Sean? Don't forget Paul, you did have a bit too much to drink last night.'

'That was last night John. I'm telling you it was definitely bloody Sean, ninety-nine per cent, even though I only saw him for a moment, as I passed him.'

Sinead and Kerrie looked at each other. 'Da,' they said in unison as they headed towards the dining room door.

Mick looked around the table. 'Well if it was Sean as Paul said,' he scratched his head. 'Then why didn't he recognise Paul?' he said, looking round the table at the lads, puzzled. 'Girls… wait…wait,' he whispered to the girls, holding up his hands, beckoning them back to the table. 'Just a minute, hang on…. hold it. If Sean didn't recognise Paul, then let's see if he recognises us, and maybe we should talk to him,' he said.

John pushed out his chest. 'Good thinking Mick,' he said, pointing at Mick. 'So what are we going to do?'

'Ok, let's see if he recognises us,' Mick repeated. 'Girls you get behind us,' he said as they made their way to the foyer. Sean was talking to a young girl and a young man as John, Mick, Paul and Craig edged parallel towards him. Rod brought up the rear. Sinead and Kerrie walked behind Rod as they all walked towards Sean. Sean looked at John and Mick as they approached him, and then he looked back at the young girl.

Sinead shuddered, her eyes froze open wide, her face pinched with tension. She abruptly stopped dead in her tracks, sucking in air between her teeth as the body and face she recognised came into view. Grabbing Rod around the neck, bringing him to a sudden halt, she swung him round, pulling him back towards the refuge of the dining room. Kerrie followed.

'What, now?' shouted Rod as she dragged him behind the dining room door, kicking the door shut with a loud bang.

Sean looked towards the dining room door.

'Shush Rod,' Sinead whispered in his ear.

'For Christ sake,' he said, pulling her arm from around his neck, pausing as he looked at Kerrie. Then he said quietly, 'Sinead, what the bloody hell's going on here! We've found your dad,' whispered Rod.

Sinead stood breathless, and the realisation of seeing him sent a ripple of shock through her stomach.

'For God's sake Sinead, what's up,' whispered Kerrie, 'it looks like you've seen a ghost.'

Sinead shuddered again, putting her hand on her chest; sweat ran cold and clammy on her skin. It was several minutes before she was able to speak as she gasped for breath trying to assemble her thoughts. 'It wasn't Da.'

Kerrie stood, looking silently confused.

Rod stared at Sinead dumfounded. 'For Christ sake! What are you talking about? It was Sean, I bloody saw him,' whispered Rod, pointing back towards the foyer.

'I'm telling you Rod,' Sinead said, taking deep breaths. She ordered herself to breathe slow and steady, the air gasped in her lungs, clogged there until she gulped for it. 'I'm telling you Rod that isn't our da, that's why he didn't recognise Paul, when Paul spoke to him.'

Rods eyes narrowed. 'You're right Sinead, he didn't recognise Paul, or John and Mick when they walked towards him.' Rod shook his head. 'Well if he's not your dad, then who the bloody hell is he then?'

'Damn it, damn it, damn it,' Sinead whispered, gulping in more air. There was a tightness in her throat now that she tried to swallow down, but couldn't. The room seemed to close in on her; she wanted to run away, as far away as she could. She took deep gasping breaths, and panic came from the pit of her stomach. She noticed that her hands were trembling, then the sensation of her inability to hold herself together yanked sharply at her insides and roared up through her like something she couldn't control. Gripping her stomach, she hunched over. 'That's our fucking Uncle Tom,' she gasped.

Rod's mouth dropped as he looked at Sinead. 'Wow, Sinead,' he said. 'You said fuck.'

'You're fucking right, I said fuck,' she almost bellowed. 'This whole thing is fucking freaking me out.' God, how the memories pounded at her mind, making her gasp for breathe again, almost knocking her to the floor.

'You can't be serious!' Kerrie nodded her head. 'How the hell…no it can't be Uncle Tom, we haven't seen him for years,' she whispered.

Sinead looked at her sternly. 'I'm telling you Kerrie, it's Uncle Tom…' 'Well, what's he doing here…?' interrupted Kerrie, walking towards the doors that lead to the foyer. Sinead grabbed her arm. 'You may think I'm crazy, but for God's sake Kerrie, don't let him see you,' she gasped.

Rod looked puzzled at Sinead. 'What the hell do you mean; he's your Uncle Tom?'

Sinead found it difficult to get the words out. 'It's…it's… Da's brother, they are identical twins.'

Kerrie came back into the dining room. 'You're right, Sinead,' she whispered. 'It is Uncle Tom; he has a small birthmark on the left side of his neck. Here,' she said, touching the left side of her neck.

★ ★ ★

Mick, John, Craig and Paul stood either side of Sean and the young girl; they watched as the reception clerk locked a safety deposit box in the back office behind the counter, and returned the key to Sean.

John and Mick nodded at Sean as he moved away from the counter.

Paul watched the young girl as they made for the swivel door. 'Nice arse,' he remarked.

'Right Paul,' said John, 'follow that arse then, we need to know exactly where he's going and get back to us later. Think you can manage that on your own?'

'No problem,' nodded Paul, 'but what about my breakfast?'

John rubbed two fingers together. 'Sod your breakfast; you'll only throw it up anyway, after last night's drinking session.'

Paul smiled. 'You're probably right. Ok, I'm on my way, consider it done.' He winked as he followed them out of the door.

'Well Paul was definitely right,' said Mick as they entered the dining room.

'What the girl's arse?' smiled John.

Mick flapped a hand at John. 'No, not her arse, in fact I didn't even look at that. About Sean, that certainly wasn't Sean, but I must say there is a bloody good likeness.'

'You're right there,' agreed John. 'So who the bloody hell is he then?

Mick shrugged. 'Maybe the girls can enlighten us,' he said, looking at the girls. 'What's up with Sinead?' he asked, 'she doesn't look too good at all.'

John stared at Sinead open-mouthed. 'So girls, if that wasn't your dad, who the hell is he?' he asked, pointing at the foyer.

Rod spoke for her. 'Apparently that's their Uncle Tom,' he said.

'Well, if that's not Sinead and Kerrie's dad,' said John, 'what the hell are we going to do now, and where the bloody hell is Sean, and our money then?'

'That's a lot of bloody good questions,' said Mick scratching his head, still concerned about Sinead. He was sensing something was definitely not right there.

Sinead was out of all the questions and answers. She needed to be alone, get away. 'Mike, take me to my suite please.'

'I'll take you,' said Rod, holding her arm.

She withdrew her arm sharply. 'I said Mick,' she snapped.

'Why, are you all right Sinead?' Mick asked softly.

'I don't feel too good,' Sinead said, squeezing his arm tightly, 'must have been something I've eaten, and I've got a thumping headache.' She felt sick in the elevator and wanted to throw up but held it back. Mick helped her to the suite door.

'Are you sure you're going to be all right?' he asked as the door shut in his face. She stumbled into the suite and was hideously ill throwing up in the sink. When she was empty, she lay on the floor and waited for the sickness to pass. When she could stand again she peeled off her clothes, leaving them in a heap on the floor as she stepped into the shower. She stood in the shower wishing there was a bit more pressure. The water dripped on to her but she wanted sharp needles to pummel her body, and wash away her demons. Instead she ran the hot water as hot as she could bear, imagining every drop of water that penetrated her skin was washing away the past. She held her hands over her face, eyes screwed shut, leaning against the tiled wall. She slumped to the floor and curled up tightly, her body rippling in wave after wave of tiny convulsions; it seemed like she had been in there for hours, all sense of time and space evaporated. Grabbing a towel from the rail and wrapping the towel around her, she crawled into bed pulling the covers over her head, letting her thoughts slide into oblivion.

Mick looked troubled as he walked out of the elevator, he had seen distress, he had been there, and Sinead seemed to be showing classic symptoms of suffering... Kerrie ran towards him interrupting his thoughts. 'What's up Mick?' asked Kerrie. 'Is Sinead okay?'

Mick nodded his head. 'I don't know Kerrie. I'm not sure, but something is amiss with her, I think you'd better go up.'

Kerrie flew through the suite door and into the bedroom. 'Sinead, Mick says you're not well, are you all right?'

Kerrie pulled back the sheets and lifted Sinead head. 'What's up?'

Sinead sobbed. 'We didn't find Da.'

Kerrie pulled back the hair from Sinead's face. Her face-hardened. 'I know we didn't find Da, but I'm confused, we found Uncle Tom. Surely that's good isn't it? We haven't seen Uncle Tom for years, ever since him and Da had that unexplained bust-up.'

Sinead shook uncontrollably. 'No,' she sobbed. 'That is not good at all.'

Kerrie sat on the edge of the bed pulling her towards her, cradling her in her arms. 'Kerrie, please stay with me for a while,' Sinead whispered, as they both lie down and fell asleep.

Sinead woke first, she felt like she had slept for hours. She was tempted simply to roll back into sleep and stay there but that wouldn't solve a thing. Although panic was piercing through her stomach like an icy poker, her gut feeling was to tell Kerrie, but not at the moment. Kerrie mustn't know yet, this was about her, and they needed to know about their Da.

'We need to see the lads,' said Kerrie, pushing herself from the bed to her feet and dressing. Sinead dragged on a clean sweatshirt and shorts. |As they made their way to the lads' suite Kerrie put her hand around Sinead's shoulders to comfort her.

Chapter Eleven
Account Number

M ick and Rod placed the burgers and beers on the centre table.

'What this for?' asked John.

'Nothing really,' said Rod, 'only when I'm stressed, I like to shag, but seeing that sex seems to be on the back burner for the moment,' he rolled his eyes, 'then eating seems to be the next best thing.'

'Shame,' replied John as Paul burst into the room. He held up his thumbs. 'Sorted John, got the bastard,' he said. 'I know all there is to know about our Uncle Tom.' He paused, catching his breath. 'Apparently he owns a nightclub called *Les Mercedes*, in the centre of town, a bar by day and at night the basement is turned in a discoteca.'

The suite door open and the girls walked in.

'Did you hear that, Sinead?' said Rod, 'Paul says that Uncle Tom owns a nightclub in town, called *Les Mercedes,* that's the one we followed him into. Paul says it has a basement, that's where he must have gone when we lost him.'

Mick gave Sinead a concerned look. 'Are you all right now Sinead?' he asked.

She half-heartedly smiled at Mick. 'Yes, I'm fine now, thanks Mick.'

Hollowed-eyed and pale, and far from fine, was Mick's judgment. 'Have you taken anything?'

'Yes, a painkiller.'

'Have you eaten anything?' asked Craig, waving a burger at her.

Sinead retched at the sight of the burger, and raised her hand. 'For Christ sake,' she snapped. 'I'm fine, look lads thanks for the concern, but I'm fine, and I don't need a bunch of bloody nursemaids you know, I am a doctor, and it's only a headache.'

'Ok...ok, we're only concerned that's all, only you don't look too good though,' said John.

Mick gave him a nasty look.

'What!' said John raising his shoulders.

Sinead could imagine how she looked. 'I wasn't feeling too well, that's all John.' Self-consciously she scooped a hand through her hair. 'As I said, it was just a headache so Kerrie and I took a little nap. I'm fine now, thanks lads for all your concerns, but really I am fine.'

'Ok, as long as you are sure,' said Mick softly. 'We'll leave it there, no more said,' he smiled at her warmly.

Paul watched Rod's face as Rod watched Sinead. There was no doubt about it, Rod was completely besotted with her, it was definitely there in his face. Paul's loud sigh held a hint of envy, but in the scramble for burgers and beer nobody heard. This was ridiculous he shouldn't fancy her, he was a married man and he certainly shouldn't care about Rod fancying her. Paul passed him a beer. 'Come on Rod drink up,' he said, as they all grabbed a beer and a burger and sat down.

Mick scratched his head. 'So what happens now? We have a bloke who looks like Sean, that the girls say is their Uncle Tom, so where the hell is Sean?'

'Hang on, let's let the girls fill us in here, because we seem to be at a loose end,' asked John. 'Who is this Uncle Tom?' he said, looking at both the girls.

'He's Da's identical twin,' said Kerrie.

'Right,' said Craig, 'that explains the likeness then.'

'Brilliant deduction Sherlock Holmes,' said Paul.

Craig stuck a finger in the air.

John leant forward on the sofa, and shook his head. 'Hum, strange…so what is he doing here then?' He looked around the room at the lads for confirmation.

'Maybe Uncle Tom's in league with Sean,' said Craig.

'Good thinking Craig,' agreed John nodding his head. 'That's a possibility you know.'

'So you're thinking that Sean got the money, and they both came out here,' said Mick. 'So that means Sean is here some…' 'No…no…' shouted Sinead, 'Da wouldn't do that, he would never… never have teamed up with Uncle Tom… never.'

'How come you are so sure?' asked Mick, looking puzzled at Sinead's outburst.

Silence.

Kerrie spoke, 'Because Da and Uncle Tom haven't spoken to each other,' she paused and thought, 'for at least eleven years.' She turned and looked at Sinead. 'We don't know why, but they had a unexplained bust-up and have never spoken to each other from that day on.'

Mick had a feeling that Sinead know more. 'Is that right Sinead?' he asked.

A cold sensation went through Sinead as she bowed her head; Mick knew there was something more that might have happened in the past. 'This is not just about Sean missing is it?' he said softly, as he leant across the table and lifted her head lightly with his finger under her chin. There were tears in her eyes; she sobbed as a tear ran down her cheek. Finding it difficult to get her words out, she said, 'I …I have… a feeling…that Da's …dead.'

Shit, Mick thought, trying hard to come to some intelligent explanation as to what had really happened between Sean and Tom. *Shit, did Tom murder his own brother and do a runner with their money?* Gazing into the middle distance he found himself locking eyes with Sinead. 'Sinead,' he said softly, pulling a handkerchief from his shirt pocket. He reached across the table, giving her the handkerchief, and held her other hand.

'I'm so sorry to have to say this, but do you think' Mick began tentatively. 'I mean and it's only a possibility… do you think your Uncle Tom has murdered your dad?'

Silence.

Kerrie's eyes opened wide. 'Why would he? We don't know,' she answered, lifting her shoulders in a non-committal shrug.

'We really don't want to think that way,' said Kerrie as Sinead sobbed into the handkerchief again.

'As much as it pains me to say this,' said Mick softly, 'I think what Sinead suggests maybe a great possibility.'

It's quite hard to imagine that Sean may have been murdered by his own brother for money, thought John as he brought his fist down slowly on the burger carton, feeling the rubbery plastic crushing it out of shape, wishing maybe prematurely that it was Tom's head if he had killed Sean.

You could hear a pin drop as they all sat in silence. It was Mike who broke the silence, 'John you don't look happy.'

John nodded thoughtfully, and folded his arms. 'I'm fine.'

'Sure?'

John unfolded his arms, while attempting to think back to that Monday before Sean disappeared. 'It's just that,' he paused, 'do you remember what I said to you right from the very beginning, when all this started.'

Mike shrugged his shoulders. 'No, what?'

Something has nagged at me, John metaphorically slapped his forehead and his thoughts drifted off temporarily. He was sure now that there was a connection between Sean and the coffee machine, the thought had been banging on the door of his consciousness for some weeks, just out of reach, and now all of a sudden it was in his grasp. He was absolutely sure now that he had unplugged the coffee machine and the heater that Friday afternoon back at the site cabin before he'd left for the pub. John sprang to his feet, strode to the window, leant his back against the frame and waved a hand towards the ceiling. 'The coffee machine,' he said, 'and the heater in the site cabin, it's just something that's niggled me.'

Silence.

They all frowned, feeling they were failing to understand John's train of thought.

Mick broke the silence. 'What on earth are you talking about John, the coffee machine? What's all this about the coffee machine and the heater, I don't get it?'

John pulled back his shoulders. 'It all hinges on the coffee machine,' he said again. 'I'm telling you somebody was in the site cabin either late Saturday evening, or early Sunday morning.' He paused. 'Mick, you told me that you hadn't been down there that weekend. So if it wasn't you, then who the hell was it that left the coffee machine and the cabin heater switched on.'

Deep furrows appeared in Mick forehead. 'So what you're saying John is... that you're thinking Uncle Tom was at the site cabin on Saturday evening or Sunday morning?'

John sighed, shook his head and held up a finger. 'Exactly Mick, God you're quick,' he said.

Rod piped up. 'Hang on Mick, John's right... it's all falling into place now. I told you that Sean had a phone call down the pub on Saturday evening, that's when he left the pub. He must have gone down to the site that Saturday night, because Cathleen said he left Saturday night, after he had spoken with you.'

'But I've told you Sean never spoke to me, and I never spoke to him,' replied Mick.

'That's what we're saying Mick,' replied Rod, 'that Sean's brother Uncle Tom called Sean Saturday evening and enticed him down to the site. He must have been waiting for him there, murdered Sean and took the ticket.'

Mick shrugged a response.

'How do we know Sean took the ticket with him?' Craig asked.

Rod tapped his head. 'Use this Craig, of course he took the ticket with him, he would have wanted to show us, when we returned to work on Monday. Anyway, how else do you think his brother got the bloody money.'

'Dumbo,' said John, pacing the room.

'He's right,' said Craig, nodding his head in agreement.

'Well, if what you say is true then Rod, then where the hell is Sean now?' asked Mick, scratching his head. 'I never noticed anything different, what about you lot?'

They all shrugged their shoulders.

John stopped pacing. 'I don't believe it,' he said, holding both his hands behind his head, his face ghostly white, as if he was just about to board the plane home. 'He bloody couldn't have,' he looked at the girls with sad eyes. 'Girls, I'm sorry but you're not going to like what I'm about to say now. If you'd like you can leave the room.'

'Mick,' said John, looking at him, and nodded towards the door. He stood. Both the girls waved their hands for Mick to sit back down. 'No,' said Sinead. 'We're not leaving, if you've got something to say John, then you say it in front of us, we are all in this together.'

'Well at least let's all have a stiff drink first. Rod, brandies all round.'

Rod went to the room's bar and poured out six brandies, and passed them round. They all took a quick drink; the girls both sipped theirs and coughed as the harshness of the brandy hit the back of their throats.

John coughed. 'Well,' he brought their attention back to him. 'This is how I see it,' he continued. 'There was something definitely strange when I drove into the site on Monday morning,' he said, nodding his head. 'I noticed something quite unusual, you would probably only notice it if you'd been in the building game as long as Mick and I have,' he paused, taking another sip of his brandy.

They all leant forward waiting in anticipation for his explanation.

John continued. 'It's all to do with sand you see,' he said, sucking his teeth. 'When were the piles of sand delivered Mick?'

Paul leant towards Craig. 'The sun's got to his head,' he whispered to Paul, 'bloody sunstroke. Two waltzers shy of a fairground, he's gone bonkers.'

Mick scratched his head. 'The sand you say, right, yes it's been there for some time, it was brought in for the second phase of the housing project, but as you know that was put on hold.' Mick nodded his head. 'So yes, as you say, it's been there at least three or four months, maybe longer.'

'No,' said Craig, 'don't forget we had a delivery of sand on Monday.'

John scratched his head. 'You're right Craig,' he said, pointing in his direction, 'but let's get back to my original question. What happens to sand when it's been standing for some time? Ok, Mick,' said John, 'I say to you again, what happens to sand when it stands for any length of time?' 'No... for Christ sake,' said Mick, 'you're not suggest...' 'Yes I am suggesting,' interrupted John, nodding his head... 'No he couldn't have,' interrupted Mick.

Paul nudged Craig. 'They've both gone bloody mad now, what the hell are they both going on about?'

'What,' said the girls, not having a clue where Mick and John were going.

'We know that one of the piles of sand had been moved,' said John.

'How?' said the girls in unison.

'Well,' said John, holding up his hands and tapping his fingers. 'One, when sand stands for some time in the sun, it gets what they call a crust on it,' he looked at both the girls, ' a hard skin that is,' he explained. 'And two, there were three piles of sand on the site. As Craig said one pile was delivered on the Monday. Two of the other piles of sand were delivered some time ago as Mick said, so there should have been no variation of colour in the old sand, so both of the old piles of sand should have been the same colour. And they were definitely the same colour when I left the site on Friday afternoon. And when I returned Monday morning for work, one of the two old piles of sand had changed colour.'

'I never noticed that,' said Rod.

'Well you wouldn't have, would you Rod,' said John, deciding that it wouldn't be appropriate to bring up the weekend Rod had with the two young ladies.

'You're right John,' said Craig, wishing that he could say something about the two tarts Rod had picked up at the pub, but he wouldn't be so cruel. 'So you're saying one of the piles was moved.'

'Correct,' replied John, 'one was definitely a different colour. I'm telling you that the hard skin had been broken on one of the old piles, and the colour change was different because the pile had been turned over exposing the damp sand.'

'Jesus Christ John, now that's what I call classic bloody Sherlock Holmes,' said Paul.

'John's right,' said Craig. 'Elementary, Paul, elementary, dear Watson. The pile that John said had been moved was the same colour as the pile that was delivered on Monday. So one of the old piles of sand must have been moved.'

'All right, you're so clever Craig, how the hell did Uncle Tom move so much sand?' asked Paul.

'I don't know, bucket and spade maybe,' smiled Craig, 'I haven't a bloody clue...' 'Nearly,' said John interrupting Craig, noticing that the girls weren't smiling. 'Mick d'you remember, the wall safe key, the one you had it in your pocket, so I couldn't lock the safe up when I left on Friday....' 'Jesus,' interrupted Paul, turning towards John. 'You're not saying that Uncle Tom used the JCB to conceal Sean body?'

Rod's mouth gaped open; he laid a hand on Sinead's shoulder.

Mike moved over and sat next to Kerrie.

Finally Rod spoke, 'My God John, you're saying that Sean is buried at the site, under a pile of discoloured sand.'

John shrugged his shoulders. 'All I'm saying is that the sand had been moved,' *not wishing to tell the girls that what Rod was saying he believed to be true.*

The girls both sobbed. As Mick put his arm around Kerrie's shoulders she fell into his arms and cried; he felt her body trembling with grief as Rod was feeling the same feeling with Sinead.

'Let's take some time out here lads,' said Mick. 'Let's give the girls some fresh air,' as Rod and Mick walked them to the suite door, and down into the street.

'I'm so sorry,' said John, as the girls, Mick and Rod returned back into the suite. 'Girls, you know that Sean, your dad, was a very good friend to all of us, and if what we have just discussed is the case, then he is going to be sadly missed, especially for your poor mum Cathleen.' John raised his hands. 'Let me suggest, Sinead and Kerrie, that at the moment this is only speculation on our part, so let's not jump the gun until we know for sure.' John paused, not really wishing to go on but he had to. 'But… we need to get to the money before Uncle Tom gets any notion that we know it's him. Is that ok with you two girls?'

Both the girls nodded in unison.

'Right, believe me Sinead and Kerrie when I say this,' said John, 'if what we've discussed is the case, then while we have got any breath left in our bodies, the lads and I will find out for you what happened to your dad.'

They all nodded in unison.

'Girls you go and have a rest,' said Mick softly, 'and we'll talk about it when you're ready.' The girls without a sound left the suite, as Rod collected the glasses and poured out another round of brandies.

Mick had called a meeting in John's suite.

'I've ordered beers for the lads and wine for the girls, room service are bringing it up,' said John as they all sat down. 'Well,' he continued, 'this is as I see the problem we have at the moment…' A knock on the suite door interrupted his flow. 'Shit,' he said as he opened the door. 'Good, the beers,' he said. 'Put them over there, on the table,' he said, pointing the waiter towards the table. They waited until the waiter left. The girl entered the room as the waiter left…. 'Ah good, you're back, wine,' said John, pouring the girls a drink, and passing around the beers. 'Right,' he continued. 'We were just discussing what to do next,' he said, looking at the girls. 'This is how I see our problem. At the moment we've got no Sean, but we've got Uncle Tom, who we know owns *Les Mercedes,* so where do we go to from here?' John raised his eyebrows at them. 'Well, we can't just walk up to Uncle Tom…' 'Hang on,' said Paul, interrupting John. 'Would anybody mind if we refrain from calling him bloody Uncle Tom? It's winding me up knowing what he's done to us, and what he might have done to Sean, and the girls. Let's go for a pseudonym.'

John raised his eyebrows, puzzled. 'What's a bloody pseudonym,' he asked.

'Another name,' replied Mick.

'Right, good idea,' said John, nodding his head.

'I'll go with that,' agreed Mick. 'What do you have in mind?'

'The bastard,' Paul suggested.

They all gave a nod of approval.

'Ok, the bastard it is then,' agreed John. He continued, 'as I said, we can't just walk up to the bastard and say where's our eighteen million, he'll just do a runner.'

'You're right John,' agreed Mick. 'So what are we going to do then?'

Silence.

Mick broke the silence. 'I know,' he said, holding up a hand, 'the key to all of this is the key.'

Rod, Paul, John and Craig looked puzzled.

'What key?' asked Rod… 'Firstly,' interrupted Paul, 'don't we need to prove the bastard murdered Sean, and then get our money. That's what we're here for isn't it?' he asked.

'That's why we need the key,' replied Mick. 'We need to get the key to prove the bastard stole the money, and then we can prove he murdered Sean.'

'What key!' asked Rod again…. 'Ok Mick,' said Craig, ignoring Rod's question. 'So you're saying we need to get this key that the bastard has got, then what do we do with it, when we've got it?'

'What fucking key?' shouted Rod.

Startled, they all looked round at Rod.

'What key,' he said again softly, holding out his hands.

'When John and I were at the front desk,' said Mick. 'It's the key the bastard had at the front desk, he's got a safety deposit box in the hotel, we saw it, didn't we John?'

John nodded, confirming what Mick had said.

'We need to get that key.'

'Why do we want the key?' asked Craig.

Rod pointed to his head. 'Use this Monkey man,' he said, as he was now up to speed with what was being said.

Craig pointed at Rod. 'That's it, the bastard's going to die,' he said as he got up and walked towards Rod.

'Here we go,' said John sitting forward grabbing his beer, waiting for contact.

'It's rumble time,' said Mick.

'Stop! Stop it!' shouted Sinead, putting herself between them. 'This is ridiculous, do you two always go at each other this way?'

John sat back and sighed. 'They do,' he said, picking up his beer, gulping it down, 'they enjoy it don't they?' he said turning to Mick… Mick nodded… 'Anyway,' said John, 'it give us a bit of satisfaction to watch them.'

'I'd enjoy landing Rod one on the chin.'

'Try it,' Rod angled his chin.

Sinead looked at Craig.

'Craig, wine please,' said Kerrie smiling, holding up her glass and trying to defuse the situation.

Craig waved a contrite hand at Rod, filled Kerrie's glass, sat down and looked at Mick. 'Mick, why do we need the key?' asked Craig again.

'Because that's where he probably keeps all of his important documents, you know passport etc, in the safety deposit box.'

'Why in the hotel?' asked Paul.

'It's probably cheaper than a bank,' replied Kerrie.

'No, I mean,' continued Paul, 'why doesn't he keep them at the club, or wherever else he lives…?' 'Crime,' interrupted Rod.

'What's that got to do with a safety deposit box?' asked Craig, who was now back on track with Rod.

'Well think about it,' replied Rod, 'the crime rate in this part of the world is horrendous, a hundred times worse than Peterborough,' he paused. 'And I presume that the bastard lives alone, so the club and wherever he lives would be easy targets for criminals. It's a fact that most ex-pats use safety deposit boxes in hotels, as there is always somebody there to keep an eye on them, it's good security, and as Kerrie says it's cheaper than a bank.'

Paul paced the room. 'Yer, and I bet the bastard knows something about criminals,' he said… 'But this is the eighteen million pound question… How the hell are we going to get the key?'

'Good point Paul,' John agreed, pointing at Paul. Silence hit the room again.

Kerrie coughed softly as they all looked at her.' You spoke Kerrie,' John asked… 'No, I was just thinking.'

'Thinking what Kerrie?' asked Mick.

'As you've all said, what we need to do is get that key.' Kerrie held her hand towards Sinead's. 'You're lucky Sinead's here, because that's her department.'

'What do you mean her department?' asked Craig, looking puzzled.

'Sinead can get the key for you,' replied Kerrie.

Mick looked puzzled at Sinead. 'How can she get the key, the bastard would recognise her.'

Kerrie had dropped this on Sinead like a thunderbolt out of the blue and sweat popped out of her skin. Her hands clenched into small balls digging her fingernails into her palms until she drew blood. The thought of going anywhere near him made her stomach convulse. She took a shuddering breath. 'I can't... I... I can't do it.'

Kerrie looked bewildered at Sinead's refusal. 'You have to Sinead, there's no one else who can do it, you must do it for Da.' She turned towards Mick. ' My big sister is brilliant at disguising her voice, in fact we thought that when she left school she'd become an impressionist, but Dad said she had to go to Med school first; I'm telling you she's excellent at changing her voice. You know, a bit of a Rory Bremner. Go on Sinead; do them your Cilla Black impression. She used to do it all the time when we were children.'

Rod was finding out a new side to Sinead's talents. He raised a sceptical brow.

Sinead blushed. 'Certainly not,' she said, looking firmly at Kerrie. She hadn't given it much thought, or attempted it since they were all little girls. And she'd certainly never done it on the open stage before; she only did the impressions in the privacy of their own bedroom, just to make her sisters laugh.

'Go on Sinead, let's hear Cilla Black,' said Craig, encouraging her to participate.

Mick could see by the expression on Sinead's face that she was uncomfortable with the prospect of herself having to perform in front of the lads, so he stepped in. 'Now, don't embarrass her lads.' But still, I'll keep hold of the concept that Kerrie had spoken about.

'Bugger it,' said Craig, 'I wanted to hear her Cilla Black.' He gave them his rendition of Cilla Black, pushing out his front teeth, and pulling back his hair. 'Her the girl with the fair hair.'

The girls laughed in unison.

'Don't give up your day job,' said John.

'Thanks to Sean I haven't got a bloody day job,' replied Craig.

'Kerrie it's not just the voice,' said Mick, ' just look at her, the bastard would recognise her straight away... 'Don't worry about that Mick,' interrupted Rod, 'we could change her appearance.'

Sinead rested her head against the back of the sofa, her eyes widened. 'And you think Uncle Tom's going to go for that?'

'Trust me, I know he will,' said Rod, shaking his head.

'So if as you say Rod, you did change Sinead's appearance and she did get the key, then how the hell are we going to get into his account?' asked Craig.

'Well that's where I come in, now you're in my backyard,' Kerrie interrupted with a smile. 'Maybe.... she paused... 'Maybe I can get into Uncle Tom's, sorry, the bastard's account and transfer the money... But...' 'Shit, I hate buts,' whispered John... 'I'll have to have some information first though. What I need is the bastard's account code number. Can you imagine, without it I'd have to search the world's account code numbers for his. I'm afraid you would all be very old men by the time we found it. I would have to break it down by date transfers, the transaction from the UK of the eighteen million pounds, get all the account numbers and sort them one at a time, do you see what I mean, and that's if the bastard is using his own name. Well, if the bastard's using another name, it's impossible, then I'm sorry but you can kiss your eighteen million good-bye.

'Shit,' said Mick. 'Anyway let's recap, so far we have no Sean, but we have the bastard, his club, and the key, and that's if Sinead's going to get us the key and Kerrie's going to tap into his account. Then we are home and dry.'

They all nodded… Rod was looking decidedly jaded with the whole conversation. 'Ah, well, as you said Mick, home and dry,' he said, 'don't let me put a spanner in the works, but if what Mick has said is factual, I'll go along with what Monkey man said. How the hell are you going to tap into the bastard's account? I'm sorry, but I can't see the bank just letting Kerrie walk in and ask the cashier to hand over Mr Walsh's account code number, or anybody that has transferred eighteen million pounds within the last six months, then explain that the bastard stole the eighteen million pounds from us, and we want it back, thank you very much and good day. There's got to be something we can do.'

Paul pulled at his hair with both hands, showing signs of frustration. 'Well, as Rod said,' he agreed, 'the bank aren't going to give you that information, are they?'

'Unfortunately not,' replied Kerrie.

'It's more complicated than we thought. So how are you going to get in there?' asked Paul.

'Not wishing to blow my own trumpet Paul, but I am the computer expert around here as you know, and I know my job. You get me the code, and I'll promise you all I'll get you your money.'

'That's it then,' said Rod.

'It's that easy,' Kerrie held up her hands. 'Rod, once we have got the account code, I just access the Amax mainframe that all the banks use, and make the changes.'

'If as you say, it's that simple,' said John, scratching his head. 'Then I'm impressed, but,' he said pausing, 'how the hell are you going to do that, just whip out your lap-top, modem it up, and *hey presto* eighteen million pounds?'

'No,' Kerrie said, looking confused by John's question. 'No I'll just go into the Citibank. When of course I have the information I require, and use their system.'

'And you're saying the bank are just going to let you walk in?' asked Craig.

'Yes, I'm afraid they will. Yes, it's as easy as that,' replied Kerrie.

Mick tapped Kerrie's arm. 'Isn't Amax the International Banking Organization?'

Kerrie tapped his hand. 'Clever boy Mick, yes it is sort of but a bit better than the I.B.O; the one I'm taking about is the International World Banking System.'

'I'm impressed,' said Mick. 'Are you saying you can get into their system?' he asked.

'And why not Craig?' she said, returning to Craig's question. 'That's my job; I can get into any banking system in the whole world. It's not so difficult really,' she continued, 'all you need to do now is get me the bastard's account number code, I'll get into his account, and I'll just clear it out for you, no problem, then it will all be done and dusted.'

All the lads smiled in unison at Kerrie's confidence.

John looked at the girls. 'Isn't this going to be dangerous for the girls? Don't forget lads, we haven't got anything to lose.'

'Only eighteen million pounds,' Paul reminded him.

'Money's not everything Paul,' said Mick.

'Right,' smiled Paul sarcastically. 'It is to me,' he mumbled.

Mick cringed, looking back at John. 'Now that worries me too,' he said, 'good point.'

'I'll keep an eye on the girls,' said Rod

'What like you did the bastard?' said Craig.

'Touché,' replied Rod. His expression looked genuine, he would put his life on the line for both the girls, and John knows he would.

John touched Mick's arm. 'Let Rod do it Mick, he won't let us down, I know, not on this issue anyway, Rod has a vested interest.'

'Yer, money,' said Paul.

'Not this time,' John replied, 'and enough said.'

Mick looked at John and smiled.

John winked an eye, and nodded his head slowly.

'Cheers John,' smiled Rod. 'I promise you, hand on heart Mick, they won't come to any danger, I'd give my life for this lady.'

'Don't worry Rod, if anything does happen to them, it's your life we'll be asking for,' said Mick.

Sinead looked at Rod. 'You better take Mick seriously Rod. I think he really means it,' she said. Rod noticed a small sparkle in her eyes that he had never seen there before. He smiled his boyish smile. 'No he don't, its just hot air,' he shrugged.

Kerrie coughed... 'Well, I'm afraid we don't have any other choice, the bastard would recognise me straight away, we need to get close to him.' Kerrie held up a hand. 'We don't even know where he's living; we know it's definitely not a hotel. As you know, we've checked every hotel in Barcelona. I mean the bastard could have bought a villa on the outskirts of Barcelona, who knows,' she raised her hands, and shrugged her shoulders. 'So, I'm afraid we have no other option but to get somebody to meet him, and as you say, get the key.' Kerrie looked round at them all. 'I don't wish to offend you lads, but I know for a fact that none of you boys have got the equipment to entice the bastard.'

'No offence taken,' replied John.

'Hum... Tristram,' said Paul. 'Maybe we could fly him over, he'll sort the bastard out.'

'You're joking,' said John. 'I don't want to be within ten feet of that gay boy. In fact this is the sort of distance I like between us.'

'Joke John, joke,' smiled Paul.

Mick looked at John and laughed, shaking his head slowly. He turned towards Kerrie, looking at her firmly. 'Now, as for you young lady, I'm telling you this,' he pointed a finger at her. 'We don't want you putting yourself in any danger; don't forget that the bastard may have murdered your dad, and you're not to put you or your sister in any danger, understand. If anything happened to you or Sinead, Cathleen would never forgive us. So any sign of danger and we'll pull you both out, Ok?' Kerrie smiled, 'Very sweet Mick, thanks for your concern, but we need to do this lads if you want your money. So it's all up to Sinead.'

'And how are you going to get this key then, Sinead?' asked Mick.

'They all looked at Sinead.

Sinead shivered, giving a non-committal shrug.

'It's for Da, Sinead,' Kerrie said.

Sinead went to speak, as Rod touched her arm. 'Leave this to Sinead and me lads,' he said, looking at Sinead. 'Don't worry Mick; we have a few good ideas.'

Chapter Twelve
Sinead's Switch

Rod heard a soft rap on his suite door. 'Come in,' shouted Rod. 'The door's not locked.'

Sinead entered, attentively closing the door behind her. 'Where have the lads gone?' she asked.

'Nowhere, they are having a siesta,' replied Rod. 'Paul and Craig can't hack the heat, and John and Mick are conserving their energy levels for the sting as we may be up a little too late for them. Past their bedtime, you know.'

'Bless them,' Sinead said as her thoughts revisited the position she had been forced into; *she couldn't bear the thought of seeing Uncle Tom ever again...* Rod interrupted her thoughts. 'Penny for them,' he said.... *If only he knew, but she wasn't going to tell him...* 'Ok Sinead it's time, everything's ready,' he said, pushing a chair in front of the mirror. 'Come sit, let's see what we can do.' He held up a pair of scissors and a bottle of dye. Sinead sat playing with her hair, twisting the long strands with her fingers. Her flowing red hair was to go, it was part of her, and it had been with her since she was a little girl. She twisted in the chair looking up at Rod with an apprehensive expression. 'I'm not too sure about this, are you sure you know what you're doing?'

'Oh, what me?' Rod blinked with surprise. 'Um…listen here young lady,' he said, 'I wasn't always a plumber, you know. Before I got into the plumbing game, I was a hairdresser up West.'

Sinead looked confused.

'Sorry West End, London, I was a stylist in a London salon, in Soho, used to style some of the most famous and beautiful people in the world, mostly models. I've styled Kate Moss's, Naomi Campbell's and, I've even styled Madonna's hair, just to name a few.' He held up a bunch of her hair, 'Ok, are we going to make a start, or what?'

Sinead nodded her head half-heartedly, as her hand rose to her neck, her long, slender, beautiful neck.

Rod sensed some disagreement but smiled anyway. He took up his scissors and comb. 'Right let's put this plan into action and create a new woman for you,' he said. Snipping off a segment of her hair he smiled at her for reassurance, and dropped the cut piece into the bin.

Sinead shook her head slowly, needing to vent her irritation. 'Rod, I don't wish to be offensive, *you're really starting to annoy me,* but you really talk shite, sometimes. I don't mind you talking shite, but talking it to me is really starting to annoy me. I'm tired, upset about Da, and to cap it all I have a throbbing headache.'

'Sorry,' replied Rod: all he could think about was his throbbing hard-on. 'Believe me,' he said, rubbing his shorts with his comb, 'I'm really not trying to annoy you Sinead. Ok, let's give it twenty minutes,' he said, as he washed his hands and looked at his watch.

'Sorry Rod, forget what I just said, take no notice of me, I'm just a little scared about the hair going. God knows why.'

Rod smiled, laying his hands on her shoulders. 'Don't worry, you're in good hands, it'll all be over very soon if that's any help. I think you're handling the whole thing very well, you know, about your dad and all that.'

Sinead shook her head. 'That's because I'm Irish,' she replied, brushing his hands from her shoulders.

Dejectedly Rod applied the colour, and looked at his watch again. 'Right let's give that twenty minutes, do you want me to get you an aspirin?'

Sinead massaged her forehead. 'No it's fine, it will go in a minute. Thanks anyway,' she looked at him and smiled.

'Let me do that while we're waiting,' Rod said, removing her hands from her forehead. He massaged her temples softly, and the back of her neck. 'Do you mind if I play some music?' he asked.

'No,' Sinead replied sleepily.

Rod slipped his Julio Iglesias *Non Stop* CD into the player and pressed play; *if I ever needed you I need you now* filled the air. This was definitely not a first for Rod, having a beautiful woman in a room on her own. Normally girls initiated sexual advances towards him, but it felt strange being on the other end, of having to make the first move. Enjoying her closeness even though she wasn't particularly participating.

'Mmm… that's great…Rod… you should have been a masseur,' she said, purring with pleasure as his hands pressed lightly across her shoulders. She closed her eyes and lay back in the chair.

Rod sang softly, *'If I ever needed you I need you now, there's nothing in my life, I've been more sure of since I've fallen into your love and I promise I'll make up for the hurt somehow.'*

'A singer as well,' Sinead said, 'I love the French accent,' opening her eyes.

Rod's face went red with embarrassment.

'No... no...' she said, feeling his embarrassment, 'honest, you have such a gorgeous voice.'

'Karaoke,' said Rod shyly. 'This is my favourite song.'

'Really,' she said. Their eyes made contact; he could have swum in her deep green pools. 'Rod,' she said softly, 'do you mean the words you've just sung?'

'Of course I do,' he said, unable to take his eyes off her.

'Who are they for, a girlfriend?'

'Certainly not, there's only one girl in the world who deserves those words sung to her.'

'Who's that then?' she asked, almost fearing the answer.

'You of course,' replied Rod, moving around her, pulling her up from the chair.

Shit, she tensed, but allowed him to make his move.

'Sinead?' He just wanted to cover her mouth with his. It was no good, something had to be done, somebody had to make the first move, but for the first time in his life, he had no idea what to do. Sinead never encouraged his advances. He had never been in this situation before. Their eyes met again as he placed a finger attentively on her cheek. 'I hope this doesn't put you off,' he said as he softly laid his lips on hers, feeling his whole body tingle with pleasure. Loving Sinead, and allowing herself to be loved was worth the risk, if the odds were in his favour, but they quite clearly weren't. Her body was giving off clear and unambiguous signals that she wasn't interested.

She stiffened, not moving a muscle and her eyes stayed open locked onto his, watching like a moth trapped by the bright light, pinned by the hallucinating light. She'd have jumped out of her skin if he'd laid a hand on her. But it was only his mouth, soft and easy on hers.

Rod withdrew; everything in her body language seemed to imply resentment to his advances. His inner voice was screaming *shag her; for God's sake shag her.* God he wanted to. Three weeks ago he would have, without any thought other than his own self-gratification, but his conscience was saying *Go on give in to the only other weakness to man, other than money.* He shook his head *No.* She was different, he smiled into her eyes, but her eyes were guarded. She didn't smile back. He tried to fathom out what was going on behind those tears that filled her eyes. He'd lost her and he prepared himself for rejection but he hadn't expected for her to be so scared. What was she scared of? Was she scared of him? That seemed to be the message he was getting from her, a rigid terror in her body that could easily turn into repulsion. So he didn't make any further moves to touch her, as much as he wanted to, not even a gentle brush of fingers down her bare arm. If she stepped back, he'd do nothing to stop her, but her absolute stillness was her own defence. Rod realised, watching Sinead closely, that he had truly no idea, no awareness of his inability to communicate with her – God, maybe with all the other women he'd been with, but this one gave not even the tiniest gesture. He felt his blood galloping through his veins as he nodded, stepped back and pulled himself away. For a moment her eyes had stared past him to a place he couldn't see. He kept the situation light despite a gnawing in his stomach that was more than a stir of desire for her. It was a cold fear for whatever had hurt her.

She turned away from him, taking a deep breath. 'I can't have sex with you Rod, if that's what you want.'

'Wow, hang on here,' Rod said, holding up his hands. He wasn't the sort of man to comfortably fall victim to emotions. 'Where the hell did that come from Sinead?' This kiss was becoming very complicated. 'Don't assume that I was after sex Sinead, if you did then I'm sorry, that wasn't my intention.' *You lying bastard* he thought. He paused, and looked puzzled. 'Anyway if that was my intention, why not?' He shrugged his shoulders looking for an answer.

Silence.

She looked at him. Her face showed signs of non-committal, as she turned away.

'What… what's… the matter Sinead? What are you afraid of, not me I hope,' he said, placing his hands on his chest. 'You're a grown woman, d'you think somebody's going to come along and slap your wrist for enjoying yourself?'

She turned, trying to steady her voice. 'You don't understand Rod, there's a difference between us.'

Deep furrows appeared in Rods forehead, *God you're right there is a difference between us, just look at you. He paused his thoughts and looked at her deeply. God, please don't say she's a transvestite.* He'd heard about how his mates had gone on holiday to Asia, and one of them got off with a woman, and when he got down to the nitty gritty, you could get rid of the WO in WOMAN, fruit and veg, a bloke. *No… not… Sinead for God's sake,* he shook his head at the thought, looking at her more closely. *No it was definitely not possible, no transvestite could get it that perfect.* 'Hang on,' he said, trying to lighten the conversation. 'Me Tarzan, You Jane,' he said, cupping his hands and banging his chest.

He detected just a very faint smile on her face as she turned away. 'Sorry Rod, but I can't talk about it.'

'Can't or won't?' Rod asked, taking a step closer to her, watching her eyes and the emotions that flickered across her face. He dropped his raised hands that were intended to rest on her shoulders to comfort her.

'Sorry,' she said shaking her head.

Rod held up his hands again, knowing that this conversation was going to go nowhere. 'Right,' he said, 'let's put the finishing touches to the hairstyle,' as he sat her back down in the seat, blow-dried and brushed. 'Well, that's how it looks,' he said, moving to one side allowing her to look in the mirror.

Sinead gave her head a small shake and looked at her reflection in the mirror. 'Good God is that me, magnificent.' Her eyes shone with delight at the transformation. 'Jesus Mother of God, I take back all that I said about you,' she said in awe, 'you're a genius Rod, is this really me?' She touched her hair with her hands, almost not recognising the reflected image.

In the mirror Rod spotted a nerve twitching at the corner of her mouth, the nearest she had ever come to smiling. 'Auburn or blonde, Sinead, you're one hell of a beautiful woman.'

Sinead stood and turned. 'And you are one hell of a kisser, but one swallow doesn't make a summer Rod. Be patient with me,' she said as they momentarily fell into each other's arms.

'*Shit women,*' said Rod to himself under his breath, and smiled.

Chapter Thirteen
The Kiss

R od didn't sleep well, he'd spent half the night pacing his room. Sinead seemed to fill his head, he needed to help her, but what could he do? He'd decided on an early morning swim to clear his thoughts. Feeling the warmth of the early morning sun rising up from the sea, he sat scanning the beach seeing nothing out of the ordinary for five thirty, only early morning bathers on the beach. He kicked holes in the sand. What went on in her head? How did it get there? Who put it there? ....
Mick interrupted his thoughts... 'Hi Rod, you're up early mate, couldn't you sleep?' he said, coming up from the sea, shaking the water from his ears.

'Just a bit of a problem, what about you Mick?' Rod looked at his watch, 'not like you to be up this early, couldn't you sleep either?'

'No, I slept fine, I'm just taking Kerrie's advice, getting in a bit of swimming practice, nice and quiet this time of the morning,' he said, rubbing himself down with the towel. 'I'm just going back for breakfast, you coming, lad?' he said as he started off towards the hotel.

'Yer Mick, I'll be along in a minute... Listen Mick,' Rod shouted over his shoulder, his voice trailing off trying to think how to put together what he needed to say.

'Listening,' replied Mick as he walked back to Rod and sat down beside him.

'Can I speak honestly Mick?'

'I don't know, can you?'

Rod let out a snort of frustration. 'Very funny Mick,'

He said, half-heartedly smiling. 'There's something strange going on with Sinead. Something happened between Sinead and me last night,' he steered his sights unfocused out to sea.

Mick nodded. 'Thought so. A… ha,' he teased, ' and you want to tell me about it?'

'No… no… it's not what you think,' said Rod, waving a hand and looking back at Mick. 'You know we all talked about changing Sinead's appearance?'

'Yer, so what?' asked Mick.

'Well I did the change for her…' 'Hang on,' said Mick, interrupting him. 'Come to think of it Rod, I haven't seen her about since the switch.'

'I know, she said she's not coming out until the night she does the deed.'

Mick angled his head towards Rod. 'Why?'

Rod shrugged, and held out his hands. 'I don't know why Mick, you might as well ask me why women are women.'

Deep furrows appeared in Mick's forehead. 'It's right what they say, that women are really from Mars,' he said.

'Women aren't from Mars Mick, they're from Venus, you stupid twat.'

Mick looked puzzled at Rod. 'Are men from Mars then?'

'Don't you know anything,' muttered Rod, slapping his forehead and turning away. 'God, and to think I'm going to ask you for your advice,' he turned back towards Mick. 'Of course men are from Mars. Mars is the planet of war Mick, and Venus is the planet of love.'

'Right,' said Mick frowning. 'Anyway what were you telling me, about, you don't know?'

'Don't know what?'

'Why, isn't Sinead coming out of her room?'

'Right,' said Rod, raising his eyebrows. 'As I said, I don't know,' he replied, 'anyway, Sinead said she needed to prepare herself,' he held out his hands, 'whatever that meant. She'll only let Kerrie see her. That's women for you. As I said Mick, I did the switch, and transformed her into this beauty,' he waved his hand, 'not... that I'm saying Sinead wasn't a beauty anyway. I'm telling you Mick you wouldn't recognise her. She's so stunning, she looked so beautiful, I couldn't help myself, and as you know, one thing normally leads to another...' 'Don't tell me Rod you took advantage of her,' interrupted Mick... Rod raised his hand again. 'No...no...' he paused. 'That was the problem Mick, I just kissed her, and nothing happened.'

'Oh, Noooooo,' said Mick, with exaggerated sympathy. 'So nothing happened, good God Rod, was that all... not a lucky night for you then,' he replied, a weak effort at humour. Mick crossed his arms and grinned at Rod. 'I'm sorry to hear that, better luck next time maybe...anyway it wasn't a complete waste of time then, at least you got a snog.' *Good girl* he thought, smiling.

Normally Rod would have laughed at Mick's wisecracks. 'If all I'd wanted was a snog, as you put it, somewhere wet to put my tongue, then I'd have bought a fucking ice cream wouldn't I? If all you're going to do is be bloody sarcastic then I might as well shut up.' He stood up, pacing the beach and kicked the sand.

Mick shrugged his shoulders. 'Only trying to help,' he grinned.

Rod frowned, looking back at Mick, 'Well you're not, and you're not listening.' Mick's grin didn't convince Rod of his sincerity on this point. 'Believe me Mick, I'm telling you this is serious stuff.'

'Okay sorry, go on, so what's your problem?'

'It's not anything like you think it was. My problem is that I did everything I thought was right and it all worked out wrong. When I kissed her, the kiss manifested into a cold unwilling response from her to my kiss.'

Mick shook his head in disbelief. 'So you're telling me you kissed her and nothing happened...' 'Right... Mick please,' interrupted Rod. 'I'm telling you the truth, God, I wanted something to happen, I prayed that something would happen, but, nothing happened, all I could feel was her body shaking, her skin was stone cold. It was her reaction, I didn't know if it was.... me or what! She expressed no nascent sexual interest in me whatsoever, in fact she seemed to disappear into a little world of her own, and the door was slammed in my face. What I can't handle Mick, is that I actually got blown out, and that's never happened to me before. If you'd placed a bet on anything happening between me and her, you'd have got pretty short odds on that bet.'

'And that's unusual Rod, getting blown out,' asked Mick.

'For me Mick, yes that is very unusual, it's never happened to me before, ever... what's happened with Sinead and me has shaken my confidence, you know,' replied Rod.

'Your pride I think.'

'Maybe.'

Mick shrugged. 'Ah well,' he said, 'don't worry, John gets knocked back like that all the time.' He laughed.

Rod looked at Mick sternly. 'And why doesn't that surprise me Mick,' he said, waving away his feeble attempt at humour. 'Mick I've told you, this is not funny, and I'm serious.'

Mick held up a hand. 'Sorry Rod, go on.'

'As I said Mick, it's unusual for me to be rejected by a woman, that has never happened before. As you know I've been out with enough women to know the outcome of a kiss. Our lips touched, but she never returned the kiss, if you know what I mean, she never reciprocated my interest, it was like kissing my Auntie Violet,' Rod wiped his lips with the back of his hand at the thought. 'Now I know the meaning of the old Irish saying, kissing the blarney stone. In fact it was like kissing marble, so cold...' he paused, 'so what does that mean?'.... Maybe you're losing your touch,' interrupted Mick.

Rod frowned. 'Are you questioning my ability to chat up a bird?'

'Wouldn't dream of it.'

'Good... I haven't let a woman slip through my fingers since my art teacher Linda Ferris in my fourth year at school. And that was only because she moved to Canada even before I had a chance to snog her…. Hang on a minute though, you could be right, d'you think it's me, that I'm losing my touch?'

'Of course you're not losing your touch lad, I was just joking,' replied Mick. 'You get women looking at you all the time…. he paused and shook his head. 'But Rod, I just think Sinead is getting to you. Look at it this way, don't take her rejection so bad, there's probably a perfectly good reason for her acting the way she did.'

'Such as?'

'You're vain, self-absorbed and not particularly intelligent…' 'What!' interrupted Rod angrily. 'Not particularly intelligent,' he repeated, 'for Christ sake Mick, I want to a private school you know…' 'There you are, you said it private school, a dog might be born in a stable, but that doesn't make it a horse Rod,' interrupted Mick… that want straight over Rod's head, he ignored it. 'What about private schools?' interrupted Rod. 'That's the key Rod no girls mate,' interrupted Mick.

Rod closed his eyes. 'Crap, crap, crap, I had a woman teacher, what the fuck has that got to do with anything?'

Mick held up his hands. 'Wow, calm down Rod. I don't really know. Just you know maybe…' 'And your point is Mick?'

'I'm just saying, girls Rod.'

'What *are* you getting at?' Rod stared at him.

'That was a woman Rod, I'm talking about girls, you never learnt about girls, and you're not girl intellectual.'

Bollocks, he's right, but this is not about me, Rod thought, he shrugged. 'I might agree with what you suggested

Mick, but, this wasn't about me, it's the way Sinead reacted.'

'Right, well don't forget she's Catholic.'

Rod shook his head in disagreement 'Na... naaaa... Mick that's not it.'

'Maybe.... maybe she's worried that what you want is just a "thing" to you, a passing affair. Also maybe she's a bit old-fashioned and doesn't want you to think she's easy.'

Rod looked confused 'what...firstly it's not just a "thing" I want as you put it, and secondly, as for old-fashioned, that's the last thing she is, maybe it's you that's old-fashioned Mick.'

'Cheers mate.... maybe it's women's problems then.'

'No it's definitely not that, I never even got in the front bloody door. It's so bloody obvious that I fancy her, so what's her problem.'

'Well... maybe... it... is... because of you, as you said being so obvious. Perhaps the thought of you and her getting together frightens her. Perhaps she's not ready or perhaps... maybe... she doesn't think you're the one for her.'

Rod looked baffled. 'What you're saying is that she doesn't like me, or she's too good for me?'

'No!'

Rod looked at Mick questioningly. 'You are, you're saying she's too good for me.'

'I'm not...' Mick shrugged, 'I don't know, but don't take what I'm about to say the wrong way Rod, and I know this might hurt your large ego a little, but have you ever thought that maybe… just maybe Sinead doesn't fancy you, or perhaps it's just not meant to be.'

Rod twisted round in the sand and looked sharply at Mick. 'What!' he said, shaking his head. 'That's not possible, of course she likes me, I'm a muffin magnet Mick, how could she not like me, what's wrong with me?'

'Maybe, as I said, you're not her type. She's an intelligent, beautiful young lady you know,' he paused, 'have you ever been out with an intelligent woman?'

Rod frowned at Mick. 'I'm not sure I follow you; I've been out with beautiful women. 'He paused.

Mick shrugged and shook his head. 'Rod, I think you know what I mean.'

'Are you suggesting Mick, that I haven't been out with an intell…'he paused again, *come to think of it, Mick was right, although life had thrown plenty of women in his direction, none had been of great complexity. He's right; he hadn't ever been out with an intelligent woman. Their brains weren't his main priority at the time. Give this question a wide berth Rod, this argument was going nowhere.* 'Anyway Mick, let's not get away from the issue… What was the issue?' he asked, scratching his head.

'We were discussing Sinead's type.'

'Right… I know… I am… I know I'm her type; I saw it in her eyes.'

'So now you've started to look into women's eyes, that's a change for you Rod, whatever happened to your routine habits?'

Rod looked puzzled. 'What routine habits Mick?'

'Like, looking from the floor up, and stopping at their breasts.'

'Ha…ha…very funny Mick.' *He had to admit that he had an uncontrollable urge for women, all women to him were a challenge, his objectives being clearly defined, get whatever you could. But he must admit that it did leave him without a vocabulary to deal with women, only as a lover, shagging was easy talking was pointless.* 'I've told you Mick; I don't look at Sinead like that, she's different. But, I think she has a problem in trusting me.'

'Noooooo, you don't say,' Mick answered sarcastically.

'Sarcasm is the lowest form of wit, d'you know that Mick?' Rod said and continued. 'But then I thought she doesn't know me, so I'm sure the fear she was showing wasn't coming from me. So what can I do?'

Mick scratched the back of his neck. 'Well it is said that the eyes are the windows to the soul, so, maybe you did see something in her eyes.'

'Are you and John in cahoots Mick?'

'No… why!'

Rod looked suspiciously at Mick, tilting his head to one side. 'You're sure?'

'Yes, of course I'm sure,' Mick snapped, 'why?'

'What you said about Sinead's eyes, John said something to me about women's eyes, that it's all in their eyes. Anyway, what you said about the eyes: I did see something in Sinead's.'

'Maybe you did, but I shouldn't read too much into them, Rod.'

'Maybe…' Rod paused… 'John said that if you think anything of a woman you must work at it. I've tried Mick, and I just can't seem to get close to her, the closer I get, the further she seems to pull away from me,' he shook his head, 'there's something definitely disturbing her.'

'Right,' said Mick, 'so you're taking advice from John about women now, are you? I imagine that that must have been a very short conversation then, since everything John knows about women you could write on the back of a postage stamp.'

Rod frowned. 'I don't know about that, but for the first time in his life he did seem to know what he was talking about Mick.' 'Hang on Rod; we are talking about John here, you know. He knows as much about women as Prince Phillip knows about changing the tyre on a Ford Fiesta, or the Queen, bless her soul, shopping at Tesco's.'

A faint smile appeared on Rod's face. 'Does she, I didn't know that Mick.'

Mick looked puzzled. 'Does she what?'

'The Queen shop at Tesco's.'

Mick shrugged his shoulders, 'Joke Rod, joke, anyway,' he said, 'you like her, right?'

'Who,' asked Rod, 'the Queen?'

Mick raised his eyebrows, giving Rod a stern expression. 'Rod, now you're trying to bloody wind me up,' he said. 'Not the bloody Queen, Sinead.'

Rod sighed, a weak smile fell from his lips again as he looked at Mick. 'Of course I like her, it's hard not to like her, you know it is. I've never met anybody like her before, and I never felt like this before about anybody else, that's why I didn't take it any further...' he paused... 'You're good with women, and women do tend to confide stuff with their female friends, don't they?'

Mick shrugged his shoulders. 'I'm not with you, so what's your point Rod?' he asked.

'Well, look at it this way Mick; at the moment all I have is you, the male, but no female. I need somebody to talk to Sinead, and all I seem to be doing at the moment is batting bollocks. I'm sure she's hiding something; she strikes me as being deeply unhappy. I'm worried about her Mick.'

Mick looked at Rod sternly, waving his hand. 'Nothing doing Rod,' he said, 'I don't pry into other people's business, that's definitely not me, if that's what you're thinking.'

'But Mick...' Mick held up his hands again. 'No buts Rod, I can't do it.... and it's not your problem.'

'That's a really bad attitude, Mike.'

'Maybe, but it's not an attitude at all Rod, it's a fact.'

'Ok, as you say, maybe it isn't my problem Mick, but I'm worried about her.'

Mick saw the concern in Rod's face. 'Hang on here Rod,' he said. 'We seem to have a bit of a breakthrough here. Did I hear you say you're worried about somebody else and not yourself for once?'

'I know,' said Rod, 'go on say it, that's a first.'

'I'm not saying a thing; but, it comes to us all Rod. Ok... ok... Let's say Sinead is hiding something, what's that got to do with you?'

Rod shrugged his shoulders. 'I don't know, but I just can't help it Mick, I have a soft spot for her and I'm going to get Sinead if it's the last thing I do.'

'Don't you go getting ideas young Rod,' Mick said, reaching forward to scoop up a handful of smooth sand and let it run through his fingers. 'As long as it's the soft spot in your heart Rod, and not the hard bloody spot in your trousers. Remember your past insecurities with women are so obvious. What about all your other girlfriends, you know like,' Mick held out his hands and tapped his finger, 'A for Abigail, B for Bonny, C for Camilla, D for Denise, E for Erica, shall I go on? Oh! and yer and F for Fanny, and you've got all the way up to your latest, M for Michelle, I thought you were going through the alphabet.'

Rod gave a wan smile. 'Thanks a lot, Mick, give me a break.'

'Anytime.'

Rod waved a contrite hand. 'Those ladies are long gone Mick. Well and truly in the past. Sinead is different – she could cure me.'

'Maybe, so why is Sinead any different from all the others?'

Rod stopped pacing. He looked Mick straight in the eyes, 'because I love Sinead, Mick. I'm in love with her, and I've never loved another women in my life, except my mum of course.'

Mick raised his hand, looking at him like he'd just passed wind. 'Hold it right their Rod.'

Rod stared at him blankly. 'What!'

'You know exactly what! The L word, you just said it.' He waved his finger at him. 'You did. You did. You know you did, don't even attempt to make out that you didn't.'

'I'm not.'

Mick cocked his head to one side and his look turned to one of suspicion. 'You're not?'

'No I'm not, I said it, and I meant it. I love Sinead.

I knew it the very first time I set eyes on her. I'm telling you I've never felt this way before about any other woman.'

Mick's mouth gaped; he was struck dumb for a few seconds. 'Hang on,' he said, wiggling his finger in his ear. 'Let me get this straight, you say you love her. My God, I never thought I would hear you say that you loved someone apart from yourself. D'you know what love is Rod?' he asked.

Rod looked surprised at Mike's question, but gave it some thought anyway. 'Of course, I know about love, and I know I love her.'

'How do you know that then?'

'She's the girl, seriously beautiful. The superbabe. She's the one I've been looking for all my life, ever since I met her at her house, I've known I was in love with her, she's all I've thought about since. I want to be near her all the time, I know this might sound a little strange,' he paused, 'I just want to be near her, she makes me feel comfortable, she make my skin tingle, she's definitely the one for me, I know it.'

'So you love Sinead? Is that what you're trying to tell me?' Is that just in a physical way?'

'Certainly not, this is not about sex Mick, the physical thing's not important to me any more, and certainly not with Sinead. Love is much more than just sex Mick.'

'You sure?'

'Of course I'm sure Mick; she has given me a different perspective on life.'

'Like what?' asked Mick.

'I'm holding out for someone I really fancy and that's her. I want something more…you know…commitment…someone to love… And as I've said not just in the physical sense.'

'D'you want to know what I think?'

'Of course I do Mick, but for God's sake be positive.'

'It's about your revelation that concerns me.'

'Well, what about it?'

'Don't take this the wrong way… but I think you feel humiliated…' 'Not at all, fuck off Mick,' Rod interrupted… 'Ok…ok, but just let me finish what I was going to say before you jump down my throat.'

'Ok.'

Mick continued. 'What I think is that you feel humiliated, because Sinead is the first person ever not to give you all her attention. So you're coming up with this hugely elaborate justification about love and how you feel about Sinead. I don't think it's your feeling for her, I think it's your brain, and your dick, and all your emotions are playing a game with you which you have never played before.'

Rod stared at Mick sternly. 'Profound Mick, but bollocks, since when did you become a psychiatrist?'

'Since Kathleen and Elizabeth were killed, it makes you look at the world and people very differently.'

Rod saw the hurt in Mick's eyes. 'Sorry... yes... you're right Mick. But, God no, I swear that's not the case...' 'Just,' interrupted Mick. Rod held up a hand. 'Ok...ok I know in the past I have been a little bit emotionally immature, I'd admit that, and scared shitless of ever entertaining the thought of committing myself to anybody...' 'What do you expect?' interrupted Mick. 'You're a bloke, and that's part of the job description for being a bloke...' 'But that's definitely all over, it's unquestionably not the case now Mick,' interrupted Rod.'

'If that's not the case then Rod, then it's the first time you have had a rational thought about a woman and your emotions.' Mick rolled his eyes. 'Do you respect her?'

'Of course I do. I'm telling you Sinead means everything to me.'

'Ok but if you... if anything happens and you treat her badly, I'll kill you myself!'

'I've never treated a woman badly in my life Mike. In fact it's them that have treated me badly.'

'Right that what they all say.'

'Its true Mick, you know it's true.'

'Just you...tread carefully mate. This is serious, she isn't a joke!'

'I know... I know!'

'Ok...let's move on then. So we've established the fact that you love her, and respect her, so, have you told her?'

'Jesus… no… not yet,' Rod answered, pointing a finger at Mick, 'and I don't want you telling her, or anybody else, especially the lads, it needs to come from me, understand?'

Mick held up both his hands. 'Of course,' he said, nodding his head, 'but as much as I would like to shout it from the rooftops,. I promise not a bloody word from me.'

'Good, as long as we have got that straight, I'm telling you Mick she's exactly who and what I've wanted all my life.'

'All right Rod, but I needed to make sure Sinead's not going to be another one of your trophy women.' Mick wagged a finger back at Rod. 'You mess with Sinead, and I'm warning you Rod you will have me to answer to. You can fool some of the people some of the time…' 'But not all of the time,' Rod interrupted, raising his hands. 'I know…I know… philosophical Mick, very philosophical, but the fact is, I'm not trying to fool anybody,' snapped Rod, 'but, a fair warning Mick, I intend to treat her with the highest respect, I've told you I love her.'

'Good for you Rod, I hope at last you are really learning about what makes young ladies tick. Anyway, let's get back to talking with Sinead, what about Kerrie?' asked Mick.

'What about Kerrie?'

'Well she is her sister for Christ sake,' replied Mick, 'she'll know if there's anything wrong with Sinead surely, can't she have a word with Sinead for you?'

'Probably,' Rod paused. 'Yes, but if Kerrie did know anything, I don't think she'll tell me. But I think Sinead will tell you Mick, you get on so well with both the girls.'

'That's because I don't want anything from them Rod,' Mick paused. 'God, you're asking me to ask her... probably some very personal things, hang on.... are you suggesting I'm a bit of a woman?' he started to laugh, but stopped when he looked at Rod's expression. 'As I said it's not just about the kiss Mick, there's something else going on, I know there is.' Rod paused, running his fingers through his hair. He continued, 'She's a beautiful young woman Mick, a bloody doctor at that, she's single, and got nothing in the world to hold her back.'

'So if it's not just about the kiss, what are you getting at?' asked Mick.

Rod tilted his head looking puzzled. 'So why is she so standoffish,' he shook his head and deep furrows appeared in his forehead. 'I don't know why, but I have a gut feeling, that... that... there's something definitely wrong with Sinead. I'm sure it has got to have something to do with her past, but I just can't put my finger on it. There's some kind of case study there that Freud would have killed for Mick... I'm telling you Mick there's no other possible explanation.'

'Maybe, maybe not, Rod, but rightly or wrongly, we all have skeletons tucked away.'

'What, skeletons like Kathleen and Elizabeth?' asked Rod.

Mick frowned at the thought. 'Sure,' he agreed, thinking how he'd suffered holding in the torment of their deaths, but now it was out he must agree with Rod, he felt better. It was easier to cope with; a trouble shared is a troubled halved. He nodded his head. 'I know Rod, since I've spoke about Kathleen and Elizabeth's death it's helped me to come to terms with my loss. But for some people Rod… for whatever reason they won't let anybody in…' 'No…no…' interrupted Rod, 'Sinead's got to, there is something that needs to be brought out into the open.' He paused and bit his lower lip. 'This is just a guess but I think something bad has happened to her a long time ago,' he shook his head. He shrugged his shoulders. 'I don't know what, but I'd give my right arm to know…' He paused and looked eye to eye with Mick. 'And it would be nice if she could share it with somebody… she needs a friend… somebody, as you said, who doesn't want anything from her. Somebody who can talk to her about whatever's happened, and she's not ready to confide in me, that's for sure, she probably thinks that I'm only after one thing, so that rules me out. So that leaves only you Mick, I couldn't ask Monkey man, Paul, or John now could I?'

Mick shook his head. 'You're probably right. But for God's sake Rod, I'm not any good at that kind of thing.'

'Yes you are Mick, there's one thing that you're bloody good at…' 'What's that?' interrupted Mick.

'You're very positive.'

'How's that.'

'Look how you handled…' Rod paused; he wasn't sure whether he should continue.

'What?' asked Mick. He was intrigued with Rod's questions.

'You know,' replied Rod.

'For Christ sake Rod get it out, or we are going to sit here all day.'

'Your emotional disorder, and how you've dealt with it, when you wife and daughter were sadly killed…' He paused. ' I know Sinead trusts you, and you are looking out for her welfare, she needs our help. See if you can spend some time with her. Do it for me, please Mick, do it for me. You know there's nobody else in this world I could ask, or trust.'

They stared at each other for a few minutes. 'If you won't help me make this step in the right direction, then you're…. you're…. a wanker Mick.'

'You don't have to make such a big deal out of it.'

'Mick, this is the rest of my life here and you're the one making a big deal out of it. All I'm asking is for a little help, I want Sinead to be safe, mate.'

'Ok! Ok…' said Mick, 'get my arm from up my back.' He pointed a finger at Rod. 'But I'm telling you this now, don't you hurt that young lady, I'm doing this for Sinead, not for you. And how do you suggest I approach this subject? We'll need to get her clear of the lads. What d'you have in mind…?' 'I know, take her shopping,' interrupted Rod, 'she loves shopping, and shopping is the key to a woman's heart. They say shopping is the next best thing to sex.'

'Excuse me?'

'Shopping, Mick, it will give you a chance to get her on your own ground, then you can have a chat with her.'

'Give us a break Rod, I haven't been shopping with a woman since my Kathleen and Elizabeth died. Good God I haven't got a bloody clue about shopping…' 'You don't have to Mick,' interrupted Rod. 'She'll do it all for you, as I said, she loves shopping. Just follow her around, take her out to dinner, something like that...' 'Ok... right... just follow her around, you say,' Mick nodded his head, unsure. 'Ok, I think I can do that. Hang on, you said Sinead's not coming out of her room until the deed is done...' 'Take her breakfast up to her room Mick,' interrupted Rod.

'What! To her room, she isn't going to like that...' 'Mick, I'm telling you Sinead likes you, I know, you can talk to her, believe me.'

Mick gave him the smile of a wise old man who'd been through it all. 'God, I hope you're right Rod; I guess I can do that... ok... let's go get some breakfast.' Smiling, Mick clapped a hand around his shoulders in a jovial manner as they made their way back to the hotel. 'It's very refreshing to see your feminine side Rod.'

'Right,' replied Rod. 'But don't get carried away Mick,' pushing his arm off his shoulder.

★ ★ ★

Mick tapped lightly on Sinead's door.

'Hello, who is it?' came from inside.

'It's Mick, Sinead, I've brought your breakfast to your room,' he said, holding up the breakfast tray so she could see it through the spy hole.

'What's all this in aid of?' she said as she opened the door.

Mick entered and stood still. His first thoughts were, Wow. His mouth fell open for a few seconds as he failed to comprehend what he saw standing in front of him. He looked back at the door. 'Is this the right room?'

'Right,' she smiled, fluffing up her hair. 'What do you think, do you like the change?'

'God, do I like the change, does the Pope pray Sinead?' replied Mick. 'Goes without saying Sinead, beautiful, absolutely beautiful.'

She smiled and blushed at Mick's sweet talk.

'Anyway,' Rod said you weren't coming down for breakfast, so here it is,' he said. 'Service with a smile.' He held the tray out in front of him. 'I hope you didn't mind me bringing it up for you.'

'Shut the door Mick,' Sinead said quickly. 'No, that's very sweet of you Mick, thanks.'

'My pleasure,' said Mick, kicking the door shut with the back of his foot.

'My God,' Mick muttered moving forward. Rod was right she looked absolutely beautiful. 'Where do you want this?' he held up the tray.

'Oh… on the veranda would be nice,' she said, pointing to the table. 'Where's yours?'

'Had it,' said Mick standing awkwardly.

'What's all this in aid of then,' Sinead asked again as she sat down.

'Rod said you wasn't coming out of you room until the deed was done.'

Sinead shivered at his question, her expression taking a turn for the worse. 'That's right.'

Rod was right, there was something in her expression that said this wasn't the time to talk. He clapped his hands together and smiled. 'Ok, Sinead, I was wondering if you'd like to go shopping today.'

She looked at him suspiciously. 'Why?'

'I need to buy some stuff, and I think they need a woman's point of view.'

Her expression never changed.

Deep furrows appeared in Mick's forehead. *You've got to do better than that Mick, play to her sensitive side.* 'And not being blessed with having a woman myself I thought you might be just the person, and I know you are so good at shopping, and maybe we could look out for something for you. For the deed, if you know what I mean, so we can help each other, what do you say?' He smiled.

She smiled faintly. 'But I don't want to see the others until you know when Mick.'

'That's why I brought your breakfast up. Don't worry about the others, they are going out. Is it a date then?'

Sinead winked, 'Ok Mick it's a date then, but remember nobody else.'

Mick smiled. 'I promise,' he said, holding his hand on his heart. 'So I'll pick you up after breakfast, we can go out the back way just in case.' He turned to leave.

'Oh, Mick,' she said. 'Thanks for the breakfast, very sweet of you.'

'No problem, thirty minutes, I'll pick you up,' he said.

'Make it forty-five,' she said as he closed the door behind him. He leant against the door and smiled. 'You smooth old devil, you haven't lost your touch,' he murmured to himself as he whistled, making his way back to the elevator.

Chapter Fourteen
'Shopping Mick?'

Mick wiped the sweat from his forehead with the back of his arm. 'Long day, huh?' he said, holding up the shopping bags. 'Let's eat, my treat. The Lobster Pot has some excellent sea food, what do you say?'

'Fine,' Sinead replied, falling into step.

'How are things going with Rod?'

She felt her fingers tingle. 'What about Rod?'

Mick shrugged his shoulders. 'You and Rod,' he commented, looking out for the restaurant. 'You know what I mean, Sinead.'

Sinead looked at Mick sternly. 'Oh, and what about Rod and me then,' she said uneasy, knowing where this conversation might be going.

'I thought you might tell me,' Mick stopped. 'Wait… here we are. Right, in here,' he directed her, pushing open the door to the restaurant with his backside.

'*Hola,*' said Mick to the man behind the counter, grabbing an empty table overlooking the beach and dumping the shopping bags in the corner as they sat down. It was late afternoon, but the place was still jammed packed. Sea air wafted through the open wicker windows. He shifted, stretching out his legs. 'They've got all kinds of sea food here,' he said, handing her the menu. 'If you're up for it, that is?'

'Sure, why not, I'm game.'

'Great, is there anything you don't like on the menu?'

Sinead scanned the menu. 'No, it all looks fine to me, I'll leave the choice up to you.'

Mick slid out from the table. 'Drink?'

'Just water, please.'

'Coming up.' Mick walked to the counter and placed the order. Sinead watched the way Mick joked with the man behind the counter. The way he hooked his sunglasses in the pocket of his shirt, stretching his strikingly toned and tanned arms out for the drinks. The cheeky smile on his face as he walked back to the table. She pushed a hand through her hair. 'What were you laughing at? she asked.

Mick laughed again, placing the jug of ice-cold water and two glasses on the table, looking back towards the counter. 'The man behind the counter said what a lucky man I was to have such a beautiful woman.'

'What did you say Mick?'

Sinead grinned. 'In my dreams, I told him, only in my dreams.' Although he sensed that it was an effort for her she rubbed her hand up and down his arm. 'You are a good man Mick, and if you were younger maybe then it wouldn't be in your dreams.'

'Be off with you Sinead, you're teasing me,' he said, tapping away her hand, 'but thank you for that nice thought anyway.' Mick sat. He needed to make a start if he was going to find anything out at all. Pouring out two glasses of cold water, he pushed one towards her. He sipped the cold refreshing water and laid the glass back on the table. 'Rod said that you kissed him?'

'What,' Sinead snapped. 'I never kissed him at all, let's get one thing straight here Mick, he kissed me. I didn't ask him to kiss me.'

'Ok… ok…said Mick softly, 'you're a grown woman, nothing wrong in that at all. So he kissed you.'

'So, he kissed me,' she snapped again, taking in a deep breath. 'What did he say about me then?' she asked with a disdainful look on her face.

'Wow,' said Mick holding up a hand. 'He hasn't said a word about you at all. Only that he's concerned about you.'

'Why would he be concerned about me?'

'He said that when you both kissed…' he paused, hoping she wasn't going to take what he was about to say the wrong way… 'He felt that you were holding something back.'

'He wanted sex Mick.'

Understandable, 'Look at you, what young man wouldn't want…you know what…' 'Sex Mick, sex, that's what he wanted,' interrupted Sinead… 'But,' Mick interrupted, shaking his head. 'Rod seemed to think that that wasn't the problem.'

There was a long silence, which seemed to grow increasingly intense as Sinead began to blink faster and faster, her breathing becoming heavy and irregular. 'He should mind his own business Mick, and he doesn't need to be concerned about me, he doesn't know me.'

Mick leaned forward and spoke very gently. 'He would like to know you better Sinead. I know you can trust Rod, he's a good lad, and very protective. If there was something wrong and I'm not saying that there is, but maybe...' he tried to tread softly, 'just maybe, he could help you.'

'You tell him from me Mick that I don't need his help or want to know him, thank you.'

'Hey Sinead, we're friends aren't we? Don't shoot the messenger. I think he's only trying to be your friend,' he smiled at her, 'I just think he wants to get to know you better. Why can't you just approach him?'

Sinead half-heartedly smiled for him. 'Sorry Mick,' she said softly, 'but I know it's not you. Just tell him, I don't need any friends at the moment, especially men friends.'

Mick smiled, his head cocked sympathetically to one side. 'Sinead... is it Rod that worries you... or is it men in general?'

Sinead jabbed her forefinger at him. 'Look Mick, which part of I don't need friends, didn't you understand?' she said through her teeth. 'I'm not interested in him or anybody at the moment, and you can tell Rod that I don't like being handled.'

Mick shook his head, affirming her request. 'Ok...ok... if that's what you want. I'll... I'll... tell him,' he said. 'But I must confess Sinead, that I don't blame him, you are such a beautiful young woman, that you are. What man wouldn't want to know you better?'

Sinead didn't respond as she looked down into her lap.

Mick watched Sinead's face, trying to scan her facial expression. He was starting to get a nasty feeling in the pit of his stomach that Rod was right; there definitely was something amiss here. 'I'm sorry to have to say this

Sinead...' Sinead looked up, slowly fixing her eyes straight into his. 'Well don't say it then Mick,' she said slowly and direct... 'I must,' interrupted Mick.

'Why?' she looked back into her lap.

It was killing Mick not to get to the point and just to keep quiet, but he didn't know what else to do. He felt a lump in his throat. 'Because I'm sensing there's something wrong here. Well... it's totally up to you, but... if you do want to talk about whatever's happened, I'm an excellent listener,' he reached across the table, and gently lifted her chin with his finger. 'And I have a very sympathetic ear.'

She slumped a little, sipping her water and glanced out to sea, pushing a strand of hair away from her face. She didn't answer.

Mick stared at Sinead's chest rising and falling with deep, heavy lungfuls of air. 'Ok, you don't have to talk to me,' he said, as he took another Tiger prawn from the plate. 'But,' he instinctively sucked in air as he popped the prawn into his mouth. 'I think maybe it would be good for you if you talked to somebody about whatever happened.' He wanted to press her further, but thought better of it. If she didn't want to talk about what happened, then he wouldn't press her; he didn't, waiting for her to take the initiative.

Sinead shook her head, throwing her hair back and looked back towards Mick, but she was seeing past him, looking at the wall, remembering that terrible night so long ago, going back with great clarity, breathing. In... out...in... out. Slowly swallowing to ease the tightness in her throat. She sucked in her cheeks; this conversation with Mick had unsettled her. Partly because he'd made her question things that she never wanted to revisit. Unlocking a pile of dormant terrors, he'd shaken them awake in her head when she wanted the whole issue to stay in the back of her mind. Was she ready to reveal her feelings to a mere stranger? Maybe… just maybe Mick *was* the right person. She was sure Da would have approved. Finally, and very slowly, she raised her head back up to look at him. Her eyes were full of tears, quivering, hovering and waiting to fall. Eventually she spoke. 'I know,' she drew in deep breaths again…'No…no,' said Mick, holding up his hands, shaking them from side to side. 'If you don't want to talk about whatever…' 'No,' interrupted Sinead… 'No…. it's not that, it's more like I don't want to think about what happened.'

Like a flower in spring Mick knew she was ready to open up. 'What happened? I mean that's only if you want to talk about whatever happened, you don't have to say a word, if you don't want to,' he pointed out again.

'I know… but I do want to tell you Mick.' She shrugged as they both took long drinks from their glasses of cold water.

'I think we are going to need something stronger than this,' Sinead said as she lowered her glass to the table.

Mick held out his hand. 'Hold it there,' as he jumped up from the table, rushed to the bar and was back within seconds placing two glasses of brandy and a bottle on the table. 'Ok, go on, in your own time,' he said as he sat down.

'Physically, I know it's all over now Mick, it happened a long time ago.' She paused, pressed her lips together as if trying not to go on and lifted her hands, dropping them back into her lap. 'I still don't understand, how or why I became the victim,' she paused and drew in another deep breath.

Mick had a feeling he was preparing himself for something that might easily have been the worst thing he'd ever heard since Elizabeth and Kathleen's death.

Sinead blew the air from her cheeks. 'I'd came from a solid, steady family background, as functional as any family could manage to be, there was love and happiness in our house. I was bright, well educated, just getting my independence, starting college, a free lively spirit. Of course there had been some boys in my life.'

Mick nodded his head in agreement.

'But nothing really serious, only what happened to a normal sixteen-year-old girl, healthy… happy… relationships.' She trembled as she spoke. Pausing, she swallowed her shot of brandy in one gulp, and coughed.

Mick watched her; the inner turmoil showed clearly in her eyes. He nodded, his eyes not losing their concentration on Sinead's face. 'When you're ready,' he encouraged her softly, patting her arm. Now she'd started, he wanted to know everything, everything he could possibly know about all that had gone on. He wanted to be in touch with what had really happened in her life. To try and understand just how she was feeling, he wanted to explore her innermost feelings.

With a small shrug, she placed the glass back on the table.

Mick topped up her glass.

She worked hard to keep the tears from flowing, turning her head away. The background sounds of the restaurant became a soft mumble to Mick's ears as Sinead spoke. 'I was sixteen,' tears showing in the corners of her eyes, 'he'd baby-sat many times before, for Ma and Da,' she inclined her head as the tears trickled down the side of her cheeks. She spoke slowly as if they were in a time warp. 'He said he was looking out for my interests Mick,' her voice was almost inaudible.

Mick leant forward, wanting, but in some very sad way not wanting, to miss a word.

'I didn't know that anything was going to happen, I trusted him Mick. Whenever I pleased him he gave me little treats. God it disgusts me to think how easily I was manipulated by him.' She gave an involuntary shudder. 'He was baby-sitting for my baby sisters Caitlin and Una; Kerrie had gone out with Ma and Da, college intake or something... it was terrifying.'

Mick was trying to gauge how far he could go. Finally on impulse, he leaned further forward and said 'Go on.' He wished she'd hurry up because he wanted to know everything as fast as possible: there were questions he couldn't wait to ask, but he didn't risk interrupting her. His face registered shock, he never thought that his heart could accelerate that fast again, but it did. 'What happened?' he nodded, bracing himself for the worst. His question hung in the air for a while, before Sinead took a long sigh, drying her face with a napkin. She could barely get the words out, gazing at him across the table, eye to eye. There was an immediate wobble to her voice... 'He.... he... raped me.' She shook her head to get a grip. 'Mick... he... raped me, and there I was, this sixteen-year-old, abused, raped, and trapped.'

This unforeseen piece of news had thrown him completely off balance. He looked at his watch as if this was an event he needed to register like he did when J.F.K. was assassinated, when Elizabeth and Kathleen were killed, and when Princess Diana was killed in her horrendous car accident. Yes, this was as important as any of those dates, he was horrified, shocked beyond all measure. For a few moments he looked immeasurably concerned, but his expression was extremely gentle, he'd lost his power of speech. It was as if the shock of what she'd just said caused his vocal cords to seize up. Then he managed to clear his throat, and find a few words. 'Who...who... did this to you Sinead?' he asked softly.

'It...it... was,' she breathed deeply; this was much harder than she had envisaged, emotions forcing her to pause. She lifted her glass, drank, and breathed deeply, steadying herself, not wanting to ever get the words out, but she willed her eyes to meet Mick's in a bravely prolonged gaze. Mick looked incalculably apprehensive. His expression was gentle. .... 'Uncle... it was Uncle Tom,' she whispered.

Mick's eyes burned with shock. He tossed his head back and necked his brandy down in one gulp. The drink burned down through his throat. 'Oh, my God Sinead, I'm so... so... sorry.' Mick's voice was softened in sympathy, he sat back jamming his hands in his pocket, feeling absolutely useless, hanging his head in disbelief for a few seconds. He leant forward again, putting his hand softly on her arm. 'Everything's going to be all right; it's going to be fine. He's not here Sinead. He can't hurt you anymore I won't let him.' He seemed to want to say more but restrained himself; with a horrified face he leaned further forward and held her hands, kissing them softly.

The pressure in her chest was making her head light, she sipped her brandy, forcing herself to think; she looked across at Mick, fear in her eyes. 'Can't he? He's here,' she snapped, thumping her heart, 'and, in here,' tapping her head, 'and mentally the lasting pain that rape causes a person. He's never gone away, or stopped hurting me. He thought of no one but himself, and his pleasure became my Achilles heel. I hate him so much Mick, I wish he was dead.' She rubbed her fingers on her temples, trying to get him out of her head.

Mick could tell she was reliving the past. The bastard was an animal. He felt sickened at the picture conjured up by his overactive brain, he could visualise her pain graphically. He didn't like the look on her face; it was grim, so set, her eyes glassy and pale, like someone about to go to war. He could see in her eyes that a lot of damage had been done to her; he couldn't proceed with anything other than infinite care until her permission was granted for him to continue. He couldn't just sit there and say nothing though, she was in pain. He needed to reach out to her verbally. 'Don't do that Sinead,' he said taking a hold of her hands. 'Be angry with him. Not at yourself, it's not your fault.'

She didn't bother to look at him. Staring into space. 'I am …I am… angry with him; I wanted to kill him, for what he did to me. God I've never been able to talk about it to anybody. I never thought I could.'

Mick gave Sinead a questioning look. 'Do you want to tell me the rest?'

She stared at him her eyes narrowed, tears rolled down her cheeks. 'I'm not sure.'

'Take your time,' said Mick, pulling a handkerchief from his pocket and handing it to her. He couldn't stand to see her cry; he couldn't stand to see her sitting there, trembling, her face so sallow. 'You don't have to tell me...' She looked him straight in the eyes. He could see the pain in her eyes, deep. The pain had been set in there for a long time... She interrupted him, 'Please Mick,' I have things I need to say.'

'Go on,' said Mick softly.

She spoke in a quiet tone, finding it difficult to get it out. 'Uncle...Uncle Tom put Caitlin and Una to bed and asked if I wanted to help him, I tucked them into bed. I read to them both, their usual story and when they both fell asleep I crept out of their room.' Her voice trembled. 'Uncle Tom stood on the landing and asked me where I slept, and asked if he could see my bedroom.' She felt her heart beating faster as she recalled the scene. 'I couldn't see any problem with that so I showed him my room and when we were in my bedroom, he locked the door; he threw me on the bed, he was like a wild animal. His heavy body laid on me, his hands all over my body,' she fisted her hands in her hair, tugging until the pain stiffened her spine. 'I wanted to scream, but he put his hand over my mouth, I couldn't breathe Mick, he had torn my dress right up the front,' she held her hands close to her chest gripping her dress as if it was happening again. 'I tried to push him away Mick,' she wiped the tears from her eyes, shook her head, 'but I couldn't. He tore my pants from my body. My body was crushed beneath his weight, he held me with one arm, his other hand moving between my legs and touching me, then he unzipped his pants, and I felt his thing against me. I cried for him to stop, but he just wouldn't stop, he hurt me Mick. Then he heard the front door open, and got up from my bed. I crawled under the covers, wrapping myself into a cocoon as he left the room. I heard Da's voice downstairs, and Ma was putting Kerrie to bed. I heard the front door close, and Da's footsteps on the stairs. He came into my room, switched on the light, and sat on the bed. I shivered. Da felt my body shaking through the bed covers.'

'Sinead, my princess, what's up, are you ill?' Da said as he pulled back the covers, I just fell into his arms and wept.'

Mick face was drained of blood. 'My God,' he said, his jaw tightened, his body shocked. 'I'd have killed him there and then, Sinead.' He reached out, closing his hands over hers, gripping her hands tighter in a sympathetic squeeze; he doubted that she was aware that he had tears in his eyes. 'What did Sean say?' Mick looked to the side and saw people looking wide-eyed at Sinead. 'Seen enough?' shouted Mick in anger, as they returned to their meal. 'Go on,' Mick whispered softly, tapping her hands.

She sobbed and blew into the handkerchief. 'Da carried me downstairs, and we sat on the sofa in the lounge, he rocked me back and forth for comfort. Tears streamed from Da's eyes, he mumbled to himself as he held me, and all I heard Mick was, 'the bastard has raped my princess.'

For a father it must have been the worst feeling in the world, what could he do? Thought Mick.

'Ma came downstairs, and into the lounge, Da stood up, and handed me over to Ma, all he said was, 'Ma the bastard's raped our princess' as he left the house. I never knew to this day what Da had done, and we never talked about it again, Caitlin, Una and Kerrie were never told. She looked at him sternly. 'And Mick they are never to be told.'

Mick put his hand on his heart, 'If that's what you want Sinead, I promise nobody will ever hear it from me.'

She smiled faintly, seeing the sincerity in Mick's eyes. 'We never saw Uncle Tom ever again until now, I hate him Mick, I hate him.'

'I know...I know...' Mick clenched his hands on the table, his knuckles white under the pressure. It was hard for him to come to terms with what Sinead had told him. 'I'm so sorry you've had to go through it again Sinead.'

Sinead sobbed, she had lifted a little of her excess baggage, and placed it squarely onto Mick's shoulders. He moved round to her side of the table, he ground his teeth wishing he could say something to take away her pain, but there were no words of comfort for someone who had been raped. Mick moved his chair round to her side of the table. She sobbed and fell into Mick's arms, burying her head in his shoulder, sobbing harder and louder, as he pulled her tighter against him. She shed more tears. Mick stroked her hair for comfort as she buried her face into his chest, gripping his shirt with her hands. 'I tried to stop him,' she cried. 'I know... I know...' Mick said, rocking her gently for comfort.

'You must tell Rod, Sinead, he's not silly, I believe he knows there's something wrong, he's concerned about you, he's told me he's never met anybody like you.'

'I know Mick...I know Rod cares for me, I can see it in his eyes, and I need somebody like Rod for his strength, but that's part of it, I don't know how I'd begin to tell him Mick, I haven't got his strength,' she sobbed.

'Shush.... shush' Mick whispered into her ear. 'You speak to him in your own time. You'll know when the time is right Sinead,' he said, tapping her back gently. 'I promise you Rod will listen.'

'Thanks Mick,' she said, 'thanks for your strength, normally I would rely on Da.' Lightly she kissed him on the cheek. Mick felt the warm tears on his face as she nestled back into his shoulder. Her body trembled. Her warm tears soaked through his shirt, as Mick rocked her backwards and forwards as Sean did several years back.

Chapter Fifteen
Wise Old Man, Mick

Rod tried getting Mick's attention across the room without the others noticing. He nodded hard, and then he coughed.

'What's up?' John asked.

'Nothing,' replied Mick quickly. 'I think Rod wants a word with me, you get yourself another drink John,' he said, slapping John on the shoulder. 'I'll just have a word with him,' he said as he walked towards Rod.

'Well Mick, what's your verdict?' asked Rod.

Mick looked around holding his finger to his lips. 'Shush,' he whispered, ushering Rod into the foyer. 'Ok,' he said, slowly looking back at the foyer doors to make sure none of the lads were listening.

Rod tugged at his sleeve a worried expression on his face. 'Well?' he said again.

'Right, I did as you asked, went shopping, had dinner, had a word,' Mick nodded his head slowly a dark look crossed his face. 'Rod that's one very sad young lady,' he held up a warning hand.

'I knew it,' said Rod. 'I knew it…' 'Wait,' said Mick. 'You're going to have to be very patient here, no kicking off, and especially patient with her, if you and her want to move on.'

'Oh, my God, Mick. It's that bad then?'

'I'm afraid so,' replied Mick, 'she's going to need all the support you can possibly give her, remember what you said to me at the beach.'

'Yes.'

'Well, you're definitely going to have to pull out all your stops, and do what you said. This is nothing like you have ever had to deal with before.' Shaken yet again by what Sinead had told him, Mick explained to Rod what Sinead had told him.

Rod's face paled with anger. 'Well that seems to explain a lot of things, I knew it… I bloody knew it,' he said, clenching his fists and punching the wall. 'Shit,' he continued, pacing the foyer, 'I knew it… I fucking knew it… the dirty… bastard,' he pulled at the back of his neck, he had never before felt such an overwhelming protectiveness towards any one individual woman as he did for Sinead. He stopped and stood pointing a finger at Mick. 'I swear when this is all over Mick, mark my words, I'm going to kill the dirty bastard.'

'Hang on Rod,' Mick held up a hand. 'Knee jerk reaction son, that's just anger talking. Think lad, think, all that bottled up anger might help you feel better, but that wouldn't do you or Sinead any good at all. At least it's good to know what we're dealing with, isn't it?'

'Maybe,' replied Rod, sadness showing in his eyes. *What he had done to her, as if the rape had only just happened, then for Rod it had. Shaking his head, still unable to believe that somebody could do such a thing to such a beautiful young girl.*

Mick laid his hand softly on Rod's shoulder, his voice broke into his thoughts 'Rod, keep the anger inside but use it to your advantage, and let's get him back to the UK, and let him serve his time, son.'

'He deserves to die Mick.' Tears showed in the corner of Rod's eyes.

Mick held up a hand. 'I know he does Rod, and I felt exactly the same as you do now when I heard it for the first time lad. I love Sinead too, in a paternal kind of way, and I wish to God that I myself could kill him for her, but that's not going to help us at all, now is it?' Mick sat down, patting the sofa and encouraging Rod to sit.

Rod fell heavily into the sofa next to Mick. 'Killing him would be justice for what he did to Sinead though, Mick,' Rod buried his head in his hands, tears streaming down his cheeks at the very thought of what Sinead had gone through.

Mick placed a hand on his shoulders. 'I know lad... I know... but that would only bring us down to his level, and we don't want that do we?' he said softly. He bought himself and Rod a strong brandy, giving Rod five minutes to compose himself and come to terms to what he had told him. Rod gulped down the brandy hoping to numb the pain he felt. It didn't. 'Well...' he paused for a moment to think, 'I suppose you're right, but where do we go from here then?'

Mick turned sideways, looking straight at Rod and held up his hands. 'Rod... I.... don't know, but we must let it ride for the moment. I know that's going to be difficult for you, but Sinead is the most important thing here at the moment, and this conversation is to go no further than you or me as the only people who know are Sean, Cathleen, and now me and you, and of course the bastard...' 'But Mick,' interrupted Rod. Mick lifted the third finger of his hand and flexed it. 'No buts Rod,' he said, looking at him sternly, 'do you hear me, no further than here, I've promised Sinead...' 'My God Mick,' interrupted Rod, 'do you think I'm going to tell anybody else,' he wiped the tears with the back of his hand, 'but I only wish she had come and told me first.'

'Believe me Rod it was no easy task for Sinead to tell me, she blames herself for what happened.'

'For Christ sake Mick, it wasn't Sinead's fault.'

'I know it wasn't her fault Rod, I've told her that, and that's why we have got to help her through this. We are going to have to be strong for her, so that she can lean on us for support.'

'I know and I'm going to do whatever I can do for her.'

'Good lad, said Mick, tapping Rod lightly on the shoulder. 'I knew you would come up trumps lad; there's hope for Sinead if we stick together, our love for her will prevail, and maybe there will be hope for you and her.'

'I hope so Mick... I hope so. You are one hell of a wise old man, Mick.'

'Wise yes, but not so much of the old, young man.'

Rod smiled faintly. 'Hang on Mick, what about the bastard and the key? I've made plans for Sinead to go to *Les Mercedes* and get the key, we can't let her go anywhere near the bastard now we know what he did to her, can we?'

'What was she like when you mentioned it. Did she seem all right about it?' asked Mick.

'Hum… she seemed terrified about the whole suggestion of meeting the bastard, now I know why. But because she hadn't told anybody, she's just going along with it.' Rod frowned. 'God Mick, we've forced her into it…' Rod paced. 'We could pull her out. Why don't we get another woman to do it, we could pay her?'

'No… much too risky Rod, anyway who would we get, we are in South America you know,' replied Mick.

'I am aware of that Mick.' replied Rod, shrugging his shoulders, 'we could get somebody form the British Embassy to help…' 'No…no…' interrupted Mick. 'We can't trust anybody else, one whiff of what's going on, and the bastard would disappear like a rat up a drainpipe, and it would probably take us bloody months, no… maybe years to find him, plus he would be more careful if he knew we were behind him.'

'Like what,' asked Rod, 'what could he do?'

'Think Rod, what could he do, he's got eighteen million for Christ sake. He could hide the money, change his name, and probably change his appearance and disappear off the face of the earth. This is our only chance; he's been careless only because he hasn't got a clue that we are after him.'

Rod reluctantly agreed. 'I know, you're right Mick, as usual.'

Mick looked worried. He shook his head. 'But tell Sinead, if she really doesn't want to do it then we won't force her.' He paused. 'But remember, I'm afraid we haven't really got any other options at the moment.'

'What about Kerrie?' said Rod.

Mick shook his head from side to side, 'No, that's definitely a no... no. Kerrie won't do it you know she won't Rod. As Kerrie said before the change, Sinead is the only one that can pull it of. You've done the change, and she's ready, we hope.'

'I know Mick, and I hate bloody saying this again, but you're right, but I'm telling you Mick, she's bloody scared.'

'I'm not bloody surprised, I'm bloody scared for her now that I know what I know, and I hate the fact that we have got to let Sinead do it. But it's our only option. I'd do it for her if I could bloody get away with it.'

Rod waved a finger at Mick. 'But I must admit that when I asked her about it, she did say that she wanted to do it for her dad.'

'She's one hell of a brave young lady Rod, I'm not happy about her doing it, but if she says she wants to do it for her dad, we can't stand it her way, but assure her we are certainly not going to let her out of our sight, not for one second. She won't be able to take a dump without us knowing,' he said. 'And as you said Mick,' interrupted Rod, 'I know she's one hell of a brave lady, that's why I love her.'

Rod lent on the veranda railing looking down at the swimming pool. Sleeping never seemed to be his problem, but now at night he was suffering from bouts of insomnia, no matter how much he tried he just couldn't sleep...something was wrong. Of course, all insomnia they say is melodramatic, he thought, staring at the pool, and turning to stare at the flashing LED of his alarm clock: 2:32 am. Why does insomnia make you feel like you're the only person awake in the entire world? Ever since he'd first meet Sinead his brain had worked overtime. When she was not in sight he wanted her, making excuses to be near her He needed to take his mind off her, allow himself a few quiet moments for thought and reflection on where he was going with Sinead, that's if she would let him go anywhere. Deciding to take a swim in the pool he changed into his trunks, snatched a towel from the bathroom and made his way to the pool.

Sinead was suffering the same fate as Rod, insomnia problems and she needed to clear her head. She drew a irritated breath, folded her arms and leant over the veranda handrail. Overlooking the hotel pool, she watched Rod's dark silhouette as he threw down the towel and entered the water. The thoughts of her conversation with Mick flooded back; she needed to talk to Rod. She dressed and made her way down to the pool. She sat on the edge of the pool and dipped her feet in the water, watching Rod's muscular body swimming, streaking through the water as if he was in a race. A thought invaded her head, which would never have happened a week ago – what it would be like to have him crouched over her, in her.

Rod caught a glimpse of her as he turned, moving rhythmically in and out of the water in time with his strokes. He pulled up in the water and swam towards her.

'Hi, couldn't you sleep as well?' asked Rod.

'Nice night, huh, but too hot,' she said, cupping her hands and scooping water from the pool, splashing her face.

'I spoke with Mick today.... he told me about the rape.'

She froze, making a face, lifting her head in the air. 'Shite,' she hurled at him. 'Nice one Mick, did he tell you everything that happened?'

'Mick was only thinking of you Sinead. He found it very difficult to tell me, but some of it, probably not all, and I'm so...' To Sinead's surprise, Rod's voice went husky; he had to wait a moment before he could continue. 'I'm so very *angry*, not with you of course, and so very *sorry* for what he did to you. Why didn't you mention any of this before?'

Sinead swallowed, her voice taking a softer tone. 'I thought it was more appropriate to keep the rape dead and buried. That's why I didn't want a man.'

'Are you sure?'

'Of course I was sure,' she snapped, 'that was until you and Mick came along and now I have the two of you. I never believed that Mick would be the ones that I'd want to confide in... or that the nature of our relationship was going to be such as to invite intimate revelations.'

'Mick loves you, you know, in a fatherly sort of way.'

'I know, where would I be without Mick's support?'

Rod stared intently into her eyes. 'How come you didn't speak with me first?' he paused, glancing at her as if expecting some remark; but when she said nothing he continued in a mild tone, 'why Mick?'

'Because, as you said Rod, Mick loves me, and he doesn't want anything from me, no ulterior motives, you know what I mean,' she snapped.

Rod frowned. 'What do you mean?'

'Mick cares about me, for who I am,' she said, placing a hand on her chest, 'and he's a good listener.'

'Good old Mick.' Rod's eyes narrowed, his lips tightened. 'Just a minute,' he was silently treading water, trying to clear his head. 'And you think that I wasn't capable of doing that,' he never waited for an answer. 'Ok...ok... the truth is I'm only human and yes you're right; at first I did have an ulterior motive. I would love to have jumped into bed with you. In fact from the first time we ever met in your mum's kitchen, I wanted to, and every day since that first day I met you. But it's always seemed to be a one-way street, now I know why you shut me out.'

'Now you're angry.'

'I am angry, to think that you don't trust me. But, one look at your face and my anger goes. I hated not being given the chance to help you, or being shut out; especially when I haven't done anything wrong.' Rod raised his eyebrows. 'Or maybe I have.' He turned to face her, 'Why didn't you tell me, did you think I wouldn't understand?'

'No…no… it's not you, you don't understand. I believed if I told you…. you wouldn't want me.'

'Jesus Christ, Sinead… why… do you think I've been spending all this time with you?' He slapped the water with his hand in frustration. 'I don't know why I'm bothering here?'

'I'm sorry if it doesn't suit you Rod,' she exploded.

'For God's sake Sinead, this is not about me, it's about you, and it's you who won't let me into your life, and now all of a sudden you're telling me what I want. Don't you dare presume to tell me what I want, be so kind as to let me make that decision for myself, I am old enough you know?' he said softly. 'And you're not getting away from the question. Why, then didn't you tell me?'

'Just because,' she said, tears stung her eyes.

Rod shook his head. 'For God's sake Sinead, I hate this, be fair with me – throw me a line, I'm dying here, how can I get to understand what's going on if you don't tell me how you feel,' he whispered, 'believe me Sinead, all I want to do is help you, then maybe we can work it out.'

She took a deep breath. Her expression didn't change, but he heard the concern in her voice. 'Why do you want to help me Rod?'

'Just because,' he said, pulling himself onto the ledge of the pool. He was silent as his lips brushed her forehead. 'Can't you see, or are you that blind, it's because I like you.'

She moved her head sadly from side to side. 'Just a little?' she asked.

'More than just a little,' he said, 'a lot in fact.' Gently stroking her hair he tucked the strands of loose hair behind her ear, and his fingertips brushed feather light across her temples thumbing a line on her jaw. 'Sinead, you're going to have to help me along here, I'm not very good at dealing with situations like this.' She held up her hand. 'No you're right, nor am I... but at the moment it's the wrong time and place...' she said, placing a finger on his lips as he opened his mouth to speak again. 'Rod, wrong time,' she said softly, 'the one thing I don't want from you is a few wild, physical moments in a hotel room, I'm sorry but I need more.' She paused, 'Like gentleness, security, and most of all a solid relationship, this is all much too soon for me.' Her voice quavered she stared at him, tears welling and just starting to fall down her face. 'You... you... know at some time we need to talk about what happened to me a long time ago. It wasn't my fault you know that.'

Rod nodded in silence and let her continue.

'But as much as anything explains anything, it probably makes more sense to you now as to why I haven't been able to make love to you, even though at times I've wanted to.'

Rod stared into her eyes. *You what! Make love to me* he thought, *it was there in her eyes*, Mike and John were right, he could see the sincerity in her eyes. He smiled at the thought of a chance of making love to her.

'But I didn't want to complicate your life.'

Rod stood up and pulled her to her feet. He took his time, as he had to say the right things without showing anger, his voice low and intense. 'Christ Sinead, probably you think that's very sensible, but shouldn't I have some say in that, seeing as it's my life? You don't have to hide anything from me, what's done, is done.' He skimmed her hair away from her face, and rested his hands on her shoulders comforting, supporting her. 'We can make things happen Sinead, but only if you want to!'

She pressed a hand against his shoulder and pulled away; *she should turn away, run away and hide.*

'Ok fine,' said Rod standing back, 'but if you do want to talk, and tell me yourself what happened to you, you can. But I can't help, if you don't talk to me.'

'You can't help me at the moment,' she said dully. Her hands held tightly at her sides. She had to stop to steady her voice and she moistened her lips. She swallowed.

Rod shook his head. 'I will if I can, and you let me.'

She blinked back tears. 'It hurts, Rod, God it hurts. You don't know what it was like, what he did to me.'

'Hang on Sinead,' Rod said quietly, 'there's no need to continue now, I can imagine.'

With intent she looked into his face through glassy eyes. 'No you can't, you haven't been there,' she snapped fiercely. She punched his shoulder with her clenched fist. Her heart was pounding too hard. She had to keep her breath under control.

'I know this is easy for me to say Sinead, but don't become a prisoner. A terrible darkness was forced upon you, I know, but you can't surrender to it because of what the bastard did to you, you're stronger than that, you have to let go and forget the past, it's past. But don't forget who and what you are Sinead; you're a beautiful intelligent young woman, with backbone enough to make a life for yourself. Whatever he did to you, think, he will never break you.'

Sinead's jaw tightened and she let out a little breath to ease the pressure in her chest. 'He did though Rod, he took my confidence, my self-respect, and my courage,' tears rolled down her cheeks. 'I was so scared.' She sniffed. He passed her his towel. She blew her nose and raised her head.

'I know,' said Rod, moving his hand slowly towards hers until he was just touching the tips of her fingers, which immediately went sort of pins-and-needlesy.

There was an awkward pause. 'Forgive me,' Sinead said, stealing a peek at Rod, and yes he was looking at her meaningfully. She dropped her eyes again. 'My hesitation to tell you was, I know now, incomprehensible.'

'Until now Sinead,' he said, 'from today I want you to trust me. I will support you in whatever it is that you want to do, but you must tell me how you feel, and from then on we can rebuild your life together.'

She wiped the tears with back of her hand. 'It's not easy to rebuild those things, I can't explain to you, what it was like.'

'You don't have to explain it to anybody, or me. You didn't do anything wrong Sinead. In time, we can work it out.'

She stamped her feet in frustration. 'All I want, Rod, is a normal life, is that too much to ask for?'

'Of course it's not, all I can promise you, is that you will... you will...' Tears appeared in the corner of Rod's eyes. 'You will and I will help you to find a normal life, I know whatever it is you want me to do, I will do it for you.'

Sinead looked up into Rod's face; she saw sincerity and love in his eyes. She wanted Rod to hold her, and he wanted to hold her too; she could see it in the tension of his body. Unable to resist, slowly she stepped forward. Reaching up, she cupped her hands around his face, thumbing the tears from his eyes, warm air whisked over her body.

'You're still worried I'm going to let you down.'

'I'm not! It's not you I'm worried about.'

'Prove it,' said Rod, taking hold of her hands.

Nervously she held his hands in hers; they felt strong as his hands curled around hers. Her pulse was galloping. She fell into him, he felt so good, it was ok to lean on him now, to take from him. But not at this moment, she needed to clear her thoughts. She closed her eyes and whispered. 'I have to go,' she said softly. Without warning the skies opened and lightning cracked, silhouetting their shadows on the pool as the rain fell in a torrent, a tropical storm.

'In a minute,' Rod whispered back, as the rain lashed, soaking their bodies. The rain mixed with the tears that soaked their faces. He tightened his arms around her, pulling her close. He whispered into her rain-soaked hair, 'I need this, and if ever I needed you, Sinead, I need you now.' They pressed the elevator button, the doors swished open and the elevator ascended to the fourth floor. They stopped at her suite door. Rod pulled her softly against him, covering her mouth gently with his in a warm tender kiss. She tasted of fruit, smelling of strawberries, and for a split second he let himself drown in the scent of her body.

Her body felt alive as warm air whisked over her body. Her stomach became hot as desire began to build inside her for him. Blood rushed to her head leaving her dizzy, weak and achy. She leant into him as one strangled moan escaped her lips, gripping the edge of the door for balance.

Rod pulled himself back slightly, letting his hands run over her shoulders and down her arms before linking his fingers with hers. 'That wasn't so bad,' he said as he studied her face, the colour seemed to have retuned to her face. He lowered his forehead to hers and kissed her again lightly. 'Sinead,' he said, 'let me love you, let me love you as you deserve…' 'Meaning …what?' asked Sinead before she could stop herself.

'Meaning Sinead, I'd like to share your life, to be with you in every sense, if that's possible?'

'That I promise you is certainly a possibility,' she said as he moved away.

'Take your time Sinead,' Rod held up a hand, 'just remember without an end, there can't be a beginning, and as long as you remember what he did to you, then he wins. I've got my whole life to wait for you, and I will wait, that I can promise you,' he said, smiling. He didn't look back but he could feel her eyes on his back as he walked towards the lift.

She watched him stand at the lift, and then closed the door leaning against it.

'Shite, Rod,' she sighed wearily.

★ ★ ★

'Sinead,' whispered Kerrie, beckoning her from her suite door. 'Well,' said Kerrie as they both sat on the bed, 'what's going on between you and Rod?'

Sinead shook her head, wiping her hair with the towel. 'I've been doing a lot of thinking,' she paused and looked away, 'about sex. I wasn't sure I'd ever want to be with a man again, especially somebody like Rod, but there's something about Rod that seems to make me very itchy.'

'What! You've had sex with Rod?'

Sinead frowned. 'No,' she said sharply, 'certainly not Kerrie, you don't have to have sex because you feel itchy. I mean itchy when a man touches your skin.'

'Well why don't you do something about it? Scratch the itch?'

'I never thought I would ever consider making love to Rod. We just talked by the pool. I was floating on air as he walked me back to my suite; he makes me feel as if I'm the most important person in his world.'

'Well don't go putting up barriers. What happened next?'

He kissed me good night at the door, the kind of kiss that lifts off the top of your head and spins it around. He made me feel so comfortable.'

Kerrie breathed excitedly. 'Well, what happened next?'

'Then he went to his room.'

Kerrie's face dropped. 'Sinead, didn't it occur to you to drag him inside your room, toss him on the bed, and rip his clothes off?'

'Kerrie, what would Ma think?'

'Sinead, Ma's not getting it.'

Sinead laughed. 'I couldn't do a thing like that; I wouldn't know where to begin.'

'Visualize,' Kerrie said wickedly, 'visualize.'

Chapter Sixteen
Les Mercedes

'You two up for a bit of clubbing it tonight?' asked Rod.

'We couldn't,' said Mick, 'especially John he certainly hasn't got the energy, you lads go. John and I will go for a nice quiet drink, and see you later.'

'You've got to go,' snapped Rod. 'Sinead said that if you two didn't go then she's not going to do it, and you can kiss your money good-bye. She needs you there Mick.'

'Ok... ok...' Mick held up his hands, 'if Sinead wants us there, then we'll be there right John?'

John nodded his head in agreement.

'What time?'

'Be ready at eight, the taxi will pick us up outside the hotel.'

'What about the girls?'

'Don't worry about the girls they'll make their own way there, you just be ready at eight.'

Before coming out that night, the talk amongst the lads of going to a nightclub made John feel edgy. Nightclubs, or discotheques – whatever you called them these days – was not his thing; he'd rather have stayed in and watched the television, but there was shit-all on, and what was on, he couldn't understand anyway, and Rod said that they all had to be there.

At eight thirty the taxi pulled up outside the club. Blue, pink and green neon signs flashed *Les Mercedes discoteca*. The lads piled out as Mick paid the driver. The evening was humid and the club was getting hotter as they made their way down the iron staircase to the basement into the dim lighting accompanied by flashing lights. The club was already heaving, with bodies pressing against each other. The air was heavy with the smell of smoke and sweat mingled with perfume. Now John was there, he didn't feel any better; he felt like a fish out of water standing at the bar. The bar's backdrop of neon blue lights made everyone's face look a bit peaky except for Mick; the blue light seemed to enhance his looks, making him better looking, he looked like an older Cary Grant. This definitely wasn't John's normal crowd. The dancers on the floor thrashed to the music, nothing at all like his hometown pub, the Black Swan back at Farcet in Peterborough. No dartboard, no Zimmer frames in the far corner or the recognisable sound of erratic banging from the cribbage board. Maybe this was the sort of place for Rod, Craig and Paul. But definitely not his and Mick's cup of tea: they had no idea of the modus operandi. It had been a long time, if ever, that they both had been in a place like this. The last time John could remember being in any place that had music and women was when the Beatles sang *She Loves You,* where the women danced with each other and men watched from the sidelines. Mick's thoughts weren't far behind

John's. He felt both old and inappropriately dressed and wondered whether he had remembered to apply deodorant; he sniffed under his armpit. Thank God he had as the sweat was beginning to show. The beautiful Latino ladies were on display; scent drifted, vaporising after the women as they brushed past him.

John and Mick leant against the bar drinking a bottle of warm beer while Craig went to the toilet.

'Where's Rod?' asked Mick, scanning the club. 'I didn't think he would miss a session like this.' He glanced sideways at the Latino ladies gyrating on the dance floor.

'He said he was staying at the hotel.'

'Why?' asked Mick, smiling.

'Don't ask me Mick,' said John shrugging his shoulders. 'All Rod said was that we needed to be down here to-night.'

'That's funny, he never said anything to me either,' said Craig.

'Mick, Paul, Craig, another warm beer?' said John, clicking his fingers at the young woman behind the bar; John pointed at the four bottles, *'mismo otra vez, cuatro cerveza por favor.'*

'*Gracias,*' said John as she pushed the bottles across the bar.

'You seem to be picking up the lingo,' said Paul.

'Case of having to, if you want a bloody drink,' replied John. 'Nobody around here seems to speak fucking English,' he said, looking around the club, when a woman in a short black dress with legs as long as a giraffe's neck came down the stairway. It was the beautiful long legs that grabbed John's attention. He felt something catch in his throat as she descended the stairs. He nudged Mick. Mick nudged Paul, Paul nudged Craig, and Craig nudged some Latino woman standing at the bar.

Rod smiled as they all watched her as she descending the last few steps.

'That dress was made for her,' said Paul. A tight-fitting little black dress, the fabric fitted like a jet-black second skin, setting off her golden hair and deep green eyes. 'Forget it John and close your mouth you're catching flies,' smiled Mick. 'Generation gap there, mate,' he said, 'I'm off to the toilet.'

'Fuck it,' murmured John, snapping his mouth shut.

'I hope it's just a piss Mick,' shouted Paul.

Mick gave Paul a stern look as he moved off.

Paul was back on the case. 'Shit,' he shook his head, 'is that one hell of a women, or what,' he said, and yet there was something familiar about this young lady. She was tall; her face was striking, surrounded with a pageboy blonde hairstyle, her figure absolutely neat and well proportioned. Her expensive and intensely flattering dress made him almost want to turn away because he could not bear to look at her without feeling he was doing Gale, his wife, a disservice by looking. He turned towards John. 'Your eyes will pop out of your head John,' he said, imitating the way that he stood leaning on the bar.

'That's you know who,' said Mick as he made his way back from the toilet, pulling his beer from the bar. 'Cheers,' he said, taking a sip from the bottle.

'Who?' asked John.

'You're right,' said Paul, 'I knew I'd seen that figure before.'

John looked at them both. He craned his neck in her direction again. 'You've bloody lost me, who the hell is it, for fuck sake, WHO?' he shouted again.

'Sinead,' said Rod, standing behind Craig.

John spat his beer over Mick, and paused. 'For fuck sake,' he gasped, 'Rod you're bloody joking,' glancing back at her with renewed interest. As he did so, their eyes met. She smiled faintly at John; he felt like a weak-kneed teenager, this absolute beauty was smiling at him. She raised a hand at Craig, John, Mick, Paul, and Rod.

'What happened to her?' asked John. 'How the hell did you…' his words trailed off as he stared at her in disbelief. For once John was lost for words.

Rod tilted his head slightly to one side as he considered the answer. 'I happened to her,' he said smiling, 'I changed her hair, and did her make-up.'

'Shit, you've completely changed her appearance,' Paul said, agreeing with John.

'Shit you're quick Paul,' said Craig, 'that was the whole idea.'

'Good God, bloody good job there, Rod,' John remarked, 'I wouldn't have believed it if I hadn't seen her with my own eyes.' Watching her departing back as she passed them he grabbed Rod's shirt. 'Don't tell me she's going for the key.'

'I told you all Sinead and I had a plan, and you know that the bastard at the other end of the bar has the key.'

'Right,' said John, releasing the grip on his shirt. 'But you take this as a warning Rod. If she gets hurt I'll take it personally.'

Rod rearranged his shirt. 'So… how… else were we going to get the bloody key?'

John looked at Mick. 'Nobody tells us fuck all, do they?'

Mick smiled at John, 'I hate to say this, but John's right Rod,' he agreed, turning back to Rod. 'Remember, you don't let her out of your sight, keep your eye on her at all times,' he said, 'and tell her good luck from us all, and we're right behind her.'

Rod laid his hand on Mick's shoulder. 'Don't you worry Mick, she'll be safe with me,' he said. He looked in Sinead's direction. 'Must go lads, there's work to be done, I've got to instruct Sinead on her protocol,.'

'Famous last words,' Craig tutted. 'She'll be safe with me,' he repeated Rod's words.

Paul shook his head and smiled, agreeing with Craig. 'Comforting to know that Sinead is in such reliable hands,' he said. 'Right who's for another drink?'

Sinead blinked hard. Rod detected tears forming in the corner of her eyes. He put his arm around her. 'Hey, what's all this, we are all here with you. I know how you feel Sinead, and I know you don't want to do this, but, just breathe deeply and remember what you've got to do.' He shook her arms. 'Sinead listen, he may have been your demon at one time in your life, but time has a way of changing things. Remember life is just a circle – it takes power away and gives it to those who once had none. Right now your Uncle Tom is the one who is going to be destroyed. It's your time now, and you are the one who is going to destroy him. Believe me he can't hurt you anymore, Sinead he's nothing!'

'I'm telling you now Rod, if he touches me, I'll kill him.'

'You won't have to do anything Sinead,' Rod said, tapping her purse. 'Remember you have the control here in your purse. But I'm telling you if the bastard so much as lays a finger on you, don't worry, I'll kill him for you.' He smiled without a hint of humour.

Her body shook with the fear at the thought of standing in front of him, let alone speaking to him. 'Shite, he makes my flesh creep. I'm so scared Rod. Do you think he will go for it? What if he recognises me?' she asked.

'What! Just look at you. He won't recognise you, you're a different woman, and you haven't seen him for years. Anyway the lads never even recognised you,' Rod affirmed, holding out her hands and standing back. 'You're the best looking woman in this place, believe me, you look absolutely fantastic, who the hell could resist you, I bloody can't, and that goes for the lads as well. Remember,' he said, shaking her arms again. 'We're all here, right behind. You look so beautiful,' he reached out and stroked her cheek.

'Thanks,' she said, hugging him. She smelt faintly of jasmine. He closed his eyes and breathed her in, feeling her breath on his cheek as he buried his head in her hair;

for a moment he was seized by the urge to nuzzle her neck, but he thought better of it. He really wanted her, wishing that it was him she was going to spend the night with. He shook his head trying to eradicate the perfume as she released him. 'Anyway,' Rod continued, 'he'd have to be gay or blind, and I didn't see a white stick, or a guide dog did you?'

She smiled wanly.

Rod nodded towards John and Mick. 'Or the bastard would have to be as old as them two not to go for this package.'

Sinead smiled faintly. 'Don't be so hard on them Rod, they've both got a good heart, and anyway, John talks well of you, you know.'

Rod narrowed his eyes. 'John, yer right,' he sneered. 'Anyway John's not our problem at the moment. Right, let's get back on track. This is what you need to do, engage him in conversation, chat him up,' he said.

'Shit Rod I'm so scared, do you remember that record, *if I ever needed you, I need you now.*'

'I know… I know… as I've said we'll be right behind you. You can do it Sinead, don't forget this is for your dad. Believe me, you can do it,' Rod said again, shaking her arms gently. 'Remember; just tell him that you're a journalist from England, doing an article about Brits abroad. Apparently, the bastard loves the ladies, so he shouldn't give you any problems, he'll be too busy looking you up and down.'

Sinead frowned. 'I know,' she snapped, 'we need to talk later.'

Rod saw the concerned look in her face. 'We will. Smile,' said Rod. 'And don't you worry, we won't be far behind you.'

Sinead looked uncomfortably in the bastard's direction, fear knotting her stomach. She looked at Rod, drawing in great gasps of air. Rod contemplated her thoughts. 'Go on doctor, do your stuff,' he said, 'you've got everything.'

'Yes,' she said, tapping her small purse.

'Right smile,' said Rod, 'let's go and do it then.' *God she smells good, he wanted so much just to take her away,* he thought as he kissed her on the cheek, hoping that one day he might get close enough to her to relieve the permanent hard-on he seemed to acquire every time she stood near him, in fact ever since the first day in the kitchen when she mopped the blood off his head. 'We'll see you in an hour?'

'One hour.'

'One hour,' assented Rod, inclining his head, 'your carriage will await you.'

'Don't forget, Rod, we need to talk,' Sinead said again as she turned and walked towards the bastard.

'We will, we will,' said Rod softly to her disappearing back. He watched her as she pushed her way through the crowded dance floor. He turned, grabbing the club photograph, '*hula, ingles,*' he said.

'Yer bud, I'm Australian,' replied the photographer.

'Ok, can you see the girl in the back dress, over there?' he said, pointing in the direction of Sinead.

'Yep, who could miss her, the stunner with the nice arse mate, no V.P.L.,' he said.

'What?' shouted Rod.

'Visible Panty Line mate, no underwear.'

Rod looked at him sternly; if he didn't want him to do something for him, he would have punched his lights out there and then for that remark. 'Just save your bloody eyes for the viewfinder, mate. I just want you to take her photograph with the man she's standing next to and make sure their smiling,' he snapped.

'Sorry mate I didn't know it was your old lady.'

'It's not my wife, bud,' Rod snapped, 'just a friend. When you've got the photograph, I'll be over there,' he pointed towards the lads.

'Ok mate no problem. Over there you say,' he shouted as he disappeared into the crowd.

'I hate fucking Aussies,' Rod mumbled to himself as he pushed his way back through the crowd towards the lads.

'Right everything's set, contact made,' Rod shouted above the din. 'What you all having to drink lads? Mick, you keep your eye on Sinead,' he said.

'Who's that bloke Rod?' said Craig. 'He's waving something at you,'.

'You'll see,' said Rod, waving the Aussie over.

'Here you are mate, and they are smiling as you said.'

'How much?' asked Rod, diving his hand into his back pocket.

'25 euros to you mate.'

'Here's 25, keep the change.'

'Cheers,' he held up his hand, 'have a good night lads. Tight pommy bastards,' he muttered under his breath as he turned and disappeared back into the crowd.

'Let's have a look,' said Paul. 'Not bad,' he said as he passed the photograph around.

'He bloody does look like Sean,' said John, squinting at the picture.

'Jesus, you couldn't tell them apart,' said Mick.

'What do you want that for Rod?' asked Mick, passing him the photograph. 'Sinead's not going to be very happy with that.'

'You never know. She'll be all right Mick, trust me,' he said, slipping the photograph into his shirt pocket.

'Rod… Rod… Sinead's on the move,' John shouted, looking over the heads of the crowd of gyrating dancers.

'Right I'm off,' said Rod, gulping down the last of his beer. 'See you all back at the hotel.'

Mick grabbed Rod's shirt. 'Remember Rod, you guard her with your life,' he said.

'Don't you worry Mick, watch the shirt,' Rod said, pushing his hand away and straightening out his shirt. 'We'll see you all back at the hotel later lads, it's going to be a long night.' Rod waved and disappeared into the crowd.

'Thank fuck for that Mick, now we can go,' John said, drinking the dregs of his beer. 'Paul, Craig are you coming or staying?'

Paul looked at his watch. 'Not yet, it's only bloody eleven o'clock. No, you and Mick go if you want, get an early night, we'll see you later.'

'Mick, John, are you going to get a round in before you go?' asked Craig. All Craig and Paul saw was John and Mick's V sign in the air, as they left the club.

'We'll take that as a no then, shall we Craig?' said Paul. 'Get them in Craig,' he said, pushing his glass across the counter and raising his hand at the barman.

Chapter Seventeen
Rohipnol

Rod leant against the wall and looked at his watch: 3:10am. He paced up and down outside the perimeter wall of the spacious villa, listening to the rasp of the crickets; he could only see the rooftop of the villa as the foreground was covered with tropical trees and deadly spiked throng plants. The rest of the villa was covered by bougainvillea, masses of green and deep-red clusters of flowers. He looked at his watch again, impatiently kicking the wall that surrounded the villa.

Back at the hotel Mick paced the hotel room.

John slapped the arms of ᵗhe sofa. 'For Christ sake Mick will you bloody well sit down and have a drink, you're wearing out the bloody carpet. You're bloody acting like me when Kaylie's out on a date.'

'I can't help it John,' replied Mick, moving towards the door. Opening it looking towards the elevator, listening for any audible sound.

Nothing.

Mick went to close the door as the elevator doors swished back and Paul and Craig fell out of the lift, breaking the silence. He looked at his watch. 3:30am.

'Well?' shouted Mick as they both staggered towards the suite.

Craig and Paul held out their hands simultaneously. 'Well what Mick?' asked Paul. 'Did we have a good skin full?'

'What does it look like?' replied Craig.

'No, you pair of idiots, have you seen Sinead and Rod!'

'I can hardly see in front of myself,' said Craig.

'That's because you've had too much to drink Craig,' sniggered Paul, looking back at Mick with glazed eyes. 'Nope, have… have…you?' he asked.

'Of course I bloody haven't,' replied Mick, now ranting on nervously. 'If I had I wouldn't be asking you now would I? Never mind' he ended, looking back at the elevator. He slammed the door and looked at his watch again. 3:40am.

Rod heard a door bang slam shut. A security light filled the air with light and large moths bombarded the light that surrounded the front entrance as he heard the sound of her shoes on the path, coming towards the front gate. He opened the gate as she came through.

She held the key in the air, as they made their way towards the car. Rod opened the passenger side door. Disaster, he knew the moment she got into the car.

Sinead threw in her shoulder bag and slid into the passenger seat. The interior light of the car picked out the troubled look on her face.

'What's the matter?' asked Rod as he turned towards her.

'I don't know how to put this Rod.' She looked away out of the passenger window. As a car sped past she turned back to face him, her hands trembled she bit her bottom lip. 'I'm sorry I'm not going to be able to give you what you want.'

'What, we've got it,' he said, holding up the key.

'It's not about the bloody key,' she said as tears appeared in the corner of her eyes.

'The bastard didn't fucking touch you did he?' asked Rod as he moved to get out of the car.

She grabbed his arm. 'No...no...Rod, he didn't touch me, he didn't do anything he just gave me that sick smile and collapsed.'

'What then, for God sake Sinead, come on tell me what's the matter?'

Sinead took a deep breath. 'What happened the other day, do you remember when you changed my appearance, and we kissed?'

'God yes and I shall never forget that kiss, I haven't washed my face since,' he said smiling, trying to lighten the conversation. Her face never altered; normally he'd have got a faint smile. *God he'd changed her appearance and she changed her mind about him, in his heart he knew that was what she was going to say, he looked up into the air. God please don't let her say that.*

'I know when I kissed you I wrongly led you on, that there might have been more. I shouldn't have.'

'Hang on Sinead, how do you know what I'm looking for, or what I want?'

'It isn't fair for me to give you the impression that there could be anything more between you and me.'

Rod waved a hand. 'God Sinead I think you know in your heart that there is something between us, that kiss said it all, even if you're pretending there wasn't. But that doesn't change the way I feel about you.' He looked into her eyes, tears rolled down her cheeks. 'Sinead the fact that we haven't slept together or made love, doesn't change the way I feel about you either. That night we kissed,' he took a deep breath, 'sadly I was only thinking of myself, but deep down I felt you weren't ready. It would have been a mistake, maybe for you, but certainly not a mistake for me,' he said, holding his hand on his chest. 'I presume that if I'd wanted to I could have taken you to bed that night, but what good would that have done. It would only have satisfied my lust for you. Sinead, you need to give yourself freely, which is more important than me just taking what I need, and the satisfaction for me is not just taking what I need, and I'm going to be truthful here, I do need you.'

Sinead moistened her lips. 'You presume a lot, but thanks for your concern Rod, and probably yes, you're right about making love, that's my problem.'

He'd never seen the act of making love before as anything more than just sexual gratification, but Sinead was right, she certainly wasn't a case of sexual gratification; this would certainly be a case of making love to her. 'I seem to think you're frightened of sex,' he asked.

'Maybe it is sex,' she wiped the tears with the back of her hand as Rod passed her a tissue. 'But as sex is never going to happen, then I'm not prepared to go into that.

She decided even if she told him the truth it wouldn't matter, the other night wasn't going to go anywhere.

Rod wanted to probe more deeply but instinct told him that he needed to tread carefully, she wasn't going to let herself go, not just yet anyway, but he wouldn't pursue any further. Even though there were tears that clouded her eyes, he saw deeper into them and all was not lost, but it had to be in her time, not his. 'Ok,' he said finally, turning the ignition, gunning the accelerator. 'Let's get back to the hotel, they're all concerned about you, especially Mick, he'll be worried all night.'

Sinead and Rod walked into the suite.

Mick jumped up from the sofa, – when he heard the door open looking at his watch –3:55am. 'Are you all right Sinead?'

'We're bloody glad you're back Sinead,' said Paul,' Mick's been shitting bricks all night.'

Sinead hugged Mick, 'Thanks Mick,' she said, 'no problem.'

'I…I… was worried too,' said Paul positively oozing concern. 'Give us a hug,' he said, holding out his arms towards John.

Sinead grabbed his arms and hugged him, kissing him on the cheek. 'You're the best,' she whispered in his ear.

Paul smiled at Rod, as Mick sat down breathing a sigh of relief that she was back and safe.

'Good, now you're safely back Sinead, how did you get on?' John asked, impatient to know what had happened. 'Did you have a good look round?'

'Of course.'

'She got it,' replied Rod, raising the key.

'Shit, she's done it,' they all said in unison.

'How did you leave him?' asked Kerrie.

John gave Sinead a pointed look. 'Dead I hope,' he shouted.

'No, not yet I hope,' replied Craig, 'we need our money.'

Sinead ran her fingers through her hair. 'No, I left him out cold,' she replied, *although she wished that he was dead.* 'He'll be ga-ga for about six hours and he's going to have one hell of a serious hangover in the morning; he won't remember a thing.'

'What did you do to him Sinead?' asked Mick.

'Rohipnol,' replied Sinead.

'What the hell's Rohipnol?' asked John.

'Helmet Kohl, grassy knoll, or for whom the bell tolls as it's commonly known,' replied Rod.

Mick looked puzzled he shook his head and turned to John. 'What the bloody hell is he going on about?' he asked.

John shrugged his shoulders. 'Haven't got a bloody clue Mick,' he replied.

'Rohipnol's a date-rape drug,' said Rod.

John looked at Paul. 'And of course Rod would know all about that,' he said.

Rod's face twisted. 'Sod off John; I've never had to use anything like that at all. Unlike you and Paul I use my good looks and charm. Rohipnol's for the likes of you sad, ugly bastards who would have to use it to get a bird into bed.'

John and Paul lifted their arms together, as if holding handbags. 'Wahoo, sore point,' they said in unison.

Rod looked at them sternly.

'Take no notice of them Rod,' said Craig, trying to relieve the tension. He was looking puzzled. 'I didn't think Rohipnol had any other purpose than for date-rape.'

'Well it does,' Rod snapped, but took Craig's advice and ignored John and Paul. He looked back at Sinead and smiled. 'Well, Sinead tell them what happened.'

Sinead had poured herself a drink, and took a sip from the glass. 'Well, I slipped the bastard the Rohipnol in the club, and he tried it on when we got back to his apartment.'

'Tried what on?' asked John.

'What do you think she meant John, he tried on a dress?' said Craig.

John shrugged his shoulders. 'You never know, look at Tristram.'

Paul held out his hands towards Sinead. 'Would you try on a bloody dress with something like Sinead standing in front of you?'

John nodded. 'Excuse me Sinead but don't take this the wrong way,' he said. 'But I'd be ripping her dress off, metaphorically speaking though.'

'Right, that's what we meant by trying it on John, SEX,' said Paul.

Rod looked sideways at Sinead, knowing that she shuddered at the thought. Sinead didn't know whether to be offended or take what John and Paul said as a compliment.

'Dirty bastard,' hissed Mick, 'his own bloody niece.'

'But he didn't know it was his niece,' said Craig 'look at her, wouldn't you go for that?'

'That's neither here nor there,' said Mick, this time age did matter to Mick. 'He's still a dirty old bastard,' he said, 'she's half his age.'

'Well don't everybody worry. It was all ok Mick,' said Sinead, 'because nothing happened, he passed out.'

Rod scratched his head. 'Hang on, now we have the key,' he explained holding the key in the air.' Right,' interrupted Craig, who was right behind Rod's thinking. *We can't just go and open the box.* 'How are we going to get to the box, Rod?' he asked.

Silence.

'I don't know,' said Rod finally.

'Well you're the brains Rod, what can we do?'

'I don't bloody know,' snapped Rod, rubbing his forehead.

John threw up a hand. 'Craig's right, how the hell are we going to get into the safety deposit box? And you Rod,' he said pointing at him, 'are saying you don't bloody know how to get in there.' He slapped his hands to his side. 'We're all bloody sunk kiss the money good-by.'

Rod thought about what John had said for a few minutes then gave them all a brief nod. 'No...no... we're not sunk at all…' he smiled, turning towards Kerrie. Holding out the key, he smiled. 'Kerrie can do it.'

Mick narrowed his eyes. 'Kerrie can do what?' he asked.

'Yes, good point Mick,' said Kerrie, looking back at Rod. 'Do what? What, do you have something in mind Rod?' she asked, holding out her hands, looking backwards and forwards from Mick to Rod.

'Yes Kerrie,' replied Rod, 'you're the only one that can do it.' he continued, 'for her it will be a piece of cake,' looking at the others. 'It's easy.'

'And what do you propose that Kerrie's got to do,' asked John.

'Just look at her.'

They all looked at Kerrie. 'Call me dumb,' John said to Mick. 'I'm sorry, but I haven't got a clue what he's getting at, what's your point Rod?'

Mick nodded. 'John's right, I'll go along with that,' he agreed.

Craig and Paul knew exactly where Rod was coming from.

Rod held out his hands again. 'Look at her, I'm telling you she's got the equipment,' replied Rod.

Kerrie frowned. 'I don't like the sound of this,' she said, 'what equipment?'

Rod ignored her question and continued. 'It's easy I'm telling you,' he said, looking down at Kerrie again.

'How easy?' asked Craig.

'I know for a fact that the bloke on the reception desk fancies her.'

'He can't,' said John quickly, 'he's bloody foreign. Anyway she's got a boyfriend.'

Craig ignored John's racial remark. 'How do you know that he fancies her?' he asked.

'Haven't you seen the way he looks at her when she walks through the foyer?'

'No,' they all said in unison.

'Well that's where you lot differ from me. I know when somebody fancies somebody, bloody hell I've spent enough time practising. In the past of course,' he said, turning towards Sinead, raising his hand.

They couldn't argue with what he'd stated.

'Jesus Christ,' continued Rod, 'I'm not asking Kerrie to bloody marry him. If Kerrie with her equipment can just keep the bloke at the reception desk occupied, one of us could slip into the back room and open the safety deposit box, and, *hey presto* we'll have what we need. Kerrie can get the information, photocopy it,' he paused, 'they must have a photocopier.'

'They have,' said Craig, 'I've seen it.'

'Good,' said Rod, 'you see, Monkey man has got his uses sometimes. Once we have got the info we require, then all we have to do is put the information back.' He held out his hands. 'I'm telling you, nobody will ever know that anything was missing.' He raised his eyebrows. 'We could get a key cut tomorrow, and return the key back to the bastard's villa. We know where he lives. We could just drop the key on his driveway near his car. He'll think the key fell out of his pocket when he got out of the car pissed up. What do you think?' he looked round at them all.

They all looked at each other; finally John spoke, smiling at Rod's inventive mind. 'Good bloody thinking Rod, I can't fault your plan, you've certainly got it all worked out,' he said, pointing at him.

Rod tapped his head and smiled.

Kerrie mulled over what Rod had said in her head as they all looked at her. 'Right,' she said finally smiling, 'seeing as Rod said I haven't got to marry him.' She looked at her watch. 'No time like the present.'

'What are we going to do then?' asked Mick.

Kerrie stood up. 'Strike while the iron's hot Mick. Right, Rod, give Paul the key,' directed Kerrie. 'You and Sinead stay here you've done enough for tonight. Mick, you go to bed you looked knackered and Craig you get an early night as well, I shall need you tomorrow morning. Paul and John I want you two to come with me.'

John looked puzzled. 'What do you want us to do?' he asked.

Kerrie went to her briefcase and pulled out a bundle of files. 'Just follow my lead John, and keep out of sight. You'll know when to make your move; you know where the safety deposit boxes are, don't you Paul?'

'Yes I do, as Craig said they are behind the front counter,' answered Paul, 'I noticed them when we booked in.'

'Good, ok, wait here, and talk amongst yourselves, won't be a minute,' Kerrie said, throwing the bundle of files on the tables. She left the suite and emerged minutes later in changed clothes.

'Shit,' said John, 'that's the quickest I've ever seen a woman get changed.'

'Wow, look at her,' said Mick, 'I've always said that clothes make a difference.'

Kerrie looked professional, intelligent, and sexy as hell, dressed in a black pencil skirt, white silk blouse and a black jacket slung over her shoulders. 'You've got to look business- like,' she said, fluffing her hair. 'Perfect,' she muttered, picking up the bundle of files. 'Well, what are we waiting for boys?'

'You,' replied John, raising his shoulders.

'Right let's go.' Her last words cracked at them like a whip, startling them into action. She led the way out of the suite.

John looked at Paul, raised his eyebrows and laughed. 'A woman in a hurry, let's not keep her waiting.' He trailed after her.

'Seems that way,' replied Paul.

'Pssst,' said Rod, slipping something into Paul's hand as he made his way to the door and caught up with John.

John nudged Paul. 'There's something sexy about a woman in charge, and I love it,' John whispered as they followed Kerrie to the elevators.

Chapter Eighteen
Safety Deposit Box

'Right, what's the plan,' asked John as they waited for the elevator.

'No plan John,' said Kerrie. 'We'll play it by ear, but Paul, you must get the information to me as soon as you get it out of the safety deposit box, ok.'

Paul looked at Kerrie puzzled, 'And how am I going to do that?'

'You'll know when Paul.'

Paul didn't look convinced that he knew what was going on. 'Don't you want me to bring the information up here…?' The bell of the elevator interrupted him.

'No, we need to have it all over and done with in a few minutes,' replied Kerrie as the elevator doors swished open. They entered and Kerrie pressed the ground floor button.

'Paul, key,' said Kerrie as the doors silently closed.

Paul held the key out in his hand.

'Right, don't forget Paul, you stay out of sight until I shout, NOW, and John you watch the front door.'

John did a mock salute.

Kerrie undid the top two buttons of her blouse, exposing her cleavage.

'Here we go again,' said Paul.

'What's that for?' asked John, pointing at her blouse buttons.

If she's anything like her sister, thought Paul. He held up a hand. 'Believe me John, I know where she's coming from,' he whispered.

Kerrie never answered, she just winked at them both. The elevator bumped to a halt, the doors slid back. Kerrie dragged her fingers through her hair and fluffed it up as she walked out.

'He doesn't stand a bloody chance,' said Paul as they slid to one side of the elevator, just keeping the front desk in view. Kerrie walked towards the front counter, her high heels tapping on the marble floor; the clerk was young, probably in his twenties, jet-black hair with a handsome Spanish face. She coughed and smiled at him, placing the bundle of files on the counter, holding her cleavage together.

The first thing the clerk looked at as his eyes came up from

his book was her cleavage, his eyes massaging their way across her chest.

Kerrie waited until he had clocked the vision.

His eyes left her breasts and travelled up to her face; he looked at his watch. *'Buenas tardes senorita.'*

'Puede ayudarme, por favor.'

' Si'

' Hebla ingles?' Kerrie asked.

' Si senorita, a little,' he replied, giving Kerrie's figure an appreciative appraisal from her waist up.

'Have you got a photocopier?'

'Si senorita.'

'Good.' She flipped the front leaf of the files open. 'I know it's late,' she said, looking at her watch, 'but I was wondering if it's possible to photocopy some important documents. I need them for an important meeting early tomorrow morning at the bank.'

'*Si senorita.*'

'Now,' she snapped impatiently, looking at her watch feeling he had had enough time to get acquainted with her breasts.

'Pardon, *Si senorita,*' averting his eyes from her cleavage, 'won't you come this way.' He held out his hand to the room behind him. 'The photocopier is in here.'

'*Shit,*' Kerrie said under her breath as she snapped the files shut and lifted them from the counter.

John nudged Paul. 'What's she doing?' he whispered.

Paul waved a hand at him, and peered around the corner. He looked over his shoulder at John. 'The buttons bloody worked, she's moving away from the counter.'

Kerrie walked to the corner of the counter, turned and slipped on her ankle. She screamed as she fell to the floor, hitting her head on the edge of the counter. The folders flew from her hands and the papers they contained fanned out over the marble floor. The clerk rushed round to the front of the counter as Kerrie lay on the floor stunned.

' *Senorita…senorita…*' shouted the clerk, 'are you all right *senorita,*' he said lifting head.

John tapped Paul's shoulder. 'For Christ sake Paul, what's happening?' he whispered.

'She's fallen on the floor.'

'Is she alright?'

'Shush,' whispered Paul.

Kerrie sat up dazed.

'Are you all right *senorita*,' said the clerk again, as small droplets of blood dripped onto Kerrie's white blouse. She raised her hand to her forehead, as the clerk took a handkerchief from his top pocket, and dabbed gingerly at the blood. She winched 'Ouch.'

'Sorry,' senorita he said easing off.

'Can I have a glass of water?' she asked, dazed.

'*Si senorita,* but I will have to go to the kitchen for the water, will you be all right if I leave you?'

'Yes... yes... I'll be all right,' she said, holding the handkerchief as he ran off towards the kitchen.

'NOW,' she shouted, waving a hand at Paul.

'Here we go,' said Paul running towards her. He bent down. 'That looks bad, are you all right?' he said, looking at her head.

'I'm fine, go on... go on, get the information,' she snapped.

Paul ran behind the counter, unlocked number ten, and slipped the photo in the passport that Rod had given to him. Withdrawing the contents he thumbed through the paperwork. 'This is it,' he shouted, tucking paperwork inside his shirt and returning the rest of the paperwork into the box. He slammed the door shut, locked it and ran back to the front of the counter.

'Now what Kerrie?' he said as the clerk approached them water in hand.

'Here we are *senorita*,' he said. As he bent down he looked at Paul.

'What happened?' Paul asked.

The clerk shrugged his shoulders. 'I don't know *senor*, the *senorita* she just fell over,' Antonio said as he gave Kerrie the glass of water. 'Drink it slowly senorita.'

Kerrie placed her hands in Antonio's hand. 'Can you help me up,' she said.

Antonio offered her his arm she slipped her arm under his, he lifted her easily to her feet. Paul removed the information from his shirt, picked up the scattered paperwork on the floor, laid the information inside the top file, and placed the bundle on the counter.

'Are you sure you all right *senorita*?' said the desk clerk.

'Yes…yes… I'm fine now,' she said. 'I'm sorry, but I do need to get my papers copied, do you mind?'

'No, *senorita,* let me help you,' he said, picking up the bundle, and carrying the files to the photocopier.

'*Shit,*' Kerrie thought as Antonio stood watching her every move. Pulling out two bogus pieces of paperwork she ran them through the machine. She picked each sheet up and read them as she walked towards the counter, picking up the glass. 'What's your name?' she asked.

'Antonio Juan Velazquez Gonzalez, but everybody calls me Ant.'

'Thank God for that.'

'Sorry *senorita*?

'Doesn't matter,' Kerrie said, waving her hand. 'Ant, would you be a dear,' she smiled as she held up the empty glass.

'*Si senorita.*'

'Can you run the tap a bit longer, that last glass was rather warm.'

'*Si senorita,*' Antonio said, as he ran off with the glass in the direction of the kitchens.

Kerrie slipped the account statements into the machine and ran off six copies. 'Paul,' she shouted, 'key.' Paul threw the key over the counter as she returned the paperwork to the safety deposit box and locked it; she threw the key back at Paul.

Paul caught the key and returned to John. 'Done,' he whispered, holding up his thumbs as they watched Antonio return with the glass of water.

'There you are *senorita*, nice and cold,' he said as Kerrie closed the bundle.

'Thank you, Ant' she said, smiling as she took the glass and sipped the water, and handed him back his handkerchief.

'No...no...you keep it *senorita*,' Antonio said, pushing it towards her.

'*Muchas gracias por su syuda,*' she said as she handed him the glass and picked up the bundle.

'*De nada senorita, encantada de concerle,*' he said.

'And you Ant, *buenas noches,*' Kerrie smiled, as she made her way back to the elevator.

The elevator doors slid open; as they entered John pressed the button for the fourth floor and the doors whooshed shut. 'Are you all right?' asked Paul.

'Fine, just a little scratch,' said Kerrie, 'that's all, I've always been a treble bleeder.'

'So has John,' laughed Paul.

John ignored his remark, being more concerned about Kerrie. 'Are you sure you're ok?' he asked, looking at her forehead and dabbing it with the handkerchief; he went to wipe the blood from her blouse.

Paul gave him a harsh look. 'I wouldn't if I was you,' he said.

John held up his hands. 'Sorry,' he said as he backed off. 'I tell you what though,' he said.

'What?' asked Kerrie.

'You had him eating out of your hand.'

'I know John, now you know what the button on the blouse was for.'

'Dirty bastard,' said John, putting his hand to his mouth. 'Sorry, do you want me to go down there and kick his head in?' His hand went to the ground floor button.

Kerrie grabbed his hand. 'No John that was the whole idea.'

'You sure!'

'I'm sure.'

'Ok…but he didn't have to look.'

Paul rolled his eyes at Kerrie.

'What?' asked John.

'Nothing,' said Kerrie, doing up her blouse.

Paul frowned. 'I think you need to get Sinead to look at that bump, you're going to have right shiner there.'

'Well I'll tell you something, that if I had a bloody Oscar,' said John, 'I'd give you one right now…' 'I hope you mean the Oscar, John,' interrupted Paul.

John looked at Paul, puzzled, and frowned. 'Of course I meant the Oscar, what else did you think I meant?' he asked.

Kerrie laughed.

'What!' asked John, lifting his shoulders.

Paul waved his hand over his head. 'You were wasted as a plumber John; you should have been a limbo dancer.'

'Why?'

'Completely over his head,' Paul said, smiling at Kerrie.

John was listening but not following the general idea of the conversation. 'Anyway,' he continued, 'you were bloody marvellous.' He gave her an impromptu kiss on the cheek.

'Well for that peck on the cheek John,' said Kerrie, tapping her files, 'it was all worth it.'

They all roared with laughter.

Chapter Nineteen
Six Separate Accounts

'Good swim Mick?' asked John.

'Not bad,' replied Mick, 'I'm taking Kerrie's advice, getting more confident every day.'

'Good for you Mick,' smiled Kerrie.

'Sorry I never stopped up…. he paused. 'Shit, what happened to your head?' he asked touching his head.

Kerrie flapped her hands. 'Oh…. don't worry about that it's just a scratch thanks for your concern, it's all part of the big plan.'

'You should have seen her Rod,' said John, 'she was bloody great,' Paul nodded his agreement.

'Right so how did everything go last night?' asked Rod.

'Champion,' replied Kerrie, tapping her briefcase. 'Paul and John were a great help. Craig and I are away to the bank straight after breakfast.'

Craig grabbed some breakfast from the breakfast bar.

Mick whistled as Craig made his way to the table. 'Well look at you, all suited and booted. First time I've ever seen you in a suit, Craig. You definitely look the city gent.'

'Do I look like a banker though?' he asked.

'Yes, quite the little banker,' he remarked.

Rod went to speak.

Mick looked across the table and held up his knife towards Rod. 'Don't,' he warned him.

'And probably the last,' said Craig, pulling at the collar of his shirt. 'I feel like a trussed-up turkey.'

Rod was dying to butt in but filled his mouth with fried egg instead.

'What! You look very smart, as Mick said, quite the city gent,' smiled Kerrie, pulling down the back of his jacket.

Craig returned her smile. 'Thanks for the vote of confidence Kerrie,' he said as he sat down.

John leant forward to finger Craig's lapel, it was a nice suit, a very nice cut. 'Is it new?' he asked.

Craig slapped his hand away and rolled his eyes. 'No, I brought it with me, you twat, of course it's bloody new,' he said. Sinead went shopping with me this morning early. She chose it, apparently it's a Paul Smith.'

'Good choice, Sinead,' said Mick.

'Well that's us lot sorted,' said Kerrie, 'and what are you three up to today?'

'We were thinking of improving our language skills,' answered John. 'Just a bit of bar room Spanish.' Paul and Rod raised their thumbs in unison. 'Definitely,' they said in unison.

'Ok, we're off then,' said Kerrie tutting. 'Come on Craig,' she said, lifting her briefcase.

'Good luck,' they all shouted as they left the dining room.

Chapter Twenty
El Banco

'*H*ola, la senorita, puedo ayudarle?'
Kerrie produced her identity card from her bag
and waved it under the bank manager's nose. '*Hebla
ingles?*' she asked.

'Yes madam,' he replied in perfect English, holding
out his hand. 'My name is Rodrigo Esteve.'

'Kerrie Walsh,' she said. Taking his hand, she smiled.
'And this is my colleague, Butch Cassidy.'

'Hi Butch,' Rodrigo said, holding out his.

Craig looked puzzled and shook his hand, 'Pleased to
meet you.'

'Pleasantries over,' said Kerrie. 'We would like to use
your computer system to transfer some money
transactions from the UK to Spain.'

'Of course…of course, would you both like to come
this way,' he said, holding out his hand as he led them
through the card-swiped security doors. The final door
swung open as they stood in the heart of the bank, the
monitors taking the best part of the centre of the room.
'There you are,' he said holding out his hands toward the
machines. 'Would your colleague and yourself like a cup
of coffee?'

Craig nodded.

'Please,' said Kerrie, 'both white no sugar.'

As he left the room Craig whispered. 'Butch Cassidy,' he said, 'where did that come from?'

'Just a little joke, bank robbers, you know,' smiled Kerrie.

'Right, a bit surreal though,' said Craig smiling. He touched Kerrie's arm. 'Why did you say UK to Spain, surely you meant Spain to the UK?'

'Craig bear with me, everything I say is for a purpose.'

'What like Butch Cassidy?'

'Touché,' replied Kerrie, 'it's because the Spanish don't like large amounts of money going out of Spain. If I had said from Spain to the UK, they may well have asked too many questions.'

'Right, so that's why you said UK to Spain, good thinking,' Craig said.

Kerrie smoothed down her skirt and sat down, punching in her access code. 'That's it,' she said, 'we're in.'

'Craig, account code number please,' she said as Craig lifted the lid of his briefcase. Kerrie placed her hand on the lid and stopped him going any further as Mr Esteve came into the room with two coffees. He held the coffees in the air. 'Two coffees, white,' he said as he laid them on the table and stood back.

Kerrie swung round on her seat and looked at Mr Esteve. 'Sorry, Mr Esteve,' she said, holding out her hands, 'confidential accounts, you understand, client's confidentiality.'

Mr Esteve held up a hand. 'Why of course, sorry,' he said as he walked from the room, turning at the door. 'If you need any assistance, don't hesitate to give me a call.'

The door swung shut behind him.

'You're wasted here,' Craig said, smiling and pulling the account number sheet from the briefcase. As Kerrie punched Uncle Tom's account code number into the system and his account scrolled up on the screen, she checked the account, running her finger down the screen. 'Well it seems that Uncle Tom has invested in a large sum of money or borrowed on the assets as the account stands at a very, very tidy sum.'

Craig was looking round at the door as he heard noises in the corridor. 'What's that?' he asked.

Kerrie turned from the keyboard. 'You are going to be very shocked at what's in here.'

'How much then?' he asked, impatient to know.

'Wait,' said Kerrie, swinging her chair back to face the keyboard, her fingers poised over the keys. 'Right, how much?'

He shrugged his shoulders.

Craig bent down and whispered, 'In for a penny in for a pound, let's clear the lot.'

Kerrie smiled and took an enormous breath and let it go slowly, and then she said, 'Why not?' looking up at Craig. 'As I said that will give you all considerably more than you were expecting. Then I can give you my bill,' she said, smiling as she looked back at the screen.

Craig patted her on the shoulder and smiled. ' Ok, I bet you come very expensive,' laughed Craig.

'You don't want to know my price Craig.'

'Right, then definitely clear the lot,' he said.

'Right, that's no problemo,' said Kerrie, as she broke the money down into six separate accounts. Her fingers flew across the keyboard, transferring the money into the separate accounts. She looked up from the computer, her face breaking into a smile as she pressed the print button. She looked at Craig smiling, the print machine whirred into action and the printouts fell into the tray. Taking her eyes off him, she looked down again at the printouts as the last one fell into the tray. She pulled them from the print tray and turned them over, checking them one by one. 'That's it, the money's been transferred into separate UK bank accounts,' she said, leaning back in her chair and folding her arms without taking her eyes off him. 'There you are, all six,' she said again, handing him the printouts. 'Six separate account numbers in your own names, not a bad day's work.'

Craig eyes narrowed, as he looked down at the printout sheets, not sure whether the noughts were in the right place. His face paled…'Shit… shit…' he said, turning over the printouts one by one. 'This is much more than we expected, how come?' he said, shaking the statement.

'As I said before,' replied Kerrie, 'he either invested the money, or lent money on the existing windfall of your lottery winnings,' she shrugged her shoulders, 'who knows?'

'But this is six point five million…' 'Each,' she interrupted him.

'Shit,' he said again, 'the lads are going to go bloody ape shit, especially Rod.' He smiled, kissing the statements one by one, then grabbed Kerrie and kissed her on both cheeks.

Kerrie blushed, 'Craig you're a married man.'

He folded the statements, placing them safely in his briefcase and snapped the briefcase shut. 'I know I'm married, but I'm sure Maria wouldn't mind, it's not everyday you make her six point five million pounds richer. You've done a bloody good job here, and in my book you're one hell of the cleverest young ladies I've ever meet.' He tilted his head, 'Except for Maria of course.'

'Of course,' Kerrie smiled. 'I know but thank you anyway,' she said, shutting down the computer. She pushed out the chair and stood. 'Ok we're done here,' she said, tapping the monitor, 'now we can give the lads the good news, let's go.'

Craig put a hand on Kerrie's shoulder. 'Hang on Kerrie, will you do me a favour?'

'What?' asked Kerrie, turning. She looked puzzled.

Craig smiled. 'Don't ask me now, but when we get back to the hotel, will you play along with me just for a bit, and you can follow my lead this time.'

Kerrie was even more confused. 'Why?'

Craig held up a hand. 'You'll see later, it's pay back time, just watch Rod's face,' he said, taking her arm. 'Let's go.'

Chapter Twenty-One
Transfer Complete.

Craig and Kerrie giggled as they pushed through the revolving door and walked over to the lads as they sat in the foyer.

John turned in his seat. 'Ok, talk to us,' he called out, impatiently tapping his foot as soon as Kerrie and Craig came through the swivel door of the hotel.

Craig and Kerrie sat down. 'First a stiff drink's in order, a strong one for me,' said Kerrie.

'I'll get them,' said Mick quickly as he stood up. 'What will it be?'

'Brandies all round I think Mick,' said Craig.

'Coming up,' he said as he walked to the bar.

Kerrie looked round the foyer. 'Where's Sinead and Rod?'

'Shopping,' snapped John, tapping his other foot.

Mick placed the tray on the table. 'That's the best brandy money can buy,' he said, passing them round. 'So I bloody hope it's good news you've got us.'

Kerrie sipped her drink. 'You're right Mick, it's very smooth.'

John pulled himself forward on the sofa, grabbing the brandy and gulping it down in one sharp move. His inner voice was screaming, *come on, for God's sake, come on tell us,* as he tapped his fist on the arm of the large sofa.

They all looked round as the foyer door revolved. *Thank God* John thought, as Sinead and Rod came through the revolving door laden down with shopping bags. *Now maybe we can move on, any bloody longer and John thought he wouldn't live long enough to know what Kerrie was going to say.*

Sinead threw down her shopping bags and collapsed on to the large sofa. Rod and Sinead smiled, looking at them all. 'Sorry, were you all waiting for us?' she said as Mick stood and went for his wallet. 'Drinks?' he asked.

Paul sat back and ran a hand across his face, looking at Sinead's red eyes. 'Sinead have you been crying?' he asked. They all looked at her.

'Hay fever,' she said, pulling a handkerchief from her pocket and blowing her nose.

'That's funny,' said Craig, 'I wonder why I haven't got it, I suffer from that you know.'

Sinead bit her lip. 'It's different for everybody, I get what is called tropical hay fever,' she informed them.

Craig gave a minuscule smile. 'Is that right,' he said, 'I didn't know that, well you should know you're the doctor.'

'Drink Sinead,' asked Mick, quickly drawing them off the subject.

'Please,' replied Sinead. 'Just cold water for me Mick, that will do nicely, I'm absolutely sweating,' she said, flapping the front of her dress. 'I thought I could shop but Rod's a born shopper.'

'Rod.'

'Just a lager, please Mick.'

'Right, coming up,' said Mick, 'Rod, give us a hand.'

John was growing impatient. 'Shit,' he mumbled, *'Deja bloody vue.'*

'What was that John?' asked Rod.

'Nothing Rod, just get the bloody drinks in,' he said, waving his hand in the direction of the bar, 'and make it quick, there is some important business we need to be getting on with.'

'Well, she told me Mick,' Rod whispered.

'Good, I'm glad,' whispered Mick as they moved towards the bar.

'Well, what did you buy?' said Kerrie, excitedly rummaging through one of the shopping bags and pulling out a sarong. 'That is absolutely beautiful,' Kerrie said, holding it out in front of the lads, 'just look at all those colours.'

'No for God's sake no don't say it,' thought John.

'Who brought the skirt?' asked Paul.

'Rod brought it,' replied Sinead.

Craig and Paul fell into bursts of laughter.

'What's wrong?' asked Sinead, not understanding their outburst of laughter.

'Take no notice of them Sinead, they are so juvenile,' said John, looking at Paul and Craig firmly.

'Rod brought it for me.'

'Wahoo, that was close,' they said in unison, wiping their foreheads.

'Here you go,' said Rod, passing them their drink. He sat down.

'Rod brought a skirt for Sinead,' said Paul.

Mick looked swiftly at Rod, and then at Paul, and then looked across at Rod. 'It definitely was for Sinead,' he said laughing.

John's teeth were gritted. 'Jesus Christ,' he snapped. 'Are we ever going to move on, this sounds just like I'm back at bloody work, listening to all of your bloody ramblings.'

'Ok...ok...' Craig said. Holding up his hand he picked up the briefcase. The smile had gone from his face. Kerrie moved the drinks tray aside as Craig bent down and laid his briefcase on the low table. 'Watch Rod's face,' he whispered to Kerrie flipping open the brass clips.

'That's it,' Craig said, pulling out the copied statements from the briefcase and holding them up. 'Nothing,' he said, pausing as he let them take in what he had said. 'The bastard had absolutely nothing in his account.'

They all looked at Kerrie as her fingers began to twist at the loose ends of her hair. Holding back a smile, she held out her hands, and nodded her head in agreement. 'We gave it our best shot, but as Craig's said, there was nothing in his account. The bastard must have know we were here and cleared out the account.'

Craig nudged Kerrie, winked and nodded his head towards Rod.

Mick, John, Paul and Sinead sat with their mouths gaping; all hoping that this wasn't happening.

Rod's face paled.

'I see what you mean,' Kerrie whispered in Craig's ear.

'You'll have to excuse me Sinead, but it's got to be said,' Rod apologised, turning his back on them and looking towards the bar. 'Fuuuuuuuuuck it,' he shouted, 'how the fuck did the bastard know we were here?' Antonio looked over from the reception desk at Rod's outburst.

Rod threw his hands in the air. 'Christ, this just gets worse. So you're telling us that all of this was for bloody nothing.'

Craig passed the statements around one at a time. 'Right, that's yours Mick, and yours John. As you can see,' he said again, 'nothing.' He tapped his top pocket and pulled out the statement. 'I've already got mine.'

'You fucking bastards,' shouted John smiling.

'What!' said Rod, turning back towards them. 'What!'

Mick looked at Craig, 'John's right, you are a bastard Craig,' he mouthed.

'I know exactly why you did it Craig, pay back time,' Paul said, looking at Rod.

'What!' said Rod again, holding out his hands.

'From Monkey man,' said Craig, slapping the statement in Rod's hand.

Kerrie burst out laughing as Rod looked at the statement. He shook the statement at Craig. 'I'm telling you this Craig, I'm going to buy a fucking zoo with this money and lock you up forever, you bastard, and feed you fuck all.'

'Every Monkey has its day, so they say,' replied Craig.

'Dog, you twat,' said Rod, smiling and looking at the statement again.

After their initial shock, there seemed to be an unusual stillness in the foyer that only money seems to bring, as they studied the statements. Then came the shouted echoes of 'Fuck... fuck... fuck... fuck... fuck.' Antonio looked up again from the reception desk.

'Six point five million each, that's more than we expected, how come?' gasped Rod, looking at Kerrie for an answer.

Kerrie shrugged her shoulders. 'Don't know, could have been anything. Who knows what the bastard was into, could be drugs money...' 'I hope not,' interrupted Mick, who frowned looking at the statement dubiously. 'I wouldn't want anything to do with drugs, dirty money,' he said, placing the statement on the table.... Craig nudged Kerrie, as he knew Mick would upset the apple cart with her suggestion of drugs money. 'But Mick,' said Kerrie quickly, it's probably not drugs money, more like investments borrowed against your lottery money.'

Mick smiled. 'Well in that case, that's alright then.' He pulled the statement back off the table. 'As you said,' he said, shaking the statement, 'it was our money anyway.'

Rod's face lit up, acquiring a permanent smile. 'What the fuck am I going to do,' he said, unable to take in the sizeable amount of money that he had just come into, 'Six... point... five... million... pounds? This is brilliant!' His eyes shone. 'This means...I have enough money to...' he shrieked. So many things were passing through his brain that he couldn't put his finger on just one thing.

'To do what?' asked John.

'What ever I bloody want.'

'Spend…spend…spend,' answered Paul, looking wide-eyed at the statement. 'That's much more than we expected,' he said.

John shook the statement in the air. 'Shit, at last, we've got the bloody money,' he said, kissing the statement.

The only two in the foyer who never joined in the lads' excitement were Sinead and Kerrie. All the money in the world would never make up for the loss of their da. Their only happiness would be to see the bastard behind bars.

'And it's all because of the girls,' said Mick, 'you know without them we wouldn't have got a penny of this money.'

'You're bloody right Mick,' agreed John. 'Anyway dinner's on me tonight ladies.'

Paul held up his hands. 'Hang on did I hear right John?' he said, wringing his finger in his ear. 'Did you say you're paying?' he asked sarcastically.

'You can pay for yourself Paul, it's the ladies I'm taking out.

Whatever you want ladies, is on me.'

'Yes, well done you girls,' Mick said, hugging Kerrie and then Sinead, feeling their sadness flowing through their bodies as he hugged them. 'Right,' he said as he sat back down, 'what happens now?'

John's fear of flying had gone. 'Book me the fastest plane back to good old Blighty,' he shouted.

'Right,' agreed Paul, 'and then we can start spending.'

'You don't need to go back home to draw on those accounts,' Kerrie said, 'I have given you access over here, you can start drawing on them now.'

Paul tilted his head. 'It that right?' he said, raising his eyebrows.

'God, Kerrie, you shouldn't have told him that,' John said, 'there'll be no holding him back now.'

'When we going home then?' asked Craig.

Rod and Mick were the only two who knew what the girls were feeling. Rod went to speak. Mick held up a hand, knowing exactly what he was going to say. 'Hang on, before you jet back to the UK, what about the girls?' he asked.

'What about the girls?' asked Paul, shrugging his shoulders.

'Think,' said Mick, pointing to his head. 'Sinead and Kerrie didn't come out here for the money, did they Paul?'

'No,' Paul replied, 'but they are not going home empty- handed, they will get Sean's share. Rod couldn't hold his tongue any longer. 'Paul, for them it's not about money for fuck's sake, it's about their da; they came out here to prove that their da didn't steal the money from us.'

'Well he didn't, they've proved that, haven't they, we know their da didn't steal the money,' said John, 'their Uncle Tom did.'

Sinead spoke. 'That's the point, Uncle Tom...' she shuddered at the name. 'What's going to happen to the bastard?'

'We could let him rot here bloody penniless,' said John.

'I'm afraid we can't just walk away,' said Kerrie, 'we only know that the bastard stole the money. We really don't know whether he...murdered Da, it's only speculation on your part, John.'

'Well, I'm sorry about your dad girls, that goes without saying,' said John, 'but I'm 150% sure that the bastard murdered Sean.'

'We're going to have to confront him then,' said Craig.

Rod smiled one of his rare smiles at Craig. 'Now Craig, you're talking the girls' language,' he said.

Paul looked puzzled. 'So, right, let me get this straight, what you're suggesting is that we walk up to the bastard's front door and say, excuse us Uncle Tom, we are from the UK. I hope we haven't caught you at a bad moment, but we were wondering before we return to the UK if you could tell us if you killed your twin brother Sean, and as an afterthought, when he goes to slam the front door in our faces we could tell him that we have cleaned out his bank account.'

Mick was in deep thought taking in only part of Paul's sarcasm. 'Something like that,' he said, 'maybe not the front, but we could go in the back door.'

'I was joking Mick,' said Paul.

'I'm not,' replied Mick.

John was giving what was being said some serious thought. He was watching Sinead and Kerrie's faces as the conversation was going around the table. 'Uhmm...' he said, 'Mick and Rod are right; when we needed the girls they helped us in lots of ways and got us the money. Now the girls need us and we are not going to just walk away from them. If they want to know what happened...' he paused. 'We are certainly not going to get any answers sitting around here, and if the girls need me then I'm in.' John looked at the girls; their smiling faces said it all. 'The girls don't need to say a thing,' he said, 'well, are we going to find out what really happened to Sean for them, are we all agreed?'

'Well said,' said Mick, patting John on the shoulder. 'You can definitely count me in.'

'And me,' said Rod smiling, holding up a thumb. 'Good on you John.'

'Well Craig?' said Mick.

'Count me in,' said Craig as they all looked towards Paul.

Paul's thoughts went back to the shopping trip in the UK, how could he let down a lady that he had seen naked, and she let him... John interrupted his thoughts. 'Well Paul...?' 'What can I say?' said Paul, shrugging his shoulders and looking around at the lads and then at the girls. 'I suppose I'm out-numbered, but count me in,' he said. 'Hang on though, I must say that when the going get tough, we can always rely on John to get us up to our necks in shit.'

They all roared with laughter. 'Thanks,' said Sinead and Kerrie as they kissed John on both cheeks.

Mick noticed the tears in Sinead's eyes. 'What's up?' he asked softly, as she fell into Mick's arms and sobbed on his shoulder.

John looked puzzled. 'What is it, not something I said?' he asked, looking at Kerrie and raising his shoulders.

'Probably,' replied Paul.

Craig interjected. 'John only said that we were going to help them...' 'It's not that,' said Sinead, waving a hand, interrupting Craig, and wiping the tears with the back of her hand. 'If Uncle Tom did as you said John...' she sobbed again, 'murder Da, then who's going to tell Ma?'

Mick tapped his forehead. 'Christ, you're right Sinead,' he agreed, 'Cathleen hasn't got a clue, unless you girls have been ringing her,' he looked at both the girls.

Both the girls shook their heads in unison. 'We've only spoken about where we are, and general conversation that's all,' said Kerrie.

'Well somebody's got to tell Cathleen,' said Paul.

'Uhmm...' said John as they all looked round at him. 'This is what I propose we do,' he said, hands spread wide. 'Firstly before one of us rings Cathleen, the girls need to know if Uncle Tom did murder Sean.'

'I can tell this is going to be the shit bit,' said Paul.

'Well take a clean set of pants with you Paul,' smiled John. 'Anyway, so what I suggest is we go to his villa early tomorrow morning, and I mean early,' he said, looking at Paul and Craig. 'Five-thirty am...' 'We're what?' interrupted Paul, 'all going out at what time in the morning? He asked.

'You heard,' replied John. 'Five-thirty am. Sharp!'

'You're joking.'

'No sodding way,' Craig agreed with Paul.

'Listen to me,' said John, 'this is no game we're playing here, we're going to have to get to the villa early so there is nobody about.'

'That seems sensible to us,' agreed the girls.

John smiled at the girls. 'Right, so no late night tonight, Craig and Paul.'

'Is nine o'clock all right then John?' said Paul and Craig in unison.

'Just make sure you are in early, no piss-ups.'

'You can tuck us in if you like John,' said Craig.

'For God's sake will you two shut up and listen to what John has to say,' snapped Mick.

Craig and Paul sat back in their sofa chairs.

'Cheers Mick,' said John, 'anyway, Sinead and Rod know where Uncle Tom lives.'

Paul put up his hand, like a told-off schoolboy.

'Go ahead,' said Mick, looking at him sternly.

Paul had deep furrows in his forehead. 'Why so early in the morning?' he asked.

Craig raised his hand, Mick pointed at him.

'Good point Paul,' said Craig.

'You're right Craig, good point,' repeated John. 'Well, as I've said about nobody being around, also have you seen *Crime Watch UK* on the television? When the police arrest somebody they go in early morning, so that the person is disorientated.'

'That's hasn't a clue, to you Rod,' said Craig.

'Like you Rod,' said Paul.

Rod ignored them both. 'John's right,' he agreed.

'So…. does that answer your question why we are going in so early?' asked John.

Craig and Paul nodded.

Mick looked round at them all. 'As John says, tomorrow we'll go in the back door and *hey presto* we grab him.'

Paul held up his hand again.

Mick pointed at him.

'Any dogs?'

'Another good point, Paul,' said John.

'John hate's dogs,' said Rod smiling.

'It's not that I hate dogs it's just that I love my fingers,' replied John looking at his fingers and turning to Sinead. 'I nearly had my fingers bitten off the last time we tried entering a house.'

Sinead nodded her head. 'I never heard anything,' she said. 'When I searched the kitchen, I didn't see any signs of dogs, no plates on the floor or dog food in the cupboards.'

'Good, so that's settled then, tomorrow morning early,' confirmed John.

They all nodded their heads in agreement.

'Hang on though,' said Mick, 'that doesn't answer Sinead and Kerrie's earlier question,' he said. 'Who's going to tell Cathleen about Sean? If we do find out that Sean was murdered by Uncle Tom then she has got to know before we get home.'

'Shit, that's a difficult one Mick, you're right though,' said John, agreeing with Mick and lowering his head, 'Cathleen's definitely got to know,' John paused, pondering the question. 'It can't come from the girls; it will be much too upsetting for them. Paul or Craig, haven't got the finesse.' He looked at them both. 'They unquestionably couldn't do it.'

Rod waved a hand towards John and nodded, 'NO.'

John looked at Mick. 'I'm afraid that leaves you and me Mick, and I don't think I could do it, I wouldn't have a clue what to say or where to start.'

'Forgive me for saying this Mick,' said Craig, turning towards John. 'But John, I think Mick's our man; he's been through it once before, what with what happened to his wife and daughter. He knows exactly how Cathleen is going to feel.'

Mick nodded his head, 'I can't do it, it would be too upsetting for me.' He looked at both the girls.

'Please… Please… Mick,' said Kerrie as both the girls sat next to him. Kerrie rubbed his hands. 'We'll be there with you when you tell Ma, please Mike. You are the only one that can do it, and Ma has a liking for you.'

Mick looked at Sinead and then at Kerrie with their sad eyes. 'Does she?' he asked.

'She does and if Da has been murdered then she's going to need somebody strong to help her through the grieving period. We trust you, and we know you can do it Mick.'

Mick's eyes watered. 'Ok if you say so, but you've both got to be there with me, when I tell her.'

'We will Mick… we will, we'll be there.'

'Ok, I'll do it for you all and Cathleen, when we find out if Uncle Tom did murder your dad.'

Kerrie hugged him tightly, and whispered. 'You know, we all love you very much Mick.'

★ ★ ★

Mick ordered two more pints, and sat down.

'Where's everybody tonight?' asked John, looking around the bar.

'Paul and Craig have taken Kerrie out for a curry.'

'Where's Rod and Sinead?' John asked.

'A bit of quality time together I think.'

'I hope you don't mean that Rod's trying it on with her.'

'I think Rod may have changed a bit since he meet Sinead.'

'Changed,' John tutted. 'Mick, never be fooled by the leopard, it never changes its spots believe me. I'm telling you Mick, that Sinead's a very sensitive young lady, you know, too sensitive for him.'

Mick nodded. 'Maybe you're right John, who knows.'

'I know Mick, if there's one thing I do know that's something about young ladies, got a young teenager of my own, as you know,' said John gulping his beer.

'Yer, maybe,' said Mick,' 'anyway she's spending some time with Rod. They said they were going to check out the bastard's whereabouts, and stake out his villa.'

'Good for them, anyway I've given Rod a few words of wisdom.'

'I think they are going to make it,' said Mick, 'Rod's really fallen for her, hook, line and sinker.'

'I don't know,' John looked at Mick confused. 'D'you think so?'

'I do,' replied Mick.

John nodded his head. 'Na…. I don't think so Mick,' he replied. 'I think Rod's got two hopes Mick, Bob Hope and no fucking hope. I'm telling you Mick, it's in Sinead's eyes, and her eyes are saying no chance here Rod my son, you're not getting your hand in my drawers.' He held up his glass. 'Anyway, more important things to think about, what are you having?'

'Same again,' said Mick, smiling.

Chapter Twenty-Two
This Could Be the First Time

'Come on, come in,' shouted Rod, 'you don't know what you're missing: it's lovely and warm.'

'I can't, I haven't got a costume on,' she shouted.

'Don't worry, I won't look,' shouted Rod, placing his hands over his eyes, but splitting his fingers so he didn't lose the perfect image of her form in the light of the moon. 'Come on…come on, it's really warm.' He gazed as Sinead lowered her hands and gripped the hem of her T-Shirt. She toed off her shoes.

Rod trod water. 'I can't promise that I'll keep my hands off you once you get in here, I want you wet and naked Sinead, I just plain want you.'

'If I wanted you to keep your hands off me I wouldn't be here now, would I?' She took a deep breath and started to peel off her shirt.

'Hey, hey!' they shouted.

'Shit, there's no fucking God,' mumbled Rod as the lovely glimpse of her creamy flesh vanished under Sinead's hastily tugged down shirt, and she turned away.

Sinead put her hands over her eyes. 'Yes?'

'Is that you Sinead? It's us,' Kerrie shouted, waving her hands towards them.

'Over here,' she called.

Kerrie turned around. 'It is, lads, I told you it was Sinead and Rod,' she shouted at Craig and Paul, as she took off down the beach towards Sinead.

'The lads and I have just been out for a curry. What are you doing down here all alone?'

Sinead pointed out to sea. 'Just…' 'Right,' Kerrie interrupted, straining to see and spotting Rod in the water. 'Right, I see,' she said, shaking her head and smiling. 'Well, Paul and Craig suggested we went for a swim,' she held out her hands. 'So here we are, shame I never brought a swimsuit, still never mind. Let the boys go in, we can sit and watch them.'

Rod finished dressing, sat and slipped on his shoes. 'Jesus Christ I never thought they would go.' He stood, wrapping his arms around her waist. This woman in front of him didn't remind him of any of the women he'd ever known; Sinead circled her arms around his neck for a moment. 'I'm sorry about the other day,' she said.

Rod put his finger to her lips. 'That's ok,' he replied, feeling uncomfortable when he'd said that's ok. 'Not the you know what, I mean,' not wanting to say rape. 'That's definitely not ok.' They stood, lips a breath apart, while his body shivered with anticipation. Mouths brushed lightly, retreated, brushed again. It was she who moaned for the first time as she crushed her lips onto his in a hot spurt of hunger. She'd been isolated from her feelings until now but the kiss triggered a spreading warmth throughout her body, followed by a tight cluster of sensations like she had never felt before; she needed his strength, the press of his hard muscular body, the ripe flavour of him, and the heat, the silky dance of his tongue and the teasing nip of his teeth, the edgy thrill of feeling his heart pounding against hers. She let out little gasps of pleasure when he changed the angle of his kiss; she dived in again, setting off aches in her body that throbbed like pulse beats. Never wanting to let go. Quiet sounds of need hummed in her throat and burned in her blood, her skin feel like hot satin, and the feel of her skin under his touch sent erotic images, demands that needed for them to be horizontal. She wanted to take him to bed that very minute.

Pulling away from the kiss, 'Jesus Christ Sinead,' he said, breathless. 'What do we do now?'

She smiled at him; her eyes were alight, filled with trust and pleasure. 'What do you think?'

'Are you talking…like…maybe… consummation?'

She shrugged. 'That sort of area, let's go, we have to get inside, unless you want to do it right here.'

'Right. Wow, let's go.'

Time never existed from the beach to the hotel elevator; it was as if they had been beamed up into the elevator. The doors closed behind them. Sinead's breathing had become ragged as they wrestled with each other's clothes. The elevator doors opened and they stumbled into the hallway, buttons popping off his shirt as he picked her up and half carried her towards her suite door. They ended up in a heap on the bed, half on and half off.

'My... God... Oh God...' She shouted as her fingers worked on his belt.

'Wait,' he shouted, 'the door, let me close the door.' Rolling off the bed, he could have done the four-minute mile, if his trousers weren't pulling at his ankles. He kicked the door shut, and hopped back towards the bed.

'The CD,' she shouted.

'What!' he shouted breathless.

'The CD player,' she pointed at the player. 'Switch on the CD player.'

He hopped towards the player removing his shoes, and pressed play on the CD. Hopping back, he jumped onto the bed.

'This CD is how I feel about you, Rod,' Sinead whispered as the room filled with Westlife's Unbreakable.

You took my hand, touched my heart, you were always there, by my side, night and day... through it all. Baby come what may, swept away on a wave of emotion. We're caught in the eye of a storm, and whenever you smile I can hardly believe that you're mine. Believe that you're mine.

They tore at each other's clothes, rolled and tugged. He caught glimpses, beautiful, erotic images of tanned skin, soft curves, and delicate lines.

This love is unbreakable; it's unmistakable, and each time I look in your eyes, I know why, this love is untouchable, I feel in my heart just can't deny, each time I look in your eyes I know why...

And whenever you smile, I can tell you're mine, together we are strong in my arms that's where you belong….

He wanted to stop and wallow in her beauty. No time now, he wanted her, he felt himself shaking inside, he'd never felt this urgency before with anybody, not until he'd meet Sinead, and his loins seemed to be vibrating with a hot energy every time he undid a button or clasp. He shook his leg trying to rid himself of the one trouser leg that wouldn't budge; he gave up and lowered his mouth to hers. She poured all she had into the kiss, vibrating beneath him – a volcano on the brink of erupting. What she hadn't been able to put into words to him, she could make up now with her heart, her body. A skim of his fingers, a brush of his lips, her skin purred under the brush of his fingers. When he touched her, those thrills, those soft and fluid aches were welcome. She felt the room spinning around her as flashes of white-hot heat raced through her system, she was ready, arching under him, not an offer, but a demand. His muscles rippled as she ran her fingertips lightly up and down his back, arousing him. She felt as if she was falling deeper and deeper, as if she'd leapt on Oblivion at Alton Towers, and all that she could grab hold of was the glorious weight of his body, hoping for the ride of her life.

He felt her breasts, cupping them in the palms of his hands, pleasuring them both with his lips, tongue and teeth, the tips hardening under the soft bite of his teeth. The taste of her intoxicated him, a flavour he could come to crave as much as his next breath.

Her heart began to beat under his mouth like the endless pulse of the sea. And as the beat quickened, she rose beneath him with a single breathless gasp. 'Now,' she commanded, gripping his hips; freely she opened herself to him.

'Now.'

He lifted her hips and gently entered her with one smooth strong motion, that moment's pleasure was what his body needed, gentle rising and falling, letting his body take over, letting his mind go. There was nothing left but extraordinary passion, body-to-body, mouth-to-mouth, touching and tasting. From that moment on nobody else existed, and no one would ever come between them. Rod knew from this time on Sinead was his only soul mate, as Sean had said.

She closed around him, he felt her tighten, stretching herself like a bow beneath him, with a kind of ruthless endurance.

'God,' she gasped.

He shot screaming to her peak. Her climax rippled through him like madness. He could feel her body shivering with pleasure, trembling with the delirium that had pulsated through her. She was free, she wrapped herself around him, clinging tighter, and she was his.

And with her feeling of sheer pleasure he knew she was never going to be hurt again, not while he drew breath.

Rod woke. His ears were still ringing; it had been the most wonderful night of his entire life. Change is definitely a good thing, just what he needed. He'd found something far more profound than mere gratification and Sinead had represented a major breakthrough in his life. This wasn't because the sex had, in physical terms, been fantastic: for the first time in his sexual life he'd concentrated hard on trying to give her pleasure without paying too much attention to his own sexual needs, and to top it all this beauty slept quietly beside him, This was the first woman he'd woken up with, with her name on his lips. He looked at his watch. 4.30am, *we've got an hour*, he thought. His hand gently brushed her cheek. 'Sinead…. Sinead.'

She moved drowsily.

He kissed her. 'How'd you sleep?'

'Mmm………. fantastic, the sleep of sexual satisfaction.'

He knew exactly where she was coming from, it was the best night's sleep he had had for months.

She felt the feeling of slow warmth flowing through her body. Curled by his side, all her fears and worries had been washed away. 'Rod, I love you,' she whispered softly. She reached up, kissing him with great tenderness. 'I have so many reasons to be so grateful to you. I scarcely know where to start.'

Rod placed a finger gently on her lips. 'Start nowhere. You owe me nothing. It's me that owes you Sinead,' he hesitated. 'God you don't know how long I've been waiting to hear you say that you love me, and it's been so hard waiting for you to say that to me.'

Sinead raised herself on her elbow, the sheet slipping across the contours of her body. 'I couldn't say anything before, and if I've hurt you through my silence then the fault is mine, not yours and I beg your forgiveness.'

He watched and listened transfixed at what she'd said; a bead of sweat trickled its way from around her neck, past the creases of her tanned skin between her breasts.

'What are you thinking?' she asked.

'I don't need to forgive you Sinead, I love you, absolutely love you, and you're the only woman I have ever loved.' He said it with such force that there could be no doubting his sincerity. He looked at her beautiful face, feeling her fingers sweep through his hair; she was everything he needed, and his journey was over. 'I know you couldn't say anything before, but why now?' Rod asked, looking for reassurance that Sinead felt the same as he did. With the point of his little finger he traced the passage of the droplet, which made a sudden rush to her navel.

'Can't you guess,' she paused. 'Because, when you're near me Rod,' she smiled, 'I feel safe, and everything inside me lifts and sighs, and because love is the most precious gift, and I wanted to give mine to you, I can't imagine life without you now or forever.'

Gently he stroked his hand across her cheek, into her hair. Tenderly he kissed her forehead and cheeks. *He knew he had found the perfect partner, sex was just the icing on the cake, but this cake was the real thing to him, not your sponge with fake icing, this was the real thing fruity, spicy, with every bite more delicious than the first. He had tried many women trying to fill the empty void in his life, but nothing had worked, the other women he'd known had been a pretence, maybe an attempt to prove his virility, but now he knew in the end it was a pointless exercise, like drawing a picture with a broken pencil, pointless. Afterwards he always felt alone. But the presence of Sinead in his world, so close – and in bed with him – had made him realise that. From now on he knew what the rest of his days would bring. He faced the rest of his life with every aspect of his existence being alive with this new excitement of really loving someone, and that love being returned. He knew now that falling in love had corrected the one-sidedness of his life, and Sinead's fears had been washed away, no more trip wires, no more hidden horrors for her, he had taken them on for her, they were in love.* 'I want to spend the rest of my life with you, you know.'

She pushed a hand through his hair. 'Is that what you really want Rod?'

'I want you more now than I ever did, remember when I first saw you at your house?'

She nodded and smiled at the thought of him squirming under the padded TCP swab.

'There was nothing honourable about my intentions towards you then, I wanted to have sex with you there and then on the kitchen floor, but now it's different. If I'd never got to lay a finger on you, I'd still love you, now I want you for different reasons.'

She looked puzzled. 'What reasons?' she asked.

'Why do I want you? Why?' said Rod. 'Well...well, let's see,' he paused. She punched him on the shoulder.

'Ok...ok maybe because you're one of the most beautiful women I've ever seen in my entire life.'

She blushed.

'And now,' he continued. 'All I want is you for life, as your dad said to me once which seems a long time ago now. He said about me finding a soul mate. Well now I know I've found just the soul mate that I needed, and all I can think of is you.'

Sinead pulled him in closer, as the palm of his hand slid slowly past her belly button, her breath quickening. 'Christ Rod we've got to go down for breakfast,' she panted. The blood was beginning to rush once more. Her body was desperate to make up for so much lost time.

'I've ordered breakfast, it should be here any minute,' Rod said. Reluctantly she diverted his hand to the outside of her thigh; if she let him continue they would be their forever. 'We must go, the lads will be waiting for us,' she muttered. She leaned over and kissed him before rolling out of bed.

He watched her get out of bed and head towards the bathroom. 'Jesus Christ you have one hell of a figure, young lady.'

She looked back and shook her hair back. 'Thank you, you're too kind sir, so have you,' she grinned at him. She'd never intended for this to happen, but it seemed inevitable. A knock at the door interrupted them. 'Rod get that will you, it must be breakfast. I'm taking a shower then we'll have breakfast, and go down for a quick coffee with Kerrie and the lads.'

Rod couldn't resist Sinead as he watched her figure through the opaque shower screen. 'Wash your back, young lady,' he said as he slid back the door and stepped into the steamy abyss. Watching the water run down each other's hair, neck and shoulders. He felt warm and solid as she leaned against him for a minute. 'God,' she said as he pushed against her. Turning she slipped her hands around his neck, 'Sod breakfast, it can wait another ten-minute,' she said as their lips touched.

★ ★ ★

Sinead and Rod walked in together, gazing into each other's eyes.

'That's a good sight,' said Mick as Sinead and Rod walked into the breakfast room practically holding hands.

'What?' asked John, shovelling a spoonful of fruit into his mouth.

'Matching grins,' replied Mick, waving a finger at Sinead and Rod and signalling to John that Rod and Sinead had come into the dining room.

The others looked at each other. Convinced that Sinead and Rod appeared to be having some kind of relationship. Mick went quiet. Finally he spoke, knowing what they were all thinking. 'It's none of our business, I expect.'

'I know,' replied Paul, looking over at them. 'But I wouldn't mind having a smile like that on my face,' he said. 'Something's definitely been going on there. Rod looks fucked.'

'Well, well, just look at them, its love's young dream,' laughed Craig. 'I think it's the other way round, it's Sinead who's got...' 'Don't you dare say what I think you're going to say,' interrupted Mick, 'there's no need for that.'

'Ok,' Craig held up his fork in defence. 'Sorry Mick it probably would have been inappropriate, but you must admit that he has shagged Sinead.'

'Craig's right, it seems that somebody got very lucky last night, definitely a case of hiding the sausage I think,' said John.

Mick tutted. 'For God's sake listen to you, you're both beginning to sound like Rod.'

John held up his spoon. 'What! It was merely an observation Mick, that's all,' he said, shrugging his shoulders.

'You're not going to squeeze him for the full details are you?' asked Mick.

'Please Mick,' answered John, 'you know me better than that, now would I do such a thing to them.' He spooned in another mouthful of fruit.

Paul smiled at Mick. 'Do bears shit in the wood Mick?'

'Does the Pope pray?' said Craig.

John smiled and shrugged his shoulders again.

Mick tried to change the subject. 'Nice…breakfast?' he said, then winced at the pathetic question, knowing that John wouldn't move on the subject. He continued. 'John, don't you dare say a word; you'll only embarrass Sinead. Ssh,' whispered Mick, 'Rod's coming over.'

Craig only had to see the bounce in his walk towards the table to know he had shagged Sinead.

Sinead spoke with Kerrie at the breakfast bar as Rod sat down with his coffee, clocking Craig's reaction to his arrival.

Rod sat down and looked around the table. 'What have you all gone quiet for?'

'Nothing,' they said at once.

'Busy night Rod,' John commented.

'You bet,' replied Rod, unfolding his napkin. He shook it and laid it on his lap. 'Went for a late night swim.'

'I don't think it was your late night swim that put that smile on Sinead's face,' winked John.

Paul nudged John. 'Yes you're right John,' he said, nodding unconvinced. 'Definitely the look of a girl who spent the night in the throngs of passion,' he said, *the lucky bastard has had sex with that bloody heavenly body; imagining Sinead would be just as tasty as the bowl of fruit John was necking back.*

'Well?' they all said.

'What?' Rod replied, trying not to smile.

They all stared at him across the table, in mounting silence.

'Aren't you going to tell us what happened?' John said eventually.

'Out of ten Rod,' asked Paul.

Rod swallowed a forkful of scrambled egg and took a gulp of coffee, avoiding Paul and John's questions.

'So you and Sinead got down to a bit of the old mattress samba, then?' said John. ' Come on Rod, just a little information, about what happened,' he asked, holding his thumb and index finger 10mm apart.

'So you actually shagged her?' asked Paul again. 'Come on tell all?'

Rod looked at their faces severely. 'Shut up, piss off, the lot of you, I'm not talking about my sexual activities.'

Paul rolled his eyes at John. 'Well there's a first,' he said, 'any other time Rod, that's all we'd bloody hear.'

Rod ignored Paul, and went straight to John. 'John, have I ever asked you about your sex life?' Paul interrupted Rod. 'John would probably tell you Rod, that's if he was getting any,' he laughed.

Mick and Rod roared with laughter.

John looked sternly at Mick. 'I'd expect that reaction from Rod, but you Mick, I would appreciate it if you laughed with me, and not at me.'

'Sorry John,' said Mick, holding up a hand to his mouth.

Paul leant forward. 'Come on Rod what happened? You look like a cat that's stolen the cream.'

Rod looked over his shoulder. Sinead was still in deep conversation with Kerrie and he hoped she wasn't informing Kerrie of what went on last night. He turned back towards the lads. 'Can't you guess?'

'You shagged her,' said Paul.

'You're jealous. It's so obvious you're jealous.'

'Course I am, you idiot. Course I'm jealous.'

'Why?'

'Well if you had seen what I had seen John,' whispered Paul, 'you would be jealous.'

'What!' asked John.

Mick tapped the table with his fork, 'Paul!'

Rod held up a hand, 'that's all right Mick, yes and as you so crudely said, Paul, shagged was not the word I would have used. What I did was make love to her, and I can tell you this, it was the most perfect night, commendable; I've never met anybody in my life like Sinead.'

'Aaaaah! I knew it,' Craig said, slapping the table. 'I'm telling you he's actually shagged her, and I said it would happen one day.'

'Shut up!'

'And?' asked John.

'And what?' replied Rod.

Mick looked puzzled. 'What do you mean, and what John?'

'Rod knows, how was it?' John asked, looking at Sinead at the breakfast bar.

'Was what?'

'Was it? You know.'

'Yes.'

'Yes what?'

'Fan… Bloody…. tastic!'

'Really?' Paul sipped his coffee in an attempt to regain control of his mouth muscles, which seemed to have formed themselves into a fixed grimace. *The dirty lucky bastard's been pawing that perfectly formed body; still, he resigned himself to the fact that he'd been lucky enough to see it before Rod.*

Craig smiled. 'Oh…Mmm…' He ran his tongue over his lips. 'Don't stop now.'

Rod smiled. 'Me and Sinead – we're just…'

'Just what?' asked John, waving his spoon.

'I know we're – you know lads – we're very compatible.' 'Really,' interrupted Paul, 'what sex-wise is that?'

'Everything wise mate, it was just perfect; we're perfect for each other. I think we broke a few of my previous personal demons last night…' 'Now you're bragging Rod,' interrupted Mick, 'it's inappropriate.' 'Shush, that's all right Mick,' said Paul, waving a hand, 'he's among friends. So what are you going to do about you and Sinead now?' he asked.

Rod looked over his shoulder; Kerrie and Sinead were still deep in conversation. He looked back at the lads. 'I'm telling you Sinead is completely different from any other woman I've… you know lads…been with…there is nothing casual about this lady.' They all sat, spoons in their mouths, listening with intent.

Rod looked around at Sinead then back at the lads and continued. 'Honestly, it was like we weren't just having sex, we were actually making…' 'Don't say it,' snapped Paul, pointing his spoon at Rod.

Mick shrugged 'Don't say what Paul?' he asked.

'Just don't say it Rod,' repeated Paul.

John looked at Paul. 'What?' he asked.

Paul shook his spoon at Rod again. 'He's going to tell us he was making love to Sinead last night. I'm telling you if he does I'm going to puke all over my breakfast.'

'But we were.'

Paul placed his fingers in his mouth and heaved.

'Piss off Paul,' snapped Rod. 'And I'm telling you all now lads, that I want to share the rest of my life with Sinead, grow old with her. In fact… I want to marry her …' the sound of cutlery echoed around the breakfast room as their spoons, knives and forks hit their plates in unison.

Chapter Twenty-Three
Let Me Kick His Head In

They all met in the foyer at 6:30 am on the dot. John looked around the foyer. 'Where the hell's Sinead and Rod, and Craig' he snapped. 'I bloody told them all to be...' Mick held up a hand. 'Don't worry,' he interrupted. 'Sinead and Rod are bringing the car round the front, John.' Mick looked around the foyer. 'Mind you, I don't know where Craig is.'

John frowned at Paul.

Paul shrugged his shoulders. 'Don't look at me like that, John,' he said, 'I don't know where he is; I'm not his bloody keeper. I was in bed by nine o'clock last night, like you said... the car horn interrupted Paul.

'Well, there you are John. There's Sinead and Rod outside,' said Mick.

John looked at his watch. 'Well, we can't wait for Craig any longer.' He took a last look round the foyer. 'Let's go and kick Uncle Tom's arse,' he said as they made their way out to the car.

'*Buenos dias senorita*, how is your head?' Antonio shouted across the foyer from the front desk, pointing to his head.

Kerrie waved. '*Buenos dias* Antonio, it's fine, thank you,' she shouted across the foyer, raising her hand to her forehead as they all disappeared through the revolving door.

They all jumped into the car, Rod looked round. 'Where's Monkey man then, Paul?' he asked.

'Why does everybody keep asking me about Monkey Man,' Paul snapped, shrugging his shoulders. 'I don't know, I'm not his bloody keeper.'

Rod looked at John, waiting for the command to move.

John looked at the revolving door. 'Sod him,' he said, looking at his watch again. 'Ck Rod, let's go, we can't wait for him any longer.'

Rod pulled away but he'd only got a hundred yards when he noticed a large pair of arms waving in his rear view mirror. He hit the brakes screeching to a halt.

'Shit Rod,' shouted John, Mick, Paul, Kerrie and Sinead in unison, as they all lurched forward.

Rod grinned. 'Look it's bloody Monkey man,' he said as they all turned and looked through the rear window, watching Craig as he ran towards the car waving his hands in the air.

'I've never noticed it before, but Rod's right, he has got long arms,' said Kerrie looking at John.

'We think it's genetic Kerrie, a family thing,' said John. 'Where the fuck have you been...?' Craig doubled up, panting at the passenger door. 'Sorry,' he interrupted... 'Sorry... I'm late, but... but...Maria was having the baby.' He was still trying to catch his breath as he opened the passenger door. 'That's why I was late.'

'What! She was having the baby?' asked Paul.

'Yes, I told her about the six point five million, and she went into labour, lucky though, her brother was with her,' replied Craig as he jumped in.

Rod twisted in the driver's seat to look at Craig. 'Nice thought, Craig, that her brother was there, but I don't think so,' he said pulling a face. 'How inconsiderate, I hope you told her we were busy.'

'I didn't have time,' he said excitedly. 'Anyway, you wouldn't believe it if I told you…' 'But you're going to tell us anyway,' interrupted Rod. Craig ignored Rod's remark. 'It was over in minutes and Maria had the baby while I was on the phone. Would you believe it while I was on the bloody phone,' he repeated unable to control his excitement. 'I heard the baby cry, when they slapped it.'

'You sure they didn't slap Maria,' said Paul smiling.

'Piss off Paul,' replied Craig, 'it's our big day and I don't give a shit what you say.'

'Well said and well done Craig,' smiled Sinead and Kerrie.

'I wished they had bloody slapped Craig,' whispered Rod. 'Well! What is it?' he asked.

'It's a baby.'

'Jesus Christ Monkey man, we know it's a bloody baby,' Rod raised his eyes at John. 'Was it a boy or a girl, or a chimp?' he said laughing.

'Very funny, piss off Rod; it's a beautiful little boy, apparently, looks just like its mum.'

'Phew, that's a relief,' said Rod, wiping his forehead with the back of his hand.

'Shut up, this is Craig's big day Rod give it a rest. How's Maria?' asked Mick.

Craig grinned at Rod. 'Thanks Mick, she's tired, but doing fine,' replied Craig.

'Well, what you going to call the little chimp... chap Craig?' inquired Rod.

'Maria said she wanted to call him Richard, after her dad.'

'Nice name,' said Mick. 'Richard's my middle name,' he said, nodding his head in approval.

Craig looked at Mick. 'No offence to you of course Mick, but I said no way,' he nodded his head. 'Sorry but definitely not Richard.'

John looked puzzled. 'Why not Richard?' he asked, shaking his head. 'Richard sounds a good enough name to me.'

'I'm telling you John, no; maybe Richard was all right for her dad. His name was Richard Tate, but not with my surname.'

John never got the connection. 'Enlighten me,' he asked.

Mick was already in front of the rest of them, as he had seen Craig's wage slips on many occasions. He smiled. 'You're right Craig, you can't call him Richard, the poor lad would never live it down.'

'What! You didn't call him Sue?' asked Rod, thinking of the Johnny Cash record, *A Boy Named Sue*.

Craig ignored Rod's remark, turning towards Mick. 'That's exactly what I told Maria,' he said.

'Are you two going to let us in on your ramblings, or what?' asked Rod.

'Right,' agreed John. 'Bloody time's ticking by here,' he snorted, looking at his watch. 'Well, Craig's surname is Edwards,' explained Mick.

John shrugged his shoulders, making a vague gesture with his hands. 'So?'

'Well what's short for Edwards?' asked Mick.

'Ed,' replied John.

'Right,' said Mick, 'and what's short for Richard?' asked Mick.

'Dick,' answered John.

Rod roared with laughter. 'Dick Head,' he roared with laughter again. 'Like father, like son.'

'Excuse me ladies,' said Craig. 'Bollocks Rod, why don't you shut your big mouth up?'

'Oh excuse me,' Rod said loudly. 'Hit a raw nerve there have I?'

John turned to Craig and in between bouts of laughter he said, 'Shit, you're right, now I know why you didn't want to call him Richard Edwards.'

'So what did you decide to call him in the end?' asked Mick, trying to keep a straight face.

'Maria said we'll leave his name open until I get home,' replied Craig.

'Good,' said John, looking at his watch again. 'Anyway congratulations Craig, but are we going to make a move to day, or shall we leave it until tomorrow? Rod, for Christ sake move this bloody car now,' he shouted.

Rod pulled out, turned down a side road and the hotel was soon lost to view. Five miles later he pulled into the kerb and stopped. 'That's it,' said Rod, pointing at the villa.

'Very nice,' said Mick as he got out of the car, 'must have set him back a bob-or-two.'

'Cost us a bloody bob-or-two,' John said, making his way round to Mick's side. They stood in front of the large white villa in its own grounds that were surrounded by what seemed to be tropical gardens. They all moved away from the car to the front and stood outside the ornate wrought iron gates. Uncle Tom's Mercedes convertible stood on the drive.

'Let's do it then,' said John rattling the gates. 'Shit they're locked,' he said.

'Back there,' pointed Craig. 'I noticed a dip in the wall we could climb over it.'

'What are we waiting for,' said John, moving in the direction that Craig had pointed.

John looked around making sure the coast was clear. 'Paul and Rod you get up on the wall and help the girls over,' said John. Mick and John cupped their hands as Rod and Paul climbed to the top of the wall.

'Ok, come on girls, up you go, and wait on the other side,' said John as Mick and John cupped their hands again. The girls were up and over in seconds and dropped down the other side into the garden.

Mick and John jumped off the wall into the garden. 'Are you all right girls?' asked Mick as John led the way to the back of the villa. John held out his hand to stop them. 'Shit,' he whispered, 'look at the fucking size of that,' he whispered stepping back. A large tarantula walked slowly up the white painted wall, they all skirted around the horrific spider making their way to the back door. Paul cupped his hands against the patio window.

Mick gave the large patio doors the once over 'Locked,' John whispered. He was eyeing up the small window to the left of the back door. He held up a thumb: a simple latch job that opened outward. John pulled out a credit card and slipped the latch. Pulling the small window open, he stuck his arm through the open window, slipping the bolt to the back door. 'Hey presto,' he whispered. 'Let's hope we've got the right bloody villa this time,' as they entered the back door. Slipping into the kitchen, they closed the back door behind them. Mick made a small hand gesture for the girls to stay put. 'Make sure no one walks in on us.'

The girls stayed, pushing the bolt on the door home and locked the back door again. They all walked slowly and silently through the villa. 'Pssst,' John mouthed. 'Sinead, the bedroom?'

'Over there,' mouthed Sinead, pointing to the bedroom from the safety of the kitchen door.

John jerked his thumb towards the bedroom door.

Sinead nodded.

It was as if everything was frozen for a moment as they stood outside the bedroom door. John put his ear to the door. 'All's quiet,' he whispered.

Paul touched John's arm gently. 'John. Let me do this, I've always wanted to do it,' he whispered, as he stood back. John nodded as Paul ran towards the door and shouldered the door so hard it nearly burst off its hinges. The side locks and bolts splattered the framework as the door burst open with a startling force. A loud scream came from inside the darkness of the room. Craig pulled open the shutters and light flooded into the bedroom.

'Michele's,' shouted Paul, staring wide-eyed at the naked female who sat up on the bed screaming, clutching at the bedclothes and dragging them around her naked body.

Craig's eyes widened.

John pointed a finger at the naked girl. 'Don't move,' he shouted as he dragged Uncle Tom from the bed, naked.

'What the fuck's going on, what the fuck are you doing in my villa,' shouted Uncle Tom, as he dragged himself up from the floor. He stood motionless, like a goat in the stare of a python, thinking that it was one of his drug deals that had backfired.

'I hope we didn't startle you by just showing up at your back door unannounced,' said John sarcastically, 'and watch your language, ladies present,' he shouted.

Craig rolled his eyes at Paul, who wasn't interested in John's reaction to Uncle Tom's swearing, as he was still gorping at the girl's naked body sitting up in the bed.

John slapped Uncle Tom hard across the face; he fell back hard against the bedside cabinet. As he got up Tom's hand disappeared into the drawer. John kicked the drawer shut; Tom yelled with pain. 'For fuck's sake, you've broken my finger,' he screamed with pain. John slapped Uncle Tom again as he removed his foot, pulling the gun from the drawer. 'Nice piece,' he said, rotating the gun in his hand and holding it in the air, clicking out the magazine.

'Shit, you've broken my fingers,' Tom screamed again holding his fingers.

'It's loaded as well. Expecting company were you?' John said as he snapped the magazine back into the gun pushing it into the back of his trousers.

Uncle Tom stood in front of them holding his private parts with his good hand; seesawing the bed covers between him and the naked girl.

John pointed down at the naked girl, 'How old are you?' he shouted at her.

'*No habla ingles,*' she screamed. '*No habla ingles.*'

John's face tightened as he looked at Rod. 'Help us out here Rod for God's sake,' he said, holding out his hand towards the girl.

Rod waved his hands at her to calm her down. '*Como viejo hey,*' he asked.

' *Tengo diez y s…diez y sels,*' she said in a quivering voice.

'*Como te llamas?*' Rod asked, with a smile on his face.

Her lips trembled. '*Me llamo… Conchita…Conchita….Maria Delores de Triana,*'

John looked at Rod.

Rod's face glowed red with anger, *as he looked at the naked young girl knowing that she was only a year older than Sinead, when the bastard had raped her. What could he do, any outburst now would only make the lads suspicious, but he wanted to kill him.* 'Her name is Conchita Maria Delores de Triana, and she's just seventeen,' he said.

John turned to face Tom; Uncle Tom's face seemed to have drained of blood while John's had filled with anger, almost as if there'd been a transfusion of sorts between the two of them. John shook his head, his tight face snarling with sheer distaste. He made a derisive grunt. 'She's just a baby, you dirty little pervert,' *thinking of his teenage daughter.* Uncle Tom's face came level with his own, he never saw it coming as John head-butted his face.

Uncle Tom staggered back to the wall, eyes glazed, mouth open, gasping for air. 'What the hell was that for?' He screamed in pain, blood pouring from his nose. He held up his hands to his bleeding nose. He bawled, 'Look, shit, you've broken my nose.' He pushed his face towards John. Bad move – John took the opportunity to hit him again.

'It doesn't look broken to me,' said John twisting his nose between his fingers. Another scream of pain came from Uncle Tom; he staggered as he swiped the back of his hand over his mouth and smeared blood. He hated the taste of blood in his mouth. He slurred his word through his swollen lip. 'If... if... you're her father, I... I... swear, I didn't know she was only seventeen,' he protested. He held his hands out towards her, 'Just look at her.'

'We are ... we are,' said Paul, his eyes wide.

John tossed Uncle Tom a pair of shorts. 'Put these on, we have got somebody we think you'll like to see,' he said. 'Anyway, you're not that big a man, you know,' he said, looking down at his penis.

Paul scratched his head. 'Maybe it's fear, John,' he said. 'It's fear and cold water have a habit of doing that,' he remarked, pointing at Uncle Tom's private parts.

Rod stared angrily at Uncle Tom. 'Do you remember this young lady?' he asked as Sinead stepped forward from behind him. A shudder ran through her as she stood in front of him again, her mouth felt dry, her throat hot.

He narrowed his eyes. 'Yer, she's the reporter I met at the club a couple of nights ago.' He held up his hands, 'I never bloody touched her, I passed out, too much to drink, I promise I never touched her, ask her.'

'That's not our concern,' replied Rod, placing his hand on Sinead's shoulder. 'So, you don't recognize this young lady then?'

Tom screwed up his eyes, taking his glasses from the bedside table. 'No, as I said, she's the lady from the club.'

Sinead for the first time held his gaze, she never looked away or cowed from him. Her eyes blazed, boring into him with all the hatred she could muster, letting him see how much she hated him. A look intended to convey all her years of anger. The next thing that happened shocked them all. Sinead hand curled into a hard fist and drawing her fist back she made contact with Uncle Tom's face. *Whack*, it sent him reeling to the floor. His glasses flew across the room, as they all watched paralysed by dismay.

Craig's jaw dropped. 'Shit, what the hell was that?

'I think Uncle Tom pissed Sinead off, and she lost her rag with him,' said John. 'Shit, that was some punch, Sinead.' He'd seen the effect Uncle Tom had had on Sinead; what he couldn't see was that he had been part of her problem she needed to release. 'Would you believe it,' he said, slapping his hands together, dragging him up off the floor.

Rod and Mick's mouths gaped open, but they knew where Sinead's punch had come from.

'What the fuck was that for? I didn't bloody touch you,' shouted Uncle Tom holding his jaw.

Sinead leant forward grabbing what little hair he had left and whispered in his ear, 'Maybe not this time Uncle Tom.' There was hatred in her voice when she mentioned his name, wishing he were dead. If she hadn't taken her Hippocratic oath *"never to do anybody any harm"* when she'd graduated as a doctor then Uncle Tom's position might well have been dramatically different.

'Ok,' said Rod, 'you may not recognise her, but there's one thing you won't forget and that's her punch,' he said, 'so if you don't recognise that young lady, what about this young lady then?' Kerrie walk out from behind Mick.

'Hello, Uncle Tom,' said Kerrie.

Uncle Tom felt his body shaking, blood pouring from his nose. He felt his stomach seizing up; he was struck dumb, shaking his head, his throat tight, and his mouth gaping open, as if he'd contracted lockjaw. His vision blurred at the edges, but he could see well enough as he looked back at them both. He swallowed inaudibly, and finally he spoke, 'Kerrie,' he said, his gaze narrowing on their faces, looking quickly back at the club reporter. 'Sinead, my God is that you?' he asked, his head going from one to the other, not being able to comprehend what was happening. 'What the hell are you doing here, am I dreaming?'

They both stared back at him not hearing a word.

John took a deep breath, and let it out. 'Well, if you are dreaming,' he said, 'we are your worst nightmare. Get dressed,' he shouted at the young girl in the bed, 'and make some coffee.'

She looked puzzled at John, her forehead rippled, as she looked frantically between John and the others.

John heaved a sigh sharply and looked at Rod. 'For God sake Rod will you tell her?'

'*Obtener el vestido,*' said Rod, throwing her a dressing gown, '*y hacer algunos el café.*'

She clutched the dressing gown and ran towards the kitchen. 'Paul, follow her and keep an eye on her,' said John, 'while we have a little chat with Uncle Tom.'

'My pleasure,' said Paul as he followed her to the kitchen.

'Let's go into the lounge, I hate sordid bedrooms,' said John, grabbing hold of Uncle Tom by the arm, pushing him towards the lounge.

'What the hell's going on,' said Uncle Tom as they entered the lounge.

'Firstly, our money,' John said.

Uncle Tom shrugged his shoulders. 'What money, what's that got to do with me?'

'Ok, let me give you an example,' John said, 'we've got plenty of time. I'll make this easy for you. What would you do if somebody robbed you?'

Tom looked on, helpless.

John rubbed his chin. 'Ok, let's just say you had eighteen million pounds, and you lost it. How would you feel?'

'I don't know,' replied Tom.

'More to the point, some fucking dickhead walks up and takes it from you. What would you do?'

'I don't know,' answered Tom.

'I'm not getting the right answers here,' John sighed. 'I'm asking you a simple question, Tom, and we want an answer. I bet you'd be pissed off. Wouldn't you?'

'I suppose,' said Tom, wiping the blood that trickled down his face with the back of his hand.

'We're trying to do a quid pro quo with you, like you're not helping us.'

'All right, I suppose I'd be upset.'

'You're bloody right you would, that's what all this is about,' said John. 'You're the dickhead who took that money which belonged to somebody else.'

'What money?' asked Tom.

'Eighteen million pounds ring a bell?' asked John. That got a reaction.

'That was Sean's money,' said Tom, 'he gave that to me.'

'Oh, and why the fuck would Sean do that?' asked John.

'Investment,' said Tom. 'Sean said he won the eighteen million on the National Lottery and asked me to invest it for him, that's why I'm here. I'm investing his money.'

'You lying bastard,' spat Rod, 'it was our money, and Sean would never have done that to us.'

Tom held up his hands. 'Ok, I'll give you your money back,' he said. 'I only need to get in touch with the bank, you can have it back in full by tomorrow

morning and I'll throw in a million, just for good will…'
'I'm afraid you've got nothing to offer us Tom,' John interrupted, nodding his head. He held out a hand. 'We have all our money back, thanks to Kerrie.'

It all fell into place now, Tom knew why Sinead had approached him in the club, and why he'd got drunk so quickly she must have spiked his drink, and found his safety deposit box key, that's why he found the key on his driveway…. John interrupted his thoughts. 'So what's happened to Sean then, where is he?' he asked.

'He's still working as a plumber as far as I know, I ring him every week.'

Sinead swallowed to ease the tightness in her throat. 'Uncle Tom, what happened to my Da?' she asked.

Tom moistened his lips, and sniggered, and shrugged his shoulders in a non-committal manner.

'So you haven't seen Sean lately? Asked John.

Tom shook his head emphatically. 'I swear, I don't know! As far as I know Sean's back in England.'

'Liar, the bastard knows,' said Rod. He would just as soon as snap his neck like a twig as stand there listening and looking at him. 'I know you know, tell the girls you bastard,' he shouted.

Silence.

Tears appeared in Kerrie's eyes, her words spluttered. 'You… you… did, you killed Da, didn't you?' she said.

Tom stared at both the girls. 'What! You're not suggesting that I killed my own brother?'

John put a finger to his lips, and looked round at the lads. 'No, we were thinking it was somebody else actually.'

Tom grimaced at John and looked back at the girls, pleadingly. 'I swear I haven't kill your da, Kerrie,' he said quickly, holding out his hands. 'I know we wasn't the best of friends, but why would I want murder my brother?'

Rod stared at him. 'He's lying,' he stated flatly, directing his observations to the others. 'I'm telling you the bastard's lying,' he said again. 'I've got a knack for knowing when people are lying.' He shook his finger at Tom.

'John doesn't like people who tell lies.'

John had his hands planted on his hips. 'Rod's right, you're a lying bastard,' he said, 'you had eighteen million reasons why you'd murder your brother, we know you murdered Sean.' He nodded his head angrily. 'Your own bloody brother.'

'Our da,' said Sinead and Kerrie in unison, both holding back their tears.

'You have absolutely no evidence,' screamed Tom, 'that I murdered anybody.'

'Oh yeah?' John frowned, his face glowing redder by the minute with rage. 'Fuck off, Tom; I suppose Sean just gave you the eighteen million pounds then.' He paused, turning towards the lads. 'Fuck, he's bloody asking for it, and I'm just in the mood to give it to you,' he said, moving towards Tom, making a rolling-back-sleeves gesture, although he was actually wearing a white T-shirt with *Plumb-It* written across the front. His knuckles whitened as he clenched his fists. 'I'll ram your teeth down your throat. Fuck it, just let me cave the bastard's head in.'

Tom raised his arms in defence as John moved towards him. Craig grabbed him. 'John, that's not going to do us any good at all, and it won't bring Sean back.'

'You...' John paused, pointing at Tom, pushing against Craig's restraint. 'Fucking did call Sean down to the site on Saturday and you had a cup of coffee in the site cabin, because it was you who left the coffee machine on all weekend. *That had bugged him for months, now he knew he'd switched it off.*

'Fuck off and prove it,' Tom yelled, feeling confident now that John was being pulled back and restrained by Craig, but Tom hadn't anticipated Mick's proximity. There was a short silence as John glanced at Mick knitting his brow into an angry frown.

Mick's shoulders were stiff with suppressed tension, his head dropped, his eyes watered, and his mouth was dry with anger. The red mist came down in front of his eyes, he was blinking rapidly, trying to brush away the mist of rage and clear his thoughts. The anger wasn't subsiding as he clenched his hands by his side, his nails digging into his palms. All his pent-up emotions of Elizabeth and Kathleen's deaths rushed from the back of his mind, and the horrific agony that the bastard had put Sinead through. At the time of their deaths he needed to vent his anger but he'd never found any physical outlet for his anger, nobody deserving enough to vent his anger on. His face glowed redder, showing the signs of deep anger. He raised his eyes to the ceiling for a moment trying to get his anger under control. It didn't work. He lowered his head slowly. He glanced over at Sinead and Kerrie. 'Excuse me.'

They nodded.

'Fuck it,' Mick whispered as he lashed out, his fist hitting Tom squarely on the jaw, sending him sprawling across the room like a marionette that had had it strings cut.

Paul turned his head in the kitchen, at the sound of broken chairs and a crashing table as Tom crashed through the chairs and over the table, cracking his head on the terracotta-tiled floor.

Nobody moved.

Sinead and Kerrie froze to the spot and screamed, holding their hands to their mouths without saying a word.

John's mouth gaped open.

Tom laid still and never moved.

'Shit, I think Mick's bloody killed him,' shouted Paul. Rushing from the kitchen over to Tom he bent down, pushing his head from side to side. 'He isn't bloody moving.'

'Why did you fucking do that Mick? What good has that done us now,' shouted Rod, holding Sinead and Kerrie and looking wildly at Mick.

Mick shifted his gaze from face to face. 'That was for my late wife Kathleen, and my daughter Elizabeth, Sean, Cathleen, and the four girls,' he spoke softly. He paused, wiping his wet eyes with the back of his hand. 'And that was for John and I, it will make us feel a lot better,' he said, raising a triumphant thumb towards John, rubbing his hands together. 'Shit, that hurt.'

'Not half as bloody much as it hurt him, I bet. Cheers Mick,' said John as Craig let him go.

Tom groaned, moving his head back and forth.

'Thank God,' said Paul as he walked over to Tom and bent down. He looked at Mick sidelong. 'Thank God Mick, he's coming round. Now, you leave him alone Mick. You really must learn to channel your aggression you know, it's not good for you.'

'Mick,' John paused. 'Fucking excellent punch, have you ever thought of taking up boxing? Paul, put him in this chair,' said John, pushing a chair with his foot towards Paul. John found some duct tape and threw it at Paul, 'Tie him up.'

John stood in front of Tom and grabbed him by the neck, pushing him deeper into the chair. 'So you don't know anything about your brother Sean?'

Blood poured from his nose and lip. 'I told you; I don't know where Sean is. I haven't seen him since I came over here.'

John rubbed his chin. 'Well here's my theory, you were at the site on Saturday night, and it was you who phoned Sean.' He paused. 'How am I doing?'

'I haven't a clue what you're talking about.'

John walked to the bedroom, picked up Tom's mobile from the bedside cabinet and returned to the lounge waving the mobile in the air. 'For starters, the call will be listed on your phone account.'

Uncle Tom shrugged his shoulders. 'So what do you think that proves. I phone Sean all the time, that doesn't prove a thing.'

Rod pulled the gun from the back of John's trousers. He pulled back the chamber: the mechanism clicked and slammed home. 'Let's blow his fucking kneecaps off,' he said, holding the point of the gun to his right kneecap, slowly taking up the tension on the trigger.

Mick leant forward and held the gun. Looking Rod straight in the eyes, he shook his head. 'We can't Rod, as much as you would like to do it, in fact I would be just as happy to pull the trigger myself, but think Rod, that would cause us an awful lot of problem, like involving the police etc...' 'You're right of course Mick, but I want to kill the bastard for Sinead,' Rod whispered, slowly raising the gun. 'I know, don't we all,' whispered Mick as he took the gun and handed it back to John.

John wiped the sweat from his forehead as he replaced the gun in the back of his trousers. 'We need to know where Sean is and the sooner you tell us, the sooner you'll be on your way back to anonymity.'

'Tell you what exactly?'

'Everything you know,' Mick growled. 'Like how you got hold of the ticket?' What happened the Saturday night you murdered Sean?'

John opened his arms expansively. 'Start wherever you want.'

Uncle Tom shook his head. 'I don't know what happened to Sean.'

John rubbed his fingers on his chin strange that Sean's disappearance seemed to coincides with you coming out here.'

'Did it bollocks,' snapped Tom defensively.

'Then why did you come out here?'

'A man's got a right to go wherever he wants,' Uncle Tom said defiantly.

'Only if he has a good reason,' argued John, 'we're curious as to what your reasons were.'

'What if I said it was none of your business.'

'Then you would be making a big mistake, and I'm afraid that's not good enough; you've got to do better than that,' John said, looking around at the others. 'We need to put the fear of God into him.'

Craig nudged Kerrie, 'Jesus Christ, fear of God,' he whispered in her ear, 'I would have sung like a bloody nightingale and soiled my pants if that was me sitting in that chair.'

John turned and looked at the girls. 'Girls, does he have any pet hates that you know of?' he asked.

The girls looked at each other, Sinead bit her lower lip. 'I know,' said Kerrie, holding up her hand. 'Spiders,' she said. 'I know he hates spiders.'

A huge smile appeared on Mick's face. 'Let me,' he said.

John shivered at the thought. 'Be my bloody guest,' he said as Mick left the room.

Mick re-entered the room, his large hands cupped.

'So you don't know where your brother is?' asked John.

Tom shook his head.

John looked round at the lads. 'Maybe this will jog his memory,' he said as he stood back.

'I would stay completely still,' said Mick as he moved forward. Leaning down he uncapped his hands, laying the large hairy tarantula spider carefully onto Uncle Tom's leg. The tarantula momentarily stopped, getting its bearings, and started walking slowly up towards his groin. Uncle Tom's eyes were wide with fear as he stared down at the tarantula's movement; not a muscle on his body moved, sweat poured from his whole body as the tarantula passed the waistband of his pants. Tom felt the large front legs attentively probing his sweaty skin.

'Well?' asked John.

Silence.

'Get me a stick,' said John. 'Let's aggravate our friend a little,' he said. The spider moved up his chest. 'Here,' said Mick, passing John a stick. He prodded the rear end of the spider. As it moved quickly up to his neck and slowly onto his face, Tom was trembling with fear. Mick cupped the tarantula and took it off his face.

Tom exhaled and breathed in deeply. 'Jesus fucking Christ,' he shouted, violently shaking his head, wishing he could rub his face with his hands.

'Now, where is Sean?'

Silence.

'Ok Mick, put the tarantula back on his face.' John waved the stick at Tom as Mick moved forward.

'This time he's going to bite you Tom.'

'Ok... ok... I'll tell you where Sean is, but get that fucking thing away from me.'

Mick stepped back.

John waved the stick like a concert pianist in front of his face. 'Right we're all listening,' he said.

Tom's voice trembled with fear. 'He's... he's... at your building site.'

'So you did ring him,' asked Rod.

'Yes, I rang him on the Saturday night.'

'Where at the site?' John asked.

'Under a pile of sand.'

John nodded his head. 'Yes… yes… I fucking knew it,' he said, 'so you did murder your brother.'

'He bloody deserved it,' shouted Tom. 'He gave me a severe beating eleven years ago; I spent six months in hospital thanks to him.'

John looked puzzled, 'Why?' he asked.

'Because I…' John never saw it coming. As Rod and Mick moved forward, Mick beat Rod to Tom and landed him a punch that Mike Tyson would have been proud to lay claim to. This time he knocked him backwards on the chair, and clean out.

John looked round at Mick amazed by his actions. 'For Christ sake Mick give it a rest,' he advised.

'John's right. For fuck's sake Mick,' agreed Paul. 'You know, you're going to have to spend your lottery win on a bloody anger management course when we get back to England, if you keep beating people up.'

'You got what we wanted to know,' said Mick, rubbing his hands together. 'He murdered Sean, that's all we needed to know. Right now that bit's over. The hard bit now is I'm going to have to call Cathleen, but I want a quick word with Sinead first.' He waved at Sinead to follow him to the patio out of earshot of the others. 'Right Sinead,' he whispered, 'you're going to have to keep the bastard drugged from now on, we don't want him mouthing off to them about,' he looked around, 'you know what, do we now?'

She nodded her head in agreement. 'Thanks Mick,' she said, hugging him and kissing him lightly on the cheek. 'Don't you worry he won't say a word,' she said, pulling a small leather case from her bag and waving the case at him. 'I've got a hypodermic in here: a shot in his arm, he'll stay on his feet but he won't know what time of day it is.'

'Champion, let's do it then,' Mick said, smiling.

Sinead removed the hypodermic from the case. Placing a tie around his arm and pulling tight, exposing the vein, she pushed the needle into the cork of the glass phial and pulled out the plunger, filling the syringe. She flicked the syringe with her fingers and smiled, *the shoes on the other foot now you bastard, how do you like having something pushed into you don't want.* She pushed the needle in to his vein. 'That will do fine,' she said, 'he may come round, but he will be incoherent.'

'How long will he be like that?' asked John.

'An hour or so out cold, and then just partly conscious.'

'How long before the drug wears off?' inquired Craig.

Sinead looked at her watch. 'Approximately four hours, then I'll give him another shot.'

'We don't want him coming round at the airport, Sinead,' John said.

Sinead held up a hand. 'Don't worry, John, I'm going to pump enough medication into the bastard to slow an elephant down. He'll go into a catatonic state, no movement.' She raised his hand as it fell unaided back to the floor. 'See, no movement at all, he won't speak, he'll just sit and stare; he won't know what day of the week it is.'

'John you're a bit like that, and that's without medication.' Rod smiled.

Sinead laughed and smiled at John.

'Bollocks,' mouthed John. 'He'll be fit enough to stand trial when we get him home, I hope,' he asked.

'No problem,' replied Sinead. 'I'll make sure he's fitter than a butcher's dog when we get back to England.' She looked at Mick. 'Mick are you going to ring Ma now, you said as soon as we knew anything, you would ring her?' asked Sinead.

'Ok let's sit outside.' Mick waved his hand at Kerrie. 'Kerrie we're going to ring your ma.'

They all sat down. 'Ready?' said Mick to the girls, breathing deeply. They both nodded as he punched in her number and pressed call. Sinead held his hand.

Cathleen answered the phone on the third ring.

'Hello Cathleen, it's Mick.'

'Hi Mick, it's nice to hear from you.'

'Maybe not Cathleen, I'm sorry but I've got some bad news. Is there a chair handy? I want you to sit down.'

There was a silence at the other end of the phone. All he could hear was Cathleen's soft breathing. 'Are you still there Cathleen?' he asked.

Cathleen sat down. 'Yes, sorry Mick, I'm still here.'

Mick detected the sorrow in her voice. 'That's ok,' he said, 'take your time.'

Cathleen took slow deep breaths. Finally she spoke. 'Mick I think I know what you are going to say; I was expecting this phone call.'

Mick raised his eyebrows at the girls, showing a puzzled expression. 'How did you know?' he asked.

'Because when you all left for Venezuela, I was going through Sean's clothes in his wardrobe. And you know when you were round here?'

'Yes,' answered Mick.

'Well, we said that Sean had taken his passport with him.'

'That's right we did.'

'Well he didn't, his passport was in one of his suit jacket pockets, so he couldn't have gone aboard, so he's definitely not in Venezuela.'

'You're absolutely right Cathleen, I'm afraid Sean's not in Venezuela, as you said,' replied Mick.

'The girls told me you have found your money.'

Mick rubbed his forehead. 'Sadly, yes we did find the money, that was with the girls' help of course. They have been absolutely marvellous, Cathleen,' he said, patting Kerrie's knee. 'Did the girls tell you who it was that took the money?'

The girls nodded *no* in unison.

'No,' replied Cathleen.

'Shit,' said Mick under his breath.

'What was that you said, the line's bad?' Cathleen asked.

'Pips,' he said.

'So who was it in Venezuela then?' Cathleen asked.

Mick took a deep breath. 'Uncle Tom,' he said, hearing a sharp intake of breath from the other end of the phone.

'Good God,' said Cathleen. 'Sinead how is she, is she all right?'

'Don't worry about Sinead, Cathleen, she's fine, you can speak with her in a moment. But before I hand you over to the girls I need to tell you something.'

'Ok go ahead Mick.'

'You need to phone the police,' Mick informed her, 'and tell them about Sean, tell then that we believe he has been buried at the building site. Tell them to look under the pile of sand that has recently been moved, and ring us back if you get any news,' he detected a few sobs at the other end of the phone. 'Is that ok Cathleen, can you do that for us?' asked Mick.

Cathleen sobbed. 'Ok... ok... yes, sorry Mick, I'll ring you back as soon as I've got any news.'

'Ok Cathleen, I'm so sorry I had to make this call, but be strong. I'm going to hand you over to the girls now; it won't be long before they are home with you again.' Mick passed the phone to Sinead.

'Hello Ma.'

Sinead let go of Mick's hand as he walked away, his eyes wet with tears, knowing exactly what the girls and Cathleen were going through. He kicked the grass waiting for the girls to finish the call.

The girls finished their call and both walked towards Mick, tears in their eyes. They both held out their arms. 'We are so sorry you had to make that call Mick...' 'It's not the call,' interrupted Mick, 'its you girls, I'm sorry about your dad.' They both cuddled him as he fell into their arms, and it was the first time they had all wept together.

Chapter Twenty-Four
Going Home

R ight, I've booked the flight,' said Rod.

'Mick, I need to shower,' Sinead whispered, 'I need to wash the stench of that bastard off me,' she looked at her watch. 'How much time have we got before we have to leave for the airport?'

'We've got at least four hours before take-off,' said Rod, looking at his watch.

'Right,' said Mick. 'Sinead, you need to go back to the hotel anyway, go with Kerrie, and settle up the bill. Rod, you go with them. Be ready to move in,' he looked at his watch, 'in three hours that should give you enough time, we're going home.'

'Ok we'll be ready,' said Rod as they went to the car.

'Oh by the way Rod,' called Mick, throwing a key at Rod. 'Take the bastard's key and open his safety deposit box. Empty the lot, and don't forget to bring his bloody passport or we won't get the bastard out of the country. 'And Rod,' Mick said as an afterthought, holding up a hand. 'Just a shower please,' winked Mick.

Sinead smiled. 'Just a shower Mick, no problem,' she winked. 'Leave it with us.'

Mick smiled, rubbing his hands together as he walked back to the villa; lovely jubbly, everything was falling into place at last.

Chapter Twenty-Five
El Agente De Policia

'Hi Antonio,' Kerrie smiled as they walked to the reception desk. 'I need the contents of this safety deposit box,' she said, pushing the key across the desk.

Antonio picked up the key, checking the number on his computer. 'Si, it's not possible senorita,' he said, pushing the key back towards her.

Rod put his hand over his mouth. 'Shit,' he mumbled.

Kerrie frowned. 'Why isn't it possible?' with more authority in her voice.

Because, senorita, that key belongs to a senor Walsh,' he said, pointing at the key.

'I know...' said Kerrie, pushing the key back to Antonio. Interrupted by a cough from behind them, they all turned; there stood two police.

'We're in deep shit now,' Rod whispered in Sinead's ear.

'*Que pasa,*' the older police officer asked Antonio. He explained the position to the two police officers.

'*El passporte, por favor,*' the older officer said, holding out his hand, as Rod noticed the young officer unclipping his weapon holster.

'Si... Si...' said Kerrie, rummaging through her bag. 'He wants your passports,' she said to Rod and Sinead.

Rod already had his passport in his hand, passing it over to the young police office so that he'd take his hand off his gun.

'*Viajan juntos?*' the older officer asked.

'Yes,' answered Rod, 'we are together.'

The officers scrutinised their passports as Antonio explained the position again, handing him the key. The officer showed Antonio the passport and looked at the computer screen and tapped the passport on the screen.

Antonio nodded. The officer slid the key across the counter closer to Antonio. Antonio disappeared in the back office and came out with the content of the safety deposit box, laying the contents on the counter. The older officer picked up Uncle Tom's passport. '*Si fotografica en este passporte,*' he said, Passing the photo over to the younger officer, he placed the photo against one of the girls' passport, and then the other, and looking at Sinead, he nodded.

'*Siento haberle molestado,*' the officer said, handing the photograph to Sinead. She looked puzzled at the photo and then looked at Rod. He smiled.

Kerrie smiled, 'That's no problem officer, you have a job to do.'

'*Muchas gracias, siento molestar,*' he said, handing them back their passports. The officer spoke to Antonio. Antonio nodded uncompromisingly. '*Adios, buena suerte,*' the officers said in unison, as the younger officer clipped up his gun holster. They moved off smiling, tipping their hats.

Antonio smiled. '*Firme aqui, por favor senorita,*' he said, turning the book round and handing her a pen. Antonio looked at Sinead. 'The officer said you looked like your father.'

Sinead shuddered at the thought.

'She does, doesn't she?' said Kerrie quickly as she signed the book as Antonio pushed the contents of the safety deposit box towards her.

'Thanks again Antonio,' Kerrie said smiling. She waved as they made their way to the elevator.

Sinead looked puzzled. 'How the hell did that photo get in the safety deposit box?' she asked.

'I said it would come in handy,' replied Rod. 'They slipped it in there the other night, back with the information they got out.'

'That was a bit too close for comfort,' said Kerrie, as the elevator doors whooshed open.

★ ★ ★

Kerrie's mobile rang.

'Hello! Ma... yes Ma, Mick's here. Hang on, I'll get him for you, hold on...Mick,' Kerrie shouted, waving her mobile at him, 'it's Ma on the phone, she wants to speak to you.'

'Hang on,' said Mick to the flight manager as he ran towards Kerrie. She handed him the phone.

'Hello Cathleen how are you?' *Silly bloody question* he thought as he said it, *of course she's not all right.*

'Mick the police have found...' she paused, 'found... Sean's body, you were right. Sean was at the building site. I've had to go down there to identify his body...' She paused. 'I'm... so... sorry Cathleen,' interrupted

Mick softly. 'Caitlin has videos of all the news reports, we'll show you when you get back home, and the police are interested in speaking with Uncle Tom. They said they would meet you off the plane at Heathrow and take him from there...' Mike looked at his watch. 'We are changing planes at Madrid, but we should be at Heathrow in nine hours, tell the police we will be arriving at Gate Sixteen, British Airways flight number VEZ 7640...' 'Ok Mick, you have a safe journey home now, and I will inform the police, bye Mick. Oh... oh... by the way, the girls have given me a glowing report about you, thanks for looking after both the girls, bye Mick.' The line went dead. *Mick smiled, wanting to hold Cathleen to try and make everything all right, but how could he go about making her husband's murder fine?* Kerrie interrupted his thought, 'How's Ma?'

'As well as can be expected,' replied Mick, 'where's everybody?'

'In the bar,' said Kerrie. 'A pre-flight pint for John I think, and Uncle Tom's having his pre-flight booster.'

'What you having to drink Kerrie, Mick?' shouted John.

'A white wine for Kerrie, and a orange for me, will do nicely John.'

'Hang on, we're not going to have trouble getting the bastard on the plane?' said Mick, as Sinead and the bastard came out of the toilets. 'Look at him, he's out of it.'

John looked at the bastard. 'I know,' he said. 'I asked Sinead to give me some of that stuff, but she said it wouldn't be wise, so I've got to rely on this,' he said holding up his pint. 'Medicinal purposes to give me a bit of Dutch courage.'

Mick gave Sinead a worried look. 'We don't want any trouble now, not after what we've been through.' Sinead had stuck a Band Aid plaster across the bridge of the bastard's nose to hold it straight, his eyes and nose were shades of black, blue and green. 'Look at the bloody state of him…' 'Don't worry Mick,' interrupted Sinead. 'It's not going to be a problem; I've spoken with the flight attendant and informed them that I'm a doctor. I've explained the bastard's condition to them, and that we need to get the bastard back to the UK for an operation, tumour on the brain…' 'Look at the bloody state of him,' interrupted John, agreeing with Mick, 'look at his eyes and his broken nose.'

Sinead held up a hand. 'Don't worry. I've told them that the black eyes and the nose are just part of an injury when he blacked out, and that it's the medication that's making him incoherent, and that I need to look after the bastard, and give him his medication during the flight. I informed them that the flight would not be compromised by his condition; in fact they have arranged a special bay for us.'

The bastard staggered in a strange half-sleep which allowed hallucinatory images and odd narrative patterns to flicker rapidly across his consciousness as they made their way through passport control.

The first boarding announcement went out. *'Would all passengers on British Airways flight VEZ 7640 to London Heathrow, please go to gate 15, as the flight is now boarding for take off,'* came the disembodied voice.

John's face drained of colour. 'One more for the road Mick,' said John, pushing his glass across the counter. 'Lads?' he asked, as they all pushed their glasses across the counter.

This is the final call for flight VEZ 7640 to London Heathrow. The gates will close in five minutes.

They half dragged, half pushed him into his seat, as the bastard sat between Rod and Sinead in their allocated section. Rod looked at Sinead, he took a deep breath and mouthed, 'Marry me.'

'What!' she laughed.

Rod took another deep breath, his heart beating unsteadily. 'Marry me. Please. I want to marry you, there.... Oh, God I've said it.'

'Oh, God,' repeated Sinead. 'Why?' she asked, turning her head away from him, a faint smile played about her lips as she mulled over what he'd asked.

Rod held up his hands. 'Why... you ask I mean, I thought it was obvious. Because you make me happy, you fulfil my life, we can be happy forever. What we've got is perfect. It couldn't be any better. We care for each other – we will look out for each other – we should be together. Forever.'

'You assume.' said Sinead. 'And now I don't know what to think.' She looked at his face creased with disappointment. 'Please marry me,' interrupted Rod.

Sinead looked at him. With the weeks bleeding together, the process of grieving over the rape had come to an end. She was tired of being sexually unhappy, until Rod had come along. She needed a radical life-change, and marrying Rod would take all the pain from her. Suddenly with Rod's proposal an escape had been offered to her. Now she could only look ahead instead of dwelling on the past, and a proposal of marriage was above all a vision of her future. Rod had proved himself to be strong and protective, sensitive to a woman's needs. She was definitely attracted to him, more than anything by the fact that his physical strength – his large, powerful body – carried not an ounce of threat towards her, only to protect her. 'Ok, I think you'd run a mile if you had the slightest glimmering that I'd take you seriously.'

'Try me, you never know.'

Sinead raised her eyebrows, 'But...' Rod's face creased with frustration. 'Do you really want to be with me, Rod? Properly? You want to settle down and have a family and everything? The whole nine yards?'

'As you said the whole nine yards, I think of nothing more than spending the rest of my life with you,' he held up his hands, 'what else can I say?'

'Ok, in that case, then yes, Rod, I will marry you.' The love in Sinead's beautiful green eyes told him she'd follow him anywhere. He knew that he now had an uncomplicated lady, and at last he figured he had it all, as Sean had said, he had found his perfect soul mate.

They all sat round as Sinead switched on the television. The television flicked into life. 'Shush,' she said, pointing towards the television. They all sat forward, as Una pushed in the videotape.

The music faded in: Dong...Dong...Dong... 'Good evening, this is the Ten o'clock News. I'm Trevor McDonald. Today Tony Blair has been admitted to hospital, after losing the general election.

Flash floods in Asia have killed fifteen hundred people.

An unknown body was found today, on a building site at Lipton.'

'Shit, we're on the national news,' said John.

Mick placed his finger to his lips. 'Shush,' he said as Una fast-forwarded the tape. 'Here we go,' she said, pushing play. The camera trailed past officials and forensic scientists in white suits, gloves, and masks and settled on a wind-swept young female reporter holding a microphone. 'Good evening, I'm Sally Briton in Lipton, it seems that the police have been informed from some unknown source that a body would be found on this building site. After contractors had been called in to remove several tons of sand, the police came across a car and a single male body was found hidden in the trunk of the car. The body has not been named until the next of kin are notified. Police are expecting to have a man in custody shortly to help them with their inquiries.

News at Ten, I'm Sally Briton reporting from Lipton.'

Una switched off the tape.

'I still can't believe it,' said John, looking around at them.

'At lasts the bastard...' Mick put his hand to his lips and looked at Cathleen. ' Sorry, I mean Uncle Tom has got his just desserts.'

Cathleen smiled. 'You're absolutely right Mick, revenge is a dish best served cold, so they say.'

Chapter Twenty-Six
Three Weddings and a Funeral:
Three Months Later.

S ean's body had been released. Everybody attended the funeral, except Uncle Tom who was going to spend the rest of his life in prison.

Mick had been seeing Cathleen for some five months since Sean's funeral, and they had become very close. They walked through the gates towards Sean's grave, to lay some fresh flowers. Cathleen knelt down and replaced the flowers; tears appeared in the corner of her eyes. Mick reached out a hand; she took his hand and stood. He traced the outline of her tears with his fingers, wiping them to one side. 'No more tears,' said Mick.

She smiled.

'Maybe this is not the right time or the right place, and please tell me if it's not. But I have never kept any secrets from Sean, and this would be the only place to ask you.'

Cathleen looked puzzled. 'What Mick?'

'Marry me Cathleen?'

'But why?'

'Because…. I just want to snatch you up and take care of you. Above all, I want to be with you forever, and we get on so well, I'm fond of you… no the word is not fond of…I love you Cathleen and have done for some time, and the time has never seemed to be the right time.'

Cathleen looked at the new cold grey headstone, and knew that Sean would approve. She turned towards him. 'Mick I don't know what to say.'

'Please, Cathleen,' Mick pleaded. 'Just say yes.'

Being with Cathleen all the time – it seemed too good to be true. Cathleen reminded Mick so much of his first Kathleen; they were both so similar in many ways, kind, loving and stable, which was good for Mick, he needed Cathleen so much. He knew that Kathleen would have accepted Mick's decision to marry Cathleen. He kissed Cathleen lightly on the nose as their hands interlaced; at last Mick felt that now he truly belonged to somebody. They never heard the shouts of good luck as they walked towards the wedding car.

Epilogue:

John retired and became a professional grumpy old man and his daughter Kaylie gave up smoking and went on to university to study law. Still not giving up the dream of becoming a supermodel.

Paul and Gale moved the family to Florida.

Craig and Maria moved to the country in Surrey and called their baby boy Sean.

Kerrie went on to become chief executive of the World International Bank.

Una became the posh fisherwoman, counting fish stocks in the Philippines' coral reefs.

Caitlin finished her law studies and became a top QC alongside Cherie Blair QC in family law.

Sinead and Rod married and moved lock, stock and barrel back to Venezuela. Rod opened a beach bar, and Sinead became Chief Surgeon in the Venezuelan International Hospital and had five boys called Sean, John, Mick, Paul, and Monkey.

Mick and Cathleen married and moved back to County Kerry, Ireland.

THE END